FATED

Pack of Dawn and Destiny Book 3

K. M. SHEA

For my community,
for rallying around me when I needed you most.

Thank you.

Chapter 1

Pip

The tree branch I was crouched on creaked ominously, like it was contemplating breaking.

"Don't you *dare*," I growled at it. I was trying to reach a higher, thicker branch, but the cold was turning my fingers numb, making it increasingly harder to climb.

"Everything okay, Pip?" Shania called from the safety of the ground.

"Yep! Everything's great up here. Just dandy. How are you? Any signs of packmates?" I wrapped my arms around the tree trunk and inch-wormed my way up it, holding on through sheer stubbornness.

"No wolves in sight," Shania reported. "Sounds like most of the Pack is out on the Pack run tonight." She turned in the direction of the sing-song howls—which were faint and echo-y to my ears, but probably crystal clear to Shania thanks to her werewolf hearing.

"This is so stupid," Wyatt very helpfully said. "Why are you risking your neck like this?"

"Because if I go through the front door, the entire Pack will be able to follow my scent trail." The rough bark scraped my hands in a burning sensation, which briefly stabbed through the numbness of cold.

"I think it's enlightening," Aeric said. "I never knew you always got Alpha Greyson's schedule by going through the window."

"Yep. I'm so clever," I said between clenched teeth.

I didn't *feel* clever. I was crawling out across a bare tree branch that shook a little from the wind, trying to reach an office on the second floor of the massive Pack lodge. Wyatt was right, this *was* stupid.

But my entire life had been turned upside down this year, and I'd do a lot of stupid things to feel even a little better about it.

The branch grew parallel to Greyson's office window, and with the practice of a hundred times, I hung from the branch like a sloth and used my fingers to push the window sash up a few inches.

"Pip, for real, why are you doing this?" Wyatt asked. "You don't need to grab his schedule for interested female were-wolves anymore. *You're* his mate."

At the reminder of what I was oh-so-healthily trying to avoid thinking of, I puffed up like a cat. "I'm trying to regain a sense of *normalcy*, that's what!" I hissed, my voice progressively going higher in pitch with the thickness of my emotion.

"By breaking into Greyson's office during a Pack run?" Aeric asked.

"You lead a much more exciting life than I realized if breaking and entering is normal for you," Shania said.

I swung a little hysterically from my tree branch. "One thing! I just want *one thing* to be normal! Is that too much to ask?"

Over the past few months, I'd discovered I had magic that

made me a very rare kind of werewolf hunter commonly referred to as a Wolf's Kiss. I'd also found out I was Greyson's long-missing mate and that the bond just hadn't taken because I was a hunter, leaving Greyson in a mental limbo.

As Greyson was the Alpha of the Northern Lakes Pack—the largest Pack in the Midwest, which I'd been unofficially adopted into after my hunter parents died when I was a kid and a werewolf couple took me in—and he was also the unofficial heir apparent to Pre-Dominant Harka—the strongest wolf in the Midwest who served as the top werewolf in the region—the mate thing was a big deal.

Fueled on by my rage, I stretched my leg out and shoved my foot in the gap between the window sash and windowsill, then pushed up until the window was opened wide enough for me to wriggle through.

"Wow, hunters are more bendy than I realized," Aeric said.

"Pip, just give up and climb down," Wyatt said.

That was another change.

I'd been friends with Aeric and Wyatt for a long time, but since news that I was a Wolf's Kiss had gotten out, Greyson had practically chained the pair to me to act as bodyguards.

That was why they were here with me instead of joining in on the Pack run—something I was banned from since it was for wolves in their wolf forms only.

"Normalcy, Wyatt. *Normalcy!*" My voice was a tad too close to hysteria for my liking, but Shania, Aeric, and Wyatt didn't seem to notice.

Though if they notice, that might be preferable. Then Wyatt won't push for more information.

Yes, I was doing this because I wanted to do one normal thing—well, normal for me. But also because if I knew Greyson's schedule, it was a lot easier to avoid him.

Aeric and Shania clapped as I flung myself at the windowsill and grabbed it.

The Pack lodge resembled a ski chalet…if the designer had unlimited funds and a thing for timber and huge windows. So I was able to wedge my feet along the timber and climb up the wall. I crawled through the open window while Wyatt barked off some pretty serious censures on my hunter ancestors.

I landed inside in a crouch—thank you, hunter instincts—and waited for my hunter senses to kick in.

I could tell there were a few werewolves in the lodge, but there always were. Just as long as I was in and out of Greyson's office before they came to investigate the noises I made, I was fine.

I turned around and yanked the window a little more open. "Ta da!" I waved down at the trio. "Aren't I cool?"

"Not in the slightest," Wyatt said.

"Come on, Wyatt," I said. "Lighten up! This is only the second floor. If I fell out of my tree I'd survive."

I didn't have the powers of a werewolf, but being a hunter came with a few nice bonuses, like having pretty decent night vision and being tougher, stronger, and faster than the average human.

I'd get bruised like a banana if I fell from this height, but I wouldn't break anything.

"Maybe, but if you break a fingernail we are all going to die," Wyatt said. "At the hands of our own Alpha."

"Is *that* why you've been so concerned about her?" Aeric asked.

"You think it's an unfounded fear?" Wyatt asked.

Aeric scratched his head, temporarily ruffling his red hair, which seemed to glow in the soft light of the moon.

"It's a valid point," Shania said.

I rolled my eyes and turned away from the window. I rubbed my hands together—trying to restore feeling to my numb fingers—as I surveyed Greyson's office.

It was meticulously organized with every file in its place

and every pen in a mesh pencil cup. His schedule—a leather-bound, weekly calendar—was helpfully placed in the very center of his desk, next to his sleek black keyboard and computer monitor.

I flipped the schedule open and got to the right week—it was surprisingly empty considering it was the last week of November. I dug my cellphone out of my pocket and took a picture. I then shut Greyson's schedule book with a satisfying snap and started to shove my phone back into the pocket of my puffy jacket, when the door creaked open.

Heart pounding in my throat, I flicked my eyes to the door, then released a gurgled hiss of air.

"Pip? Something wrong?" Aeric called up to me.

I couldn't answer. I was too busy being frozen in horror.

Lounging against the doorframe—oozing charm and danger from every pore—was the one person I was desperately trying to avoid: Greyson.

Tall and lean with intense gold eyes and hair that was either a dark blond or light brown depending on the lighting, Greyson wore power like it was an old t-shirt he was familiar and comfortable with.

"Pip," he said.

"…That was Alpha Greyson's voice," Shania said.

"Every wolf for themselves!" Wyatt shouted. His voice grew quieter as he presumably sprinted off into the darkness.

I spun around and peered out the window. "Hey, wait up!"

Wyatt was already halfway across the meadow the lodge claimed from the endless forest of trees around us, and Aeric and Shania were tearing off in a separate direction, running for their lives.

"Cowards!" I lunged for the window, but Greyson already there, yanking the window sash down with a loud thump.

He turned around and leaned against it, pinning me in place with the look in his gold eyes. "It's been a while."

"Ahah, yeah, well, you've been busy. And I've been… helping Shania." It seemed like a good excuse, besides, she owed me after turning tail and running like this.

"Really? It seems to me like you're avoiding me," Greyson said.

I sheepishly laughed, but made myself meet his eyes. Eye contact was important to werewolves, and looking away would be like admitting defeat. "Why would you think that?"

"Because I haven't been able to speak to you alone since the night you figured out we're mates." Greyson—wearing a t-shirt despite it being below freezing outside—purposely moved his arm, flashing the bottom part of his mate mark, a black wolf paw print that magic had emblazoned into his bicep.

Acting on pure instinct, I yanked his sleeve down. "Are you *insane*? You can't just flash that around! The rest of the Pack might see!"

Only a handful of wolves knew we were mates. Hector—Greyson's beta and the second in command of the Pack—his wife Ember, Aeric, Wyatt, and Shania. That was it.

I was hoping to keep it that way—when the rest of the Pack found out it was going to be pure chaos.

Greyson smirked down at me, and I had the feeling he was wearing the t-shirt just to be provoking.

I cleared my throat and straightened up. "And while we haven't spoken alone, I've seen you plenty. You made the arrangements for wolves to guard me at work."

"Whenever I've seen you we've only talked about you being publicly outed as a Wolf's Kiss," Greyson said.

In all fairness, my getting outed was a pretty big deal.

The Pack knew about my powers, but we'd been keeping it quiet because a Wolf's Kiss was an incredibly rare thing, and thanks to my magic it gave the Pack some pretty hefty advantages—namely more humans who attempted the change became werewolves, and all of them survived when the nation-wide average was death.

But a few weeks ago someone had sent out an email to all of the Midwest Alphas, announcing what I was.

Things had kind of been on fire since then.

"Don't get me wrong," Greyson continued. "Addressing your safety is important. We don't know what weirdos will come for you with that news broken. But we haven't had a chance to talk about us."

My throat tightened. "Oh, so *now* you want to talk about us? Never mind that you were completely happy to keep me in the dark that I was your *mate* even though you've known for months?" Some of the bitterness I still felt about the issue crept into my voice.

Some of Greyson's relentless strength seemed to soften a little as he studied me. "I'm sorry. I didn't know what to do."

I couldn't look at him—it was too dangerous. From the set of his mouth to the slant of his eyebrows, he appeared way too reasonable and repentant considering the situation.

Greyson and I were in trouble.

Mate bonds were special, inseparable bonds that rarely popped up for wolves and shifters. You felt what your mate felt, and you became one heart in two bodies.

And that was the problem. As a hunter, I had natural immunity to things like Alpha powers—which could influence and even force a wolf to obey the will of an Alpha. Mate bonds fell under the same kind of mental-magic category, which meant I had no way to complete the mate bond, and because Greyson was a stubborn wolf who had accepted the bond *knowing* this, he was doomed to forever wander around with half of a bond, while I felt absolutely nothing.

I pressed my lips together, and the hurt that had been burning in my gut since the moment I'd figured out I was

Greyson's mate was enough to push me into shattering the silence between us. "You still should have told me."

Greyson blinked.

"This—the bond—is a huge deal. It directly involved me, and I had to figure it out myself even though you *knew*." The words I'd been hanging onto came out in a rush. "Was it because you wanted to break it without me finding out—"

"Never." Greyson's voice was deep and unmovable. "I didn't tell you because I thought it might make you run, and I couldn't survive that." Raw emotion flickered across Greyson's face, and he took in a ragged breath.

It was my turn to be silent, but I had to stare at Greyson's forehead because if I met his gaze I knew I'd crack.

"But you're right. I should have told you." Greyson said. "I apologize. I never meant to hurt you."

He's being truthful. As much as I want to hold this against him because it would make everything easier, he really is sorry.

I exhaled, the fight deflating out of me. "I'm glad you see how wrong it was." Tired—of everything—I scrubbed at my face, my fingers unpleasantly cold. "Why did you accept the bond, Greyson? You always said you were going to reject your mate if you could."

"I told you already," Greyson said. "I would have rejected anybody except for you."

"But this can't be okay! You have a half-completed bond—forever. You've signed up for a life of constant pain with that kind of imbalance." I mashed my eyes shut. "I know you had to come to the Northern Lakes Pack because of my powers, and I am sorry about that. But this? You could have prevented this." I popped my eyes open again to scowl at him.

Greyson quirked an eyebrow. "Did you ever consider that —for me—perhaps the pain is worth the relationship?"

I stared at him, not knowing what to do or say. I could see in his golden eyes that he meant what he'd said.

But what do I think about Greyson?

The question alone scared me.

For the past few years I'd tried diligently not to let anyone get too close to me.

After losing my parents, then Papa Santos and Mama Dulce, and finally when Hudson and Lynn had left, I'd decided life was a heck of a lot easier when you kept everyone at arm's length.

Objectively, I knew Greyson was amazing. But what did he mean to me?

Did I have the same kind of dedication for him? Could I?

I slammed the door on the thought before it could grow and spread like a tree fungus. Thinking about my feelings wasn't necessary right now. Hopefully not for a very long time.

I sucked my cold hands up into the sleeves of my jacket. "What do we do, Greyson?"

Greyson's expression was casual as he reached for me, but I didn't miss the way his entire body relaxed when he draped an arm across my shoulders.

It's the bond...he must be in pain, and I can't do anything to make it easier on him.

"For now, we focus on the most pressing issue: that someone dropped the news that you're a Wolf's Kiss on the Packs."

"Really?" I frowned so hard my forehead wrinkled. "That's still the issue you want to deal with first?"

"It wasn't," Greyson said. "But based on how you're acting now, I'm guessing I shouldn't press my luck. Besides, your safety will always take priority."

"It's really that bad that the other Packs know, huh?" I asked.

"It is." Greyson's voice was grim. "Desperate wolves do stupid things. And when word gets out about what you can do, there will be plenty of desperate wolves to go around."

This has already been a terrible year, let's just top if off with some power-hungry werewolves. Seems like a recipe for a good time.

As sour as my thoughts were, I couldn't shake the nerves that churned in my gut—or the dread.

Greyson watched me for a moment, until his cocky smile flared to life. "Try to curb your disappointment, Lady Hunter. I know the priority list must be sad for you, since you were obviously just dying to spend quality cuddle time with me."

When I stared at him, he gestured to his desk with his free hand. "Why else would you come here just to find out my schedule? Don't be so shy, Lady Hunter. Just text me when you want to see me."

I groaned, wholly aware that breaking the moment was exactly what he'd been aiming for. "I'm leaving now."

"I'll walk you out." Greyson let his arm slide down my side, stopping when it rested on the small of my back. "And check on your supposed bodyguards." I could feel the heat radiating off his hand even through my thick jacket.

"You told them they needed to stick with me in case I was attacked. You never said they needed to guard me from you," I pointed out.

"Or from your own stupidity," Greyson added.

"Hey! I've done this every week practically since you arrived. It's almost a tradition by this point."

"Maybe, but that doesn't mean it's still not stupid."

Chapter 2

Greyson

It was about three in the morning when I scented another wolf.

Disgruntled, I peeled my head off the canvas covered dog bed I was sitting on—which was quite comfortable in my wolf form—and sniffed the wind.

Stale swamp water and wet dog intermingled with the icy fresh smell of air and the more pungent smell of pine and wet, decaying leaves.

Must be a Low Marsh wolf.

I stood, silently yawning and stretching, then climbed off the dog bed and sauntered across the porch, my nails clicking on the wood planks.

I stalked across the lawn and got to the edge of the woods before I glanced back at the log-constructed cottage I'd been dozing in front of.

The lights were off, and everything was silent.

Good. Pip is still sleeping.

Maybe I'd be able to handle this without waking her up.

I slipped into the forest, feeling a little refreshed from my nap.

Pip hadn't questioned it when the dog bed had showed up on her front porch the day she figured out she was my mate and the email dropped revealing her as a Wolf's Kiss.

I camped out for her safety, but one of the unexpected benefits of the job was that the gaping hole I felt in my heart where a piece of Pip should have been didn't twist as painfully when I was this near to her.

The ache of missing her—the lack of connection where she should be—was…less than desirable. But I'd bear it. She was worth it, and I'd never regret cementing the bond.

I raised my nose, sifting through the scents of the forest. I filtered out the smells of the trees and wet dirt. There was a nest of squirrels nearby, and…wet fur. Homing in on the interloper's scent, I silently made my way through the forest.

I didn't sleep on Pip's porch every night. Aeric took quite a few turns given his vested interest in the place. Shania, his girlfriend, was living with Pip until she was better able to handle all the new powers that came with being a werewolf.

The wolves who were on watch duty during the day frequently lounged on the bed as well.

I stalked through the shadows of the trees, following the scent. My instincts were torn with half of me demanding to go back to Pip's cottage, and the other half bent on eradicating whatever threat stalked through the forest.

The bond is getting stronger, even if she can't complete it.

I tried pushing the bond as I stalked through the woods, trying to glean anything from Pip that I could through our hazy bond.

I couldn't tell what she was thinking, but I'd known she was avoiding me because her guilt was a sharp prickle at the back of my throat.

That feeling was a double-edged sword. It'd made it hard

not to track her down over the ensuing week and demand we talk.

I'll have to be careful, or she could become an obsession.

That was part of the danger of an incomplete mate bond —it was easy to tip the scale from a fierce love to a twisted obsession.

Not only was Pip likely to shoot me if I went down that path, but it was also completely inexcusable, and a sign of low mental strength. That was something I couldn't indulge in when I had the Northern Lakes Pack to lead and a Wolf's Kiss as a reluctant mate.

I cannot let myself be weak and slip. Pip deserves better.

The thought was an itch I couldn't scratch, but I ignored it and scented the air once more before stalking through the underbrush.

I found the wolf—he was raising a racket, stepping on every twig and branch between him and Pip's place as he tried to get closer. He was in his wolf form, but he was an embarrassment with how little he was paying attention to his nose and ears as he shouldered his way through a dead bush, the scent of stale water wafting off him in a strong enough scent to tickle my black nose.

So Vant is interested in Pip. I'll have to fix that.

I waited until he cleared the bush before I lunged, flattening him to the ground and biting at his throat.

The wolf fought back, trying to kick his legs into my gut as he tried to wriggle away.

I grabbed him by the scruff and tossed him into a tree trunk, then was on him before he could even try to get up.

The wolf yipped, almost immediately showing me his belly as he whined and curled his tail underneath his rear, attempting to placate me.

You were attempting to spy on a member of my Pack, and my mate. That isn't going to work.

I growled, and snapped my teeth close to his ears, then backed off just a little.

He shot to his feet, and I bit him on the hindquarters—puncturing his hide but not ripping it—as a warning.

He yipped and ran off, disappearing into the dark forest.

I took a few steps after him, then glanced back at the cottage.

I can't leave Pip unprotected.

I howled, lifting my muzzle up to the sky as I called out to my packmates.

It took a few moments, but someone answered: Roanne and Ember.

I shifted the notes of my howl in a tone that requested backup, then cut off my song and ghosted after the intruder.

I was going to make sure he left my territory, and by morning Vant was going to learn why you didn't enter Northern Lakes Pack land without permission.

Chapter 3

Pip

I squinted and leaned closer to my computer as I checked the bleed margins for the pamphlet I was working on for next year.

The Pack always changed up the park/walking path pamphlets each year, and I had to go over them to make sure everything lined up and there were no typos. It was only the end of November, but if I wanted to get these back in time for New Years I needed to finish them and get them to the printer as soon as possible.

"I should print out a black and white copy to make sure." I hit print and listened to the ancient laser printer situated with me in my hexagonal shaped desk rattle to life.

Deep in the gift shop, I heard a thump.

"You okay in there, Shania?" I called.

"Yep!" Shania said. "Just putting my werewolf strength to use and rearranging some of the keychain spinning rack things."

Though it had only been weeks since she'd been changed,

Shania was back to working with me at the Timber Ridge Welcome Center. She couldn't work on the computer or do anything that involved a light touch, but she'd gotten enough control over her werewolf strength to restock shelves, which was great because I'd been in over my head when it was just me staffing the place.

The welcome center served as a place to educate humans about the Northern Lakes Pack, advertise Pack-owned businesses, and sell merchandise in the small but exceedingly popular gift shop.

The tiny bell on the door jingled, and two ladies with sunshine blond hair slipped inside, laughing. They were impeccably dressed with wool coats, alpaca fur hats, and polished boots with thin heels I'd never be able to walk in.

When they smiled at me—their eyes, which were the bright blue of the sky, only added to their incredible beauty—I tilted my head.

Ah. They're fae.

"Hello, welcome to the Timber Ridge Welcome Center," I chirped.

"Greetings," one of the fae said. "I must say your little village is positively delightful. Our friends did not steer us wrong at insisting we visit."

"Are you a member of the Night Court?" I asked. For a variety of reasons, Timber Ridge had become a popular tourist destination for fae from the Night Court.

"No, we belong to the Day Court," the second fae said, surprising me. "But our friend who spoke of this quaint place is from the Night Court."

"I see. I'm glad you decided to take your friend's recommendation and visit us. How can I help you?" I asked.

"We're here for the gift shop, and to view the portraits," the closest fae said. She strolled up to the desk and rested her hand on its wooden surface.

"Portraits?" I asked.

"Of the top officers of the Northern Lakes Pack."

"Hmm. We have some canvas prints of Grey—er—Alpha Greyson and his beta, Hector, over on this wall. The gift shop is over there." I started to slip out of my standing desk area, but I was blocked from leaving, so I pointed to the wall that had the gorgeous photographs of some of the Pack members, then swiveled and gestured in the opposite direction to the gift shop that was walled off so it muted some of the sound the various howling keychains and toys made.

"Simply wonderful."

Together the fae drifted away from my desk and headed toward the gift shop.

I watched until they disappeared between two rotating magnet displays, then carefully twisted around so I could address my furry roadblock.

"I know Greyson said you needed to stay close, Ember, but don't you think this is overdoing it?" I asked.

Ember was splayed out on a memory foam dog mattress in her wolf form. She was beautiful as a wolf with her tawny colored fur and cream colored cheeks and chin.

She'd been snoozing since I started my morning shift—apparently she'd had a long night—but when I spoke she peeled a yellow eye open and peered up at me.

The bed was positioned in front of the only exit out of my hexagonal desk, trapping me in so I couldn't get past without crawling over her. (I hadn't put it there; she'd dragged it in about ten minutes into my shift.)

"I could pull your bed over to the statues." I pointed to the few exhibits we had—our effort to educate visitors on the intricacies of werewolves and Pack life. "You'll blend right in. If there's a fight you'll be able to launch a surprise attack."

Ember stared up at me for several heartbeats, yawned, then flipped over to her other side and ignored me.

The bell on the door jingled, and three fae—males this time, two of them wearing woolen mid-length trench jackets but the last one dressed in a bright yellow snowboarding jacket with a furry brim on its hood—entered the welcome center.

They smiled politely at me, but their eyes swept the room.

One of the fae women I'd directed before stepped out of the store and greeted the man while holding an all-white wolf stuffed animal. "Did you find the Sweets Shoppe Lady Theodora recommended?"

"We did," the parka-wearing male fae said. "I bought you two pounds of the gingerbread fudge you wanted, but I suspect you'll want to see it for yourself."

"They didn't sell any tea—bagged or loose leaf," one of the other male fae reported with obvious disappointment.

The group moved into the gift shop, their voices fading into murmurs I couldn't completely make out.

Must be more Day Court fae. They're so…shiny.

The door whipped open—this time with such force it jarred the bell.

I was unsurprised to see Mayor Pearl storm into the welcome center.

Perpetually wearing jackets with shoulder pads so pointy she could stab someone with them, trousers pulled up to her chest, and an umbrella that she wasn't afraid to whack people with, Mayor Pearl was a force of nature.

Her snow-white hair was hair-sprayed into a cement-like helmet of curls. The jowls of her cheeks were pronounced due to the scowl she always wore, and although her legs were thin like toothpicks I was glad I was behind my desk and out of kicking range.

Pearl was the mayor of Timber Ridge, but since her husband was the chief of police, she ruled the city with an iron fist—or, in reality, an excessive number of fines and tickets. She hit city residents for everything, ranging from smacking the wolves with fines for public indecency after they made the shift from wolf to human, to hitting humans with noise violation fines for lighting more than one firecracker at a time during summer celebrations.

And she's coming straight for me—oh goodie.

I put on my best Timber Ridge Welcome Center Smile—the one I busted out for angry tourists. "Good morning, Mayor Pearl! How can I help you today?"

"Those were fae," Mayor Pearl stated.

"Yes," I confirmed.

The older woman swung her umbrella and grunted. "There've been a lot of them around for the past month or so."

"Yes," I agreed. "Greyson made an alliance with the Night Court Queen since Chase—one of the Northern Lakes pack-mates—is working for her. They've been coming up here for…tourism."

It was my best guess. I wasn't entirely sure why the Night Court fae were so taken with Timber Ridge. They'd seen plenty of werewolves in their home city of Magiford.

"Hmmm." Mayor Pearl stood on her tiptoes to peer over my desk, her eyes landing on Ember. "I see you have company again today."

"Yeah, Greyson's getting paranoid in his old age." I laughed.

Mayor Pearl didn't.

I awkwardly scratched my elbow and tried to think of anything to say.

The Pack typically tried to keep our mess—in this case, the bombshell that I was a Wolf's Kiss and the other Packs knew it —to ourselves, unless it put the humans at risk.

As there hadn't been any trouble in Timber Ridge yet we hadn't said anything to our human counterparts.

Not that I know how we'd even begin explaining if we decided to.

"That's Ember, isn't it?" Mayor Pearl set her hands on the counter as she stared.

Ember uncurled from the ball she'd made and stood up, stretching her large body out before nodding at Mayor Pearl.

"Hmph. Alpha Greyson must be concerned to have Ember stay with you," Mayor Pearl said. "I suppose that explains the new wolves."

I stood up straighter. "New wolves?"

Mayor Pearl waggled her umbrella at the front doors. "A bunch of out of towners just descended on Main Street. They look awfully werewolf-ish. I figured it had something to do with you—it always does."

I bolted from my desk, but Ember was faster than me and was halfway to the door before I'd cleared her bed.

She huffed at me as she waited for me to open one of the doors, and together we stuck our heads outside.

Over two dozen unfamiliar wolves were outside, eyeing each other. They were mostly male, but there were a handful of females, too.

There was a huge variance in their fashion style and even the way they held themselves.

The two old guys in flannel shirts—one with a faded Green Bay Packers hat, the other a Vikings cap—had to be from Wisconsin and Minnesota. But standing next to them was a model-tall woman with ebony colored skin and a spotless white pantsuit, and next to her was a scruffy looking guy who was built so he could probably crush watermelons between his thighs—and his beady eyes darted around with a greedy expression I didn't like.

They're all Alphas. I tugged my phone out of my black slacks, my fingers moving automatically. *I can feel their power from here.*

The stifling feeling that always accompanied an Alpha's powers flooded the street as the unfamiliar wolves eyed one another.

"*Something wrong?*" Greyson said, picking up my call.

I startled—I hadn't even realized I was calling him. But as I stared down the beady eyed guy, I was glad I had. "Yeah." I swallowed, trying to get my throat to work. "A bunch of Alpha wolves just showed up in downtown Timber Ridge."

"*On my way.*"

I ended the call as Ember pushed her way forward so she was in front of me, but still standing in the doorway.

"Do you think I should call anyone else?" I asked.

Ember moved her ears, but gave no other indication she'd heard my question.

I rubbed my thumb on the smooth door handle and chewed my lip.

Shania and Moira are both here if we really need backup, and Scarlett and Radcliff both have a shift now at Howl-In Café.

Having extra hunters around might make the wolves think twice before starting trouble, but with so many Alphas sniffing around town it still gave us horribly uneven odds.

"Why do you think they're here?" I asked.

Ember finally looked up at me, staring me down with a flat gaze that managed to communicate just how silly she thought I was acting.

They must be here for me. To see if they can convince me to leave the Northern Lakes Pack and join their Pack.

Hopefully they'd stick to convincing and not kidnapping or violence like Greyson seemed certain would happen.

I glanced back inside at my hexagonal shaped desk where Mayor Pearl and—more importantly—my backpack was.

I carried one of my silver edged daggers on my person—which would irritate Mayor Pearl if she knew and get me slapped with a fine the moment I unsheathed it. But one dagger was hardly well armed. *Do I go back to the desk and retrieve my second dagger—and get a fine from Mayor Pearl when she sees that I'm carrying them?*

The old Alphas, who were leaning against a red truck that looked older than I was, turned in my direction. They adjusted their aviator glasses, then peered up and down the street before they crossed it with a physical ease that was shockingly at odds with their gray hair and wrinkle-lined faces.

They have to be pretty powerful to make it to old age.

Werewolves aged more slowly, but they didn't have the greatest life expectancy given that they were not a type of supernatural known for their self-preservation skills.

"Phillipa Sabre?" the one on the left—his flannel shirt was green and gold to match his Packers hat—asked.

Ember's hackles were raised with the hair on her back standing up. She didn't flash her teeth, but she was braced and ready for a fight.

My heart stuttered in my chest, but I kept my expression calm. "*Hunter* Phillipa Sabre," I corrected.

I need to make it clear fast that I won't be pushed around, even if they are all Alphas.

Movement behind them caught my attention, and I saw several of the other Alphas drift across the street, drawing closer to me.

My hunter senses were blazing from the bright spots these strange werewolves created in my mind. I didn't look away from them, but I leaned back, angling so I could shout into the welcome center. "Shania? Give Aeric and Wyatt a call, would you?"

The beady eyed Alpha shouldered his way past the two older Alphas. "That's not necessary," he said in a voice that was just as greasy as his unwashed hair. "We just want to have a little chat with you." He smiled, revealing a gold fang tooth.

I could tell when my puppy pheromones hit him—he blinked in surprise and his shoulders relaxed.

The pheromones—compliments of my mom's hunter

lineage—were a defensive hunter magic that made me smell like a puppy to all wolves.

It had absolutely ruined my chances of dating any werewolf—except Greyson, apparently—as it made me feel like a puppy to them, and werewolves treasured puppies. But it came in handy in situations like these, when tensions were…high.

"I see," I said. "You'll need to contact the Northern Lakes Pack, first. This is their territory, and you need their permission to be here."

"I'm sure the Pack won't mind us." Beady eyes took another step closer to me.

Ember snarled from deep in her throat, and he automatically backed up a step, then scowled at her. "Show some respect," he growled. "You low-leveled—"

Greyson hopped over the railing, landing next to Ember and angling himself so his shoulder hid most of me. "*Silence*," he said in a voice that was low and dangerous. "You will *not* order one of *my* wolves while in our Pack territory."

Cut off from the wolves by Greyson's wide shoulders, I relaxed, then furrowed my eyebrows in surprise.

When did I get so comfortable with Greyson that I was glad to have him help?

It wasn't a disturbing thought, but it was surprising, because I couldn't answer it.

I didn't know exactly when I'd shifted from fighting with Greyson, to seeing him as a source of strength.

Has the mate bond been affecting me this whole time? But I haven't accepted it. I can't accept it.

I shoved the thought aside—I wasn't going to moon over Greyson and the uneven bond when we had a literal doorstep full of Alphas.

"Why are you here?" Greyson asked.

"We know about Phillipa," said the woman in the pantsuit. "We know she's a Wolf's Kiss."

"So you all decided to invade Northern Lakes Pack territory without notice?" Greyson asked.

I felt the pulse of his Alpha powers as they unfurled.

Although they were all Alphas, none of them could match his power, and one by one they looked away. A few even bowed their heads, unable to face the pressure of his strength.

I licked my lips as Ember hopped down a few of the stairs, sniffing at the intruding Alphas.

"What do we do?" Although I whispered the words, I was positive most of the Alphas heard me thanks to their superior werewolf hearing.

Greyson briefly turned around, putting his back to the Alphas and wordlessly communicating just how little they intimidated him, which cheered me up.

There might be over two dozen of them, but we had Greyson, who was worth more than all of them combined.

I hope.

"Pip," Greyson said.

I raised my eyes, meeting his golden gaze.

I could tell by the furrow in his forehead he was trying to do that wordless communication packmates did, and was failing horribly.

Mates are supposed to be able to wordlessly communicate, too. He must be frustrated I can't even sense him much less hear him.

Anger with him for accepting our bond and a prickle of guilt that I couldn't do anything to fix our inability to connect boiled in my gut.

Greyson sighed and held out his hand. I immediately set my hand on his.

The tightness left his face, and as he rubbed his perpetual five o'clock shadow on his jawline with his free hand he nodded and seemed pleased with my reaction.

"You can't keep us from meeting her, Alpha Greyson," one of the Alphas from the street curb called—I couldn't see which one he was, Greyson was blocking my view. "If she's a Wolf's Kiss we have a right to talk to her."

Greyson squeezed my hand, then released it and turned around, this time standing entirely in front of me. "Wrong on all counts, Scruffy. Phillipa Sabre is a member of my Pack. I don't have to let you get within a mile radius of her. I do, however, owe her the *choice* of meeting with you all if she wants to. But as her Alpha there's no way I'm going to let you all ambush her at once like this. Leave Timber Ridge for the day, contact my beta, Hector, with your information, and we'll be in touch if Pip chooses."

The air was thick with tension—the Alphas didn't like Greyson's logical points.

But the strain dissipated when the two older Alphas stirred.

"Aw gosh," the one in the green and gold flannel said. "The kid's right. I sure do hope we didn't scare the poor thing —all of us just showin' up like this, not even bringing a dessert or casserole or nothing."

"Yeah, you betcha," the second one said—he was dressed in red and blue plaid and had the purple and gold Vikings hat. "We better head out and give 'er a bit of breathing room. Evenin', Alpha Greyson!" He saluted Greyson, then continued on in a lower tone as the pair strolled away. "Say, you know any good supper clubs in these parts?"

"Nah. What do you say we go take a drive and look for one?"

"Works for me!"

The other Alphas shifted and glanced at each other.

It was the woman in the pantsuit who moved next. "In that case, I'll be in contact. Good afternoon, Alpha Greyson, Phillipa Sabre." She walked off, her heels clicking on the cement sidewalk.

This seemed to break the spell, and soon the other Alphas left—after muttering their farewells to Greyson, given that his

Alpha powers were too potent to ignore and just walk away from.

A few lingered, including the beady eyed wolf who scowled at us and spat on the street.

When Ember growled and stalked toward him, he tripped on his own feet in his hurry to get away. Ember wagged her tail as she watched him hurry down the street to his car.

Slowly, the last few Alphas cleared out, leaving me with Greyson.

I watched Ember trot up and down the street, stopping to smell the spots on the pavement where the Alphas had been parked.

"What do we do?" I asked once I was certain they were gone. I shivered with the cold and wrapped my arms around myself. I was wearing a sweater, but the wind howled and had a frosty bite to it, so I backed into the welcome center.

Greyson followed me in. "We'll call a Pack meeting and contact Harka to let her know that they've started coming." He glanced down at me. "I'll keep them away from you if that's what you want, but now that they all know what you are, there's not much that could dissuade them."

"What if we told them about..." I trailed off and glanced meaningfully at Greyson's left bicep—where his black mate mark was. "They'd probably stop asking me."

Because no one would leave their mate—hunter or otherwise.

Greyson shook his head. "It'd make you into a target." He glanced at the gift shop—where the five Day Court fae were still perusing—then at Mayor Pearl leaning against my desk. "Besides, I don't want to reveal it until you're comfortable and you've made a decision."

I frowned. "A decision about what?"

Greyson stared at me until I blushed bright red.

A decision on if I want to be with him—even if I can't return the mate bond—or not.

He wouldn't say it, but I was pretty certain that was what he was referring to.

"Whatever." Self-conscious, I retreated to my desk. "Thank you for coming."

"I always will," Greyson said. "Keep your phone on you."

He was out the door before I could reply—probably going to join Ember in prowling the streets so he could make sure his scent was all over the city.

Wolves. They're...wolves, I lamely concluded.

———

"The meeting was called today to discuss the presence of outsiders," Hector announced.

He stood in front of the Pack—or all the packmates who lived close enough to Timber Ridge to attend the meeting, anyway—near the giant fireplace that was big enough for me to stand in.

As always, the meeting was held in the lodge's great room —which screamed "wolves" and "we have lots of money" with its stone-and-timber interior and many wolf and moon art pieces.

The packmates who had decided to use their human forms for the occasion all sat on the first floor in sturdy chairs with thick butt cushions. (The meetings occasionally ran long.)

The packmates who attended in their wolf forms were all on the second floor, their furry faces visible between the spokes of the wooden banisters as they peered down at Hector.

"Earlier today," Hector smoothed his perfectly trimmed goatee—I had no idea how he could be so casual with so many predators staring him down, "a number of Alphas representing their individual Packs arrived in Timber Ridge."

Whispers broke out on the first floor, and a few growls twitched across the second floor.

Hector watched the Pack, wordlessly demanding they quiet down—which they did.

Hector looked closer to a professor than a wolf with his tweed jacket complete with elbow patches, and his red bow tie, but that just hid his incredible strength from anyone dense enough not to sense it.

He was Greyson's beta, and I was willing to bet he was stronger than most—if not all—of the Alphas I'd seen earlier.

With the Pack's attention settled again, Hector glanced over to where Greyson and I stood by the wall of floor-to-ceiling windows, which I usually got stuck cleaning at least twice per year. (There were some downsides to being recognized as the Northern Lakes Territory's best climber.)

Greyson nodded.

Hector turned back to the Pack. "They're here for Pip."

It was so quiet, I could only hear Greyson's steady breathing next to me. The rest of the room was suffocatingly silent.

"They've requested to meet her," Hector said. "Presumably they're hoping to talk her into leaving the Northern Lakes Pack and joining theirs."

As one, the Pack turned their gazes to me.

I tried not to squirm with so many wolves staring at me—though the Pack had approximately a hundred members, only fifty or so lived around the Pack lodge, so it was a smaller group than usual.

"I'm not going anywhere," I said when it seemed they were waiting for me to comment.

A few of the wolves in the front row looked unconvinced.

They don't know I'm Greyson's mate.

Normally, that would cement Greyson and me together for life—which didn't change anything as I'd pretty much decided I wasn't leaving the Pack after I learned about my abilities anyway.

But the Pack didn't know about the bond—or at least my part of it.

"Of course you're not leaving. But since the information that you're a Wolf's Kiss was leaked to the other Midwest Packs, we've known this was coming." Hector gave me a reassuring smile, then spoke to the Pack again, effortlessly drawing their attention back to him. "Given Pip's abilities—specifically that she can drastically affect our Pack's change survivability— it's expected they'd try to convince her."

The wolves murmured to one another again, and East—a young Timber Ridge police officer who'd been turned this fall —stood up, his mop of blond hair glowing under the antler- bone chandeliers.

"Have we learned anything new about who sent the email, revealing Pip's abilities to the other Packs?" he asked.

Hector casually slid his hands into the pockets of his trousers. "Not at this point. It's still assumed it was Aspen's work, but despite the help of Pre-Dominant Harka and the Curia Cloisters, we haven't been able to trace who owned the email used to send out the message to the other Packs."

"Perhaps we could use the Alphas' presence to ask them if they knew the sender?" Klancy, a middle-aged werewolf, asked.

"Everyone who received the email was interviewed by the Curia Cloisters," Hector said.

"Perhaps, but that doesn't mean they didn't figure out how to lie to them," Klancy said.

"Interviewing them isn't important." Jack—Klancy's son who was a senior in high school—rocketed to his feet. "The bigger deal is, how are we going to keep these creeps away from Pip?"

"Alphas," Hector corrected him. "You don't have to do as they say, but you should still be respectful."

Jack scowled, but sat down when his father put a hand on his shoulder and yanked him back into his chair.

"There will be a larger guard rotation on Pip." Hector moved a little closer to the lit fireplace, and the dancing flames brought out the russet hues of his skin.

Larger? Hmmm, that could make work even more interesting. There's only room for one wolf behind my desk. Oh, but maybe we could talk a secondary guard into taking photos at our wolf photo stand with tourists!

"You will be notified if your aid is required."

"I'm volunteering," Jack chirped.

Hector smiled. "Yes, we imagined you and East would both be keen on joining the guard rotation."

East's, Jack's, and Shania's changes had all been traumatic, so they were attached to me since my powers as a Wolf's Kiss helped calm all of their raging, new instincts. As a result, I was pretty close with them.

"We are notifying the Pre-Dominant of all the Alphas in Timber Ridge at this time," Hector continued. "With so many Alphas missing from their Packs, things might grow dangerous in the rest of the region."

"Good," Jack shouted. "Then we can toss them out once we hear from Pre-Dominant Harka!"

A few wolves laughed, but most murmured in agreement.

Shockingly, it was then that Moira—my boss at the Timber Ridge Welcome Center, who also happened to be a tundra wolf —rocked to her feet. "I want Pip to stay with us as much as everyone else. But has anyone asked Pip if she *wants* to meet with these other Alphas—to give herself options?"

Murmurs swirled through the great room again, and everyone on the main floor stirred uneasily in their chairs while the wolves upstairs released a howl or two.

Wyatt and Aeric—aware of the mate bond—exchanged glances.

"Pip's not going anywhere," Wyatt yelled.

"I'm not," I repeated when more of the talk died down.

"You still need to be given the option," Moira said. "You're not tied to the Pack as we are."

"Moira is right. Pip should be given the option to meet these Alphas." Roanne—Jack's mom—stood up. "Even if we care for Pip, she is not bound to us. It's possible she may be happier elsewhere."

It was kind of Moira and Roanne to fight for a future that I could decide, but in a way it also twisted my guts.

They were right. I wasn't Pack.

Chapter 4

Pip

Not being Pack was a concept that I'd wrestled with for most of my adult life. I lived among the werewolves, but I wasn't one of them. I didn't have the same connection with the Pack, even if I was warmly welcomed by them.

Moira and Roanne seemed to expect a reply, so I forced myself to smile.

"Thank you for thinking of me," I said. "But I consider Timber Ridge my home. As I said earlier, I don't want to leave."

Roanne's face smoothed over with open relief, and Moira snapped off a nod.

"Good," Moira declared.

When Hector didn't add anything, the wolves began to murmur to one another—probably exchanging opinions on our unwanted visitors. The tones to their voices—usually musical like their wolf howls—were flat and quiet.

I glanced up at Greyson. "They're rattled."

Greyson shrugged. "It's expected. The Pack has been through a lot since the start of summer."

I chewed on my lip. "It's only going to get worse, isn't it?"

"For a while," Greyson said. "But the other Packs finding out was inevitable. Just as inevitably we'll have to tell the Pack one day, about…" Greyson trailed off, but meaningfully brushed the mate bond on his bicep—which was hidden under a long-sleeved shirt.

I froze at the idea.

How will they react? Normally they'd be thrilled for Greyson no matter who his mate was, but since I'm a hunter and I can't complete the bond they'll know he's in pain. Will they hate me?

I wouldn't blame them if they did.

"You don't have to freeze like a rabbit in front of a wolf," Greyson said, jarring me from my thoughts. "We're not telling them for a while. If they knew, they'd never keep their mouths shut, and we don't want other Packs finding out just yet."

"Yeah, that's the last thing we need right now," I agreed.

"Besides…" Greyson leaned over so his lips brushed my ear, keeping his words for me alone. "I am trying not to be so possessive and demanding that I tempt you into shooting me in the head. Which means we can't tell them before you figure out what you want to do about it."

"There is nothing *to* do about it," I said between gritted teeth. "Because you were impulsive and just accepted it without thinking!"

Greyson chuckled—a sound so low that I could feel it as my shoulder brushed his chest. It made my traitorous knees weak. "I disagree. Or you'd have already told the Pack if you thought the only option was to embrace it."

I lurched, unsteadied by the truth.

There was a part of me that was hopeful maybe we could undo the bond. Not that I didn't want to be Greyson's mate. I just didn't want to be the reason why he was put in never-ending pain.

Greyson was called from Colorado to the Northern Lakes Pack because of me—it's a miracle he doesn't hate me for that reason alone. But I refuse to further ruin his life, even if he's willing. Besides. Eventually…once the pain has had decades to eat away at him…I don't see how he could possibly still be glad for the bond.

When I glanced up at him, Greyson smiled—his lips curved at a mischievous tilt—but the good humor didn't reach his eyes as he tried to make a show for his Pack that all was fine.

"I'll work through this with you because it's *you*, Lady Hunter," he said, using the nickname he'd called me since he'd arrived in Wisconsin. "But I'm perfectly aware of just what your silence means."

"You are not," I grumpily said. "You're a wolf, not an oracle."

Greyson shook his head. "I know more than you could ever guess."

That bond—just how much is it telling him? I should look into mate bonds some more…in between dodging strange Alphas and trying to practice my Wolf's Kiss powers.

I rubbed the temples of my forehead. "I need some hot cocoa. Or a stiff drink."

Hector strolled up to us, his hands still in his pockets. "Was there anything else you wished to bring before the Pack, Alpha Greyson?" he asked.

Greyson shook his head. "Not until we hear back from the Pre-Dominant."

"Ah, yes, that does remind me." Hector whipped out his smartphone. "I received a text during the meeting and—yes—she has invited you and Pip to come to her offices tomorrow."

I frowned and looked from Hector to Greyson. "Why didn't she tell you directly?"

"Phone broke," Greyson said.

Hector smiled. "He was quite upset when you called to notify him about the other Alphas."

"Ah," I said.

Greyson had a history of breaking phones. He wasn't clumsy—phones are just incredibly *loud*, and with Greyson's wolf hearing it was occasionally enough to startle him and trigger his fight or flight response—which...was only fight, because he's Greyson.

"Tell the Pre-Dominant we'll be there," Greyson said.

I folded my hands together—something I did to help hold back the desire for vengeance when dealing with particularly difficult tourists. "Excuse me?"

Greyson glanced at me. "We'll get someone to cover your shift at the welcome center tomorrow."

"Except I've already been missing work a lot between Aspen and the wolfsbane issue in summer," I pointed out.

"You're not going to get fired, Pip," Hector said. "We *own* the Timber Ridge Welcome Center."

The Northern Lakes Pack owned most of the businesses in Timber Ridge, including a café and the famous Sweets Shoppe that no wolf could set foot in after getting busted by health inspectors so many times for wolf hair in the buildings. (The restaurant business was something the Northern Lakes Pack would never engage in for the very same reason.)

"I might not get fired, but money is a problem," I said.

Hector frowned—not one of displeasure, but something more personal. "How so? You are paid a fair wage, and you don't pay rent on your cottage."

"The Bedevilments." I was referring to the overweight cats my adoptive parents—Papa Santos and Mama Dulce—had left behind when they'd passed away. The cats were bratty, but I'd die before I gave them up since they'd meant so much to Papa Santos and Mama Dulce.

"Their food is insanely expensive," I said. "Also, I've been using my scooter all summer, but it's freezing. I need to buy a car."

Previously I'd used Papa Santos and Mama Dulce's, but their little car had finally bit the dust in spring, so I was car-less for the summer.

A sigh clawed its way out of Greyson. "I'll give you a car."

"No," I said. "You won't."

Greyson stared at me.

"You can't just *give* me a car!" I whisper-hissed. "That's not something you randomly give to packmates, much less someone on the fringe of the Pack like me."

"Of course I can," Greyson said. "You're my—"

I slapped my hand over his mouth. "Not here!"

"Fine," he said, his lips brushing my palm. "Then let's go discuss it somewhere else."

The feel of his lips on my palm was too...personal and made my stomach do bellyflops, so I removed my hand and made a show of wiping it on my pants. "There's no point. You still can't give me a car—the Pack doesn't know, remember?"

Greyson rubbed his forehead and looked irritated. "I can't believe I'm arguing with you about this."

Hector was his polar opposite with a bright, sunny smile that advertised just how much he was enjoying the situation. "You accepted *it* because it was her—it was all your choice, Alpha!"

Greyson scowled at his beta and ran a hand through his hair—which had more of a golden hue to it from the lights than its usual shade of dark-blond/light-brunette. "Thank you for your support, Hector." He turned away from Hector and settled his gaze on me. "We'll figure out the car situation eventually. For now, Pip, you *must* come see Harka. This is about your safety, and I'm not going to take any risks on such an important matter—regardless of how it looks to anyone else."

Greyson clenched his jaw, the words barely making it past his gritted teeth as I could feel his intensity in the statement.

He was serious. Greyson was going to keep me safe—no matter what it took.

It's the bond. Don't get swept away by him—it's the bond that's making him act like this, and I need to break that bond for his own good.

"Okay," I croaked. "I'll go see Harka with you."

Satisfied, Greyson turned back to Hector. "Go rein them in —we should finish the meeting."

Hector slightly bowed his head. "Yes, Alpha."

I stood with Greyson and watched Hector return to his spot in front of the Pack and wondered…just how was I going to learn anything more about mate bonds without alerting the Pack?

———

"Our options aren't good." Harka leaned back in her desk chair and crossed one leg over the other. "There's not much I can do given that I'm a representative, not a ruler. Since none of them have declared war, I can't exert much authority on them. However, by law the Alphas need your permission to be in your territory."

"I know," Greyson said. "But I suspect the Low Marsh Pack is letting several Alphas stay in their territory. I have no jurisdiction over them there."

Vant—he is such a creep. I scowled just thinking of the Low Marsh Pack Alpha.

"Unless their Alpha requests help I can't legally involve myself with that issue." Harka folded her hands in her lap and frowned. "I could hold the other Packs in check with my Alpha powers, but that would be a temporary measure I'd only like to use if things got dire. I'd run out of strength in a few months."

"A few months might be all we need," Greyson said. "If Pip

can learn to use her magic on the Pack, we'll have an easier time protecting her, and it won't matter if the Alphas try to enter our borders."

Harka nodded, and although there was a tenseness in her shoulder, the way she was sprawled in her chair was underlined with an athletic elegance I'd never be able to copy. "That's a reasonable idea. Hunter Sabre? What do you think?" She whipped her head to face me, making the tail of her black ponytail flutter.

I held in the pained groan I wanted to release and tried to smile pleasantly. "Well," I said. "It's a nice thought."

Harka's lips twisted into something that was half amusement half apprehension. "However?"

I awkwardly flicked my white hair over my shoulder, then blurted out, "The only outcome that'll bring is a fight that will last for forever. Other Packs will constantly be attempting to harm the Northern Lakes Pack, and Timber Ridge will almost certainly suffer from their close association with us. That's not a way I want to live, and frankly I don't think it's an option because Mayor Pearl will do her best to force the wolves out if it comes to that."

Silence stretched into all the corners of the Pre-Dominant's private office, and I was deeply aware I'd just poo-pooed the plan put out there by Pre-Dominant Harka and her most likely replacement.

"Ouch!" Rafe—standing in the back right corner of the office—grimaced. "Sharp, but true words that found their mark—spoken like a hunter!" He grinned at me.

Rafe was Harka's nephew and was in line to take over her Pack on the far-off day she not only retired as Pre-Dominant, but also as an Alpha.

I'd seen him a lot more since all this fuss started back in summer with the wolfsbane—an elven potion that made werewolves lose all control of themselves and turned them feral.

I suspected the sudden increased sightings of Rafe was Harka's attempt to nurture a good relationship between him and Greyson for the eventual future when Greyson was Pre-Dominant.

Ugh. Pack politics are always so complicated. I'm so glad hunter politics mostly involve shooting things.

Harka tapped her fingers on her desk. "Having met the formidable Mayor Pearl, I can't say I disagree. Alpha Greyson?"

Greyson's lips were stubbornly set on the threshold of a frown—a sure sign he was going to be muleheaded about this. "My first choice would be to challenge every Alpha and rip them limb from limb, but I doubt you'll agree to that, Pre-Dominant Harka, given that they're intruding on my territory but not showing signs of aggression."

"Correct," Pre-Dominant Harka said.

"I could compromise and let them sit around until they make enough trouble, then I'll *legally* be allowed to rip them limb from limb."

Harka slowly nodded, considering the idea.

No, no. We're nipping this idea in the bud.

"Greyson," I hissed. "You are not going to be able to fight your way through *all* the Alphas one by one! If you do that, it's going to make the other regions angry, and then you'll have to do it all over again."

"So?" Greyson asked. "I'll win."

"You cocky—"

"You think I won't?"

"Of course you'll win!" I clutched the arms of the leather chair I was perched in. "But you can't plan to fight your way through *all* the Alphas in North America!"

"Obviously I won't," Greyson said. "I just have to fight enough of them to get the Dominant's attention. I'd estimate that would be only about half of the Alphas."

I let my neck fall back on the top edge of my chair. "Unbelievable. You are absolutely insane."

Harka's chair creaked as she leaned back, and I glanced at her. "So…" she started. "You two are mates?"

Chapter 5

Pip

I felt all the blood instantly drain from my face. "No." I tried to clamp down hard on any physical reactions that would give away that I was lying—increased heartbeat, an unbelievable amount of sweat, that sort of thing.

Greyson—ever so helpful—just tilted his head like a dog.

Behind Harka, Rafe made a choking noise, but his aunt ignored it.

Harka wagged her pointer finger back and forth between the two of us. "This is setting off his protective instincts more than I've ever seen from him. Usually he's calm and in control —slow to act so he can close a trap on his prey. But now...he doesn't want those Alphas getting anywhere near you."

"Because my presence is extremely beneficial to the Pack," I said, attempting to regain control of the situation.

A hint of a smile quirked Harka's lips. "Hunter Sabre, you are admirably smart, but I am not an ornamental Pre-Dominant. I've been around long enough to know a thing or two. Besides, I've seen a mate bond up close before."

Greyson frowned. "You and your husband, Beta Colton, are mates?"

"No, just fools in love." Harka smiled. "If we were mates maybe I would have woken up sooner and realized I was in love with him long ago. No, I know about them because my older sister—Rafe's mother—and her husband were mates."

The past tense clued me in that the pair must have passed away. It was expected—mates didn't often survive one another's deaths. They either died after them, or went feral.

Aspen had mentioned her parents were mates…

Aspen was Harka's niece, and a certified psychopath—and not the genius kind, more the ax murderer kind.

All fall she'd illegally and forcefully turned humans into werewolves in an attempt to make Greyson look bad. She'd said it was because she wanted Harka to stay in power, but Harka wasn't old, and she was years away from retiring, so I wasn't certain what Aspen's endgame was.

Aspen is Rafe's sister…hearing that she was sentenced to a prison term must have been rough on him.

I glanced at him. Based on his friendly, sunny smile you'd think he was just fine, but given how Aspen had emphasized family, I couldn't imagine the situation had been easy on him, even if she hadn't been deeply involved in his life these past few years while she was a Northern Lakes packmate.

"I understand," Greyson said. "In that case, yes. Pip is my mate."

"Haha, Greyson you're *so funny*," I sourly said.

"There's no point in hiding it if the Pre-Dominant can tell. And I trust that both Harka and Rafe will keep this information to themselves." Greyson stared down the Pre-Dominant and her nephew, and I could feel a tiny bit of his Alpha powers unfurl—he probably wasn't aware they were even escaping his hold.

There are so many things that worry me about the bond, but this new priority list of his in which I rank so highly is especially anxiety producing.

I cleared my throat and tried to sound casual in hopes of knocking Greyson out of it. "Yeah, threaten the Pre-Dominant, that's a great way to get her on our side."

Harka chuckled. "Hide your teeth, Pup, I have no intention of upsetting your mate—nor does Rafe. Right, Rafe?" She briefly spun around to peer back at her nephew.

Rafe's eyes were wide, and he looked from Greyson to me. "Forgive me, I'm still trying to process this—though it does explain a few things."

"A hunter and an Alpha—never thought I'd see the day," Harka said. "Can you even return the bond, Pip?"

"I'm looking into that," I said. "Speaking of which, I'll take this opportunity to ask if you have any information—maybe a helpful guide or a Youtube clip—on mates?"

Harka slowly shook her head. "I'm afraid there's nothing official. It's mostly just spoken stories passed down through generations. I don't know that we even have physical written collections of them."

In that case, maybe I should try asking Hector who in the Pack is most knowledgeable on legends. I know Mama Dulce used to tell them to all of us kids, so perhaps there's something back at the cottage, but I can't think of anyone else who has filled that hole in the Pack since she died.

"Being mates, though, changes the situation," Harka said.

"We're not going public yet," Greyson said, his voice rough. "We're not ready for it—it could put a target on Pip's back."

"So put a ring on her—that'll give you all the legality you need to kill anyone who attacks her," Harka logically pointed out.

"No—no, no," I said to every wolf in the room in an attempt to stamp out the idea.

"Why not?" Harka asked.

"Yeah, Pip, why not?" Greyson leaned out of his chair and invaded my space.

"We're not airing our issues like this. It's something *we* have to resolve," I said.

Especially because I don't want you knowing just how much I want to free you from this!

The bond would probably make him interpret that in a really hurtful way, which was the last thing I wanted.

For real, if I was a less selfish person, I'd just let this go and get married to the handsome, rich wolf bachelor. But I like Greyson enough to want what's best for him.

"I'm so proud you even admit we have issues," Greyson whispered into my ear.

I was certain Harka and Rafe could both hear him, but I was pretty sure he wanted to fluster me as his breath was hot on my neck, and I felt his lips brush my ear.

Ignore it! We have things to do—and he may think he's awesome, but I don't need to confirm it!

"Okay." I inhaled deeply as I tried to ignore Greyson. "If my being a Wolf's Kiss is going to be a long-term issue like you all seem to think and will inevitably end in bloodshed, I think we need to tackle it in a different way."

Greyson leaned back in his chair, disappointed by the way I managed to keep calm. "Why? Violence is the best policy."

"No, it's *not*," I snarled. "Which is why we have to prepare for it, because you wolves are worse than a group of trigger-happy hunters!"

"What do you propose?" Harka asked.

"I think we need to react politely to the Alphas who have showed up and welcome them." I remembered to push my shoulders back and keep my head up—if you wanted a wolf to listen to you, body language was vital. "I don't want them to even think there's a possibility they'll convince me to leave, but as long as the Pack is respectful to them, they'll leave without any negative feelings. Or at least some of them will—those who are salty about it would be salty no matter what, so they can get kicked out."

"What does not having negative feelings do to improve the situation?" Rafe asked.

"It gives us witnesses, so in the future when those salty wolves—or the wolves who won't take no for an answer—try to stir up trouble, the Alphas will remember that we were polite and respectful, and they won't complain when Greyson ends any arguments. They'll think poorly of the other Alphas instead of wondering if the Northern Lakes Pack has too much power and should be taken down—which is a real concern if Greyson just went for it and fought any Alpha who showed up."

The wolves tilted their heads back and forth as they listened to me.

Encouraged, I added, "In a best case scenario, they might even act as our allies when the less-law-abiding-Packs attack us."

Harka whistled. "Maybe my Pack should adopt a hunter. With all that strategizing you're taught, you're downright deadly."

Greyson stood up. "We can give it a try. At least half of the Alphas camping out in Timber Ridge are known to be decent. But I'm not going to take any risks with your safety."

"If it gets to be that dangerous, we'll know my plan isn't working," I said.

"If you need any additional help, call me," Harka said. "But I imagine you'd get better results if you just let your Alpha powers loose on them, Greyson."

"That's certainly a viable option," Greyson all but purred.

Harka stood up with a groan and stretched her arms out. "All the same, good luck. Handle it well—because the more often crazy stuff happens the better-looking early retirement gets."

Rafe chuckled and shook his head. "That's not something to joke about, Pre-Dominant Harka."

"It's not a joke," Harka declared.

"You're too young to retire," Rafe said patiently, as if this was an argument they'd had multiple times.

"Age has nothing to do with my desire to retire," Harka wryly said.

"You're a good Pre-Dominant," Greyson said.

"You say that just because you want the position even less than I do," Harka said.

"Yes," Greyson agreed.

"Figures—impertinent pup." Harka laughed. "Enough chatter. There are rumors of a feral wolf in the area that I need to investigate."

"Are you going to send in hunters?" Greyson asked. "They'd be the fastest at eliminating one if it existed."

Harka grimaced. "They would, but it's a huge loss to lose a werewolf. I'd like to avoid it."

Greyson made a noise in the back of his throat.

"You disagree, Alpha Greyson?" Rafe watched Greyson with an oddly intent expression.

Greyson shrugged. "With the exception of a wolf dosed by wolfsbane—which it doesn't sound like is the case this time—it's too dangerous to keep a feral wolf alive on the vague hope that one day they might finally come back to their senses, when we know it's impossible. Once a wolf goes fully feral, they're gone forever."

"It could be a comfort to their family, if they were kept alive," Rafe pointed out.

"A false sense of comfort," Greyson said.

Rafe nodded and lowered his head, looking to the ground.

Harka squeezed Rafe's shoulder, then turned back to

Greyson and me. "I assume you two know your way out of the Cloisters—or do you need Rafe to walk you out?"

"We've got it." I smoothed out the wrinkles of the dress pants I'd worn for the occasion as I stood. "Thank you, Pre-Dominant Harka, Rafe."

"I can't do much besides offer verbal support, but you're welcome. Be careful." Tension pulled tight around Harka's eyes as she studied us. "Something tells me supernaturals can't afford to lose either of you."

Rafe smiled at us. "Have a good afternoon."

When we were through the doorway he turned on his aunt. "You have to stop threatening to retire—you'll upset the Curia Cloisters with the thought of another new member on the Regional Committee of Magic."

"Yeah, yeah," Harka said before we closed the door behind us.

Harka had a dangerous-looking secretary who I was pretty certain was a panther shifter, so I made sure I smiled and waved to him as we slipped out of the front office that contained all of Harka's employees, and entered the busy hallway.

Greyson set a hand on my lower back and left it there as we made our way down the hall. He wasn't trying to guide me along like I didn't know where I was going—I would have jabbed my elbow into his left eye if that were the case.

No, his touch felt more...casual. Like he just wanted to touch me just because. I wasn't even certain he was aware he was doing it as he kept it there while we trotted down the stairs. His hand was so warm I could feel it even through the thick fabric of my sweater.

Reluctantly, I decided to let it slide. Not because it was reassuring after the unsettling past twenty-four hours, or because his hand on my back meant I was somewhat tucked against his side and it was nice to know that nothing could hurt me or reach me there. Obviously not. Hah!

No, I let it go because… Why should I have to defend myself about this, anyway?

"Did you want to do anything in Magiford before we head home?" Greyson asked.

"Chase and Chrysanthe are waiting for us with a night mare," I reminded him.

As the official allies of the fae queen of the Night Court—who Chase, a fringe member of the Northern Lakes Pack, worked for—we were given a huge perk: access to the queen's night mares, which were magical equines who created portals. This meant the normally multi-hour drive from Timber Ridge down to Magiford—which straddled the state line between Wisconsin and Illinois—was shaved down to a quick five-minute trip through the Night Realm.

"Chase has the day off," Greyson told me.

"Wow, Chase took vacation?" I asked. "This is a special occasion!"

"I never said it was his *choice* he's off duty." Greyson said. "I suspect it's the Night Queen's effort to matchmake again. She forcibly gave him the day off and sent Chrysanthe with him to pick us up, then sent me a text suggesting that perhaps the pair would enjoy showing us around Magiford."

Chrysanthe was a fae noble from the Night Court who was smitten with Chase. I was certain Chase liked her right back. Chase, Mr. All-Work-And-No-Play, used her *first name*, after all. However, it seemed like the sneaky fae hadn't realized what a big deal something like a name was to someone as stoic as Chase.

"Huh. If that's the case, let's take a bit of a detour," I said. "I'd *love* to see how Chase is dealing with a day off, and if he's any more romantically inclined than when we last saw him."

Greyson leaned in even closer, his mouth a little too close

for comfort so his rich voice made my arms pebble in goose-bumps he thankfully couldn't see under the sleeves of my sweater. "You know, our date would be twice as fun if we dumped them and wandered on our own."

"It's not a date, Greyson!" I tried to keep my voice light and unbothered, but it cracked and elicited a dangerously deep laugh from Greyson. "And we're not going far."

"Oh?" Greyson straightened up, his curiosity getting the better of him. "Where are we going?"

"We can grab a snack at one of the nearby restaurants," I said.

Greyson made a noise in the back of his throat. "They're always packed since everyone who works here at the Cloisters or is visiting eats in the places a one block radius around the Cloisters."

"Not this place," I assured him.

Greyson narrowed his eyes, obviously suspicious, then his expression relaxed into a smirk. "Whatever you think you can throw at me, Lady Hunter, I promise I can handle it."

"We'll see."

———

"Here we are!" I opened the door of my chosen location, almost chortling as Chase, Chrysanthe, and Greyson followed me inside.

The room was a jumbled tangle of bookshelves, a few hightop tables and...cat beds.

There were three enormous, fluffy cats that I could see from the entrance—a pristine white cat with long fur sat on top of the bookshelf marked "cookbooks." A pumpkin-orange cat with bronze eyes peered out at us from his precarious position on the mystery shelf, and a calico sat on the ground below him, a cat toy hanging from her mouth.

At the back of the room was a tiny stand with two coffee carafes, a glass display of pastries, and a cooler with sandwiches and fresh salads.

Mostly bookstore, but part eatery, the room was dark with dramatic dark green and gold striped wallpaper and cozy lighting that resembled candlelight. The smell of new books permeated the air with a fruity hint of food.

It wasn't quite a café—they only offered regular coffee though they had a much wider variety of tea to cater to fae— but it did have some bakery items, and a small menu of salads and paninis in an effort to lure in wizards on their lunch break.

Lady Chrysanthe looked around in awe. "What is this place?"

"Cat Tails," I said.

"This seems a dangerous place to eat as it doesn't have any reasonable means of defense," Chase declared. "Particularly considering how easy it would be to get crushed by a falling bookshelf."

"We're just here to grab a snack, Chase, not make a fortification," I said.

Greyson turned in a circle, drinking the room in.

"Not your kind of place?" I asked.

Werewolves typically went for heavier-fare restaurants— like buffets, steak houses, and any place that offered excessive amounts of meat.

"I'm trying to figure out why it's your kind of place considering you don't like the cats you own," Greyson said.

"The Bedevilments are a special kind of torture. Not all cats are like that."

"I'm not convinced. Your hunter parents used to bring you here?" Greyson asked.

"No, actually. Santos and Dulce brought me here right after they adopted me to pick out a book in case I wanted something to read on the way home," I said.

Greyson whistled. "That was over a decade ago. Cat Tails must have a good business model to survive so long. Maybe we should take notes."

"Not necessary. Do you want anything to eat or drink?" I edged toward the counter.

"Give your orders to me, and I'll buy." Chase's eyes strayed to Lady Chrysanthe.

"I couldn't possibly impose in such a rude way—" Lady Chrysanthe started.

I slapped a hand on her shoulder. "Of course you can, and will. Tell the wolf what you'd like, and let's go look at the cats."

"Oh. If you're sure." A slightly bewildered Lady Chrysanthe gave Chase her order. I gave mine to Greyson, then shooed him off with Chase so I could drag Lady Chrysanthe to the bookshelves.

"How are you doing, Lady Chrysanthe?" I asked. I towed her all the way to the books in the front, taking her to the tiny nook dedicated to children's books.

"Quite fine, thank you—"

"That's great—I'm gonna keep this short because we don't have long, and Chase will hear us if we're any closer." I crouched down on the colorful playmat that marked out the section, then grabbed Lady Chrysanthe's wrist and tugged her down so we were huddled together.

I was sure I was way too deep into Lady Chrysanthe's personal space, but this was my one golden opportunity to nudge the two together, and I was invested.

Chase had been a part of my life since I arrived in Timber Ridge. He was important to me, and I wanted him to be happy. Plus, I really liked Lady Chrysanthe.

"When Chase offers to do or buy anything for you, *let him*," I said.

"But wouldn't that be rude of me?" Lady Chrysanthe

asked. "Queen Leila is forever bemoaning that people expect her and her people to pay for everything."

"Chase isn't a fae queen, he's a wolf," I said. "Buying you lunch like this is the subtlest way he can attempt to care for you. A werewolf is *driven* to protect and serve those he loves."

Lady Chrysanthe visibly drooped. "So I'm a packmate then," she said. "Special, but not…"

Oh my gosh. What a cross cultural communications failure.

"*I said love*! Do you need me to spell it out for you?" I hissed before I remembered how the wolf we were talking about was in the same store, and was wholly capable of hearing us.

I picked up a board book that had a squeaker shape for toddlers to press, and squeaked it while finishing my lecture to properly cover up my words. "Just…let him do stuff for you. It might feel unnecessary, or like you're taking advantage of his kindness, but he wants to assure himself you're okay." I unconsciously pressed the squeaker in a rhythm that emphasized my words. "Pay attention not just to body language—he's too used to stifling the usual wolf urge for physical touch—but to what he does for you and how he thinks of your comfort. Then *tell him* when you recognize that he's doing it for you."

"I see." Lady Chrysanthe looked at the toddler book—which I was still squeaking—with a puzzled frown, but then smiled at me. "I shall follow your advice."

I squeaked the kid's book one last time. "Good luck."

Greyson leaned against the tall bookcase that contained the store's biographies. "Pip, food." His gold eyes lingered on me—still crouched on the playmat—for a moment before his lips curved in a grin. "Unless you'd prefer to play with your squeaky book some more?"

I hopped up to full height and put the book back on display. "Coming!"

Lady Chrysanthe and I wound our way back through the maze of books—pausing to pet the orange cat, who had relocated to one of the fantasy bookcases so he could observe Chase as he meticulously arranged his food and Chrysanthe's.

There was a mound of sandwiches that I was pretty sure was Greyson's, but my place at the little table was empty.

Suspicious, I turned to Greyson, who was holding a sandwich and paper cup of hot cocoa, and a snack bag of caramel coated popcorn. "They had popcorn? That's awesome—I should go order some."

"Don't bother, this is yours," Greyson said. "Sit down." He set my food at the empty spot—which he'd moved so my chair was so close to his, our thighs would brush when we sat.

I took my jacket off and draped it over my chair. "Oh, thanks, but I didn't ask for popcorn."

Greyson raised both of his eyebrows at me. "I know. Eat."

Feeling cowed for reasons I couldn't specify, I sat at my spot and opened the bag, humming at the rich, sweet flavor.

Greyson nodded then leaned back in his chair, nursing a foam cup of coffee, and nonchalantly rested his arm on the back of my chair.

"I *do* see," Chrysanthe declared.

I blinked at her as I crunched on caramel corn. "What?"

"What you were telling me." Chrysanthe tapped the corner of my popcorn bag as Chase settled into the space next to her, having maneuvered himself so he could see all entrances and exits to the store.

"Huh?" I said.

"Allowing him to do things for—"

Chapter 6

Pip

Halfway into Chrysanthe's response I realized exactly what she was going to say, and hurriedly cut her off before she could blurt the whole thing out.

"Yes, sort of, that's beside the point," I loudly said, startling her into silence.

She thinks Greyson is—well, I mean, he is. But—oh gosh. We're not talking about this. Topic change!

I didn't dare eat any popcorn or give myself a moment— Lady Chrysanthe looked too earnest and all too likely to say something. "Uhhh, I apologize for the topic hop, but Chase, I have a question for you. How much do you remember the werewolf stories Dulce used to tell?"

Chase paused in the middle of peeling plastic wrap off his first sandwich. "What?" he asked, furrowing his brows.

Greyson's shoulders shook in amusement at my obvious panic, but I ignored him. "Do you remember any of the stories Dulce used to tell?" I repeated.

"Some," Chase said.

A loud, demanding meow sounded from our feet. I peered down to see the pumpkin colored cat sitting on the ground, staring up at Greyson.

"Was there a particular story you're wondering about?" Chase's yellow eyes were bright with curiosity as he bit into his first sandwich.

"Well…" I paused, wondering just how much I should give away.

Chase is discreet—he's not going to ask me questions. And I can research mates without making Greyson even more suspicious than he already is that I'm trying to break our bond.

There was a twist in my heart at the thought, and a traitorous little voice in the back of my head wondered if maybe I could find a way to connect with the bond instead.

It was a secret, tiny hope. But while I'd look into it, I couldn't afford to let the hope grow bigger, or it'd be that much more hurtful when I found out I couldn't.

"There is something wrong with this cat," Greyson said.

When I looked down again, the orange cat had reverently placed a paw on Greyson's pants and was leaning in so his head rested against Greyson's calf.

"Maybe it likes dogs," I suggested.

Greyson narrowed his eyes at the cat, who purred.

I took a sip of my hot cocoa—which was a perfect sweetness, though not as rich as I usually like my cocoa. "To answer your question, Chase, I'd be interested in any stories you might remember about mate bonds."

Greyson didn't look away from the adoring feline at my statement, but—with his arm still slung over my chair—he rubbed my mid back, and I felt his touch straight through my sweater.

Chase flicked his eyes from me to Greyson and back as he thoughtfully chewed. "There were a few stories," he said. "But the ones I remember were all about a werewolf couple after the mate bond was established. They were typically more exciting than the straight-up romance stories about how they met, which didn't interest me as a child," Chase said, his tone apologetic.

"Yeah, those are the ones I remember too," I said.

I didn't pay attention to any of the mate stuff because it's so rare, and I was a selfish brat who didn't care about things that would never apply to me.

When I felt Chrysanthe's curious gaze on me, I put on a smile. "I'm just trying to track down some legends."

"They aren't written down?" Chrysanthe asked.

"Nah, werewolf stories are more in the oral tradition," I said.

"There are a few records, but they're hard to come by," Greyson added.

"You might want to check hunter records." Chase took another large bite of his sandwich.

I paused, my steaming hot cocoa half raised to my lips. "What?"

Chase wiped his fingers off on one of the thin, brown paper napkins he'd grabbed from the counter. "Hunters recorded some of our stories and folklore as a way to better know us—I imagine so they could learn more about their targets. They'd have an incomplete collection for certain, but I imagine it would at least have one or two stories about mate bonds to teach young hunters."

"Huh." I sipped my cocoa. "That's not a bad thought. I'll check my journals, and maybe reach out to the Quillons."

Greyson tapped my shoulder with his thumb. "Scarlett and Radcliff could ask their mother."

"Yeah, that's a good point." I smiled at Chase. "Thanks for your help."

Chase tilted his head at me. "Of course. I am available almost whenever you need it."

Before the conversation could continue, the orange cat attempted to jump into Greyson's lap.

"Okay, no. That's a line no one gets to cross until they at least buy me dinner," Greyson told the cat as he caught him mid-air.

"I wouldn't have thought cats would like werewolves," Lady Chrysanthe commented.

"They don't typically, but there are always exceptions," I said, thinking of the Bedevilments that had loved my adopted parents so deeply…and were utter brats to me, a human—albeit a human with magic.

"Stay down." Greyson set the cat back on the ground and shook his head.

I grinned as the orange cat purred and rubbed against Greyson's legs, then turned back to our tablemates. "So, Chase, Lady Chrysanthe. How is Queen Leila? I never did ask, did she ever meet up with that polar bear she was running from last summer?"

"Yes," Chase said. "He approved of her, and then Queen Leila decided she liked him, so now she has started a campaign to keep him as an ambassador of his court."

"She's named him Howard," Lady Chrysanthe added.

"I'd expect nothing less from the Night Queen," Greyson said.

"Indeed."

———

After work the following evening, I bundled up in the warmest clothing I had—fleece lined jeans, snowboarding jacket, mittens, fur lined hat, and a giant scarf I wrapped three times around my neck in a way that my neck vertebrae were going to regret by the time this was all over—and waddled my way down to the public park.

Hector was waiting there for me, along with the crowd of Alphas he had organized. (It had been decided that Hector should deal with the other Alphas whenever possible. Greyson was powerful to the point where if he wasn't keeping a stranglehold on his powers, his presence alone could drop werewolves to their knees, and we didn't need the visiting Alphas taking offense to his skills.)

"Good evening," Hector said as the streetlight he was standing under flickered. "Thank you all for attending this meeting in an orderly fashion."

Fat flakes of snow lazily drifted down from the pitch-black sky, settling in Hector's dark hair.

Despite the snow and icy temperatures, Hector only wore a scarf with his usual sports coat and trousers. The rest of the Alphas were dressed pretty similarly to him. The two old timers still only wore their flannel shirts, but the ebony skinned wolf who was flawlessly fashionable had given in enough to the weather to be wearing an unbuttoned woolen coat—as had the male wolf with angular, deep-set eyes standing with her, though his was a longer duster style and a darker color that matched his dark hair.

"Since you all have requested the chance to meet with Hunter Sabre, she's agreed to speak to you—individually— here in Timber Ridge." Hector gestured around the park— which was covered in a fine blanket of snow—then casually pointed to City Hall.

City Hall was the closest building to us, and it had cameras pointed straight at the park, which the Alphas could clearly see.

"Although Timber Ridge falls inside Northern Lakes Pack Territory, we consider the city proper to be somewhat neutral, which is why all meetings—besides invitations extended by Alpha Greyson—will remain within the boundaries of the city," Hector said.

The Alphas stared at Hector with an unnerving intensity.

It says a lot about Hector's strength that he's able to stand facing them all down like this.

"When you speak with Hunter Sabre, you will not attempt to touch her, and when she considers the conversation over… *it's over.*" Hector's voice was just barely above a growl, and his eyes glittered with a dangerous light.

A few of the Alphas stirred—irritated by his demand—but most just blinked in surprise as he immediately slipped back into his more professor-y mannerisms and smiled as he adjusted the cuffs of his jacket.

"Alpha Greyson and several members of our Pack are on hand for Hunter Sabre's comfort, including two Fletching hunters," Hector continued. "Now, Hunter Sabre—Pip, that is —is very eager to meet you all."

"Could you please run by me your definition of 'eager'?" I hissed to him.

Radcliff coughed to cover a scoff, but I heard the quiet huff of Scarlett's muffled laugh.

The brother-sister duo stood just behind me, both armed with crossbows that they held with an intimate familiarity.

Hector ignored me, and kept a friendly smile in place. "If you would present yourselves in the order we agreed on ahead of time, it would be appreciated. Thank you." Hector nodded at the Alphas, then stepped back.

Although most of what he'd said had been phrased as a request, the iron in his voice got the message across that all of it was a demand.

"Ready, Pip?" Hector asked.

"As ready as I'll ever be," I said. "The Pack is watching?"

"Yes. We've got an additional twenty in the woods besides the five present." Hector casually nodded at the tree line that boxed the back of the park in, then glanced at the Northern Lakes wolves who were mingling in their wolf form.

I saw East, Ember, Rio, Klancy, and River, and some of the tension I was holding in my spine eased out of me.

I glanced at Greyson. He was in his wolf form, but was holding his Alpha powers fairly tight. I could feel them even though he was halfway across the park, standing back at the tree line that edged it in. He'd only unrolled enough to make the air feel a little heavier than normal—a reminder to the other Alphas of whose territory they were in.

"He'll be fine," Hector said, catching my look. "He's strong. It's why he can handle...it."

He's referring to the mate bond.

Hector flicked one end of his scarf over his shoulder, patted the top of my head as if I were a puppy in need of pets, then slunk off, taking up a seemingly casual position about twenty feet down the line of waiting Alphas.

"Okay." I chewed on my lip, then smiled at Scarlett and Radcliff. "Let's get this circus started."

The first wolf stepped up, and immediately my hunter senses—which were already lit up like a Christmas tree from all of the werewolves in the area—flopped around in my chest.

He appeared to be clean cut for a wolf, with copper-blond hair that was slicked back, eyes that were a wolf blue most girls would go gaga over, and a gray sweater with black slacks. But his lips were thin and wide, giving his smile a maniac edge, and there was something about his eyes that was...empty.

I don't like this guy.

"I'm Brock, Alpha of the North Dakota Grassland Pack." His voice had that nearly musical quality to it that most wolves had, but it somehow felt *too* musical and perfect. Like auto tune had been used to make him sound as pleasant as possible.

"Nice to meet you," I politely said.

"My Pack is the second largest in North Dakota, with our territory stretching through the southeast part of the state," Brock continued.

"Sounds pretty," I said.

I wasn't entirely sure what I was supposed to say or not say to the Alphas. There was no chance any of them were going to convince me to leave the Northern Lakes Pack, but being rude wasn't going to win the Northern Lakes Pack any points.

Brock peered back over his shoulder. "It seems like everyone is anxious to speak to you, so I won't take any longer, but I look forward to telling you more about my Pack, Hunter Sabre."

"Great, thank you. Have a nice night," I said.

He smiled at me—I braced myself so I didn't flinch at that sharp edge to his grin that I didn't like—then sauntered off.

I exhaled and tapped into my hunter magic for reassurance.

It's okay. Meeting them like this was my suggestion. This is for the best.

I heard the wolves shuffle forward—the long line of them made me feel like a bride in a receiving line at a wedding reception, except instead of greeting everyone I loved, I was facing down a bunch of werewolves who wanted to use me.

My hunter senses prickled in my throat, but I smiled at the next Alpha—a shorter woman whose hair was a shade of reddish brown. She was dressed in a bulky jacket, which was pretty surprising for a wolf considering how little the cold weather affected them.

"Hello." I put on my Timber Ridge Welcome Center Smile for her. "How are you tonight—"

She lunged for me, and the three Alphas behind her—another woman and two men—jolted into motion.

For a second I thought they were trying to stop her, until I saw the knives they carried.

Oh, they're trying to grab me.

My brain was calm as adrenaline dosed my system courtesy

of my hunter abilities, and I shifted my stance into something I could defend from.

Behind me, I felt Scarlett and Radcliff shift, but I focused on the lead attacker as she reached into her coat.

Weapon, I decided. *Better not let her get any closer.*

Which meant I had to take her down—and *hard*. Were-wolves didn't go down easily.

I kicked her on the side of the head before she could drag whatever hidden weapon she had out of her coat.

That jolted her to a stop and made her lean to one side from the shock I'd just delivered to her skull.

Next I jabbed her in the throat, choking her so she couldn't breathe. It was harder to do in my mittens—it cushioned the side of my hand and spread the impact more than I would have liked. But I used enough force to get the job done, and she made a sputtering, hacking noise as she clawed at her own throat.

Two of her co-conspirators moved to duck around her, but before they were within my range, they each abruptly halted, then dropped to the ground like bricks. Crossbow bolts poked out of their shoulders, each bolt armed with a fae stun spell that was so powerful I could feel it in my teeth.

Scarlett and Radcliff.

I savagely kicked the female Alpha who had started all this in the face—making sure I ground the heel of my boot into her nose.

I then pulled out one of the small throwing knives from my jacket pocket and flung it at the last Alpha. I nailed her in the arm and she cried out, but it wasn't a very bad wound—my knife was pretty small, and it didn't go in very deep.

Before I could throw another knife, a werewolf in wolf form jumped the Alpha from behind. He knocked her to the ground, then closed his teeth around her neck and growled.

"Don't kill me," the Alpha groveled, kicking up dust as she wriggled on the ground.

I relaxed, recognizing Greyson's snow white coloring. "Thanks, Greyson," I said.

Greyson flicked his eyes at me, but he didn't drop the Alpha. I could see the fury swirl in his gold eyes, and he bit down harder.

Oh. He's mad. Like, really mad.

I took a breath, and was immediately towed backwards.

I tensed for a second before I realized it was Hector, then I let him drag me off.

"I've got her—stay behind and dose that werewolf Alpha Greyson has," Hector called to Radcliff and Scarlett.

"Are we going to have to do something about this?" I muttered to Hector.

"I'm hoping that by dragging you off, he'll follow," Hector whispered back.

"So then the angry Alpha becomes my problem? Gee, thanks."

"Look at it this way—he's never going to maul you. The rest of our visitors? Not so much."

Hector dragged me all the way to the tree line, where the forest began, before he let me go.

I staggered a few steps, until my hunter night vision kicked in since I no longer had park lights glowing over my head.

Once steady, I jumped again, when I realized Greyson was standing at my side.

"Jeez—how can you be so huge and so quiet?" I asked, trying to break the moment.

Greyson's pure white fur practically glowed in the dark, but his ears were flat against his skull, and his angry growls made me reflexively tense as he glared back the way we'd come.

Hmm…he was standing over here when the meet-and-greet started… did he close the distance that fast?

"Greyson, it's okay." I eased myself down so I was kneeling on the ground.

I was going to get wet patches on my flannel-lined jeans, but this was bad.

Greyson snarled, his eyes hooked on the swarm in the Park where Hector worked with the Fletchings to tie up the unconscious attackers.

The fur on his spine puffed up, and his growl came from deep within his chest and promised bloodshed.

His Alpha powers so thickly coated the air I could feel it when I swallowed, and I was pretty sure his powers had spread enough to affect the wolves in the park because I heard several whines behind me.

"Greyson," I snapped, my voice firm. "You're better than this! Losing your emotions in a temper tantrum over a situation we—that's you, me, and the Fletchings—handled is *not* the mark of a good Alpha, and you're not just good, you're the best. Get a hold of yourself!"

Greyson stared at me, his golden eyes glowing in the dark. A heartbeat passed, then he whined.

I wasn't Pack—which would let werewolves speak to one another in feelings if not words—and I couldn't accept the bond, so I had no idea what he was actually saying.

But I'd lived around wolves for over a decade and knew how to read their body language and tones.

"I know it was upsetting," I said. "You're allowed to be upset. What you're not allowed to do is throw your powers around after everything is over and kick up a fuss—potentially blowing our secret—because you're upset."

Greyson licked his chops, but his ears peeled off his skull as he listened to me.

"You've told me yourself that's the mark of a weak leader, and you're anything but weak."

He huffed, but his fur settled back down on his spine. He

glided through the shadows and approached me, stopping a few feet away.

I held out my hand.

Greyson set his head in my palm for a moment, then slunk closer—giving me plenty of time to back away.

When I didn't, he pressed his head into my chest.

Figuring he needed the contact, I yanked off one of my mittens and stroked his shoulders, burying my fingers deep into his soft undercoat.

I could feel the tension in his body, and something in my throat tightened.

The mate bond is doing this to him.

Obviously. He'd never acted like this before he accepted the bond. Which made me wonder, just how much of his actions were sparked by the bond and how much was genuine. It was an ugly but fair question.

Greyson maneuvered his head higher and rubbed his muzzle against my cheek.

It doesn't matter if it's fake or real. I'm doing this to him. I'm causing him this pain because I can't return the bond. I have to fix this—no matter what it takes.

A minute passed, and Greyson sighed. He backed up, touched his cold, wet nose to mine, then licked my cheek.

"Stop that." I swatted him away. "Your spit will freeze to my cheek in this weather." I shoved my hand back in my mitten, then rubbed my cheek.

"Alpha Greyson?" Hector called. He was still a ways off, but when I peeked through the trees I could see he was carrying a gym bag.

Greyson howled one low and short note.

Hector stepped into the darkness of the forest with us, hefting the gym bag. "I imagine after that...experience, you'd want to be closer—and able to speak."

He unzipped the bag and got out a long-sleeved black shirt,

65

and a pair of winter boots.

Greyson stiffly nodded, then triggered his change.

Wolves take anywhere from forty seconds to a minute to change, and it's usually not a PG experience. But I didn't have to worry about Greyson flashing me because everyone in the Northern Lakes Pack wore bracelets a powerful fae had crafted for them that would create clothing that covered all the important bits.

It was an important finance-defense mechanism since Mayor Pearl was particularly offended by public nudity, and the Pack had lost tens of thousands of dollars before the bracelets were commissioned.

Greyson had sprung for the top-of-the-line bracelet, so when he finished his transformation—in a shocking twenty seconds that was pretty much unheard of—he was wearing fitted black pants.

"Thanks, Hector." Greyson's voice was rough as he took the shirt from Hector, then put on the boots without socks, which made my spine shiver at the unnaturalness.

"Hey, Greyson, you used to take thirty seconds to shift." I tapped my cellphone where I'd been watching the time. "Now you take twenty. Is that because of my Wolf's Kiss magic?" The timeline matched. About the time I first unlocked my powers, Greyson's shift speed drastically changed.

"No," Greyson said. "It's because I found my bond."

Chapter 7

Pip

My guilty heart twisted. "Oh."

Well, at least not everything about the bond is negative.

"Shall we?" Hector motioned to the park.

I exhaled. "Yeah. I've got to greet them all, don't I? To show I'm not afraid."

Hector patted me on the top of my head again. "Ember has always said you're more wolf in your heart than you are hunter."

We left the forest, Hector sticking close to me as Greyson led us.

I was pretty sure Hector was doing it for damage control—trying to give the illusion that I was important to the Pack, not just Greyson.

"Hector, you're amazing," I said as we approached Scarlett and Radcliff. "I don't think we appreciate enough of what you do."

Hector blinked in surprise, then smiled. "Thank you, Pip. But I'm happy to do all of this for the Pack—and you." He winked, then left me with the Fletchings as he drifted up to join Greyson.

"You good?" Scarlett asked.

"Yep! Everything is peachy. Thanks for the help," I said.

Radcliff caressed the fletching of the crossbow bolt he already had loaded into his weapon. "Of course, it's what we're here for. It was pretty impressive to see you take that Alpha down single-handedly—without a weapon."

"Yeah, but that was a one-on-one fight." I fussed with my mittens as I tried to figure out what to say to them. "I've never fought alongside other hunters. That was really cool."

Scarlett beamed at me, but before she could say anything more, Greyson spoke.

"What just happened will not take place again." His voice was low, and he let his Alpha powers leak out of him. "It was disrespectful to my Pack, to our territory, and to our hunter. Anyone who attempts a similar plan *will not leave our territory in one piece.* Understood?"

Greyson unleashed the full brunt of his powers, making my head swim for a moment before my hunter senses cleared it.

It hit the wolves—Alpha or otherwise—hard, forcing them down to their knees.

Only Scarlett, Radcliff, and I remained standing, and Radcliff looked like he was having to fight the impulse.

Greyson narrowed his eyes, and the pressure of his powers increased, making more than a few Alphas grimace. "Understood?" he repeated.

A quiet chorus of yeses rippled up and down the line of Alphas.

Greyson straightened, then wound his powers up. "Then continue." He drifted off.

He didn't return to the forest. Instead he parked himself under a park light, in a position where he could more easily reach me in case of another attack.

The other Alphas uneasily stood and exchanged glances, the air tense.

Thankfully, the Alpha who was next supposed to speak to me had a lot of tact.

It was the fashionable wolf and, after glancing at Hector, she motioned for the male she'd been talking with to join her.

Together, they approached me—slowly and cautiously.

The male was wearing an expensive suit that was worth more than a car under his woolen jacket—though brands weren't my thing, so I wasn't certain on the price. But his smile seemed genuine, and the last flicks of adrenaline my hunter magic had swamped me with fled, leaving me a little weak-kneed but certain my magic didn't think the pair was dangerous.

"Good evening. I'm Alpha Maya Williams of Windy City Pack," the woman said. The tan color of her wool coat really brought out the golden hues of her ebony skin, and her hazel eyes flicked from me to the Fletchings with curiosity.

"Kim Seo-Jun, Alpha of Millennium Pack," the male wolf said. He offered me a brief smile and held out his hand for me to shake.

I took it—barely feeling his hand through my thick mittens —but there was something about the pair that put me at ease. They were calmer, and I had an inkling that—like Greyson— they were holding their Alpha powers in check.

"Nice to meet you two," I said.

"We represent the two largest werewolf Packs in Chicago," Seo-Jun said.

"Ah. I imagine Timber Ridge is a very different experience for you," I said.

"It's...quaint," Seo-Jun said.

"The nature is charming," Maya said. "As is the quiet of rural Wisconsin. Alpha Greyson extended an invitation to us to roam the Lake Lycaon area, which we intend to explore tonight. But, you must forgive us for preferring Chicago life," Maya summarized.

"What about Chicago do you love so much?" I asked, genuinely curious.

Considering how advanced a werewolf's senses were, big cities seemed like they would be the worst place to live. I'd always wondered how wolves managed to survive there.

"The variety and the humanity," Maya smoothly offered—clearly she was prepared for this question. "Chicago is a city of ingenuity and beauty—the humans keep it so between their endless stores, museums, parks, and busy lives."

"We enjoy using what humanity has developed," Seo-Jun said.

"You mean like here in Timber Ridge?" I asked.

Seo-Jun shook his head. "No, we live separate lives from the humans. We cannot combine—they would never understand us—but we mingle."

"Okay, cool," I said, even though I didn't quite agree.

Their attitude isn't surprising. Timber Ridge is unique in that the werewolves are so deeply enmeshed in the city.

"We'd like to tell you more," Maya said. "But we will wait for another opportunity given the line waiting to speak to you."

"Good evening, Hunter Sabre," Seo-Jun said.

"Good evening," I echoed back to the pair before they moved on.

"Those two came prepared." Scarlett lowly whistled as she leaned in close enough to me that her shoulder brushed my back—the Pack's touchy-feely-ness must have finally started wearing off on the siblings as they used to have a personal space bubble that was at least three times the size of mine.

I briefly turned around to face them before the next wolf could move in to talk to me. "They're also teaming up together," I whispered, gambling that with the general hum of conversation the wolves wouldn't be able to distinguish my voice from the rest. "That was definitely a two-person sales pitch."

Radcliff meandered closer so the three of us were bunched together—speaking as quietly as we could. "It makes sense. They're probably betting that having a Wolf's Kiss in the same city would be better for both Packs—they might even hope they can share custody of you."

I wrinkled my nose. "I'm not a kid in a divorce settlement."

"Yeah?" Radcliff raised his eyebrows. "Seems to me like you'd feel the same way if anyone tried to pry you away from the Northern Lakes Pack. You're good and bonded to them."

"Understandably—you grew up here," Scarlett said. "But I think Maya and Seo-Jun get points for their presentation. They weren't absolutely insane like *some* of the Alphas." She purposely flicked her eyes off in the direction where the four Alphas had been dragged off by the Northern Lakes Pack.

A man cleared his throat, prompting me to turn back around to face the incoming line of werewolves.

Scarlett and Radcliff each patted my shoulders—yes, the Pack was *definitely* wearing off on them—before they drifted off so they were a few steps away from me, though they were still pointed at the werewolves and had their crossbows ready.

I smiled and beckoned the next waiting Alpha forward—a man with a gentle smile who looked like your regular, friendly, neighborhood dad.

"Hello," I said. "I'm Hunter Sabre…"

———

The introductions continued. I tried to keep mental notes on everyone, but names were pretty hard to nail down considering I met over twenty Alphas, and all of them were distinct—from the Alphas who felt more like high-powered CEOs like Maya and Seo-Jun, to the Alphas who gave me a faint sick feeling that meant I'd work to keep as far away from them as possible, like the four who had jumped me early in the meeting.

I knew Greyson probably had pictures of the Alphas and their Packs, as well as detailed bios on every single one of them, but personal impressions were important to me. It was probably part of my hunter instincts.

"Just two left, not bad," Radcliff muttered as we waited for the last two Alphas to approach—it was the two old timers who were enthusiastically pumping Hector about the best place for a fish fry.

I watched in amusement, then hopped in place in an effort to warm myself up as I peered around the rapidly emptying park.

Most of the Alphas had left—some disappearing while others wandered toward downtown, probably to get dinner.

I frowned when I thought I recognized a guy standing at the front of City Hall.

Is that...Vant?

Vant was the Alpha of a small, neighboring Pack called Low Marsh. He'd taken over after his predecessor screwed up, but I didn't really like the guy. He felt...*oily* in my mind.

I tried squinting, but it didn't help, and the guy turned away and walked off.

Maybe I'm just paranoid from the earlier attack?

"How are you holding up?" Scarlett asked, dragging my attention back to the siblings.

"I feel like a prize they're going to destroy as they tear me from one another." I made a face.

"Accurate," Radcliff said.

"But that won't happen." Greyson sauntered up to us, everything about him appearing casual and uncaring—though I could tell by the dangerous glint in his eye that he was ready to break a few bones.

Someone is still feeling violent. Although, I suppose it's a miracle he didn't immediately drag me away after the attack. It says a lot about his self-control and his powers as an Alpha.

"Everything okay?" I asked.

"Yes." Greyson's smile was flinty and dangerous. "The Alphas who broke our rules have been...disciplined and escorted off our territory." His eyes flicked past me, to Scarlett and Radcliff. "Thank you for your help."

The siblings tilted their heads down—the usual wolf sign of respect.

"Of course," Scarlett stoically said.

"It was *great*." Radcliff wriggled his eyebrows until Scarlett elbowed him.

"Any other concerns?" I asked.

Greyson narrowed his eyes. "There are a few Alphas I'd like to toss out."

"Same," I said.

"But it seems like at least half of the group will be respectful," Greyson said. "Which means I will simply *make* the other half respectful."

I eyed Greyson, deeply aware it wasn't an idle threat as I could feel his Alpha powers stir.

My hunter powers immediately activated, offering some relief from the consuming and enthralling feel of his powers.

Radcliff blinked hard and Scarlett twitched—their hunter abilities activating as well.

A part of me wanted to lean into Greyson and assure him I was fine, but it didn't seem like a good idea with so many wolves around, and I wasn't sure if I should encourage the bond like that.

I glanced at the two older Alphas—who were still talking with Hector—then tried to nonchalantly scoot my foot closer to Greyson. It was harder than it sounds since I was wearing winter boots, but I nudged the toe of his worn hiking boots with mine.

He peeled his eyes from the still leaving Alphas and stared at me.

"We can handle this," I said. "The Pack can handle it, even if the other Alphas try something. You've led the Pack to be stronger than this."

Greyson stared at me a moment, then grinned and stepped into me. "Lady Hunter, is that a sense of *Pack* Pride? From you —the ever-insistent lone wolf?"

"Go break a cellphone," I grumbled. "I'm allowed to be proud of the Pack—I'm their Wolf's Kiss, aren't I?"

"You are your own individual," Greyson said. "The Pack is your home—if *you* choose it."

"Haven't I?" I asked.

Greyson's smile turned gentle. "Maybe reluctantly. You're with us, but your heart isn't ours just yet."

I blinked. "What is that supposed to mean?"

"Incoming," Scarlett whispered.

The two elderly Alphas left Hector and strolled toward us, their hands shoved in the pockets of their worn jeans and big smiles on their faces.

Greyson made a noise in the back of his throat, then slipped past me to talk to Radcliff and Scarlett in a lowered tone.

"Hey there!" the first Alpha called—he was the one wearing the Vikings hat. "The name's Tom. This here is my pal, Dale."

"Hello!" Dale—the one with the Green Bay Packers hat— grinned as he brushed snow off his shoulders. "Beautiful weather—maybe the lakes will freeze up for some ice fishing, don't ya think?"

I slipped my thumbs into the main part of my glove—they were getting so cold they hurt. "Yeah, snow can be beautiful."

"Look here, we won't take too much of your time," Tom— the Vikings fan—said. "You've been out here in the cold, you gotta go warm up. Also, there's a football game on, and that nice beta told us what sports bar will be playin' it on the television! He said the Drunk Skunk was a good one. You heard of it?"

"Yes," I said, recognizing it as the rustic but comfy bar where Papa Santos used to go to watch Monday night football. "They don't play music out of courtesy for their werewolf clientele and their ears. They also have really good onion straws."

"Oh, good. I could eat an order or two of those! Hopefully that scuffy rat Brock isn't going there, though," Dale said. "He's already half snookered, and the Lord knows he ain't hardly got any sense in that dense head of his. Another accident or two and he'll be as dumb as a stump."

"But, hey, you look like a nice girl," Tom said. "How's the Pack treat you? Good?"

"Yeah, of course." I laughed a little. "The Northern Lakes Pack has always been very welcoming."

"That's good," Dale said. "Since it seems like none of 'em fish—talk about missing out—at least they're good for something."

"How's the love life?" Tom asked. "You dating anyone?"

I blinked. "I...what?" I swiveled slightly, looking for Greyson.

He'd ghosted closer during the conversation, so my shoulder brushed his. He had his powers tightly capped, but a muscle in his cheek twitched.

"Hooo," Tom and Dale exclaimed together.

They looked from me to Greyson, then to each other.

"Didn't see that one comin'," Dale said.

"Me neither," Tom said.

"I'm sorry, see what coming?" I asked.

Dale nodded at Greyson. "We're talkin' 'bout you being Alpha Greyson's mate!"

Chapter 8

Pip

Behind me, Scarlett made a faint wheezing noise while Radcliff awkwardly cleared his throat, but they weren't the ones I was worried about.

This is bad. If Dale and Tom really are convinced and tell the other Alphas…

I made my smile apologetic. "Sorry, I'm afraid you're wrong," I said with the confidence of someone well versed in lying to wolves as I forcibly kept my pulse and breathing normal. "Greyson hasn't found his mate—"

"Nope," Tom said. "It's you, and you know it, don't you?"

Dale scratched his jaw. "A hunter and an Alpha, never thought I'd see the day. Striking couple, though."

"Oh yeah," Tom agreed.

"But, hey, this here is a problem." Dale frowned so deeply his forehead resembled a freshly plowed field. "She's not gonna wanna leave 'er mate behind."

"Good point," Tom said. "I reckon that means she's permanently with the Northern Lakes Pack."

"Yeah."

"Yeah."

Dale squinted. "That means we've got no reason to stay."

"I guess we could head home," Tom said. "Jeepers, that's disappointing."

They were silent, giving me a chance to put on my best welcome center smile in hopes I could stop this train before it crashed. "I'm sorry," I said. "But you two are really mistaken—"

"Oh, hey, we could still stay," Dale said. "Just 'cause *we* know they're mates don't mean we gotta go telling our Packs. I don't know about you, but the wife hasn't let me have a vacation in years."

"If we stay we could go fishing!" Tom said.

"And we could get that fish fry! By golly—let's do it," Dale declared.

"Gentlemen." Greyson eased into place by me and smiled at the pair. "There's been a misunderstanding. Yes, I have a mate, but—"

"But?" Tom said. "But you didn't expect nobody to notice?"

Dale laughed. "Sonny, we have sixty years on you if you're a day. You may think you're being all discreet like, but you can't fool us. We're *married*. We know the signs!"

"The intensity, the way you two move in sync, that she can get irritated with ya, your scent is on her, but it's faded so obviously you're tryin' to present yourselves like you're *not* mates," Tom said.

"Don't worry." Dale winked. "We won't tell no one."

"Plus it'll be a real laugh when everyone *does* figure it out," Tom cackled. "I mean, your Pack knows, right?"

"Uhhh," I said.

"Your Pack don't know? Creepers—you two are on thin ice," Dale said. "You best tell 'em—or their reaction will be worse than the time my wife invited her whole family to stay at our one-bedroom ranch house for Christmas and we ran out of brandy 'n beer!"

"Oof, that's bad," Tom said.

"You can say that again," Dale said. "So you better fix it, sonny." He shook a finger at Greyson, then grinned mischievously.

"Good talk. What do you say we go to the Dead Skunk for the game?" Tom asked.

"Yeah, okay," Dale said. "I knew there was a reason I liked you—even though you're a Vikings fan."

The duo turned away and started walking toward Main Street.

"You really wanna start that fight again?" Tom asked. "Last time I broke your foot."

"Only because your giant rear fell on it."

I watched them go, my jaw dropped so a snowflake twirled into my mouth and I choked when I inhaled it. "What just happened?" I asked.

"I'm not entirely sure," Greyson said.

"Is it true?"

I turned around, uneasily lifting my shoulders to my neck when Scarlett cradled her crossbow as she looked from Greyson to me.

Greyson briefly bumped his shoulder into mine as he rubbed his jaw.

He's trying to figure out how much he can tell them.

As I looked from Scarlett to Radcliff, I remembered how for the past few months they'd been steadfast in their desire to help the Pack, to help me with my magic, and I recognized that they both wore expressions I'd felt on my own face—the deep desire to belong.

They want to know—not because they want to use it against us, but because of what it means to know.

"Yes." I scratched my forehead, messing up my beanie cap. "The Pack doesn't know—not all of them, anyway."

"But we're going to tell them—soon," Greyson was fast to add.

Radcliff and Scarlett looked from me to Greyson.

"Wow," Radcliff said. "Talk about breaking barriers."

"I didn't think it was even possible," Scarlett said.

"It's not." When I felt Greyson stiffen next to me, I rethought my words. "Well," I said. "It makes complications. We haven't fully figured out how I accept the bond."

Or if I can…

"Pip can tell you more later." Greyson gazed across the park—which was emptier but not entirely so. "This isn't the greatest place to explain it."

"Of course!" Radcliff said.

"We're just honored you told us," Scarlett said—confirming my guess.

"Yes, of course. But…how did Tom and Dale figure it out?" I worriedly gnawed on my lip.

Greyson tugged my beanie down my forehead so it was back in place. "They're very powerful."

Radcliff's mouth dropped. "Them? Really?"

Greyson nodded. "You don't get that old—or remain an Alpha at that age—without being incredibly powerful. They just keep it locked up, like I do."

"Huh. That'll teach me not to judge by appearances," I said. "But do you think that means we should be worried?"

"I'm not certain." Greyson stared at the road that led downtown. "They seemed genuine in their desire to stay out of our mess and enjoy a week off."

"Alpha?" Hector called. "Pip has met everyone."

Greyson tugged my beanie down even lower so it settled over my eyes.

"Hey!" I pushed my hat back up, but Greyson was already halfway to Hector.

Scarlett started packing up her crossbow. "Are you ready to go home?"

"Yeah," I reluctantly said.

"Good, I'm freezing!" Radcliff did a few jumping jacks, then ran in place. "We'll walk with you back to your cottage."

"That seems inconvenient," I said. "If you walk me home, you'll just have to come all the way back to Timber Ridge." The pair had lived in the apartment over the welcome center since summer, so they'd literally make a circuit to walk with me.

"We don't mind," Radcliff said.

"Besides, then I can chat with Shania. She's a lot of fun," Scarlett said. "And maybe Aeric and Wyatt will show up, too!"

"Okay, in that case let's go home. I'll make you guys a cup of hot cocoa and some popcorn—for winter weather fortification!"

———

There was a painful stitch in my side, and I was embarrassingly close to wheezing, but I tugged on my hunter-given adrenaline to keep myself going even though I just wanted to give up and climb a tree.

The small group of wolves—who were positioned around me at the start of this particular exercise—had surged ahead.

They were forced to stop and look back at me every minute or so—checking on me with twitching black noses and tails raised in alarm—to make sure I hadn't totally fallen behind.

This isn't working. Our physical abilities are just too different.

Ember—the only werewolf in human form—jumped on top of a fallen log and crouched down.

Immediately the group I was traveling with—made of six

other wolves—halted in their tracks, the blacks, grays, and browns of their fur camouflaging them in the shadows.

I raised my arms over my head—trying to open up my lungs more and not pant, a noise that would give us away.

Ember cocked her head—listening to sounds I couldn't hear with my human hearing—and flicked one of her springy curls out of her face.

We were in a mock battle—something the wolves had started including me in now that I had a rough idea of how to activate my powers as a Wolf's Kiss.

I'd say it was exciting—previously they hadn't let me join any werewolf team whenever we had a mock battle. I'd always been stuck by myself and told to cause chaos on both sides on the rare occasion I was invited. The idea that I'd actually be *with* a side and fighting *with* packmates had been pretty enticing.

But I'd learned fast it was an exercise of defeat.

Ember pivoted on top of the tree trunk so she faced me. The silvery light of the moon glowed on her darker complexion as she thumped her hand over her heart and nodded to me.

It was the gesture for me to activate my powers.

I exhaled as quietly as I could before I grounded myself, placing my legs wide and keeping my knees soft.

I closed my eyes and inwardly found the place where my magic originated.

Humans with magic filtered wild magic through their blood into a usable form. Wizards did it whenever they needed to draw on their power, but as a hunter I was always filtering magic because some of my skills—like my hunter senses that allowed me to sense nearby werewolves—were always on.

Using my Wolf's Kiss powers required me to find the spot where my magic bubbled, and then make it work in reverse.

The best way I can describe it is I essentially made the river of my magic flow uphill instead of downhill.

I felt it when my power hit the right point, and I tried to fling it out and away from me so it covered the wolves in my group.

When I pried an eye open, I peered through the shadows, trying to see if it had worked.

As I watched, Aeric, Shania, and Wyatt grew in size. As werewolves, they were already bigger than regular wolves, but now they were much larger, their heads coming closer to my shoulder. My magic churned, making them stronger and even more dangerous.

Ember hopped off her tree stump and padded up to me on silent feet. "Nicely done—that was faster than you were last week."

"Thanks, it's nice to know I'm improving." I briefly smiled —it was good to know I could reliably kick-start my magic— but when I looked at the other wolves, my grin dimmed. "Though apparently I'm not improving in all areas."

River, Forrest, and Rio—the three other wolves in the group—hadn't changed at all.

River and Forrest didn't seem too bothered. They stared into the shadows, their noses twitching as they tried to scent out the other wolves we were fighting.

Rio, however, narrowed his eyes at me and briefly flashed his teeth before turning away in disgust.

This was the problem we'd been consistently running into with my magic. It would work on the wolves I was closest with —like Wyatt, Aeric, and Shania, Hector, Ember and even Greyson, East, and Young Jack.

But that was it. I couldn't seem to get it to work on the other wolves—at least not consistently. I'd been able to cast it on Young Jack's parents a few times, and a few other wolves, too, including Forrest. But it was pretty touch-and-go.

I sighed, and Ember patted my back. "It's been just a few weeks since you figured out how your Wolf's Kiss magic works. Give it time."

"Except who I can cast the magic on hasn't improved—or even changed at all—since I started." I opened my mouth, intending to continue, but Ember held a hand up as she stared into the shadows.

A few moments passed, and I only heard the rattle of tree branches and the quiet groan of the wind.

Wyatt, Aeric, and Shania shot ahead, Rio, River, and Forrest right behind them.

"Up you go," Ember whispered to me before she ran off after them.

I found the closest tree that would be an easy climb and threw myself at the trunk. I just cleared the second low-hanging branch when a mostly brown and gray wolf with a black saddle and mask circled around the base of the tree, peering up at me. It was Young Jack—one of the wolves I was particularly close to.

He leaned into the tree, making it groan.

Wolves were among the strongest of supernaturals. If Jack was really determined—and had enough time and some help from the other wolves—he could probably topple my tree.

"No." I shook my finger at him. "You'll get in trouble."

On more than one occasion Mayor Pearl had sent the Department of Natural Resources out to the Pack lodge with the complaint that we'd cleared preserve land when the wolves got it in their heads to knock me out of trees.

The results of such visits were financially painful enough that the wolves typically left me alone—particularly since they knew I could shoot them before they got me knocked out of said tree.

Young Jack growled at me.

I heard a yelp, and I reflexively pushed more of my magic

at the wolves, then immediately panicked when I saw Young Jack—who was *not* on my side of this particular fight—grow in height and breadth as my magic brushed him.

Shoot, shoot, shoot! I hurriedly yanked the magic off him, making sure I pressed extra down on Wyatt, Aeric, and Shania so it didn't slip off them.

Young Jack put a paw on the trunk. "*Aroo!*"

I could distinctly feel his crow of laughter at my magical failure through his musical howl.

I tapped my thigh bandolier of daggers, and he immediately turned off and frolicked away, having previously learned his lesson.

I shook my head and climbed higher in the tree.

When I found a limb that was both stable and high enough to suit me, I slipped my twin silver edged daggers out of my thigh bandolier.

The first three battles I was in I'd lugged my large, fae-made rifle around, making me even slower, before I caught on to the pattern and started packing lighter.

I leaned over the side of the tree, judging to see if any of the wolves were close enough for me to throw my weapons at, but that battle was mostly over.

Aeric, Wyatt, and Shania—powered up as they were—plowed over the other wolves—a group of twelve.

Rio, River, and Forrest rounded up the opposing wolves who tried to separate from the group—like Young Jack had—and one of the powered up trio swung by to grab whomever they'd pinned and tossed them to the ground like they were a puppy.

Aeric took down the last wolf just as I finished counting up to make sure they'd gotten everyone.

"Pip?" Ember called.

"Coming!" I sheathed my daggers and started scooting my way down the tree.

When the wind blew, caressing my face with its icy breath, I was thankful. I'd worked up a sweat running after my team.

I jumped off the second lowest branch and landed in a crouch. "That...worked. I guess."

Some of the recovering wolves groaned as they lumbered to their feet, shaking their heads and bodies to right their mussed fur.

"It went well," Ember said. "You're showing signs of improvement, and Aeric, Shania, and Wyatt are getting used to their enhanced abilities."

"Yeah...but the way we're organized doesn't seem very practical," I said. "And I accidentally powered up Young Jack for a few seconds."

"That's a control problem. You'll continue to get better at it. But you do have a point about our organizational method." Ember planted her hands on her hips as she pushed some of her dark, curly hair out of her face. "When the group surged ahead while running, they left you unprotected. You would have been easy to nab if we didn't already have an idea of how we'd encounter the other team. And it seems like a waste to have you climb a tree for every battle, particularly since we have no guarantee of fight locations—as the fight in the park showed."

Young Jack wandered up to me and jabbed his nose into my thigh, then wagged his tail.

I crouched down so I could rub the itchy spot in front of his ears and on the side of his head. "I'll check the Sabre family journals to see if they have any more information, but I can't say I'm expecting a chapter that details how to fight efficiently with wolves."

"I'd expect you're correct." Ember strolled up to me. "What we're doing is new. We have to figure out what works best for us." She rested a hand on my shoulder and squeezed. "But try not to be too hard on yourself."

Before I could respond, a beautiful howl pierced the cold night air, rippling through the forest.

I was pretty sure it was Greyson. Based on the way a few of the wolves bolted in the direction of the howl, I was right.

"That's our cue." Ember squeezed my shoulder again. "Rest up, and have a good night."

"Thanks, Ember. Bye everyone." I waved, but the rest of the wolves were already heading in the direction of Greyson's call, barely able to look back at me and wag their tails before they gave chase.

I shoved my hands deep in the pockets of my jacket to keep them warm as I turned around and headed in the direction of the Pack lodge.

They want to fight with me so they can take advantage of my powers, but there's no pretending I'm close enough to the Pack to invite me on a Pack run. Got it.

It was a jealous and unfair thought that I tried to dislodge from my brain.

Pack runs were for wolves only.

Human members of the Pack weren't allowed to come—it was too dangerous for them since they didn't have the strength, stamina, or night vision. And I wasn't allowed because I was a hunter and still not quite part of the Pack.

I thought I was in a weird spot before—halfway between the humans and wolves—but it was even worse now.

I could offer the wolves more power, but it didn't seem like they were particularly keen to give me any of their close trust in return, except for the wolves I was already friends with.

Maybe that's why I have such a hard time casting my enhancing magic on any wolves who aren't close to me?

I groaned and rubbed my eyes. "All of this learning and experimenting better be worth it."

It's not that I mind the work, it's just…all the feelings *I have to deal with in myself. I prefer avoidance. It's much more comfortable—mentally speaking.*

I felt a spot brighten in my hunter senses, and I swung around just in time to see Greyson running through the underbrush.

His tail swept back and forth once, and he slowed down as he approached me, giving me a thorough sniff—probably to make sure I hadn't hurt myself in the fight.

"Hey, Greyson. I'm fine." I crouched down, which put me lower than Greyson's head. He was the largest in the Pack as a wolf—at least in height, not necessarily shoulder width, because Wyatt and a few of the other wolves were built like tanks.

Greyson pressed his wet nose into my ear, then made a quiet noise that vibrated in his chest and sounded pleased.

I petted his shoulders, smiling a little when Greyson melted and leaned into me, pressed his furry forehead against mine.

There was something so reassuring about it after my moment of jealousy, that I felt myself thaw.

It's so unbelievably selfish of me…but sometimes I can't help but be grateful for the bond.

It was a disloyal thought considering the pain Greyson had to be in, but pressed against him like this, it felt like I wasn't alone.

A few wolves howled, their voices blending in a breath-taking song.

"You should go." I patted Greyson's back, then shuffled away.

Greyson studied me with his golden eyes.

I blinked, and in that instant he licked me. Since he was so massive, one little swipe of his tongue got the entire side of my head, and then he was off, ghosting through the barren under-growth of the forest before I could lodge a complaint.

"Greyson," I called after him. "What did I say about your

spit freezing on my face in the winter?" I stood up and tried to wipe my face off on my sleeve, and maybe I actually smiled a little instead of grimly marching through the dark forest.

At least I was mature enough to admit he left me in a better mood—until I realized he could probably feel something through the incomplete bond.

Hopefully it doesn't make him feel pain when I feel pain. The bond isn't whole, so it couldn't be that cruel, could it?

"When did my life get so complicated? Ack—" I half choked myself when I ducked a branch, which snagged on my scarf and pulled tight.

I ripped my scarf free, then marched on, heading in the direction that I *thought* the Pack lodge would be in. (It was hard to tell at night. I could see, but my sense of direction wasn't great since you can't see stars super well in the forest, even with all the bare trees.)

"I know, it was Amos Fletching. When I met him, everything got crazy," I growled. "If I'd known what a harbinger he was, I would have broken his nose at least one more time. *Woah!*"

I popped into a clearing in the woods and nearly smacked into a small body.

A human.

That'll teach me to only pay attention to my werewolf senses.

I planted my hand on my heart and gulped as I peered down at the poor soul I'd nearly trampled. "Teresa?

"Hi, Pip." Teresa gave me a smile, but I could see her lower lip trembled and her eyes were puffy from crying.

Teresa was Hector and Ember's eldest child. Her curly, dark brown hair was hidden under a fur lined hat, but I could still see Ember in her eyes and Hector in the set of her chin.

"Are you okay? What are you doing out here?" I peered down at her—Teresa was tall for her age, but she was still a few hands shorter than me.

"Nothing," Teresa said.

"Does Original Jack know you're out here?" I asked. "I thought you and your siblings were hanging out with him and the other humans tonight."

"I was at the lodge with everyone…" Teresa trailed off.

Before I could prod her to continue, the wolf chorus started up again, the notes hanging heavily in the frosty air. More wolves joined in this time, adding their yips to the song, which was as multifaceted as a gem as each wolf added to the song.

I could tell they were moving away, but I peered back—just in case.

When I looked back at Teresa, tears rolled down her brown cheeks, and she took in a rattling breath.

"Oh…Teresa." I moved in, wrapping my arms around her as if I could put the broken pieces of her heart back together.

All Teresa had wanted was to be a werewolf like her parents.

Aspen had torn that choice from her when she savaged Teresa.

As a ten-year-old, Teresa was too young to change. It was a miracle she'd survived—something her parents credited my powers for.

But since she'd survived the attack, her body had built up an immunity against the compound werewolves used to initiate the change from human to supernatural werewolf.

She'd never be able to become a werewolf. She'd be a human.

I stared up at the sky, feeling like trash.

Here I'd been feeling sorry for myself for all the practice and research I was pulling, when Teresa's dreams for her future had crumbled to the ground.

The bright, silvery moon was visible through the maze of tree branches, and I stared at it—hoping it could help me keep my tears back. "I'm sorry," I said.

"There's nothing you could have done," Teresa said in a weary voice that had no right belonging to a ten-year-old. "You kept me alive. And even if I can't be a wolf...I like living." Her voice shook and turned squeaky.

I hugged her tighter and felt useless.

Why can't I do anything for her? She's not a werewolf, but she's part of the Pack. Tell me, Wolf's Kiss magic, what's the point of making supernaturals stronger if I can't make a little girl who so desperately wanted to run with her family feel even a little better?

My magic didn't answer me. It flowed through my blood, as silent as the moon in the sky.

I held Teresa, gently rocking her—the brave little soul that she was.

This isn't right. And it's not how it's supposed to be.

———

I mindlessly rubbed at one of the faded keys on my keyboard as I watched the fae buzzing around the Timber Ridge Welcome Center.

Today we had three Day Court fae, two sisters from the Spring Court, and one tight-lipped fae who wouldn't say where he was from, which had the other fae accusing him of being from the Autumn Court.

"You're here to spy on behalf of King Fell, aren't you?" one of the Spring Court sisters said. She walked around him in a circle, her eyes narrowed.

The Autumn Court fae haughtily straightened the pamphlet on all the local werewolf businesses, which he was pretending to read. "I am here as a regular citizen, drawn by curiosity of what has all of the Courts talking so incessantly about this small city." He straightened his tunic, which was conspicuously made of earthy brown and orange colored velvet —Autumn Court colors—and covered with leaf embroidery.

Fae could be subtle, but they rarely were when it came to clothes.

"Yes, he's from the Autumn Court," one of the Day Court fae decided. "Only someone from the Autumn Court can manage to speak and sound like pure, unadulterated egotism."

"*I beg your pardon?*" the Autumn fae hissed.

I mashed my lips together to keep from laughing, but Shania—leaning against one of the ridiculously heavy magnets displays she'd just moved by herself—grinned.

I glanced down at East to see if he found the situation funny. He was lying on the dog bed positioned just behind me, but from the diligent way he was positioned—like a sphinx—he made the stuffed mattress look as comfortable as rock.

He peered up at me, but the expression on his wolf face was very grave.

"Come on, East, lighten up," I said.

East blinked at me.

"You can still have fun on guard duty," I said.

East shook his head once in a very firm "no," then slightly repositioned himself so he blocked the entrance to my hexagonal desk.

I'm starting to think Greyson assigned him on watch duty because he's going to go crazy from still missing so much work on the police force. He has the work ethic of a bee.

When the quiet bell on the door jangled, I pasted on my welcome center smile. "Good morning, welcome to Timber Ridge. Can I help you with anything?"

A female werewolf padded into the center, her head tilted and a puzzled frown playing on her lips when she saw the squabbling fae.

She was pretty, with bronze hair that draped around her in wild ringlets that made her look free spirited, and a long-legged, lean build.

"Hi." She gave me a slight smile as she approached the

desk, having decided to ignore the fae—who were congregated in front of the display of wolf statues. "I was told to come here."

"The welcome center is the perfect stop if you're new in town—or visiting," I said. "Is there anything in particular you wanted to see?"

"Yes." She smiled, which made her hazel eyes light up. "I want to meet Greyson."

Chapter 9

Pip

I tried to keep my smile even and almost knocked my keyboard off my desk. "Oh," I said. "You don't say?"

The werewolf nodded. "I'm in town with my brother—he's one of the Alphas visiting Timber Ridge to check you out," she said in a friendly way that wasn't going to do anything to keep my emotions from running amok. "I came with because this is probably the only time I'll be able to meet Alpha Greyson personally, and I might as well see if I'm his mate, right?"

Feeling something uncomfortably close to jealousy, I glanced down at East.

He'd climbed off his bed and shoved his head outside my desk long enough to sniff, then looked up at me with a questioning expression that managed to communicate his willingness to get rid of the visitor.

My hands hidden from the female werewolf by my desk, I tried to shoo him off. "Of course," I lied. "It's great to be efficient."

"One of my friends came to Timber Ridge before," she

continued. "She said you were a great help. You gave her Greyson's schedule and everything."

Before I'd learned I was Greyson's mate, one of my favorite hobbies had been directing visiting female werewolves who paraded through Timber Ridge in hopes of seeing if they were Greyson's mate.

The city had profited off the unusual tourists, and Greyson was annoyed by their presence—which was quality entertainment for me considering how little I'd known about the situation.

But what can I say, knowing I'm Greyson's mate? Even if I'm not sure what we're going to do about the bond, it would feel unbelievably weird helping her. Not that I'd be jealous.

I wouldn't.

For certain.

Haha!

But I don't think Greyson would appreciate it, and it's, it just…

I opened and closed my mouth several times, trying to figure out what to say to the visitor. "Ahaha, yes. I'm very… invested in the issue," I finally said.

East grunted at me in disgust, then stalked off, circling around my desk and heading for the gift shop, his nails clicking on the floor.

"Great!" the visiting werewolf chirped in a happy voice. "Where will he be in the next three hours?"

"Uhhh, I'm not sure," I said truthfully. "I used to keep a binder of his schedule…but I haven't. Lately."

I glanced at the slot in my desk where the binder—which I'd previously updated every week with his schedule—sat with a fine layer of dust on it.

The werewolf thoughtfully frowned. "Why not?"

Think, think, think!

"The Pack was closed to visitors for a few weeks when it

was experiencing…issues with a rogue werewolf biting humans and forcing unlawful changes," I said, walking the line of truth.

"Oh, yes, I heard about Aspen," the werewolf said. "That must have been horrible. But didn't that get wrapped up at the beginning of November? It's now December."

"Ahhh," I said.

What do I say? I can't tell her Greyson banned me from helping—his reputation shouldn't have to suffer because I feel weird about this. Should I just offer to introduce her to him later? But that feels…weird.

It wasn't weird because I felt anything from the bond. It was latent for me. It didn't do anything.

Which means my reluctance is all me. Because adding my own feelings into a mate-bond-that-can't-be-completed sounds like an excellent recipe.

"She still doesn't have his schedule. She doesn't need to, because Alpha Greyson isn't taking any kind of visitors because of Pip." Shania strolled across the welcome center, leaving the little walled off gift shop so she could join me behind the desk, East trailing behind her.

"*Shania*," I growled, every nerve in my body lighting up. I felt a wave of adrenaline dose me while my hunter magic tried to figure out what threat had ratcheted up my fight-or-flight instinct.

Is she seriously going to spill our secret?!

"It's true." Shania shrugged. "Because of all the visiting Alphas—who are here for you—he's not taking visitors. He's too focused on keeping Timber Ridge safe and slamming down any weird ideas some of the Alphas might get."

I relaxed at the perfectly reasonable explanation—and was a little mad at myself that I hadn't thought of it. "Yeah, things are a little tense," I agreed. "Attempting to speak with him likely wouldn't go very well."

"That makes sense." The visiting werewolf reluctantly

nodded. "I guess it really shows how strong he is that he has all of these Alphas invading his territory, and he hasn't lost it."

"Strong Alphas—like Greyson—have to be able to control their wolf instincts," I said. "Or he wouldn't be able to handle the Northern Lakes Pack."

"Or having a Wolf's Kiss running around," Shania cheerfully added. "Our Alpha is just that outstanding."

I paused, then nodded.

Realistically, Greyson was even more amazing than we'd summarized. Not only was he mentally able to handle all the Alphas—when his wolf instinct would be screaming to force them out—he was doing that *while* dealing with his half-formed mate bond, which was a constant physical strain.

I need to prioritize dealing with it. Playing nice with the visiting Alphas just takes diligence, not brain cells. I should be doing more research —for Greyson's sake. He's already dealing with enough.

"It was worth checking on," the visiting werewolf said.

"Of course." I awkwardly cleared my throat, then got my smile back on. "While you're here, would you like any information on the Pack? There's a complimentary phone app you can download to find out information on the Pack's closest clothes drop offs—which is really important to know since the human mayor of Timber Ridge has a serious grudge against werewolf nudity."

"Oh." The pretty werewolf blinked, then smiled. "Sure. I think my brother is planning to stick around here for a few more days."

"We also have maps, over here." Shania grabbed three of the pamphlets I handed out to all visiting werewolves—they marked out the Pack rules, the details for downloading the app, and a list of werewolf-owned businesses.

She then beckoned for our guest to follow her to a larger display of maps.

I exhaled and watched the two chatter happily.

Fated

East nudged my leg with his wet nose.

"You got Shania?" I asked.

He snapped off a nod.

"Thank you. I appreciate it." I briefly crouched down to pet his shoulders and scratch the sides of his face for him.

The tinny sound of howling wolf toys wafted from the gift shop, and I stood up, resting my hands on the top of my desk —which had smoothed with age.

Another fae marched out of the gift shop.

I wasn't entirely sure what Court he was with.

For starters, his clothes were more robe like—the top layer was almost closer to a wizard jacket—and I could see a packet of cat treats poking out of one of the pockets.

His hair was a coppery shade of brunette, but his hairstyle was unusual for fae in that it was cut short on the sides but long in the back and on the top of his head—which was pulled back from his face in a braid—so he almost looked more like a viking than a fae.

He had the angular chin and high cheekbones you didn't see on anyone but fae, but the longer I looked at him the more I noticed his nose was sharper than any fae—who could use illusion magic as easily as I used my hunter senses—would have put up with, and his smile was too genuine for a typical fae noble.

He strode up to my desk with the confidence of someone able to hold their own in a fight and set two overflowing baskets of gift shop merchandise on the counter.

"Your gift shop is positively wonderful," he declared. His voice had the cultured tone fae typically have, but there was too much inflection in it.

Who the heck is this guy?

"I'm glad you found some things you liked," I said. "Can I ring you up?"

"Please do. Though I must ask, do you think this would fit

a cat?" The handsome fae dug a baby onesie out of the pile. It was a pretty blue color covered in cartoon gray wolves, and came with a little bib that said, "Will Howl For Food."

I blinked at the idea of a fae owning a cat, much less dressing it up. "It would depend on how big your cat is," I said. "Police Chief Henry bought a newborn onesie for his and his wife's seven-pound Chihuahua. Does your cat weigh more than seven pounds?"

"I would never dare to ask a lady her weight, but I daresay she does." The fae peered at the onesie. "This one isn't for a newborn, though. It's for a six to nine-month-old."

"I think it would fit," I said.

"Wonderful! She'll be delighted with it." The handsome fae smiled at me. His eyes crinkled in a way that made him more devastatingly handsome than the perfect beauty of the Autumn Fae—who was still arguing with the two Day Court fae.

"I have *got* to tell my best friend about this city," the handsome fae told me.

I scanned his onesie, then put it in the growing pile as I picked up a wooden wolf Christmas ornament. "We are pleased to announce that Howl-In Café has expanded its tea offerings."

Fae were crazy about tea. After it became apparent that our sudden boom in fae tourists wasn't a week or two phenomenon, Greyson had ordered some fancy loose-leaf teas for our new customers, which had finally come in this week.

"That is marvelous," my fae customer said. "Though he won't care about that—he's not much of a tea person. I shall have to look into it, for myself. Tell me, do you sell loose leaf tea, and do you know if it can be charmed?"

I scanned the barcode of a wooden flute that was built to mimic the sound of a wolf's howl. "I'm afraid I don't know the ins and outs of charming tea, but the Sweets Shoppe just got its first shipment of loose leaf coconut chai tea."

"How wonderful! I shall have to try it and see if it inspires any kind of charms or spells." A ringtone blasted from within another one of the fae's many pockets. It took him a moment to dig his cellphone out, which gave me enough time to recognize the tune as a funeral march.

The fae brightened and accepted the call. "Bestie! I was just talking about you. I'm at the most adorable werewolf city. You'd hate it."

I finished scanning the fae's purchases—which filled four paper bags. He finished his call as I rang up the total, then dutifully passed me his credit card—which had the Starbucks logo on it, interestingly enough.

"Would you like some help carrying these out?" I asked.

The fae paused, patted his chin for some reason, then turned to me with a puzzled frown.

"Because there are four bags and you have two arms," I said, confused by his reaction.

He brightened. "Oh! That would be wonderful. I did drive here, and I paid for the convenience of street parking. If you do not mind?"

"Not at all." I picked up two of the bags, taking the heaviest ones—fae were not known for their strength, and as a hunter I could most assuredly outlift him. "Shania, can you keep an eye on the desk for a minute—oof, watch it, East." I almost tripped when East slipped in front of me, heading to the door with the air of a bodyguard intent on constant vigilance.

"Consider it handled." Shania strolled up to the desk, leaving the visiting werewolf gazing longingly at the canvas print of Greyson—which didn't make me feel weird *at all*. Not even a little bit.

"Thanks." I juggled the bags long enough to open the door, then stepped outside into the blasting, icy cold wind.

East—warm with his thick fur—trotted out, his tail wagging as he sniffed the wind.

My teeth immediately started to chatter, but I followed the fae to his car and helped him load his purchases—though I did look quizzically at the baby seat strapped in the backseat as East sniffed a circuit around the car, inspecting all four tires.

"Thank you for your help! I believe I shall sample the treats at your Howl-In Café before checking out the Sweets Shoppe —which, I'm told, has fantastic fudge?" The fae smiled at me, seemingly not at all bothered by the cold weather.

"The best in Northern Wisconsin," I said. "Though we can't advertise that for legal reasons."

"And as my thank you for your help, here—a little tea for yourself as my thanks, nothing needed in return." The fae winked at me as he offered a little silk satchel of a single serving of tea. "It'll warm you up when you get back inside."

I wasn't sure it was a great idea to take tea from a fae who had just asked me if the stuff the Sweets Shoppe sold could be charmed, but fae rarely gave gifts with no strings attached like this. Refusing it would be rude. Besides, most fae magic didn't work on wizards or any subset of human with magic. (Though I wasn't sure if that rule applied to spells that were ingested.)

"Thank you." I took the tea with what I hoped was a smile —my lips were too cold to know for sure.

"Of course! Until next time!" The fae left, his coat swirling behind him as he hurried up the road, heading in the direction of Howl-In Café.

Before I could turn to the welcome center, East slapped one of his giant front paws on my thigh and stared at my hands.

Shivering, I crouched down and let him smell the tea in my hands.

He sniffed it, backed off, then sneezed hard enough that it jostled his balance.

"Come on, East, it's freezing." I hurried up the steps to the door, wishing I'd thought to at least put my hat on or something.

"Hunter Sabre."

I turned around, frowning when I recognized the werewolf standing at the foot of the stairs.

He was one of the Alphas who had first shown up on Main Street—the one with watermelon crushing thighs, beady eyes, and a gold fang tooth. He'd introduced himself at my little meet and greet.

What was his name again?

"Kulk," I said.

"*Alpha* Kulk," he informed me.

I would have shrugged if my shoulders weren't so cold I couldn't unhunch them. "How can I help you, Kulk?"

Kulk audibly ground his teeth at my omission of his title— which meant he was pretty weak. Only weak wolves got their tails in a knot over trying to make outsiders follow stupid wolf semantics. "After hearing more about your powers, I've made a decision."

"Have you now?" I politely asked as I yanked the door open, prepping for a fast getaway—announcements of decisions were never a fast process, but manners or not, I wasn't going to freeze out on the front step because Kulk had hair poking out of his shirt collar and his innate wolf heat.

"You may come back to my Pack with me," Kulk said.

I reviewed our conversation twice, certain I'd missed something, before I realized I hadn't. "No thanks." I opened the door all the way, intending to slip inside—though East was snarling, and his fur was standing up now.

"That wasn't an offer," Kulk said. "It was an order." He stepped up the first stair and crouched in preparation.

East bristled, and I already had my silver tipped daggers lined up to throw.

But before Kulk could jump, and just before I released my daggers, he was yanked backwards.

"And that's enough," a dry, wry voice drawled.

It took me a moment to realize Dale, the plaid wearing, fish-fry going Alpha that had picked up on Greyson and me being mates and had as much white hair as I did, casually held Kulk over his head.

Kulk was gurgling and trying to pry Dale's hand off him, but Dale stood on the sidewalk and turned to address his friend, Tom, with a scowl. "Youngsters these days are as rude as they are stupid."

"Not all of them," Tom said. "Just the power-hungry ones —and cocky idiots who don't understand power." Tom shook his head at Kulk, then folded his arms across his chest. "Or he woulda realized this fine missy was going to slit his throat before he could even touch her guard. You alright, there, Hunter Sabre?"

"Alpha Dale, Alpha Tom, good evening." I didn't put my daggers away, but my smile was genuine. "I'm fine—thanks to your help."

"Aww, shucks, you had 'im handled." Dale peered up at Kulk, then shook him by the throat so his limbs flopped and he smacked himself a few times. "But us old dogs gotta step in every now and then and discipline the pups, or we'll find ourselves an extinct race of supernaturals."

"No doubt." Tom sagely nodded.

I was starting to shiver again as my magic-given adrenaline started to fade, and I had a moment of weakness where I just wanted Greyson to show up and fix it all.

This is the second time I've been attacked since the Alphas have shown up—that's worse than I thought. I assumed the raw power of the Northern Lakes Pack would make them toe the line more. But it seems like being polite is going to be way more difficult than I realized.

I staggered a step, and East pushed into my side, whining in concern.

"Are you sure everything is okay, Hunter Sabre?" Tom asked.

I forced a smile. "Right as rain, er...snow." I frowned at the ice that coated a few bushes planted along the sides of the building.

"Pip." Greyson appeared—as if he could sense my hidden thoughts—and jumped the stairs, wrapping an arm around me and tipping me against his chest, where I immediately started to feel warm again.

I put my daggers away—I didn't want to accidentally stab him—then snuck my arms around his back and clutched his shirt in my fists.

It felt wrong to admit it considering the pain Greyson was probably in because of the bond, but I felt a lot better now that he'd arrived.

"Ahhh yes, Alpha Greyson," Tom said. "Figured you'd arrive shortly. We caught this mutt about to attack yer hunter. She seemed angry enough to kill him—rightfully so—but seemed like that would be a bother for you to deal with, so we stepped in."

"*I* stepped in," Dale corrected him. "You're too slow tonight since you ate about five pounds of potato pancakes."

Tom licked his chops and patted his belly. "They were too good to pass up."

"Thank you for your help." Greyson slightly inclined his head to the two elderly Alphas.

"Don't mention it," Dale said.

"Yeah, don't," Tom echoed. "Or our wives will find out. Then *they'll* figure out why this whole endeavor is failed, and then we'll get called home before we get any ice fishing done."

I laughed at Tom's explanation, and Greyson politely smiled before he lowered his mouth to my ear, his lips brushing my earlobe. "Head inside—you're nearly frozen. I'll handle Kulk."

"Are you just going to warn him?" I asked.

"No." Greyson's golden eyes glowed in the muted light cast

by the cloudy sky. "I'm throwing him out of our territory. With a reminder of why he shouldn't try to come back."

Kulk had given up fighting Dale and hung limply from the older wolf's fist, but at Greyson's words he started flailing again, whimpering as the tiniest hint of Greyson's powers rolled off him and filled the area.

"Great," I said. "And thanks."

Greyson wrapped his arms more tightly around me for another moment, and I automatically did the same, sinking into the brief comfort—until I realized this had to be a wolf instinct pushing him to wrap me in his scent.

I peeled myself off him, then smiled at Tom and Dale. "Thanks again—enjoy more potato pancakes!"

"Always," Tom cheerfully said as I retreated inside.

"Everything okay?" Shania asked as I shut the door.

"Yeah, there was a bit of a skirmish, but it's taken care of." I rubbed my frozen hands together and bustled back to my desk, East following so closely he almost stepped on my heels.

Shania drifted over, a look of concern settling on her face. "A skirmish?"

My shoulders jumped in a jerky shrug. "An Alpha attempted to jump me. Dale and Tom—the two older Alphas —stopped him before I had a chance. Greyson showed up, though, and is taking care of it."

Shania leaned across the desk, studying me—though I was pretty sure she was actually trying to get a whiff of me based on the way her nose twitched. "Are you okay?"

"A little rattled," I admitted. "It's been an...unusual day." I glanced at the visiting female werewolf, who was chatting with the Spring Court fae who appeared to be talking her into taking a selfie with them.

"Yeah." Shania glanced over at the other werewolf. "I was going to give you grief about all your years of diligence for sharing Greyson's location coming to bite you in the rear, but it doesn't seem appropriate now."

"Believe me, I don't need the teasing to be aware of just how messed up everything has gotten." I sighed and rested my hands on the top of my desk, sagging slightly.

The door jingled open, and I stiffened, then relaxed immediately when I saw Original Jack—wearing a buttery brown colored Carhartt jacket and holding the hand of a small kid.

I was pretty sure the kid was Rory—one of the children Original Jack frequently looked after while his parents were off on Pack business—but he was wearing a snowsuit, scarf, and hat, so the only part I could see were his eyes.

"Pip," Original Jack said, his voice as warm and soothing as a crackling fire. "Alpha Greyson texted me. Are you doing okay?"

I smiled back—though I knew it slipped a little under Original Jack's caring gaze. "Yeah. The Alpha practically told me what he was going to do before he even tried to jump me, so I was prepared."

The wrapped up kiddo said something, but it was muffled from the scarf. He wrestled it off his face and pushed his hat off, revealing that my guess had been right, and it was five-year-old Rory wrapped up like a marshmallow. "That sounds scary," he said.

I leaned farther over my desk so I could smile down at him. "Nah, it wasn't. He was really weak compared to your parents and other Northern Lakes wolves. No one stands a chance against them!"

"Even so, it's upsetting to be attacked outside your workplace. Here." Original Jack stomped his boots to clean them of snow so he didn't track slush into the center, then he ducked aside, revealing Olivia.

Olivia was a teenager—the daughter of two Northern

Lakes wolves—who had a major chip on her shoulder when it came to me.

Most of the humans involved with the Northern Lakes Pack —excluding Original Jack and the kids—didn't understand why I was included in certain Pack activities and they were not. (Since they were humans, they never had the pleasure of seeing the werewolves beat on me in practice and witness my own supernatural powers that set me apart from normal people.)

It'd only gotten worse since the Pack revealed that I was a Wolf's Kiss, which made me an even more unique entity than before.

Olivia stared at the beautiful fae—I'd say with shock, but a lot of the fae had visited Howl-In Café, which she worked at, as part of their "Tour of Timber Ridge," so it wasn't like she hadn't seen them by the dozens before. No, she was trying to ignore me on purpose.

"Olivia," Original Jack said, his voice gentle but edged with a warning.

Olivia guiltily peered up at Original Jack. "Sorry."

He smiled at her. "Remember why we're here?"

Original Jack was something like an adopted dad to all the human children of the werewolf Pack, and he was the contact point for all the humans who were a part of the Northern Lakes, typically because—like Jack—they married into the Pack.

He'd watched Olivia since she was a child—as he was with Rory. He was a fantastic father figure, even though he and his werewolf wife never had any kids.

"Yeah." Olivia copied him and wiped her boots off on the front mat before she stalked across the welcome center and thrust a black travel mug decorated with white wolves at me. "Here."

"Oh. Thank you." I took the travel mug and snapped the

lid open, smiling when the rich, creamy scent of Howl-In Café hot cocoa—made with real chocolate and topped with whipped cream—hit my nose. "That's so thoughtful of you!"

"We can't take credit. Alpha Greyson asked us to bring you some—he said you needed it." Original Jack's smile grew, but Olivia openly scowled at me.

I ignored her sour temperament and gave her an extra big smile. "Thanks, Olivia, for bringing it over."

Olivia's scowl grew. "I only did it because Original Jack was watching Rory and didn't have the free hands."

I couldn't help myself, I had to poke the proverbial bear just a little. "That's disappointing, I thought you did it because you wanted to see me." I sighed dramatically.

Olivia screwed up her face in horror.

There was a time when her open rejection and the dislike of most of the humans involved in the Northern Lakes Pack would have…not hurt me precisely, but made me feel like I was an outsider. As a hunter living with wolves and humans alike, I didn't belong to either group.

Now…maybe it was because Radcliff and Scarlett were in Timber Ridge, or maybe it was that I spent so much time with wolves, or maybe it was even just because of the sheer amount of ridiculous danger I'd lived through in the past few months, but it didn't sting like it used to.

I grinned at Original Jack. "Thanks for the delivery. I appreciate the pick-me-up."

The bell over the door jingled again, and River—a pretty Northern Lakes wolf who appeared pint sized but could have easily thrown Original Jack over her shoulder—hopped into the doorway, wearing only a sweater, leggings, boots, and a scarf.

"Hello, Pip. I'm here as backup," she announced.

Behind her, the door opened again to admit her boyfriend,

Noah. He was a human—another one I didn't get along with great, though I liked River well enough.

I waved to him, even though he ignored me, then turned my attention to River. "Is East going off duty?" I asked.

River wildly shook her head, brushing snow from her hair. "Nope."

"But East is already here as backup for Shania."

River's grin was wolfish enough that it made Rory totter a step back into Original Jack's side. "Then consider me backup of the backup," she said. "And as backup, backup, I intend to maim anyone who is stupid enough to try you."

Noah adjusted his hat. "I get that you need to stay because wolves keep trying to have a go at Pip, but I don't get *why* they want her so badly."

River smiled and patted his hand. "It's a wolf thing, babe. It wouldn't make sense to you. Have a great afternoon, I'll see you for dinner?"

Noah frowned—not at River for her vague explanation, but me, because it was obviously my fault he wouldn't understand. "Yeah. See you then." He leaned over and kissed her, then headed out.

River seemed oblivious to his displeasure. Instead she clapped her hands with glee, making East perk his ears. "This is going to be so fun!" she said. "I don't know what has Greyson in the mood for blood, but I'm ready to follow his orders and bite any Alpha who comes at us!"

"It is odd." Original Jack rested his eyes on me, his gaze thoughtful. "Greyson usually holds back and rules with pure strength of spirit on cases like this. But he seemed to take the Alpha's attack on you…personally."

River paused. "Yeah, that is weird."

This is bad—I don't want them thinking about why that might be!

I glanced at Shania—her eyes were bulging out of her head.

"Well, I am the Pack's hunter," I said.

Original Jack laughed. "That's true. That would be enough to set him off—and I'm so happy to hear you finally admit to belonging to the Pack. Santos and Dulce worried you'd always hold back, you know."

They did?

It was surprising to hear—they'd always told me I was free to leave the Pack when I wanted to. *The whole time they raised me, did they want me to stay? Was it because I was a Wolf's Kiss?*

No.

Mama Dulce and Papa Santos were two of the most extraordinary people I'd ever met. They would never do that to me.

"Enjoy the cocoa, Pip. Come on, Rory. We have to take Olivia to driver's ed." Original Jack herded the other humans out of the welcome center, leaving me alone with the fae and werewolves and my very confused thoughts.

Chapter 10

Greyson

"Yes, he attacked her on the street." I over enunciated the words with my anger, and my phone creaked in my hand, reminding me to relax my grasp or risk breaking it. "Look, I can handle threats on me, but I won't tolerate any against Pip."

"*Understandable,*" Pre-Dominant Harka replied. "*Unfortunately, there's not much I can do. You punished him and exiled him from your territory, right?*"

"Yeah. He's got a few broken bones. I can't promise he'll stay Alpha if he goes back to his Pack in this condition. Keeping that in mind, I've got eyes on the borders—and Timber Ridge itself—to make certain he doesn't come back."

"*Then hopefully that will take care of it. I imagine things will be a little crazy initially as Alphas try to test Hunter Sabre—and you. Once you make a few examples of them, things will settle down—*"

"Alpha Greyson, I challenge you for your position of Alpha over the Northern Lakes Pack."

I turned around and was very unimpressed with my newest challenger—the third since Alphas had started sniffing around Pip.

It was a female Alpha with narrowed eyes and a smirk that was way too cocky considering she was about to go against me.

She was more presentable than the first two challengers, I'd give her that—one of them had been a scruffy kid who was so young his Pack was probably four wolves total if I had to guess, the second had been an older guy that I'd been more gentle with because he almost looked old enough to be my grandfather, and Pip would be sure to find out if word got out I was beating up old people.

"If I win, the Northern Lakes Pack becomes—"

"Zip it. I don't need to hear the whole thing. Just attack," I told her before returning my attention to Harka. "You said a few examples—how many is a few? I'd appreciate an estimate."

"Did I just hear someone issue a challenge to you?"

"Yeah. She said it loud enough I imagine my phone picked it up." I watched the female circle around me, her teeth bared.

"Don't you need to get off the phone?"

"Why would I need that?"

The challenger gave a howling yell as she ran at me.

I pivoted to put more of my weight on my left leg, then kicked my right leg high. I got her square in the face, and I might have ground my heel into her nose with a little too much pleasure.

I've never claimed to be a good wolf.

The challenger was tossed backwards, smacking into the side of a tiny hill.

I pulled the phone away from my face. "Hector? I've got another challenger for you to dump outside our territory."

Hector emerged from the trees. "I heard this one howl her

challenge." He stopped just short of her and smoothed his goatee as he studied the print of ice, sand, and grit my boot had left on her face. "They aren't learning very quickly, are they?"

"No," I said. "Thanks for handling it."

Hector nodded to me, then picked the challenger up and plopped her on his shoulder with ease, even though the tall, muscled woman must have easily weighed two hundred pounds.

He then set off, his steps light—though not as noiseless as they'd been before he picked up the extra weight.

I lifted my phone back to my ear. "I apologize for the interruption, Pre-Dominant."

"*It sounds unavoidable given how…busy you are.*"

"I'm fine. It's Pip's security I'm worried about."

"*Yeah, I imagine so given what you are. Okay, how about this—after the next serious attempt, you visit my offices again and we talk it over and see if there are any other alternatives.*"

"Fine. Thank you, Pre-Dominant."

"*Anytime, Alpha Greyson.*"

I hung up the call, then exhaled and stared up at the trees that stretched over my head.

It's a Saturday. Most of the werewolf businesses are closed, but I need to start sending out reminders about tax preparations, and I should join at least one of the border patrols and territory patrols, and check in with the Alphas since we've had a few new ones arrive. Competency is a great intimidation tactic—if they are smart enough to recognize it.

I scoffed at the thought, then was zapped with an abrupt wave of emotion that originated in the painfully empty spot in my heart where my bond should have sat.

It hit me so hard and with such force I flinched, and my phone broke in my hand.

Pip?

The wolf paw print branded into my bicep—the mark of my bond—twinged. I ignored the shattered phone as I tried to track the feeling.

That's Pip—is she in trouble?

While I couldn't pick up much of her emotion since our bond wasn't complete, it turns out fear, anxiety, and a sense of danger were easy to broadcast across the bond.

It worked out well for me—I would be notified as soon as she felt she was in danger, and I could more easily find her through the broken bond than I could have before.

I let the bond tug me toward her to get the right direction, then I started running.

I was about a minute out before I recognized that she wasn't feeling fear or worry, but something very different: glee.

Surprised, I slowly emerged from the forest, curious to see what had her so happy.

She was standing in a paved parking lot located next to one of the Pack-owned lakes, surrounded by a few werewolves and humans.

The parking lot was practically a skating rink with a thick coat of ice on it, and someone—Pip, most likely—had spray painted a target on two ends of the ice slick. It was a recent paint job based on the sour, chemical smell of the paint that lingered in the fresh air.

Young Jack, Forrest, and East stood at one end of the parking lot, while Tucker, Olivia, and Amelia were at the other.

Olivia, Amelia, Forrest, and East were all holding house brooms and looked more than a little confused, while Young Jack and Tucker held disk-like weights.

"What is this called again?" Young Jack shouted across the parking lot.

"Curling!" Pip bellowed back. "I saw an article about it, and I've been waiting to make you all try it!"

"Objection." Olivia tossed her head and did her best to sound uppity and full of attitude—never mind that she was standing in the middle of a parking lot doing whatever Pip wanted her to. "This can't be a real sport."

"Of course it is," Pip said. "It's in the Winter Olympics! Now, hop to it!"

Tucker shrugged and chucked the weight so it went skidding across the parking lot.

Olivia and Amelia tottered in front of it, sweeping the ice off with their brooms.

The weight missed the target by several feet.

"Question." East raised his hand as Olivia and Amelia retreated back to their side. "Are we doing this right?"

"You're not." Pip planted her hands on her hips and laughed manically. "But that's fine, it's for my amusement!"

Tucker raised his hand. "No it's not—Jack and I are settling an argument!"

Ahhh, that explains it.

Pip—as she was neither a human nor a wolf—was frequently approached by the Pack to settle any arguments between humans and wolves. Her favorite method to do this was to engage the two sides in a physical activity—one that would be difficult for werewolves despite their superior strength because sports always required immense amounts of control.

Pip had cycled through bowling, mini golf, pickleball, volleyball, and more in her insistence at leveling the playing field for the argument.

"Yeah, and I'm going to win this fight." Young Jack fixed his hold on his weight. "But this does feel weird. It's my first time on the werewolf side—strength for the win!" He threw the weight.

Forrest and East didn't even try to chase after it. They just watched the weight arc over the ice, hit it and send icy chunks ricocheting everywhere, then bounce off a curb and chip the cement.

"I'm glad you decided to try curling on wolf territory, Pip," East announced. "The Timber Ridge Department of Public Works would be very angry with you for chipping the curb. That's going to cost a lot of money to fix."

"I'm more afraid of Mayor Pearl," Pip said. "But he's got a point, Young Jack! You better work on your strength control some more."

"Do you want to come get a Pomeranian Puppy Powerup?" Wyatt asked. "It'll make you feel better!"

"No." Young Jack puffed his chest out. "I don't need it!"

"Your loss," Wyatt said.

Pip elbowed her friend in the side. "Don't offer me out like some kind of miracle cure."

"Aww, don't sell yourself short like that!" Aeric wrapped his arms around Pip and lifted her an inch off the ground as he hugged her.

The sight didn't bother me—the Pack commonly smothered Pip in love and affection. She'd inherited magic from her mother's hunter family that made her give off puppy pheromones as a defensive technique. All wolves loved puppies, so it smoothed over a lot of potential disagreements she'd have with the Pack.

"Your hugs are magical," Shania added. "So I want one next, since Young Jack is too foolish to see that he needs one."

"Here, I'll pass her off." Aeric dumped Pip into his girlfriend's open arms.

"Guys," Pip complained. "I can't see like this."

"I'd just give up, Jack," Forrest advised as he studied his broom. "As soon as you enter one of Pip's contests to settle on a winner, it's been decided that there will be *no* winner."

Typically Pip's sports competitions ended in exhaustion

with both sides giving up because continuing it was worse than making up.

And yet they still search her out, even though they know the outcome.

It was an interesting dynamic—especially since more than a few of the human teenagers resented Pip for being allowed into so many Pack activities that humans were banned from.

"Forrest, I'm so proud of you! You're getting wise in your old age!" Pip called to him.

I was glad to see Aeric, Wyatt, and Shania were with her, as were Teresa and a couple of the other human kids.

Werewolf children were typically born as humans, but they still had some of the werewolf thirst for violence with how they *loved* to turn up for Pip's rulings on physical sports.

I might have smiled as I backed into the cover of the forest and made my way around the parking lot, popping back out of the forest in the area behind Pip's back.

She must have sensed me approach with her hunter magic, because she turned around and waved to me.

Wyatt and Aeric turned with her and lowered their heads to me—they'd probably gotten a glimpse of me earlier judging by how unsurprised they were.

"Alpha Greyson," Aeric said once I reached them.

"Hi, Alpha Greyson." Teresa shyly smiled at me.

I crouched down so I didn't loom over her so much. "Hello. Are you enjoying Pip's newest torture method?"

Teresa giggled and glanced up at Pip.

Something in me unwound a little.

I'd been worried about Teresa. She'd been through a lot in the past few months. She could have easily become angry or bitter, but the brave little thing was proving she had the heart of a wolf with her determination to keep going.

I noticed she seemed to be even more taken with Pip these days—probably because again, as a hunter, Pip was neither wolf nor human, which made her safe.

The Pack—from the children like Teresa to the adults like Moira— put a lot of trust in her.

I stood up and leaned into Pip, making sure my shoulder bumped into hers. "Settling another wolf-human score, I see?"

"Yeah," Pip said. She paused, then it seemed to dawn on her that I was there. "I'm sorry, was there something…did I…?" She hesitated, then glanced around us, unable to say anything more because of all the ignorant packmates who didn't yet know about us.

Hmm, at least she's aware of the bond.

She'd been negative about the bond ever since she found out about it. As best I could tell, she wasn't rejecting me, which was just about the only thing I couldn't forcibly fix, so that boded well.

But I didn't care for her thinly veiled intention to break our bond. She hadn't outright said it, but I could smell her guilt, and her sudden interest in werewolf lore was out of place for her.

I'm going to have to fix that…

"It's fine." I winked. "I figured out before I arrived."

Pip narrowed her eyes and studied me for a moment. She chewed on her lip—a habit of hers.

I was wondering how far I could push my luck with her— maybe she'd let me knock my head against hers since that was a common wolf thing, but I was betting holding her hand was off the table—when Young Jack had to open his yap.

"Pip, how much longer do we have to do this?" Young Jack asked. "I think I sprained my thumb on my last throw."

Pip ripped her gaze away from me. "You keep going until you're ready to apologize."

Young Jack groaned. "That's what I was afraid of."

"Tucker, are you ready to make up?" Pip asked.

"I'll wait out his sprained thumb."

"Please," Young Jack said. "I can still beat you at this game even with an injured hand."

"Not possible. Your aim couldn't be any worse."

A gentle smile played on Pip's face, and her cheeks were rosy from the cold. She glanced up at me, and her smile grew.

In that moment—with our Pack laughing and shouting in the background—I knew I'd do *anything* to keep her safe.

Chapter 11

Pip

I picked up the hunter journals of the Sabre family and the Ward family—my dad's and my mom's families—and wiped underneath them, cleaning the end table off.

"I just have to finish dusting. Then you, and you, and I have a date," I told the books.

"Are you talking to the house again, or your cats?" Shania shouted down from her loft bedroom—the only room on the second floor.

"Neither. I'm speaking with the journals I need to be reading," I said in a normal volume. With her werewolf hearing Shania wouldn't have a problem hearing me.

I straightened the books, studying them for a moment.

I was what hunters called a legacy—the last in a hunter family line. Unfortunately, I was doubly a legacy since I was the last of the Sabre family *and* the Ward family.

"Are you stress cleaning again?" Shania yelled.

"Maybe?" I wiped my cleaning cloth across the various shelves of the bookcase that had all of Papa Santos's old

119

mystery books, then sneezed. "But I also have to clean the Bedevilments' litter box, and I'm procrastinating that particular chore."

"Can't say I blame you!"

I stood on my tiptoes to reach the top of the bookcase, determined to do a thorough job.

My little cottage wouldn't take long to clean, anyways. It was a cozy size—like all the other cottages built on Pack land. Anything larger was unnecessary for most wolf families since they spent a lot of time at the lodge, and this particular cottage had been built for my elderly adopted parents, Mama Dulce and Papa Santos, long before I'd been around.

Princess slithered past me, almost making me trip.

"Princess, watch where you're going, please," I warned her.

She looked up at me with contempt, twitching her tail back and forth before she sauntered off.

Princess was nearly identical to her full brother and the second Bedevilment, Prince. They both had gray fur with white chins and paws, though Princess's fur was a tiny bit lighter, but the difference was so small it was hard to tell them apart unless they were standing side by side.

Both of them were at least three or four pounds overweight —which for a cat is a lot—and they both had attitude issues and very obviously viewed me as their servant.

I turned toward the kitchen—intending to target the cabinets next—but paused when my hunter senses tingled as I felt two werewolves wander closer.

Must be the werewolves Greyson assigned on watch duty tonight. I debated texting Greyson to tell him the wolves could come into the house to get out of the cold wind, but it wasn't necessary given their thick fur coats and innate heat.

I'll invite them in after I finish cleaning and read a bit.

I checked the cats' water dishes and moved their food dishes back into place—Prince had flung his dish across the small kitchen when I refused to give them more dinner—then started wiping down the cabinets.

Just as I finished the last cabinet, a watery crack had me spinning around. Prince, sitting on my tiny three seat dinner table, had his white paw still extended from where he'd pushed my plastic cup of water over the side of the table, splashing it all over the cottage's beautiful cherry wood flooring.

I groaned. "Prince, get off the table—you know better!" I swatted in his direction with my cloth, and he ran off before I crossed my tiny kitchen—which was about two steps from my one couch that was positioned in front of the cute little stone fireplace so it had the perfect view of the TV—the only one in the whole house—positioned over the mantel.

Prince waddled past the couch, then climbed on one of the end tables pointed in front of a window and made a big deal of arranging himself so he was staring outside, even though it was pitch black and the glare of the lights on the window meant he couldn't see anything.

Shaking my head, I picked up the green cup and put it in the dishwasher, then wiped up all the water.

I'd just finished cleaning up the mess when I heard a rip.

"Prince!" I growled.

The tubbo had his claws hooked on the lacy window curtains that Mama Dulce had made back when I was in high school. He was pulling on his claws, making tears in the curtains as he looked back at me with smug satisfaction.

I crossed my small cottage and scooped him up, yanking the curtain free from his claws before I opened the front door.

Prince—recognizing the signs—scrabbled in my grasp, his fat rolls covering my fingers as he tried to wriggle free.

"Nope! You were naughty, you're going outside!" I tossed him outside and shut the door behind him. I pressed my face against a window and peered out at him, scowling.

He yowled at me then scratched at the door a bit.

"No—you're in time out," I called to him. "Five minutes out there will do you some good!"

Whenever the Bedevilments were particularly naughty, I kicked them outside for a few minutes to remind them that as much as they disliked me, they hated the outdoors even more, so it was better to not be total jerks so they could live inside in peace.

His exile would only last as long as it took him to march his tubbo self over to the garage door, and then I'd let him inside again.

Shaking my head, I scooped up all the used rags and towels from the kitchen and opened the closet my tiny washer and dryer were built into. I dumped the towels in the washer but didn't start it—I needed to wipe down the cottage's only bathroom, which was decorated in a dusty shade of old-lady pink, before I started the load.

But first, Prince has probably learned his lesson.

I headed for the garage, intending to let the sour cat inside. I was almost to the door when my hunter senses prickled, and I felt the bright spots werewolves created in my mind move closer.

That's weird. They typically stay farther away, unless I reach out first…

I thought I heard a cat yowl just outside the front door, and my senses kicked into overdrive.

Why hasn't Prince headed for the garage yet?

A werewolf growl pierced through the walls of my cottage.

Oh no—Prince!

I grabbed my pink, metal baseball bat from my bedroom and ran for the front door.

"Pip," Shania shouted as she stumbled around upstairs, heading for the staircase. "Don't—!"

Ignoring the danger, I flicked on the porch lights and flung the door open. "*Leave my cat alone!*"

Two werewolves I didn't recognize were on my front porch. They were growling at each other, but as soon as I stepped outside they turned on me. Their teeth flashed in the dim porch lights, revealing flecks of blood on their muzzles. A tuft of gray fur blew across the porch—the same velvet color of Prince's fur.

Did they…did they kill Prince?

The wolves divided up, moving in a way that would pin me between them.

I could feel the oppressive weight of their Alpha powers, but they slid off me like oil on water as my hunter magic— already activated—roared in my blood with such ferocity I could barely hear the scrape of their nails on my deck.

Prince…Papa Santos loved him so much.

I zeroed in on the closest werewolf—who was mostly a dark gray color that faded into swirls of brown.

"Prince!" I swung my bat, my fingers vibrating when I smashed it into the wolf's shoulder.

The wolf yipped in pain, but bit my thigh.

With my adrenaline, I didn't even feel it. I was glad, actually, because it gave me a great shot at the top of his head.

Fueled by my rage, I smashed my bat on the top of his skull, downing him with one hit.

I knew he wasn't dead—werewolves were built to take hits, even something as violent as a bat to the head—though I'd probably at least given him a concussion.

I turned on my heel to face the second wolf, who was in the process of leaping at me.

I could see he had tufts of fur hanging from his muzzle— though the lighting was too poor to tell what color it was.

Prince!

A dry sob tore from my throat, and I swung my bat, cracking the wolf on the muzzle.

One of his teeth fell out, and he landed on the ground, shaking his head.

I wound up again for another strike, and the wolf recovered enough that he snarled and darted forward—aiming to bite my stomach.

I smashed the bat down on his back, and he collapsed.

"*Don't* attack my house, *don't* eat my cat!" A few tears hazed my eyes, making it hard to see, but I kept on swinging and hitting him. "You want a Wolf's Kiss? I'll bite your face off!"

Vaguely, I realized the wolf was no longer struggling and was just lying on the ground. I finally dropped my bat and sobbed.

"It's okay, Pip. You got them." Shania eased her way out of the cottage and patted my back.

"It's not okay," I wailed. "This is the third time I've been attacked since these sub-par Alphas arrived, they attacked me on my own porch, and they killed Prince!"

A mournful yowl split the air.

"Prince?" I scrambled across the porch, stepping on the whimpering Alphas on the way. I peered around the shadows of the deck, but I didn't see him.

Did he drag himself off to safety after they attacked him?

I listened for another yowl, but there was nothing.

"Prince!" My throat squeezed shut with the painful sensation of hope as I scrambled around the corner of the house.

I skidded out when I reached the garage, wildly looking on the ground for any kind of blood trail. "Prince? Here kitty, kitty! Please, Prince!" More tears burned at my eyes, so I almost missed the blobby gray shape sitting on the wooden crate nestled into the side of my garage.

I frantically scrubbed my eyes. "Prince?"

My vision cleared, and I could see Prince sitting on the crate—completely unharmed—with a crabby look on his face as he glared up at me with his usual level of dislike.

Relief flooded me in such a rush I could barely stand. I scooped him up, ignoring his displeased growl, and smashed my face into his side.

"You're alive. You're not even hurt. You're fine." I breathed into his soft fur.

I thought for sure he'd scratch me, but while he twitched his tail in irritation and occasionally yowled, he let me squeeze him tight.

It's okay. Prince is alive. I can handle getting attacked as long as they don't mess with my Bedevilments—or the Pack.

My frantically beating heart slowly quieted in my chest, and eventually I had to pull back and sneeze from Prince's fur tickling my nose.

"He's okay?" Shania asked.

"He's just fine." I had to forcibly keep myself from squeezing him tighter against my chest as I climbed onto the porch.

Prince peered up at me with an expression that managed to convey he was dissatisfied with my peasant-y display of adoration, but he let me pet him as I started to trudge back to the front door of the cottage.

Shania peered at the unconscious Alphas. "Wow. You really did a number on these guys."

"I thought they ate Prince."

Shania raised her eyebrows when one of the wolves whined. "Even so. These were two *Alphas*. You're getting stronger every time you take someone on with that bat of yours."

"They're Alphas, but they're not as trained as a Northern Lakes wolf," I said. "The two of them together are about equal to Rio."

"I think you could stop carrying your daggers if you took your metal bat with you everywhere," Shania said.

I felt a werewolf rapidly approach us, and I turned around in time to see Greyson emerge from the woods.

The mate bond must have pulled at him because he was only wearing a thin, long sleeved shirt, and even wolves wore light jackets when it got this cold.

His golden eyes shone in the darkness of the night, and I could feel the smothering, all consuming pull of his Alpha powers—which made Shania bend over in a bow to him. His breathing was ragged, not from running, but sheer emotion —*my* emotion, probably.

The bond probably lit up like a Christmas tree, and instinct dragged him here.

He crossed my front yard, his steps silent as he eased onto the porch even though he was wearing boots.

"Greyson," I breathed. I sagged with a relief that alarmed me.

"Lady Hunter." Greyson's eyes flicked from me to the two downed Alphas, then Shania, and I felt him physically rein his powers in so Shania's knees stopped buckling from the sheer power of his presence.

His nose twitched, and he scowled down at my thigh. "You're hurt," he said, his voice pleasantly rough.

"Am I?" I peered down at my leg and was surprised to see blood dotting my pants from where one of the Alphas had chomped on my thigh. "Oh, yeah. I forgot about that." I was shaking with an uncomfortable mixture of my leftover hunter adrenaline and the panic at thinking Prince was hurt, so I had to actually think about steadying my leg so Greyson could look at it.

Shania headed for the door. "I can go get the first aid kit—"

"Don't bother." Greyson brushed his fingers against my thigh, and magic slammed into me like a waterfall.

It felt *amazing*. I could feel my thigh muscles heal, and the teeth marks closed up as Greyson gently touched my leg. He slipped his fingers under the new tears in my pants, and gently rubbed around the repairing skin. The pads of his fingers were an electrifying sensation as potent magic rushed through my system.

"*Wow*." I had to use every ounce of my focus to keep clutching Prince so he didn't fall from my weakened grasp. "This is some good stuff. It's better than a fae potion. It's better than, like, five fae potions."

Greyson skated his thumb up the side of my thigh, and I had to shut my mouth before I said something really embarrassing.

"Logically. It's the healing powers of our…" Greyson glanced at the unconscious Alphas and didn't risk saying it.

It's from our bond.

Some of my giddiness from the burst of magic drained away. "It's unfair that you only feel pain, and even though I don't feel anything I get to experience this." I exhaled deeply. "Greyson…I'm s—"

"Don't," Greyson barked out before I had the chance to finish the apology. He ran his hand up and down my thigh, but the teeth marks hadn't gone deep, so everything was healed up, not even a trace of the wounds remained. Finished with his detailed inspection of my leg, Greyson shifted his gold eyes to me. "Because *I'm* not sorry."

When he looked at me—as if I was his world and he'd sacrifice anything to protect me—the desire to give in, shove Prince at Greyson, and just bawl my eyes out while leaning into him was overwhelming.

It's because he's too reassuring and strong, I let my guard down whenever I'm with him. I depend on him.

I tried to squelch the dangerous thought. I needed to prioritize researching our bond, and how to break it. If this dragged on much longer, I'd lose all motivation to dismantle it. Worse, I'd start to lov—

"What happened?" Greyson gestured to the werewolves. "I assume they attacked the cottage?"

I straightened my shoulders and was grateful for the distraction. "Not quite." I clutched Prince to my chest so I could peer over him at the still unconscious—but breathing—Alphas. "Shania and I were inside. But I heard Prince cry out here and thought they were attacking him."

Greyson turned around and inspected the front yard. "So you came *outside* to confront them. By yourself? That's not the brightest idea you've ever had, Lady Hunter."

"I thought they were attacking him," I repeated, carefully enunciating every word.

Greyson nudged both of the wolves with his boots, rolling them onto their sides so he could inspect the damage I'd done. "You hate that cat."

"I don't care. He's mine, and I'm so sick of being stalked, and if they even look at my cats I'm going to get my rifle and *shoot them!*" My voice shook with a hot mixture of rage and tears that were still threatening to loosen.

Greyson was at my side so quickly I didn't even track his movements. He wrapped his arms around me, trapping me against his chest, and squishing an extremely unhappy Prince between us.

Whether it was the leftover warmth of the healing magic, or my raw emotion from the difficult night that prompted me, I gave in and thumped my head down on his shoulder.

His hug didn't feel electrifying like his fingers had when he pulled magic through our bond to heal me. No, it was something far more dangerous: considerate.

The embrace was tight and protective, but the way he'd tipped me against him he could hold both Prince and me secure, so I didn't even feel my cat's hefty weight in my arms.

Pressed against his chest, I could feel the flickers of his Alpha powers that he held in check, and the way they flowed through him—overwhelming and ever vigilant—let me finally give up and just relax.

Why does he have to be so understanding and good at reading me? It makes him hard to resist.

Greyson nudged me closer to the house so I was better shielded from the wind. I felt it when he started to relax—the feedback from the bond was probably finally winding down—because his chest and shoulders softened.

Tonight. I have to research the bond tonight. I owe it to him to fix this, no matter how amazing this feels. He's in pain.

Unless...I can find a way to accept the bond.

"Grab your things." I could feel Greyson's voice in his chest through my cheek. "We're moving you to the lodge."

Chapter 12

Pip

I paused, and for a moment considered arguing.

For all that I was a Wolf's Kiss, I was still an outsider, straddling the line of werewolf and human. The humans in the Pack still didn't like me, and I wasn't included on the Pack runs.

But.

Fear had consumed me when I thought the Alphas were attacking Prince...and Greyson had come for me.

Maybe I'm not Pack. But I don't think I'm alone. At least...I don't have to be.

"Okay," I said.

"...*okay?*" Greyson repeated.

"Yeah." I paused. "Or do you not really want me to come?"

"No, you're coming," Greyson said. "I just thought I'd have to bribe you into it. You have being a stiff-necked mule head down to a science."

"Maybe. But I don't mess around with Prince and

Princess's well-being, and it seems like I might have underestimated how desperate some of these Alphas are when I originally formulated my plan." I stared down at Prince, a little surprised he hadn't clawed me yet. Though his velveteen ears were flattened, he seemed resigned to being smushed between Greyson and me. "What about Shania?"

"Shania can come too," Greyson said. "There are plenty of spare bedrooms. I'll even move in temporarily, too."

"Um, I don't think—" Shania started.

Greyson looked at her.

"Of course I'm coming," Shania said. "We can make it into a slumber party! Hang out time at the ritzy Pack lodge—what's not to love?"

I rested my chin on Prince's head. "Princess and Prince have to come too."

Greyson just blinked. "Sure, they can come."

"I need to get all of their stuff." I sniffed and contemplated wiping my nose on Greyson's shirt.

"Shania and I will help you pack."

"Yeah, I'll bring your baseball bats," Shania volunteered.

I finally peeled myself off Greyson and instantly started shivering in the cold air. "Thank you—both of you." As I turned to troop into the house I frowned. "How did these two get so close to the house? Didn't you assign wolves on rotational guard duty, Greyson?"

"Apparently there were originally three of them," Greyson grimly said. "Forrest intercepted the third one—he didn't know about these two. I suspect they approached your place downwind, and he never caught their scent. I'll call Harka, but tomorrow, we're going to the Curia Cloisters. It is ridiculous that you've been attacked so many times in such a short span—in areas that should be off limits. Your idea is still a good one, but we need to take more action. The Alphas' fear isn't outweighing their desperation."

"What if Harka can't help us?" I asked.

Greyson narrowed his eyes. "Then I'll remove Vant and absorb the Low Marsh Pack, because the wolf Forrest grabbed approached from their territory."

Why am I not surprised?

When I made it into the house, Prince scrabbled in my grasp until I set him down. "In that case, thanks for letting Shania and me move into the lodge."

I'd be way safer there—obviously if Greyson was staying there, too. But also because wolves were constantly coming and going from the lodge at all hours of the night, and it was deeper in the Pack's territory.

We'd never be alone, and no Alpha stood a chance of creeping up on it. After the Fletchings' attack, Aeric wired the place with cameras pointed in every direction.

Greyson gave me a weird look—it was a mixture of amusement and something affectionate. "I'll always take care of you."

My smile faded a little.

Not that I thought he was lying or anything, but because he would.

But will he take care of me because he wants to…or because the bond makes him?

———

Moving to the lodge went faster than I expected.

Shania called Aeric—who then called Wyatt, who texted Scarlett who told Radcliff, and in the span of a few minutes the two hunters and two werewolves were at my place, helping load a cat tower, cat beds, cat dishes, and the cats themselves into a truck borrowed from another packmate.

Shania and I barely had time to throw our clothes in a suitcase, and I grabbed my hunter journals before Greyson dragged me out the door.

Our friends drove the short distance to the lodge, unloaded my complaining cats' many accessories into my temporary room, then scooted out.

Aeric, Wyatt, Scarlett, and Radcliff were all performing an emergency patrol. Shania, however, had stayed behind—she was unpacking in her loaner room, which was two doors down from mine.

This left me alone with Prince and Princess to settle in.

After securing water for the Bedevilments from the attached bathroom, I showered, finally getting rid of the icy chill that had invaded my bones since the attack, and bundled up in my bed to finally crack open my hunter journals. Reading in bed, however, made me aware of how the seemingly small differences between me and the werewolves could play out in a larger way.

I need to find more blankets, or I'm going to freeze tonight.

My enormous bed only had one thin blanket—a soft creation made of blue and white fabric with a black wolf silhouette pattern.

I'd need at least two more to be cozy—the wolves kept the lodge on the cooler side.

I searched the closet and didn't find any, so I pulled on the thickest sweater I'd brought.

"I'll go rob one of the other rooms later. Greyson isn't allowing any out-of-Pack visitors right now anyway, so it'll be safe to wander." I slid back under my blanket and—satisfied with my new warmth level—grabbed the wine-red, leather-bound journal that belonged to the Sabre hunter family, my dad's family.

Prince and Princess ignored me and sat together on their cat bed, resembling loaves of bread as they judged the room with obvious disdain.

The room was on the rustic side, to match the cabin-ski chalet style of the lodge.

The light fixture was made of deer antlers, the walls were glossy, stained timbers that were a warm buttery color, and while the bath towels were thick and luxurious, the only furniture piece besides my bed was a dresser and a wrought iron lamp that had deer and elk molded into it.

The light was soft and glowy, making the room feel cozy—even if I wasn't the optimum level of warmth.

I paged through the journal, but it was mostly full of hunting tips and beautiful hand drawn illustrations of weapons.

I'd read the whole thing three times since I'd first cracked it open and found the illustration of a hunter sitting with a sleeping wolf—the *only* reference in the entire book to the powers of a Wolf's Kiss—so I didn't think I'd find anything about mates, but I still did a quick skim just in case.

I didn't have any luck, but I stared at the illustration for a while, studying the explanation that accompanied it.

The powers of a Wolf's Kiss are often useless for hunters who strive to protect humans from rogue, rabid, and feral werewolves, as the powers use magic in an opposite direction and instead aid werewolves.

"Hmmm. Only werewolves."

Not that I expected anything else. I couldn't produce magic that would work on humans—hunter magic wasn't designed for that.

The smell of fragrant pine trees tickled my nose as I considered my magic. (The lodge typically smelled of freshly cut wood, but the Pack had already erected four giant—real—Christmas trees in the lower part of the lodge, which added the tangy scent of needles to the air.)

Except a Wolf's Kiss is not an attack skill, and more of a power up. So maybe…?

Nah. But the book did specify werewolves—as in multiple

wolves. I'd been having such a hard time expanding what wolves I could cast my magic on, I'd started wondering if it was only possible to power up one or two of them at a time.

Seems like it's a me problem, not a power problem.

I was tempted to tinker with it, but the last time I'd played around with my magic I had tried cutting it off to see what happened...and then nearly had a panic attack when my hunter senses were snuffed out along with all my other natural defenses.

Apparently I did *not* cope well when I couldn't count on my own magic for defense.

I shut the Sabre journal and moved on to the journal of my mom's hunter family: the Wards.

It was made of black leather, and it had a faded black ribbon tucked into the pages that described my mom's large family tree, and metal corner protectors. It was quite a bit bigger than the Sabre journal since the Ward family was significantly older, and I remembered it had a few references to wolf legends, so maybe—*hopefully*—it had something about wolf mates.

I carefully paged through the book, trying to keep the brittle pages from cracking. Like the Sabre journal, it had hunting tactics, details on trap spells, weapons illustrations.

About halfway into the journal I found the small section of recorded werewolf legends.

Most of them were brief, single page summaries of stories I knew had to be longer when the wolves told them, but it made it easy to search for any references to mates.

I found three.

The first was a Romeo/Juliet type story about a werewolf and human mate.

"Talk about useless—everyone dies." I scratched my nose, then turned a page in the journal. "It's a dramatic—and tragic —romance. That's not going to help me at all."

The second story was about two werewolf mates who worked together to close a rogue portal to the fae realm that had opened up and had monsters spilling out of it.

"This is probably one of the oldest legends the wolves have. It predates the elves dying—but I suppose that wasn't *too* long ago in the history of the world, even though it was centuries ago." I rubbed my thumb on one of the metal corner protectors. "This story is most assuredly in the BC timeline, though. But I remember Mama Dulce telling it, and there wasn't much information on the main heroes being mates—the focus was on their valiance and the way they closed the portal."

I carefully turned to the final legend about mates that I'd found.

It was the only one of the three to have an illustration, probably because it was also the shortest and only took up half a page.

The illustration was a black wolf, peering up into the face of a figure wearing a blue cloak.

"Esta was a young wolf when she found her other half in a human-like supernatural. She loved him with every part of her being, but her other half was depraved, with a lust for bloodshed—wolves and shifters in particular—and near perfect aim with stealth like shadows."

I held my finger over Esta's black fur, but I paused, my finger hovering above the illustration—it was so old, the oils in my fingers would probably damage it.

"Esta blindly refused to see the ways of her other half, and instead brought him deep into wolf society, ignoring as he carved a path of blood through her Pack. All she cared for was the warmth of their bond and the sound of his voice. She allowed herself to become completely taken with the bond, and lost all senses. Eventually, once he'd destroyed her whole Pack, Esta's bond killed her as well, and even as the knife bit into her heart, she only thought of her love for him."

I looked up in surprise when I felt a weight on my bed, and found the Bedevilments settling at the foot of my mattress, close enough to me that I could nudge them with my feet.

Inexplicably chilled by the story, I climbed down to the foot of my bed to join them, and petted their soft fur.

Prince tucked his paws under himself and looked grumpy, but Princess let me rub under her chin.

"It's a cautionary tale...but was it meant to warn wolves not to bond with hunters? Because the sketchy guy was obviously a hunter. Or was it supposed to warn them from getting overly obsessed with their mates?"

I glanced back at the story, unable to say exactly why I was so bothered by it.

It wasn't that they made a hunter the villain of the story. The story was old enough that it predated the tenuous truce hunters and werewolves had reached since the death of the elves. It made sense they'd use a hunter as the baddie.

I think...it's that the hunter had such control over Esta. That idea terrifies me.

But Greyson wasn't Esta.

Between the two of us—Wolf's Kiss or not—Greyson was far more powerful than I was. Greyson also had excellent control of his instincts and his Alpha powers.

If I ever went crazy, he'd stop me.

But. I still don't like it. It's too close to my nightmare—that something would happen to me, and Greyson...

I didn't dare finish the thought. If I let myself think it, it felt too close to daring it to happen.

Greyson was strong, but wolves didn't typically survive the death of their mate. They either died, or—perhaps even worse —they turned feral and lost all their humanity.

But Greyson is almost too strong. If I go down in a fight, he'd go down first trying to save me.

Suddenly, my warmest sweater didn't feel warm enough.

I crawled back across my bed, shut the journal and walked it over to the dresser, trying to get it as far away from me as possible, as if I could get it out of my mind through physical distance.

I'll have to ask if anyone in the Pack heard of Esta's story. Maybe the story is wrong.

Unfortunately, the one wolf who had listened the most to Mama Dulce's stories was Lynn, my best friend who had left the Pack with her father, Hudson, when Greyson was forced to replace him as Alpha because my powers as a Wolf's Kiss were growing too strong for Hudson to suppress.

I hadn't known about my powers at the time, and I'd felt betrayed by Lynn's abrupt exit from my life.

But now...I understood. Because of me, her family had been forced to leave everything she'd ever known—and wolves *do not* easily leave their Packs.

She must hate me. How can I ask her about a story when I essentially destroyed her life?

I hopped back on the bed, feeling colder, even as I burrowed down beneath the blankets and tucked my feet against Prince.

He batted at my foot, but then settled into place just as someone knocked on my door.

"Come in," I called.

The door swung open, and Greyson stood there, holding three blankets in his arms.

His smile was tilted in a way that used to drive me crazy, but now usually made me automatically smile back. "I thought you'd need these—unless you feel like cuddling up on my couch again?" His voice was louder than necessary, and he stood outside my door while he spoke—I was pretty sure most of the wolves on our floor heard him.

I gritted my teeth. "Are you even *trying* to hide our...situation anymore?" I whispered.

He shrugged. "Not particularly." He nudged the door shut so the Bedevilments couldn't escape, then unrolled the first blanket. "I thought hiding it would protect you, but you've been attacked more in the last few weeks than I'd estimated possible. If the whole region found out, at this point I don't think it would make a difference. Besides, I don't like that in hiding it, it means I'm unable to react immediately when I know you need something."

"What do you mean?" I rolled out of the bed and picked up the Bedevilments while Greyson smoothed the first blanket over my bed.

"I could feel your shivering all the way down the hall," he said.

I winced at the blatant reminder of the mate bond, but struggled to juggle my two overweight cats. "Sorry."

"It was useful to know—though I was stuck in several meetings, so it took me a while to track these down for you." A frown twitched on his lips as he unrolled the second blanket.

I dropped to my knees so I could release the Bedevilments onto the ground, then helped Greyson with the last blanket. "I'm capable of getting my own blankets," I said. "You have important stuff to do. You shouldn't *have* to get me something like this—though I do appreciate it."

"Pip, you beat two Alphas senseless." Greyson's expression was halfway between frustration and a jaded sort of disbelief as he raised an eyebrow at me. "I *know* you can get your own blankets." His voice went so quiet, I doubted anyone outside the room could hear us. "But you're my mate. I want to make you comfortable—it's a plus of the relationship. Not a chore."

I was reminded of the lecture I'd delivered Chrysanthe—that it was in a werewolf's nature to want to care for those they loved.

I was important to Greyson.

But why *am I important to him?*

"Greyson." I sat down on my bed, sinking into the cushion of my four blankets. "How do you know what you feel for me is real?"

"I have no idea what you're talking about, and that's with my cheat code bond telling me you're upset," Greyson said.

I set my feet on the bed—I was wearing red poinsettia socks with white moose on them—and hugged my knees to my chest. "Couldn't everything you feel for me just be the bond, manipulating you?"

Greyson tilted his head as he listened to me. I actually found it encouraging that he didn't immediately try to dismiss my question—he was legitimately considering it.

I took a breath and dared to say what I'd been thinking since I found out I was his mate. "You didn't choose me. The mate bond chose me. Yes, you could have said no, but I was your *only* shot at getting a mate. And that's not much of a choice at all."

"You think I was backed into this?" Greyson asked.

"In a way. I mean, how could you reject me when you had the full force of the bond pushing down on you?" I asked.

"It would have been hard," Greyson agreed. "But I've already told you—I would have rejected anyone except for you."

"But how do you know *that* isn't the work of the bond?" I asked. "We've been around each other for a while. The bond might have been incomplete, but it had plenty of time to wear you down—why are you laughing?"

"I'm not—it's not that I find your worries funny. It's just…" His shoulders shook as he chuckled. "Pip, you *know* me. You know the lengths I go to in order to control my powers, to keep the Pack running smoothly. I don't like chaos. Do you really think that *I* would let something like a mate bond push me into falling for a *hunter*—literally the last supernatural any werewolf would willingly love?"

Well, when he says it like that…

"You think I don't know how much trouble we're going to bring to the Pack?" Greyson drew close enough to my bed that he could reach my hands and tug me to the end of my mattress. "I'm going to spend my whole life watching your back because there will always be wolves out there desperate or stupid enough to try to attack you, and no matter how competent you are I will not let you face that alone."

I tried to swallow, but my mouth was too dry as I stared into Greyson's golden eyes.

"Pip, you can be *positive* this was all my choice, because otherwise I would have refused it out of a sheer sense of duty to my Pack—and to you." He crouched down and took my hands in his. "But I've always been selfish when it comes to you. Not because you were my mate and I didn't know it, but because you're the one person I can be with and know you'll accept it all. And I'd do anything to hold on to that feeling of freedom and release that you give me."

Greyson's gaze was fiercely soft, the curve of his lips was so slight it was almost bittersweet, and he threaded his fingers through mine, boldly insistent.

I stared at him, terrified to my very core.

How can I ever muster up the guts to keep searching for a way to break our bond when he looks at me like this? But he's in pain…and there's only one other option: to figure out how a hunter can accept a mate bond.

Grimly, the story of Esta and her hunter mate prodded my mind.

I felt so confused I didn't even know what to think anymore.

One thing I knew—I couldn't doubt Greyson. He was right. He wasn't the kind of wolf who would be fooled by forced emotions.

But I don't want to be like Esta's mate, and even if he loves me now, I'm still terrified that one day—after decades of pain whittling away at him—he'll hate me. Or, perhaps even worse, he'll be too full of pain to love me.

I scrunched my eyes shut, feeling lost and defeated even though some traitorous part of me was doing cartwheels.

Greyson loved me.

As reluctant as I was to admit it, I felt something for him.

It couldn't be the bond—since it couldn't reach me, it couldn't affect me. But even before I'd learned I was a Wolf's Kiss, and that Greyson had been ordered to come to the Northern Lakes Pack, I'd started bending.

Because just as Greyson had valued that he could come at me with everything he was, I valued that he *did* come at me with everything he was.

Werewolves and humans…they were forever holding back in one way or another from me.

Greyson didn't. That meant a lot to me.

But what does that mean for us?

I felt torn in two—I wanted to run away and hide, and another part of me wanted to stay with Greyson, where it wasn't safe.

"Take a break, Pip." Greyson let go of one of my hands and stood so he could smooth my white hair away from my face and tuck it behind my ear. "You've gone through a lot these past few days, and tomorrow we need to go to the Curia Cloisters to talk to Harka. The bond isn't something we have to —or can—fix right now. Just rest. You'll feel better in the morning."

"Thanks." I smiled. "For the blankets and…everything."

Greyson slid his hand from my cheek to the back of my neck. "Of course. I'll give you everything I can, Pip."

He leaned closer so our cheeks brushed, his five o'clock shadow lightly scraping my skin. His presence was over-whelming—not because he was an Alpha, but because it was *him. Greyson.* The wolf I'd agonized over, accidentally hurt, and come to rely on like I hadn't ever before.

And yet, his Alpha powers were so much a part of him that I could feel them humming under his skin. Though they didn't affect me, the sheer magnitude of them was enough to make my head spin until my hunter powers kicked in, washing through me in a cool wave that made me more aware of him.

Our powers—opposites in nature—splashed against one another, but they didn't fight. If anything they seemed to stick together—not mixing, but mingling in a way that felt like a shot to my heart. It was like there was something that should be there, but it was cut off from me—just barely out of my reach.

I gasped in momentary pain, my lungs aching for a breath of air I couldn't inhale. For a brief moment, it felt like my heart was on fire.

Woah—is this the pain of the bond? Because if it is, how on earth is Greyson surviving this?

The pain melted away, but Greyson must have sensed it. He pulled back, his golden eyes glowing with concern as he studied my face.

"I'm okay." I squeezed his other hand that I was still holding. "I just thought for a second… I didn't feel the bond, but I felt pain because I couldn't reach it. Maybe?"

Greyson smiled—not his confident or amused smirk, but something much smaller that simmered with his power. "You really felt it?"

"I felt that I couldn't reach it," I corrected.

Greyson tugged his other hand free from mine and slid it around my back. "Close enough."

"No, actually, not close enough at all," I sourly said. "Because I can't grab it. It just points out that our bond can never—"

"You're missing the point." Greyson moved closer, and his

overwhelming Alpha powers played at my senses again. "Even if you can't complete it, you felt it. This isn't one sided."

"One sided? You've never had anything one sided in your life outside of our extremely unfair bond," I scoffed.

"Pip," Greyson said.

"What?"

"Stop talking."

Before I could snark out a reply, Greyson leaned forward, pressing his lips against mine, and the world exploded.

Chapter 13

Pip

I'd been kissed before, but this was different. I think because *I* felt differently about Greyson from how I had about anyone else.

It wasn't that he was my mate, it was that I loved him. It terrified me to my core, but I really did love him.

As afraid as I was of our relationship, I wanted to be with him. He made me feel like I wasn't alone—that I didn't have to fight the world alone. And I swear I could feel my magic straining for him.

It was addictive and exhilarating—I felt more alive!

Briefly, Greyson pulled back and studied me, his eyes taking in every detail.

I struggled to swallow. "Greyson…"

Greyson grinned and leaned in again, brushing our lips together.

I heard footsteps outside—Pack members, probably looking for Greyson.

Wait…THE PACK.

They might not be able to hear us, but they'd certainly be able to smell me on the general vicinity of Greyson's lips. They'd have more than a few questions about that!

I planted my feet on Greyson's chest and kicked.

He was a werewolf, so I didn't even make him rock, but he did lean back and raise an eyebrow at me.

I pointed at the door with both of my hands in a wild swooshing motion.

Greyson rolled his eyes and reached for me again.

"Alpha Greyson?"

My heart pulsed in my throat as I heard footfalls outside my bedroom. I rolled off my bed, and ran to the dresser where I grabbed some lip gloss and smoothed it over my lips, hopefully covering up Greyson's scent on my lips.

...that leaves my scent on Greyson's lips!

Biting back every swear word I wanted to scream, I spun in a circle and spotted Prince, sitting on the clean sweater I'd set out for the morning.

I scooped him up—ignoring his yowls of protest—then scrambled back across my room.

I skidded to a stop, and just as the door creaked open I thrust Prince into Greyson's face, wiping the top of his head into Greyson's lips.

Rio stood in the doorway with River. River furrowed her eyebrows as she looked from me, to Greyson, to Prince—who silently hung from my hands, gaping at me in apparent shock.

Rio squinted a little and looked pained. "Alpha Greyson, River and I returned from our sweep of Timber Ridge," he said.

Greyson gently pushed Prince away from his face. "Great. Let's discuss it in my office."

"Yes, Alpha," River and Rio chorused.

Greyson sauntered across my room and ducked into the

hallway. Rio was so close behind him he was on his heels—he didn't even bother to look back at me.

River paused long enough to wink at me and wriggle her fingers in farewell before she hurried after the pair.

I set Prince down and shuffled over to the door to close it, just in time to hear Greyson speak.

"Is something wrong with either of your hands?"

"No?" Rio said.

"Good. Next time *knock* before you enter Pip's room."

Greyson's order was heavy enough to make the duo gulp.

"Yes, Alpha Greyson."

I shut the door and leaned against it, groaning.

*I went from existing in a desert of romance, to now having to sort through…*this *with Greyson. Why all the drama? Why couldn't this be simpler?*

I felt a tap on my foot and looked down to find Prince, his fur bristling as he stared at me, apparently feeling wronged.

"You owed me after that porch incident," I told him.

Prince glared, but he started cleaning his paw—a sign he wasn't going to punish me.

I stroked the top of his head—making him purr despite himself—then wandered back over to the bed, collapsing into it face first.

I don't want to be like Esta's mate…and I don't want Greyson to eventually resent me for all the pain he goes through.

But if there's another way…why can't I find it?

———

The following day, Greyson phoned Chase and got us—and twelve packmates—a portal to the Curia Cloisters.

I'd thought he'd put the matter off—maybe organize things to present a case or something—but no. Greyson went in with his powers almost entirely on full blast.

"Alpha Greyson, I know you're upset." Harka held up her hands as she stood behind her desk. "This is a bad situation, and it's unfortunate Pip has been attacked so many times. But my hands are tied—"

"No." Greyson planted his hands on her desk and shook his head. "That's not good enough. My wolves are holding three rogue Alphas outside right now. You're taking them, and you're officially judging them. Because if you don't, the bodies will start piling up."

"You can't kill all the Alphas who attack Pip," Harka argued. "Losing that many Alphas in such a short span of time will throw the Packs into chaos."

"Then *take care of it*," Greyson said through gritted teeth.

Rafe stood next to me, the two of us watching Greyson and the Pre-Dominant shout it out. Rafe leaned over and asked me in a lowered tone, "Are you all right with all of this?"

"All of what?" I asked.

Rafe gestured to Greyson. "Isn't he acting a little...domineering?"

I stared up at Rafe. "Do you have any idea how many times I've been attacked in the past week?"

Rafe winced. "Ahh, yes. I suppose that would get old."

"It doesn't get old, it fills you with anxiety and paranoia at the smallest of movements, and it makes you distrust any wolf you don't personally know—something I didn't have a problem with before." I tilted my head as I watched Greyson face down Harka. "We tried things my way. While it is working, it's also revealed to me that there are more wolves who would rather steal me like neanderthal thugs incapable of intelligent thought than there are excellent werewolf leaders who have the strength to actually lead their Packs. Because of that, we're going to have to make some drastic adjustments to my plan if your aunt doesn't step in to help."

Rafe laughed. "Ouch! Sounds like some painful—but necessary—truths."

I twitched my shoulders in a shrug, but refrained from saying anything more as I watched.

"Give us a few weeks," Harka said. "I already told you I can send some of my wolves north with you, but we can't publicly let these fights be known. The fae are rallying behind Queen Leila, the vampires consolidated their power years ago with Killian, and Hazel Medeis is fast fortifying the wizards with all the House drama going on in Magiford right now. If it's known the werewolves have so much in-fighting it will make us look weak—"

"You're worried about weakness? Fine." Greyson's eyes glowed with anger. "If you don't do something about this, I will leave the Midwest and take my mate *and* my Pack with me!"

My eyes bulged at the threat.

The Northern Lakes Pack was the largest and strongest in the Midwest. If they left it would leave an enormous power vacuum in the Midwest and significantly weaken the werewolf power base here—not to mention Harka had been quite open she considered Greyson her future replacement for the Pre-Dominant position.

I knew Greyson was mad about the attacks—it was on Pack territory, and I am his mate—but I don't think I understood that he's not just mad…he's furious.

"With our strength we won't have a problem taking new territory in a different region," Greyson continued.

Rafe glanced at me again. "You're willing to leave the Midwest? That's adventuresome."

I'd been staring at the dozens of framed photos Harka had on her wall of her family and Pack—I saw Rafe in a few, as well as a woman who looked a lot like Harka, who I was betting was Rafe's deceased mother—so his question made me shift and redirect my attention. "Greyson never actually mentioned this possibility to me."

"And you're not mad about it?" Rafe asked. "That's a big threat he uttered without consulting you."

It's almost like he wants me to get mad at Greyson…

"Bro," I said, trying to keep the atmosphere light. "The Pack is all I have. If they're moving, do you really think I *wouldn't* go with them?"

I'd miss Timber Ridge, and the humans I'd gotten to know there through the years, but I was bonded to the Northern Lakes Pack, whether they considered me one of them or not.

For cryin' out loud, I'd been so miserable in college I'd only lasted one semester before having to come back—thank you, Wolf's Kiss magic.

I would perhaps be a little offended that he made such a threat without mentioning it as a possibility to me, but while I'm certain he's fully prepared to go through with it, he had to have known Harka would never let him go, and this would be enough to move her.

As if she could hear my thoughts, Harka deflated.

"Fine." She plopped down in her chair behind her desk. "We'll do something about it—you don't have to go to that extent!"

"Are you certain? Because it seems like you aren't taking this seriously enough," Greyson growled. He didn't sit down, even though Harka glanced at the chair behind him.

"I understand, now, that this is deadly serious," Harka said. "And I confess I should have known better. Of course you'd be upset—Pip is your mate. That'd be enough to make the most benevolent wolf mad. Just…" Harka shifted unhappily in her chair. "Ratchet it down a little, okay?"

"This isn't just because she's my mate. Pip is a Wolf's Kiss. She needs help, or it would be well within her rights to abandon werewolves altogether." Greyson stood upright and rolled his shoulders back. I could feel it when he wound his

Alpha powers down. Not to the level he normally did—no, he kept them at the perfectly balanced level where it submitted to Harka, but clearly indicated he was not placated.

I mashed my lips together so I didn't whistle.

I knew Greyson had excellent control, but this is beyond impressive.

"I'll judge the Alphas and issue a warning." Harka leaned back in her chair, then glanced at me with a gleam in her eye that made me feel a touch like her prey. "*If* you publicly accept the position as my successor and the future Pre-Dominant."

Greyson stared Harka down, and I finally broke ranks, dragging my feet across the tree-print rug that covered most of Harka's floor.

"Greyson, wait." I reached him in a moment, my hand latching on to his shirt sleeve. "Don't—that's a big deal."

"It's not as big a deal as you'd think," Harka said. "He'd still be Alpha of the Northern Lakes Pack. He wouldn't even have to move to Magiford since Queen Leila of the Night Court seems inclined to portal you in whenever you need a ride."

"Excuse me, Pre-Dominant Harka, but I have *only* seen you in your Pre-Dominant role, and never just as an Alpha." I struggled against the impulse to fidget as I stared her down. Since she was a wolf, it was important to meet her gaze. "Saying it's 'not as big a deal' is the greatest understatement of the year."

Harka squinted up at me. "You know, I'm kind of glad hunters can't accept bonds. The two of you would be absolute nightmares to deal with if you could back each other up any more than you already do."

"Harka," Greyson warned her.

"I beg your pardon, but that's Pre-Dominant Harka to you." Rafe strode in from the sidelines, joining Harka behind her desk. His brow was furrowed, and I could see the hot gleam of anger in his eyes. "You have not been treating her with the respect she is owed."

Greyson smiled.

Without breaking eye contact with Rafe, I reached up and slapped my hand onto Greyson's chest.

It might have looked loving—like I was concerned about him—but I was mostly concerned he was about to lose what little patience he had left and reach for Rafe. My puny strength wouldn't do much to stop him, but it would hopefully remind him why I didn't want us picking unnecessary fights.

Please, don't. We need help.

"Easy, Rafe. They've been through a lot." Harka reluctantly jolted to her feet with a groan. She smiled and rested her hand on her nephew's shoulder. She only needed that grip to bodily move him behind her.

"And in this case, Hunter Sabre is right. It would be more work, yes," Harka said. "Hector would have to take over more of your duties. But not as many as you might think since you have a Wolf's Kiss." She flicked her eyes back to me. "It'd put you in a position of leadership, Pip. I know from the reports I've received you've always been something of an underground leader of the Pack. This would be in a more official capacity."

I frowned at her. "I'm a hunter."

"And? Greyson is your mate," Harka said. "Things are going to change as soon as you tell the Pack. Whether or not Greyson becomes the next Pre-Dominant, your life is going to radically change. At least if he's the Pre-Dominant he'll have the power to stop anyone who comes after you—even the wiliest of shifters would have to agree that attacking the Pre-Dominant's mate would be suicide."

"But it'll be years before you retire," Rafe said. His voice sounded unsure, which surprised me.

Harka slung an arm over his shoulders and smiled sadly.

"I'll hang in there for a while, but I owe it to Greyson to start preparing him for the role."

Rafe nodded as he stared at the ground, his eyebrows pushing together as if he was in pain.

He didn't appear to resent Greyson for the possibility of his position—which his sister, Aspen, certainly had.

Instead, he was watching Harka with hurt echoing in his eyes. I'd experienced that feeling before, back when Hudson and Lynn left and I hadn't known the entire story.

Why would he be upset that she's considering stepping down? He doesn't seem eager to take over, and she's said previously that she wasn't going to step down as her Pack's Alpha…

"Becoming the next Midwest Pre-Dominant is a bigger commitment than I'm willing to take on when I'm already dealing with the ever-so-mature antics of pathetically weak Alphas," Greyson flatly said.

Harka scratched her chin, then shrugged. "Fair enough. But you'll have to decide soon, Greyson. You should also consider telling more of your Pack about Pip being your mate."

I cringed. "You're right, but…"

But I'm still not certain what to do about this relationship. Though maybe if we told the Pack, somebody would be able to help me figure out what to do?

It only took a moment for me to realize that was a particularly stupid hope.

The Pack had absolute loyalty to Greyson. There was no chance any one of them would even *think* of helping me break the mate bond—if that was what I had to end up doing.

Harka eased herself back into her chair. "If you're not willing to commit to being the next Pre-Dominant, I can't come on as strong." She held up her hand to stop Greyson before he could get started. "But I *will* help. We just have to figure out on what grounds."

Greyson nodded.

I relaxed. "Greyson, I'm going to skip out to tell the Pack. It looks like you're going to be a while?"

"You can tell the wolves guarding the Alphas to take them down to holding cells," Harka said. "We got some more installed with the creation of our joint supernatural task force."

Greyson snagged my hand and squeezed it. "Take the rest of the Pack out to get lunch, after. I heard Forrest's stomach on the way over."

"Got it. Good luck." I squeezed his hand, then pulled away, heading for the door.

"Are you *certain* she hasn't accepted the bond?" Harka asked as I reached the door. "You two are disgustingly lovey-dovey."

I slipped out before Greyson replied, almost knocking into Ember—who was waiting outside.

"Harka said to take the Alphas down to the holding cell. Greyson said to take the rest of the Pack out to eat."

Ember cringed. "I'll take the Alphas if you don't mind lunch duty?"

"You sure? That seems like you get the worse job."

"Believe me, it's not. Trying to get all of them to agree on one location is going to be a nightmare," Ember said. "Good luck."

"Thanks. Are they still outside?"

"Yeah. There were some human kids attempting to make snowmen on the lawn farther down the street. They were watching."

I waved to Ember, then headed downstairs, pulling on my hat and my mittens as Scarlett and Radcliff caught up with me.

"Everything handled?" Scarlett trotted down the stairs after me as she pulled her scarf around her neck.

"To an extent. We're supposed to take the Pack out to lunch—have any ideas?" I asked.

"Why not herd them down to Main Street where they can eat at any number of locations?" Radcliff fixed his hat—like me, the Fletchings were outfitted for winter. "Lord Linus and the night mare Queen Leila sent were still hanging around the Pack when we came upstairs. They might be willing to drop us off so we don't have to walk since it's a bit of a hike."

"Let's go with that. I'll text Greyson and let him know when we head out," I said.

Within minutes we'd made our way through the maze of the Curia Cloisters and popped outside through one of the side exits, into a large parking lot and mass chaos.

The eight members of the Northern Lakes Pack who had been left outside had wandered to the far end of the parking lot. Aeric and Wyatt were keeping their bromance alive by building matching snowmen modeled after each other if the twig-constructed glasses Aeric was placing on his snowman and the miniature snow cars Wyatt was building for his was any indication.

Shania and River were chatting with Lord Linus as they watched the pair, while East and Rio turned in slow circles—scanning the parking lot for any signs of danger—and Young Jack and Forrest chased a black cat across a snow dusted lawn that stretched out from one side of the building like a peninsula.

"Hey, Pip!" Young Jack waved to me as he and Forrest ran past. "Watch—when we get close, this cat sheds puffs of hair!"

Jack poured on the speed and tore after the cat, catching up to it.

The cat puffed up—its hair standing on end as its back curved—and I saw it visibly shed a cloud of hair before it was off like a shot. It zoomed across the parking lot and disappeared into some shrubbery planted in the beds that acted as traffic directors.

"Jack, leave the poor cat alone. If it's shedding hair like that it's obviously stressed and anxious," I said.

"Fiiine." Jack circled back with Forrest, heading in my direction.

"What could a cat possibly be stressed about?" Forrest asked.

"I don't know, maybe the two giant mutts chasing it?" I asked.

"But we're so friendly," Jack said. "That hurt my feelings. I need them fixed with a—"

"Don't you dare," I warned him.

"Pomeranian Puppy Powerup!" Jack swooped in and wrapped his arms around me, snuggling me close like I was a cuddly dog. "Yep, I feel better now." He squeezed me, making my parka deflate a little.

"I think you should stop hanging out with Aeric and Wyatt," I said. "They're bad role models."

"I don't know." Jack released me and skipped away. "They told me you climb the tree outside Greyson's office when you want to break into the lodge. That seems worse."

"It was for tourism purposes," I complained.

Radcliff and Scarlett laughed as we picked our way toward the others.

The Curia Cloisters salted their parking lot, but they did it sparingly since they had to use this super expensive, pet-safe salt for the sake of all the visiting shifters that arrived in their animal forms.

When we reached Shania, River, and Lord Linus I hopped over the curb and stood on the sidewalk with them.

Aeric and Wyatt drifted away from their completed snowmen. Aeric prowled up to Shania, but Wyatt—interestingly—stopped next to Scarlett and smiled at her.

When Rio and East joined us, I shoved my mittened hands into the pockets of my puffy parka. "Greyson has set us loose for lunch. Scarlett, Radcliff, and I were thinking we could head downtown."

"A marvelous plan," Lord Linus said. "I happen to be going in that direction for my darling daughter—she requested a coffee run to her favorite café since she is stuck here at the Cloisters in a meeting. I would be delighted to drop you off along the way."

I slightly bowed my head. "Thank you, Lord Linus. We'd appreciate that."

Lord Linus looked amused. "Naturally—though I must warn you to be careful when offering your thanks to any other fae. We do love bargains, and many could construe such words as an opportunity."

Wyatt stirred from his spot next to Scarlett, where he partially sheltered her from the wind. "Queen Leila has generously helped us on many occasions," he said. "I'd honestly feel better if we could repay her in some way."

Lord Linus tilted his head. "Well, she does like money."

Hmm. That's good to know—especially if Greyson does accept the Pre-Dominant position and needs frequent trips to the Curia Cloisters.

"I'll run off to find Nova—she went around the building and hasn't come back yet—and then we'll set out, yes?" Lord Linus winked at me, then trotted off, whistling a jaunty tune.

"Can we eat wherever we want downtown?" Shania asked. "Or are we staying in a group?"

"I kind of think we'll have to split up," Radcliff said. "I don't think there's one restaurant that can handle eight werewolves without being warned in advance."

"We do like to eat," Aeric acknowledged. "But some of us better stick with Pip."

"Rio and I will," East decided.

"So will Radcliff and I," Scarlett added.

"I'll come too," Wyatt said. "Aeric, Shania, if you two would eat in the building directly next to us? I'd feel better having backup nearby."

Aeric grinned. "You got it, bro."

"What about us?" Jack nodded to River and Forrest.

River slung an arm over his shoulders. "You're coming with me—we'll have to find a quiet place. You still need some help regulating your senses and strength."

"I'll go with River and Jack, then?" Forrest said.

"Sounds good," I said. "Wyatt, do you want to decide where we're eating?"

"Already looking up reviews—and Google's estimation of how busy they are. I refuse to eat in a packed place that smells like everyone bathed in perfume and body spray."

"I'll help—I want a vote, too." Aeric wandered over to his best friend and peered over his shoulder at his phone.

With everything decided, I relaxed, moving my toes in my boots to keep them warm. I was busy thinking about what had transpired in Harka's office, which was how I didn't immediately notice someone was calling my name.

"Pip? …Phillipa?"

"Pip." Scarlett nudged me. "Do you know her?"

"Hmm?" I turned in the direction of the voice, and I froze in place.

A beautiful young woman in her early twenties slowly approached our group. She was wearing a checkered red and black flannel shirt, a white puffy vest, and a baby sling that presumably held a baby, but the kid was so decked out in clothes I couldn't see more than fabric.

Her blond hair was pulled back in a neat braid, and her smile lines were more pronounced than when I'd last seen her, but I'd recognize her anywhere.

I stared, and my mouth was almost unable to form words. "…*Lynn?*"

Chapter 14

Greyson

I leaned against the brick wall outside Pre-Dominant Harka's office and exhaled.

My Alpha powers—driven crazy with the knowledge that Pip was in constant danger—pounded inside my skull, aching for release.

Meanwhile, my incomplete bond was a gaping hole in my soul and a level of pain that was hard to describe.

It wasn't so much a truly physical sensation, but a keen awareness of a great loss and emptiness where Pip should have been.

If I can get her to agree to our mate bond, I can deal with this.

I rubbed my jaw and tried to calculate the odds that Pip would actually agree to our bond.

Low. Very low.

Not because she disliked me, but because of guilt. I could see it in her eyes—she blamed herself for my pain, even though she couldn't control that she was a hunter, and none of it was her fault. Occasionally her guilt was so strong it pierced the haze between us, and I could feel it like a knife in my ribs.

That worried me more than anything.

Pip was a notorious loner since she'd lost so many people. I was pretty sure it was only sheer persistence on Aeric and Wyatt's end that had finally reached her and formed their friendship. But she was also relentlessly loyal.

If she mistakenly believed she was causing me pain…

I stretched my arms behind me as the scents of the Curia Cloisters—stale coffee, magic, fur, and the faint whiff of blood from vampires—swirled around me.

I could smell a fae—a powerful one who reeked of fae magic—but pushed the sensation out of my mind.

The most annoying part of all this is that there is no common knowledge on how to woo your mate. Everything is just supposed to fall into place.

Well, maybe it wasn't so annoying. Instant perfection sounded boring—or at the very least not exhilarating like Pip was.

The noise level of the Curia Cloisters increased as the office workers and meetings broke for lunch. I shut my eyes in an attempt to block out the stomp of feet, the buzz of pixie wings beating like a hummingbird, laughter, and the creaking of doors opening and closing.

I'll figure out a way to get to her, but first I must protect her. How can I do that when I don't want to become the Pre-Dominant, and when a total blood bath might temporarily fix it, but would cause more problems in the future?

"Alpha Greyson?"

I peeled an eye open and wasn't too surprised to find Queen Leila—sovereign of the Night Court—standing a respectable distance from me.

She must be the powerful fae I scented earlier.

Standing just behind her was Chase with four other guards,

all dressed in the Night Court colors of dark blue and purple with silver accents.

"Ah, it is you. I was wondering why Chase kept gawking down this hallway." Queen Leila smiled, making her purple-ish blue eyes sparkle as she swept her black hair over her shoulder.

"Queen Leila, hello." I slightly inclined my head to the fae monarch. "It is a pleasant surprise to see you here."

Queen Leila made a noise in the back of her throat. "Not really. It's meeting day for me, and there's a Regional Committee of Magic meeting later tonight that'll start once Killian wakes up from his beauty sleep."

Considering the "Killian" she so calmly referred to was the Vampire Eminence—the most powerful vampire in the Midwest who had a deadly reputation to match—it was no surprise that I could feel the potent fae magic that hummed around Leila.

All members of the Regional Committee of Magic were strong—they had to be, given their roles were traditionally seen as positions in which you entered the dogfight for your race.

And Harka wants to toss me in. Something to look forward to.

Queen Leila tilted her head back and forth as she studied me. "Linus said he was giving you a portal jump into Magiford today…I hope it's not for anything too terrible?"

I flattened my lips. "Werewolf politics," I said. "I'd like to kill some people. Pip would not. We attempted a compromise."

"It's not working?" Queen Leila asked.

"Not very well, no."

"Ah." Queen Leila glanced back at her guards.

Chase must have seen something in her gaze because he nodded.

Queen Leila grabbed the skirts of her black dress and lifted them slightly as she turned around and inclined her head at me. "Come on, talk with me."

I hesitated, then fell into step with the tall fae queen. "You aren't too busy?"

"Not for an ally. Besides, I'm waiting for my latte that Linus went out to get me." Her dangly diamond earrings clinked quietly when she turned her head, peering up and down the hallway.

She led me to the fae section of the Curia Cloisters, leaving behind thick, wooden furniture meant to stand up to a lot of weight for colorful thick cushions and thin chairs with vine-like backs.

"Here we go. This is a private tea room. We can be undisturbed here." Queen Leila bumped a door open with her hip.

The room was small—about the size of a large walk-in coat closet, which I was willing to bet it once had been—but what it lacked in size it made up for in luxury. Or at least what the fae perceived as luxury.

It was decked with gold foil wallpaper shaped like thistles. The wooden shelves were cluttered with different kinds of tea sets made of porcelain, fine china, and clay.

I didn't know enough about tea to recognize the origins of the sets, but the glaze on them smelled old—though that scent was nearly eclipsed by the strong smell of flowers that wafted up from the cushions of an antique fainting couch and matching armchair that were both pure white.

Queen Leila flopped onto the fainting couch with a groan and an unusual lack of fae grace.

Chase closed the door after instructing the remaining guards into a formation outside, then ducked into the small spot behind the fainting couch, leaving the armchair for me.

"Thanks, Chase. Now, Alpha Greyson. I'm a little aware of what has happened with your Pack—and Pip." Queen Leila scooted into an upright position so she could look me in the eye as I carefully eased my weight into the armchair, uncertain if it would hold up to werewolf weight.

"Yes, some weeks ago Chase asked for permission to explain the situation to you." I glanced at Chase, who stood with his hands tucked behind his back.

"Is there anything I can help with?" Queen Leila asked. "I'm not in a position to stick my thumb into werewolf politics, but we are allies. If you need support, I'd like to help—if it's not financial, that is."

Familiar with the financial woes of the Night Court—which Leila had been trying to fix ever since she'd been made queen over a year ago—I cracked a smile.

"Although I appreciate your offer, I must say that as werewolves we don't take terribly...*well* to outsiders deep in our territory, which is where we are keeping Pip, so it is better if we handle it ourselves."

"In that case, do you want me to encourage the fae to stop visiting Timber Ridge?" Queen Leila asked. "I didn't think there was any harm in it, but if it's a bother I can get them to stop. Or at least try to."

I shook my head. "Fae tourism has been an interesting addition to our lives, but it's not inconvenient. The problem is the Alphas after Pip, which is a much more finite issue."

I narrowed my eyes as I studied the lovely queen.

She had the delicate fae features and beauty, but I'd seen many fae who were far more beautiful than her. No, her real power lay in her charisma.

She's the fae representative on the Regional Committee of Magic, and she sought out that position. She's honest enough, though, to tell me if the committee really is as horrible as it sounds.

"However, I could use some of your insight," I said.

Leila perked up. "Really? Then ask away!" She fluffed her skirts over the fainting couch and chortled—sounding more like an old man than a fae queen. "This is awesome—I'll have to tell Rigel! Someone actually wants *my* insight! What do you think of that, Chase?"

163

"Your insight is not often sought after, My Sovereign, because you frequently and loudly offer it, particularly to those who don't want it," Chase said.

Leila cleared her throat and ignored Chase. "So. Alpha Greyson. What can I offer my insight on?"

"The Regional Committee of Magic," I said. "How do you like being one of the members?"

"Oh. Well." Queen Leila tapped her chin, her eyes moving as she thought through a reply.

She isn't immediately answering with some boxed "of course it's wonderful" line, which is encouraging.

"It's frustrating, or even rage inducing," Queen Leila said. "The meetings can get tedious, especially if Killian Drake is in a mood. But I joined for my Court, and the fae in general."

"To secure more resources for them?" I asked.

"No. To get them to stop fighting—to be in a position where I could fight on their behalf." Leila tapped her fingers on her knee. "When it comes to the fae, we're our own worst enemy. In my talks with Hazel, it seems like it might be the same for the wizards, too."

It seems the same is true of werewolves. The biggest threat to Pip is other Packs, and our power structure is so delicate that if I push back too hard I could topple everything.

Were shifters their own worst enemy? Not so much. I hadn't had a lot of contact with shifters—which was partially why I was reluctant to take up a position in which I wasn't only supposed to represent werewolves, but all of shifter kind—but because other shifters were so varied and they stayed, if they stayed together at all, in smaller groups, they seemed to have a better handle on what was necessary to survive.

And fighting for power isn't it.

"It's a lot of work," Queen Leila continued. "There are meetings upon meetings, and when you *don't* have meetings you need to prepare and read up on subjects that will be discussed in meetings. But it's important work. We've done so much since I became the fae representative, and that was at the beginning of this year. Magiford is changing—for the better. Supernaturals are starting to interact more with humans—and each other."

Queen Leila studied me, her eyebrows turning into a sharp V as she thought. "I'll warn you, though, I get off easy. Each fae Court is pretty self-sustaining. I've only had to get involved in physical conflicts—which are slowing down. I'm not sure how much extra work the Pre-Dominant has on behalf of werewolves and shifters that doesn't get brought before the Regional Committee of Magic."

I stifled the desire to shift in my chair. "You're aware I'm a candidate to become the next Pre-Dominant?"

"The way I hear it, you've been the only candidate for a while." Queen Leila glanced back at Chase. "I'll admit, I was surprised to hear Harka is already thinking about training a protégé. She's quite young—I thought she'd be Pre-Dominant for at least another decade or two. Any idea why she's considering retiring?"

I shook my head. "No. She hasn't mentioned anything concrete."

"Hmm. Weird. Anyway. Is there a particular reason why you're reluctant to take the job?"

"No…"

Harka hadn't been wrong. Hector was fine taking on more responsibilities, particularly with Pip to back him up. He'd be free to concentrate on the werewolf-owned businesses, and most Pack matters would likely be left to Pip, given that she was already responsible for any conflicts between wolves and humans.

"If it's the distance that bothers you, I'm sure we can make some kind of permanent arrangement with the night mares for you," Queen Leila said.

"Timber Ridge is my home. Leaving it…setting aside my responsibilities for a different kind of work…" I trailed off, not quite able to put into words what I meant.

I didn't want more power. My Pack was loyal, our expansive territory was perfect for wolves, and I'd found my mate.

Whatever politics shook Magiford likely wouldn't affect Timber Ridge, and everything my Pack had fought to establish. The position of Pre-Dominant wasn't going to do much for me…

Except help me better protect Pip. But if I become the Pre-Dominant, wouldn't that change everything?

"Do you think Pip is the only hunter who could live with wolves?" Queen Leila asked.

I straightened in my chair. "What do you mean?"

"Your Pack has benefited greatly from working with the humans of Timber Ridge, and the hunter in your midst. Do you think it's because Pip is special, or could it be possible for others?"

I blinked. "We know it's possible for others. Radcliff and Scarlett Fletching have been living among the Northern Lakes wolves for several months, now."

"Do they work well with the Pack?"

I nodded. "Their help was pivotal when we were dealing with Aspen and the illegally changed wolves this fall."

"That alone might be why Pre-Dominant Harka is considering retiring early," Queen Leila said.

"What do you mean?"

"The Northern Lakes Pack is rewriting the rules. Everyone knows it—*I* know it, and I'm just a fae," Queen Leila said.

I blinked. "*Just* a fae? You say that as if you aren't a sovereign of one of the most powerful Courts in the Midwest."

She swatted her hand at me. "You wolves and your requirement for precise words—you know what I mean. Besides,

Rime's Winter Court is actually stronger than the Night Court, so there. But that's not my point."

"Then what is your point?"

"Harka is concerned about the wolves and shifters getting left behind," Queen Leila said. "She was very kind to me when I first became queen—kinder than she needed to be, honestly. But it's because she sees the changes in the region and knows the wolves and shifters aren't changing, while many of the big players in supernatural society are. That's going to put them in a dangerous position. You, and the entire Northern Lakes Pack, represent change. Positive change." Queen Leila jerked her thumb over her shoulder, gesturing to Chase.

Harka did mention something about the other races growing in power.

I tilted my head. "Then you think it is my duty to become Pre-Dominant—so I can help wolves and shifters?"

"No, I'm just trying to give you perspective on why Harka is attempting to pull you in," Queen Leila said. "I know already you wolves have enough honor and duty in your bones to choke a hydra. I'm just trying to point out the forest through the trees for you, because I'm not entirely certain you're aware of just how amazing your Pack is."

I leaned back in my chair as I considered the fae queen's words.

For so much of my life, I've done what I've been asked to do for the sake of honor and duty. That was why I accepted the assignment to the Northern Lakes Pack…however…it has worked out.

The Pack is amazing, and I found Pip. But I never wanted to be more than an Alpha. I don't need more power.

"You don't have to do it, Alpha Greyson," Queen Leila said.

I mentally shook myself from my thoughts. "Pardon?"

"You don't have to become the next Pre-Dominant," Queen Leila said. "Harka will find someone else if you really don't want to."

I waited for a moment. "Is there a however to go along with that?"

"No," Queen Leila said. "You—and your Pack—have already accomplished so much. No matter what you choose, you'll continue to be trailblazers, and you'll continue to help wolves and shifters by being different. What's important is that you make a choice that you can live with."

"What do you mean?"

"You'll live with your choice for the rest of your life, so you need to be certain you choose the route that lets you get up in the morning and look at your reflection in the mirror. If that means concentrating on your Pack and the growth of Timber Ridge, great. If that means taking on the position of Pre-Dominant to help werewolves at large, that's also great," Queen Leila said. "Your choice is a gift."

I was quiet for a few moments. "I think I understand. Thank you, Queen Leila."

The fae queen beamed. "I'm glad I could help. Leadership is a burden—one that's hard to bear alone. Good luck in deciding what you want to do."

I frowned a little as her words burrowed deep into my mind. "Yes, thank you."

The question is then…what's most important to me? The good of the Pack? Or the good of our race?

Chapter 15

Pip

The restaurant Wyatt had chosen for lunch, Macho Tacos, smelled like garlic and cumin, and I stared unseeingly at the plastic covered menu.

"They have a taco here that's the size of my head!" Wyatt enthusiastically said.

"Great, we should get at least four of them," East said.

"Isn't one of those supposed to serve multiple people?" Scarlett asked.

"Werewolf metabolism," Rio said.

They were three tables away, but I barely heard them over the clink of cutlery, the music, and my own nerves, because across from me, bouncing her adorable baby on her knee, sat Lynn.

I glanced at Lynn, staring at the braid of her blond hair. It looked a little bit shorter than when I'd last seen her as she left the Northern Lakes Pack with Hudson—her father, the previous Pack Alpha. But her smile was still warm, and her voice and mannerisms had only sweetened as she peered at her baby—whom she had shucked of his sack-like onesie jacket and hat so he wasn't sweating in the warm restaurant.

I sipped the ice water in my plastic cup just to give myself something to do, and generally avoided eye contact. "So," I made myself say. "Congratulations on the baby."

"Thank you!" Lynn beamed at me and held up her baby for inspection.

He gurgled happily, his chubby cheeks and big eyes making him utterly adorable.

"He's such a good boy—he's already started sleeping through the night!" Lynn continued. "Dex—my husband— said he gets his sweet temperament from me, but I'm not so sure." She cradled him in her arms. "How are you, Pip?"

"Good. Really good," I evasively said.

How do I ask her if she never contacted me because she was mad at me?

Now that I knew the truth—that Hudson had been forced to leave because my powers as a Wolf's Kiss were too strong to suppress, and Greyson needed to come or I would accidentally throw the Pack into chaos—it was obvious why Lynn had chosen not to answer any of my texts or calls.

I couldn't believe she could sit across from me and chatter so happily—as if *I* wasn't the one responsible for forcing her family from their Pack, the thing that meant most to wolves.

"Dad said he saw you this summer," Lynn said. "Are you still working at the Timber Ridge Welcome Center?"

"Yes," I said. "For the past few months we've had a lot of fae tourists, so we've expanded some of our product lines in the gift shop. Howl-In Café offers some loose-leaf teas, and the Sweets Shoppe is experimenting with making green tea flavored fudge."

"That's exciting!" Lynn said.

"Yep." I took another swig of my water and wished I had ordered a margarita or something.

"They have Mexican hot chocolate here," Lynn said. "You should try some before lunch is over."

"You remember that I like hot chocolate?"

"Of course!" Lynn laughed. "Just because I left doesn't mean I forgot about you."

"Lynn…" I made myself look her in the eyes, because she deserved at least that much from me. "I know, now, why Hudson had to leave."

Her smile faded into something soft and a touch bittersweet. "Yeah. Dex's dad—he's the Alpha of our Pack—got the email about you. I figured you must have found out around then."

"A little before, actually." I tried to swallow, but my throat was too tight. "I'm sorry, Lynn."

Lynn blinked. "For what?"

"That Hudson—that your family—had to leave because of me. I swear I didn't know or…"

"I know," Lynn said.

"I'm so sorry," I said.

"Why?"

"You left your *Pack* because of me. I can't imagine how sad —or angry—you must have been." I braced myself for her reaction.

Lynn brushed her baby's cheek as he waved a fat little starfish hand in the air. "Dad told me I was going to regret not reaching out. But I still don't think I could have done it." She sighed.

"Done what? Talk to me after you left?" I asked.

Lynn nodded. "Yes. Pip, you have nothing to apologize for."

"How can you say that?" I asked. "You had to leave the only family you'd known for your entire life. You lost your home, friends, your entire *life* because I didn't control my powers."

"I'm not going to say it wasn't hard," Lynn said. "But I love my current life—I love my husband, my baby, and my new Pack." She met my gaze, her eyes filled with so much love I could barely keep my head up. "It was a sacrifice, but one made out of love."

I bit my lower lip to keep from crying, and looked away, staring at the wall, which was painted a bright orange color and had framed pictures of menu items covering it.

"I didn't answer your texts or calls, Pip, because I knew I'd break," Lynn said. "I'd tell you everything. I didn't even know about your powers until a week before Dad announced he was leaving, and it was a miracle I was able to keep my mouth shut during that time. I had to avoid you as much as possible, which felt horrible in a way I hadn't experienced before."

"Would telling me have been so bad?" I asked.

"Yes," Lynn said. "Because you're so *loyal*, you would have felt honor bound to leave the Pack. No matter what it did to you."

I jerked my gaze back to her, startled. "And that would have been bad?"

"Pip, you're a Wolf's Kiss. You bonded to the Northern Lakes Pack. Even without Santos and Dulce—and my family— you *needed* the Pack. You could barely stand the semester away at college, but if you knew about your powers you'd make yourself leave, even if it killed you. It was my choice—and Dad's—to leave. We did it because we wanted you to be happy —to be *free*."

"How could you make a sacrifice like that?" I whispered. "I'm just a hunter."

Lynn's eyes glazed with the tears I felt I couldn't shed. "Oh, *Pip*," she said, her voice broken. "You're so much more than that. You're my Pack."

"Even now?"

"Even now." She stood up—still cradling her baby—and

eased herself into the chair next to mine, then scooted closer so she could tip her head against mine. "I love the Northern Lakes Pack. But you're a part of that Pack. Dad, Mom and me? We could start over. It would be rough, but I knew we could do it. But as a Wolf's Kiss… We decided to leave because we loved you, and we knew you needed Northern Lakes."

I sniffed. "Maybe not as much as you think. I missed you."

"Yes, and then you *chose* to wall yourself off from the Pack." For the first time there was a hint of reproach in Lynn's voice.

I pulled back so I could gape at her. "How did you know?"

"Aeric and Wyatt." Lynn jutted her chin in Wyatt's direction. "They've been keeping me up to date."

My heart faltered as I glanced at Wyatt—who was laughing at something Scarlett said. "Did you ask them to be my friends?"

"No." Lynn shook her head. "They didn't reach out to me until they were concerned that you were shutting the wolves out. And they weren't the only ones who texted me about you."

I furrowed my forehead. "Who else?"

Maybe Hector or Ember? But I can't think of anyone else I'm particularly close to who would know her. Jack, East, and Shania are all new wolves, so they wouldn't really know her…

Lynn glanced at the group of Northern Lakes wolves again. "It's not my place to share, but, Pip…you mean a great deal more to the Pack than you're willing to believe. I wish you'd let yourself be loved."

Funny you say that when Rio is literally within eyesight, and he openly picks fights with me.

I gulped my ice water and wiped at the water ring it left on the plastic tablecloth of colored peppers wearing sunglasses, and wisely said nothing.

"Dad considered staying with the Pack even after Greyson arrived, but he and the Pre-Dominant decided it would be too confusing for the Pack, and possibly divide loyalties," Lynn continued.

I grunted.

As much as I disliked it, she wasn't wrong.

Heck, *I* would have done everything I could have to stir up crap out of loyalty to Hudson, and that would have made things a thousand times worse.

"In the end, I think everything worked out in the best possible way." Lynn smiled down at her baby. "I should have tried talking to you, though. I'm sorry. I wasn't strong enough at the time…"

"I was hurt." I swirled my plastic cup. "But I didn't understand everything that was going on. I didn't know what I was doing."

"Are you happy now?" Lynn asked.

I rattled the ice in my cup as I thought of the Bedevilments, laughing with Shania, stocking the gift shop while fae watched with fascination, training with the wolves, and…Greyson.

"Yeah," I said. "I'm happy."

"Good," Lynn said.

Her baby fussed, and Lynn crooned to it, her beautiful voice curling through the air almost like a physical caress.

I smiled, remembering the nights my own mother sang to me, and when Mama Dulce and Papa Santos used to serenade me as wolves to make me laugh.

Wait—I'm talking to Lynn. This is the perfect opportunity to ask her about werewolf lore!

I straightened in my chair. "Lynn, do you remember if Mama Dulce told us any stories about werewolf mates?"

"Oh yeah. There were tons of them." Lynn rearranged her baby, then tickled his chin.

I licked my lips. "Were there any about…hunters and wolves?"

Lynn snapped her eyes up to mine, and I could feel the years fade away between us.

I didn't need to say a thing.

She knows—I'm Greyson's mate.

"There was one about a wolf named Esta," she cautiously said.

I cringed. "Yeah, I know of it. The hunter used her and killed her Pack and eventually her." My stomach growled as a waiter walked past with one of the head-sized tacos Wyatt had been drooling over earlier.

"And in the end, the hunter's magic breaks."

I sat up straight. "*What?*"

That certainly hadn't been in my hunter journal!

Lynn nodded. "Yes, after the hunter killed Esta, wild magic sought vengeance on her tragic behalf and broke his ability to wield magic as penance for all he'd done."

"Huh. Well. That shouldn't be a problem," I said.

I'm never going to kill Greyson, or hurt him like that.

"When my mom told me the story, she said his magic broke because there could only be imbalance in a bond between a wolf and a hunter."

My heart thumped in my chest. "Sorry, *what?*"

Lynn pushed her eyebrows together, her expression growing worried. "She said either the wolf pays with eternal pain, or the hunter pays with broken magic. It's the price for something that shouldn't be."

"Wow. That's really not encouraging," I said.

Broken magic? I don't know if I could mentally survive *without my hunter powers. I had a panic attack when I was briefly cut off from it. It's not that I'd choose magic over Greyson, it's that my magic is so enmeshed in me it'd be like lopping off a part of me—a part of my brain. Could I survive that?*

But could Greyson survive the pain of an incomplete bond?

"That was something my Mom said." Lynn leaned into me again. "It doesn't mean it's right. Besides the story of Esta and the hunter, I don't know of any hunter-wolf bonds. And Greyson isn't a normal wolf."

"Yep," I grimly said. "Yep, yep, yep."

Lynn pressed her lips together. "I remember once, Dulce told me the legend of Esta for about the fourth time. It was when we were juniors in high school. You were with Santos, making popcorn and hot chocolate, and I badmouthed Esta for falling for the hunter's tricks."

I peered up at her, holding my breath in the hope that Mama Dulce had said something kinder.

She flashed me a quick grin, then stared down at the table as she strained her memory. "I'd said Esta was silly for falling for a hunter in the first place, since he could never return the mate bond, and they were natural enemies. Dulce…she said that hunters weren't mates not because of the bond, but because the divide between us was too wide. Hunters weren't close enough to wolves to understand our nature, and wolves weren't close enough to hunters to understand theirs. She seemed to imply it was more of a cultural thing, and that it bred distrust—which would doom a bond that is supposed to be built on trust."

I shrugged. "That was probably her trying to give you a moral lesson. She's not wrong, but the physical inability to accept the bond puts a strain on the relationship that no other mate bond would have. If it's like your mom said and maybe the hunter lost their connection to their magic, it *might* work. But could they even be considered a hunter, then?"

"I don't know," Lynn said. "Dulce seemed pretty certain."

I pursed my lips. "It's worth thinking over, I guess. But Dulce also told us that the shift—being changed from a human into a werewolf supernatural—used to be different, too."

"Long ago, yeah," Lynn said. "Do you think she was right?"

I rested my elbows on the table. "Who knows? I think only the elves would be able to remember that long ago, and they're all dead."

"There are some vampires who might remember," Lynn said.

I snorted. "Yeah, if you can dig them out of their crypts and melancholy. The oldest vampires have all given up—everyone knows that."

Lynn looked like she wanted to say something more, but her baby cried again.

"Oh, Phil, it's okay." She rocked him and smiled down at him.

I blinked. "Phil?"

That doesn't seem like a werewolf name. They like stronger names—like Wyatt, Chase, and Greyson. Phil sounds like a high-level accountant in the Curia Cloisters—still dangerous, just in a very different way.

"Yes, Phil." Lynn's smile turned mischievous as she peeked at me. "He was named after someone very special to me."

I slumped in my chair, making it creak in alarm. "You know someone named Phil? From your new Pack?"

"No," Lynn said gently. "But I do know a Phillipa."

I stared at Lynn, taking several moments to let her words sink in. "*Me?*" I squeaked when my brain finally caught up.

"You," Lynn laughed.

Instantly those tears I'd been trying so hard to fight off flooded my eyes, and I sniffed as I leaned over her baby.

"Hi, Phil," I said.

"Do you want to hold him?"

"Um—"

"You should hold him."

As I took baby Phil, Wyatt finally broke ranks and left the Pack's table so he could crouch down next to us to say hello to the baby as I showed him off. Next came East, then even Rio, and the Fletchings.

Baby Phil…I never would have imagined…Then again, I never would have ever thought I'd be Greyson's mate, or a Wolf's Kiss.

Dulce's words to Lynn…they were kind and pretty, but I knew better. I'd seen the pain in Greyson, and I knew there was no way to get around my magic unless it broke like Lynn's mom mentioned.

A mate bond between a wolf and a hunter was doomed.

———

A wolf howled.

I pressed my lips together and tried to concentrate on reversing the flow of my magic. It settled on my team, seeping into them as it bolstered their abilities.

Aeric, Wyatt, Shania, East, Jack, and Moira all immediately grew, the magic stretching their frames out and packing even more muscle on them.

Unfortunately, it did nothing to Rio and River, and it had a very tenuous grasp on Forrest and Klancy that slipped if I wasn't paying attention to it.

I tried to tamp down the twitch of irritation that flashed through me.

I have yet to ever get my magic to stick to Rio. It wouldn't surprise me if he's been rejecting it out of spite.

I'd been assigned progressively larger groups of wolves to hunt with during the fights, but I had yet to get my magic to stick to the entire group. (Though the spiteful part of me suspected my inability to cast my magic on Rio had something more to do with his attitude than my abilities.)

The team we'd been assigned to fight against flickered at the edge of my eyesight, appearing in the shadows cast by the bright moonlight on the snow covered ground.

Moira took out the first wolf from the opposing team, tossing him aside like he was a rag doll and not a full-grown wolf.

Aeric and Wyatt drove three wolves between the two of them, herding them away from our base.

I raised my daggers, preparing for the opposing team— which was about double the size of mine—to break our frontlines.

I felt Klancy slip from my magic, and I clenched my teeth as I directed more at him.

It got to him in time that he was able to body slam one wolf and bite at the throat of another, but a third packmate streaked past him—running toward me.

Shania, standing near me, flattened her ears, and something bubbled inside me, so I *knew* what she was thinking.

"I told you I *can't* bring a baseball bat to a fight like this," I said.

She glanced over at me in surprise—she was so huge from my magic, she didn't have to look up very much—then shifted her weight to her hindquarters and sprang forward. She intercepted the wolf with a snarl.

Hopping in her footprints, I joined the fight.

I saw a wolf attacking East's unprotected flank and moved in, kneeing it in the head. When it turned to me, I ruthlessly slashed at its paws with my daggers, and it retreated.

Behind me, East yipped in alarm as my Wolf's Kiss magic faltered. I threw more magic at my team, then pivoted, finding my next target.

I kicked, sliced, and then cursed whenever I felt my magic slip from me and fall off my team.

It seemed impossible to keep up without my full attention —which I couldn't give, obviously, when I was attacking a wolf.

I thought this would be something I could multitask, but maybe I'm too inexperienced? I shook my head in irritation as I forcibly threw more of my magic on my team, then had to bite back a scream when my magic flooded the area and cast itself on *all* of the wolves present.

The packmate I was fighting—Remy—started to grow, and I hastily yanked back on my magic, starting to pull it off our opponents.

The first bits of my magic returned to me, hitting me in a wave that felt…different.

I didn't have a lot of experience with my Wolf's Kiss magic, but it had a distinct, reverse-flowing feel to it. What I'd removed from the wolves had that same sensation, but it had a wolfish feeling to it—similar to how my hunter senses made a werewolf feel in my mind: bright and minty.

I paused, and for a moment both groups of wolves were oversized, as I hadn't completely stripped them of my powers, too surprised by the feeling of wolves and my magic combined.

What the…?

When I realized I was looking directly into Remy's eyes because she was huge from my magic, I startled into motion. I finished pulling all my magic off the opposing team, then dumped the weirdly flavored magic on my team, and was relieved to see nothing weird happened to them.

Remy gave a high-pitched yip I recognized as wolf laughter.

I scowled at her. "It's not funny. What if that happened in a real battle?" I kneed her in the side, and she coughed, staggering a few steps.

Both my hunter senses and my powers as a Wolf's Kiss flooded me, and I had to stop for a moment to try to shake my vision clear.

I heard a familiar howl at my back, and a cold sweat crawled up my spine.

Hector.

Years of conditioning flooded my system, and I ran.

Hector was the strongest wolf I had ever faced—because whenever Greyson and I faced off it was always abundantly clear to me he was just playing. But that was fine with me! Hector—kind, professor-y Hector—was a *terror* to go up against. I didn't need to know what someone with Greyson's power would be like.

I swerved around a bush, searching for a suitable tree that was strong enough to survive against the Pack beta, and would be easy enough for me to climb.

Got it!

I spotted one off to the side. I lunged for it, biting down a squeal when I felt hot breath on my back before teeth closed around my ankle and yanked my foot out from underneath me.

I managed to keep balanced on one leg for a moment, while I bent over and attempted to throw a dagger at Hector from my folded position.

Hector dodged my throw, then gave one more yank that pulled me back on my rear.

Before I could recover, he had his teeth at my throat.

I groaned and slapped the snowy ground. "I yield—you won."

Hector wagged his tail as he released me—back to looking like an especially wolf-ish and enormous friendly dog—then released a loud howl that filled the area.

Gradually, the wolves stopped fighting and milled around, self-sorting themselves back into their teams before a number of them triggered their shifts, making the painful switch from wolf to human.

I groaned as I rolled to my feet, brushed snow off my pants, and then sheathed my daggers in my thigh bandolier. Finally, I released my magic, and my team lost their power boost.

Hector nudged me, pressing his nose into my side.

"I'm fine," I assured him.

"Pip!"

I waved as Scarlett and Radcliff approached—both wearing bright orange like human hunters did so they stuck out against the blue of the snow. "Hey, guys."

"How'd practice go?" Scarlett asked.

Radcliff eagerly rubbed his hands together and bounced in place. "I still don't believe it—you're fighting *with* wolves! How cool is that?"

"It's taking some adjusting," I said. "I'm not used to fighting with a group. Though I suppose that's more a personal quirk than something I get as a hunter."

"Looks like the battles are getting to be larger—and longer," Scarlett said.

"Yeah—unless Hector is involved." I scowled at the beta, who wagged his tail again and looked as innocent as a puppy. "Then it's over as soon as he decides to enter the battlefield."

"What's it like?" Radcliff asked.

"Facing off against Hector? Terrifying."

"I meant fighting with a Pack."

"Oh, yeah that makes sense. It keeps changing, honestly," I said. "I still can't understand the wolves like they can understand each other, but I'm starting to pick things up from them. I don't know if I'm getting even better at reading their body language, or if it's because of my magic."

"You're rapidly improving, so I would imagine it's probably your magic, and you're connecting deeper with them," Scarlett said.

I winced. "Maybe, but I'm not improving in all areas. I still have trouble keeping my magic active—and it's still not working for everyone."

"Is it always the same wolves that it won't cast on?" Radcliff asked.

"For the most part, yeah. But then again in this fight I had a moment where I briefly managed to power up *everyone*." I peered up at the sky—I couldn't see as many stars as I could in the summer—moonlight reflecting off snow is pretty bright—but it was a beautiful swirl of silver and black.

As gorgeous as it was, it didn't do a lot to take the edge off my frustration.

Why won't Rio just accept *my magic? I know he's been through a lot and we've never been besties, but come on! The magic positively affects him—there are no downsides to this!*

I dropped my gaze, then lowered my voice. "I'm starting to think it might be a trust problem—"

"*It is.*"

Chapter 16

Pip

I turned around, surprised to see Rio—human Rio—prowling toward me, wearing only the loose, baggy shorts his fae-charmed bracelet provided.

Snow stuck to his bare feet, and he was shirt-less, but his focus was, unfortunately, on me, and not the cold.

I pushed my shoulders back and straightened up, preparing for a fight.

"What, are you too paranoid I'm going to hypnotize you into doing my bidding?" I snapped.

Rio's laugh was dark. "Oh, no, Pip. You're not pushing this one on me. The problem is you."

I scowled. "Not a chance."

"Quite the opposite, actually," Rio said. "It's the only possible explanation. Your distrust of me and the others makes it impossible for your magic to work on us."

I set my hands on my hips and gripped the belt loops of my pants. "If you think my distrust affects my magic, then *your* distrust certainly does as well. This is a two-way street, Rio."

"That's the problem."

Rio got a little closer than I normally like angry wolves to be inside my personal space, but I couldn't give up any ground —he'd really go for me, then. Instead, I took a step closer to him and tried to puff up as much as I could

"Oh really? Then enlighten me, Rio, how does *my* magic work?"

"I'm not saying trust isn't required from us," Rio said. "But you're missing the point. We already trust you."

I scoffed.

"See?" Rio jabbed a finger at me. "This is why you can't cast on everyone!"

"Please," I scoffed. "You don't trust me, either."

"Except I do!"

"No way."

"You're *Pack*." Rio put every ounce of feeling he had into the declaration—making it sound exasperated, angry, and...heartbroken.

I snapped my mouth shut, my teeth audibly clicking, and peered up at him.

"You've had my trust for years—the trust of the Pack for years—but you refuse it," Rio continued. "You're the one who insists you're not part of the Northern Lakes Pack, even though all anyone has ever done is love you."

"I'm grateful to the Pack for accepting me," I said. "And I'm aware I was given permissions that other supernaturals normally aren't. But you can't pretend that I'm really part of this when I was purposely kept out of specific Pack activities."

Rio narrowed his eyes, but looked away.

"Why don't we take a quick break before we start up the next round," Wyatt suggested.

Aeric brightened up. "We could talk about cars and winter tires!"

I managed to hold in a groan—the entire Pack had winter

tires because of Aeric's fanaticism with cars and tires. I was pretty sure most of us knew everything he knew about winter tires, too.

"I guess we'll head back to the boundary so we're out of the way," Scarlett said.

"I'll walk with you!" I volunteered. "I was getting a little mixed up in that last round. I could use some space so I can come back and refocus on who I'm casting my magic on."

Hector gave me an "*Aroo*" which I chose to interpret as permission, so I waved and wove through the forest with Scarlett and Radcliff.

"Ugh, I'm going to have to wash these clothes. My sweat glands kick in like crazy whenever I hear Hector howl." I peered down at my hunter winter gear. Since I was so active it wasn't as thick or warm as the parka and snow pants I occasionally wore. Instead, it was designed to release my heat so I wouldn't sweat—though I still did.

"Can you imagine facing Alpha Greyson?" Radcliff jumped a fallen tree, his boots crushing the thin layer of snow that covered the ground when he landed—we were in mid December, but we hadn't gotten much snow yet.

I shivered. "No. Facing him down when Aspen got him dosed up with wolfsbane was bad enough."

"I bet," Scarlett said.

We reached the boundary for our match—which was limited to a relatively small patch of forest that filled only a few acres.

"I hope you two have a great afternoon. Any plans?" I squinted up at the sun, which felt way too low on the horizon to be in the early afternoon, but December had our shortest days of the year and always threw my sense of time off.

"Yeah, we're going to do some target practice—Beta Hector told us about an area we are allowed to use." Scarlett pointed to the pile of black, padded bags that most likely held all of their equipment that they'd placed on one of the picnic tables left out year-round.

Radcliff picked up one of the black cases and brushed snow off it. "He was quite happy when we asked about it." Radcliff checked the dagger that was tucked into his belt. "Ember was with him at the time and asked if we could practice in the meadow while the Alphas come to the lodge for the Pack-sponsored meal later this week. The idea was abandoned out of safety concerns."

"Pip!"

I held my hand up to my face to shadow the glare of the low sun and make out the swaddled shape coming toward us.

It took me a moment to recognize Teresa—she was wearing black snow pants and a pink coat with matching hat, gloves, and scarf—for all that werewolves loved the cold, they seemed to fear their children would freeze and swaddled them in so many layers it could be hard to move.

I knew from experience—Mama Dulce and Papa Santos used to rarely let me leave the house without snow pants in the winter.

Teresa pulled a bright pink sled—which contained several armloads of pinecones—behind her through the thin layer of snow.

"Hey there, Teresa," I said. "Are you collecting pinecones?"

"Yeah—Original Jack is having us kids gather them up to use in extra Christmas decorations for the lodge." Teresa pulled her scarf down and peered from me to the Fletchings. "Are you practicing?"

I hesitated, trying to decide if she'd be hurt by my reference to the Pack. "I'm practicing my Wolf's Kiss magic with the Pack, but Radcliff and Scarlett mentioned they were going to do some target practice."

Teresa's eyes widened in interest as she peered up at Scarlett and Radcliff. "Target practice? With what weapons?"

"We have crossbows, handguns, and a few daggers," Radcliff said.

"You don't have a rifle like Pip?" Teresa asked.

Scarlett shook her head. "Typically hunter families specialize in different weapons. Our mother prefers a variety of guns with her magic, but we take after our dad and his magic, so we mostly use his specialty: crossbows with spelled ammo."

"Do you spell the ammo?" Teresa asked.

Radcliff laughed. "No—that's beyond a hunter's abilities. We buy our ammo from fae, just like Pip."

Teresa squirmed a little in place.

"You have another question?" I asked.

"Kinda," Teresa said. "Doesn't that mean that you don't have to have magic to use hunter weapons?"

I stared at Teresa, transfixed, and too scared to answer.

Teresa had her dreams broken—she'd wanted to be a were-wolf like her parents. She'd been understandably devastated, but…could she be thinking…?

Answer her! Answer her now, and fast—encourage her! This is what we've been wanting for her!

Unfortunately, I was so tongue-tied with hope, I could only gape at her.

"Correct," Scarlett answered her with a casual brightness that made me want to give her a voucher for a life's supply of Pomeranian Puppy Powerups or whatever else she wanted. "While hunters do have innate magic to make our job easier, magic technically isn't required to be a hunter."

"Our Dad's mom was pure human," Radcliff added. "She fell in love with our grandpa and joined his hunter family. Even though she didn't have magic, she was the best shot in the whole family."

"Really? A human can be a hunter?"

"Yes," I said, finally getting my mouth moving. "They'd have to join a hunter family, of course, because hunting alone is pretty dangerous for *any* hunter, but bloodlines and magic don't make a person a hunter. Families try to preserve their magic for the sake of tradition, but humans are always welcome to join."

"Do you have any humans in your family history, Pip?" Teresa asked.

I winced. "I'm ashamed to say I never dug too deeply into the Sabres or Wards. If I had maybe I would have been more prepared for being a Wolf's Kiss." I scowled briefly. "But I can pretty confidently say yes, or the hunter family gene pool would get too small."

"Huh?" Teresa said.

I waved my hand. "I mean all hunter families need fresh blood in their family lines."

Teresa furrowed her eyebrows. "Okay?"

"The point is, humans are welcome!" I said. "But they have to go through the training we did when we were younger, so they know how to use, clean, and repair their weapons, and know basic hunting, trapping, and tracking strategies as well as the habits of werewolves and shifters."

"There's a certification test you have to pass, but it doesn't require the use of magic," Scarlett added. "They give out different tests depending on your magic specialization. Radcliff and I had a tracking test."

Teresa chewed on her lip. "What did you have, Pip?"

I made a show of scowling—knowing that my answer was about to relieve her. "They stuck me in a room of werewolves to test the effects of my puppy pheromones. I got really spitty from all the unwanted wolf licks."

Scarlett strangled a chuckle, but Radcliff laughed outright.

"You see, Teresa?" he wheezed when he could talk again. "Magic isn't necessary."

"That's cool." Teresa fixed her grip on the rope tethered to the sled. "Can I watch you practice with your crossbow sometime?"

"Yes," Scarlett said. "We can show you the difference between it and our handguns."

"That'd be fun!" Teresa said.

I blinked, not knowing any other ten-year-old who would geek out over weapons besides a hunter.

Maybe she really could do it, and become a human hunter.

"I should go, the lodge needs these pinecones," Teresa said. "Good luck with practice."

"Thanks." I waved to her as she trotted off, her sled rattling behind her. I waited until she was out of hearing range before I turned to Scarlett and Radcliff. "Thank you—she needed that."

"I can imagine." Scarlett's face darkened, and she picked up the padded case of her weapons. "I was so angry that Aspen savaged her like that. Teresa needs hope."

"It won't be easy for her," Radcliff said. "But she's got the gumption."

"Even if she's only interested in it for a few years and it helps her get back her confidence—or shows her that humans are just as strong as werewolves but in different ways—I'll take it," I said.

"Yes," Scarlett agreed. "If she gets certified and joins a family, it will help her longing for community, too."

I hesitated, my spirits falling. "Maybe," I said. "But she still won't be able to run with her parents."

Radcliff watched her run up a slight hill. "No," he said, his voice sad with regret. "She won't."

———

"You seriously have popcorn *stores*—stores, as in, more than one?" I couldn't keep the disbelief and longing out of my voice, and my mouth dropped open as I gaped at Maya Williams and Kim Seo-Jun—the two Alphas whose Packs were both based in Chicago.

Maya laughed. "It's a chain called Garrett Popcorn. It's very popular, and considered to be an icon of Chicago."

"What flavors do they have?" I rested my hands on the table and scooted a little closer.

Seo-Jun played with the brim of his white fedora hat—which he'd taken off upon entering the lodge. "The usual: plain, cheesy, buttery. They also have a bunch of variations of their CaramelCrisp flavor, with nuts or—what I suspect you would like most—the seasonal Hot Cocoa CaramelCrisp."

I groaned and leaned back in my chair, upsetting the fork I'd left on my dessert plate, which I'd nearly licked clean—Moira had made her famous peanut butter cheesecake for tonight. "That solves it. I need a road trip to Chicago!"

I immediately straightened up and guiltily peered around the room, trying to see if anyone had heard me.

All the visiting Alphas had been brought into the great room for a Northern Lakes Pack-hosted dinner.

The room wasn't too packed—there was plenty of space between the various wooden tables—but given it was a roomful of werewolves, I'm sure most everyone had heard me.

Thankfully it didn't seem like my declaration caused any alarm, so I relaxed and returned my attention to the two Alphas I'd been chatting with.

Seo-Jun had a slight smile on his lips. "I would not have thought popcorn would be enough to tempt you into traveling."

"It's a pretty good lure," I said.

"In that case, please allow me to extend an invitation to you on behalf of all Chicago Packs to come visit, and see the city—and the Packs—for yourself," Maya said. "We'd love to entertain you, and you can see everything the city has to offer."

Oohh, that was a slick move.

Seo-Jun had to be in on her offer—he nonchalantly studied his glass chalice of water—the Pack had busted out all the stops for dinner.

The plates were china with silver edging and a snowy design, there were bottles of locally brewed beer as well as imported wine, and the cloth napkins had snowflakes stitched into them that matched the plates.

I'd say they were trying to be excellent hosts, but knowing how competitive wolves are, it was likely another way of putting the Alphas in their place. It was a show of wealth—most Packs couldn't afford a place like the lodge, much less the expensive dishes. But, then again, most Packs didn't own the majority of businesses in a tourist city.

"Thanks for the offer, but I'll be upfront with you guys: I'm not leaving the Northern Lakes Pack. And that's not going to change," I said. "The Pack is important to me, and…"

And I can't exactly just abandon Greyson.

Maya nodded. "I imagined as much given how long you've been with the Northern Lakes Pack and how well respected they are, but we had to try."

Seo-Jun set his chalice down. "If you change your mind, the offer stands. Or even if you are merely curious about our city."

"Thanks." I relaxed, grateful they were taking the refusal well.

There had been at least two other Alphas who had made similar offers when I was making the rounds during the actual dinner. Both of them had gotten mad when I'd said no.

I glanced at the female Alpha who had reacted badly—she was watching me with an intensity I didn't like.

She hadn't jumped me when I'd said no, but the anger in her eyes was obvious, as was the ominous cracking her fingers made when she balled her hands into fists.

"Yes, you'll need to be careful," Maya said.

"I'm sorry, what?"

Seo-Jun gestured around the room. "Not all the Alphas will take your refusal well."

"Which makes them fools," Maya grumbled. "Who—in their right mind—would try to swipe anything from Alpha Greyson, much less his Wolf's Kiss?"

Seo-Jun laughed and picked up his wine glass. "You're not wrong." He smirked a little as he glanced at me. "Which reminds me, to compensate us for your refusal, Hunter Sabre, I request that you put in a good word for us with Alpha Greyson."

"Sure, but why?"

"It never hurts to build a positive relationship with the future Pre-Dominant," Maya said.

I coughed to cover the wheeze of air. "Wow. Okay. So in other news I'm never going to politically cross either of you."

"It's not really political as much as it is planning ahead for our Packs. It's why Maya and I agreed to team up for our venture of talking to you," Seo-Jun said.

"We've also been meeting with Rafe—heir apparent to Pre-Dominant Harka's Pack—since he is eventually going to become the Alpha of his Pack, and—Northern Lakes Pack withstanding—it's one of the largest and strongest in the Midwest."

"Yeah, I could see the positives in that," I said.

Harka's been dragging Rafe to every meeting we have with her so Rafe can establish a relationship with Greyson, too.

I rolled my neck, pausing when I saw Hector—who tapped his watch once he had my attention. "I should probably move on to the next group of Alphas. Hector is giving me 'the look'."

Seo-Jun chuckled. "You are fun, Hunter Sabre. Thank you for a diverting conversation."

"You're welcome. Have a lovely evening." I almost staggered when I stood up—my right foot had fallen asleep—but when I put weight on it the staticky feeling receded, and it no longer felt quite so numb.

As I made my way to Hector, some of the Pack started escorting a few of the Alphas out.

Since Greyson had opted to host the dinner in the lodge, the Alphas were being personally escorted in and out of the territory by the Pack—and on a rotational basis so the lodge was never unguarded.

"Hey, Hector. Who is up next for this round of 'Pip-show-and-tell'?" I asked.

Hector smoothed his goatee as he carefully picked his words. "There's just one Alpha left, but he's not proven to be the most…*stable* of persons, and he was seen conversing with Vant when the Alphas first arrived, so I will be accompanying you."

"Sounds like fun."

"Most assuredly."

"Yippee."

"If you'll just follow me, Pip." Hector smiled at me before he led me off across the great room.

I figured out who we were meeting pretty quickly—with over half of the Alphas gone, he was the only one sitting at his table. He appeared to be clean cut with slicked back hair, a blue sweater, and khaki pants, but his smile was a little too thin and wide, so he looked a little…off.

If I remembered correctly, his name was Brock, and he was the Alpha of the North Dakota Grassland Pack.

I'm surprised he's still here. Most of the Alphas who weren't within a several hours' commute of Magiford realized they didn't stand a chance and this was a bad idea after initially meeting me. He can't possibly think I'll leave here? But Hector did say he's cray-cray.

I slapped on a smile as we approached the table.

"Hello! I hope you enjoyed dinner?" I rested my hands on the back of a chair and tugged it back so I could sit down.

Brock stared at me, his lips starting to curl back in a werewolf snarl.

Hector put a hand on my shoulder before I could sit, then pulled me so I was slightly behind him. "Alpha Brock," he said in a deep voice Hector only used when he was about to discipline someone.

I automatically did a sweep of the area and relaxed slightly when I saw Dale and Tom were still hanging around. They were sitting two tables away, reciting fishing stories to Young Jack—who shared their rare enthusiasm for water.

Not that Hector wasn't capable of pounding the shifty Alpha into the ground. But backup is always a great thing to have.

"Hunter," Brock managed to say.

I frowned. "Obviously."

Hector tapped a finger on my arm, telling me to be silent. "Alpha Brock, if you have a problem with Hunter Sabre, allow me to ask: why are you here?"

Brock looked around the room, then shrugged. "I don't have an issue with her being a Wolf's Kiss. I just don't like her as a person."

Hector discreetly sniffed—probably trying to scent out if Brock was lying or not.

His shoulders relaxed after a moment, which I took to interpret as Brock was being honest.

"I understand. However, you can see Hunter Sabre is unlikely to leave," Hector said—a nice way of saying '*She'll never go with you*.' "Thus, perhaps it is time you head back to your Pack."

Brock leaned back in his chair and shook his head. "No. I need to see how this plays out."

"I see. In that case, be forewarned that the Northern Lakes

Pack will not tolerate *any* show of aggression to Hunter Sabre," Hector said.

Alpha Brock looked past us. "Yeah, I see that now."

I peered back over my shoulder and spotted Greyson prowling toward us.

Brock sharply nodded, then pulled out his cellphone and started tapping away on it.

Hector turned around and nudged me away, herding me across the room and straight into Greyson.

Greyson set both of his hands on my shoulders and studied me from head to toe—as if I'd somehow gotten injured.

"Everything's fine," I said.

"Tell that to your emotions," Greyson muttered.

Hector motioned for us to keep on walking, and he led us out of the great room, into the darkened lodge. "Brock isn't interested—he's got an attitude against Pip that makes me think he has some variation of a small man's complex—but he's here to watch." Hector's voice was barely louder than an exhale.

Greyson nodded.

"That's it?" I asked. "You don't find that sketchy?"

"It's not surprising," Greyson said. "The Northern Lakes Pack has always attracted more attention than I'd like. Of course he's going to watch—he wants to see if anyone can lure you away, which would be a sign of weakness in our Pack."

I glanced back at the room. "I don't know...his Pack is relatively small, right? Would he really be that interested in us?"

"He will be if Greyson becomes the next Pre-Dominant," Hector said.

"Yeah..." I trailed off and chewed my lip. Hector wasn't wrong, but his—and Greyson's—explanation didn't sit quite right with me. My hunter senses didn't quiet down, either.

Maybe I'm just getting paranoid from being attacked so much?

Regardless, the one thing I'd learned in all of this was that for all their competitive shows of strengths, werewolves could be just as crafty politically speaking as vampires and fae— which was surprising since they were considered to be one of the more straightforward types of supernaturals.

Maybe Alphas are Alphas because they can do the politicking, and their Packs can't?

"Alpha Maya and Alpha Seo-Jun both told me they intend to leave for Chicago tomorrow," Greyson stated.

"I believe after tonight a good portion of the Alphas will leave," Hector said.

"Really? Why?" I asked.

"They can't afford to be away from their Packs much longer," Greyson said. "And most of them are smart enough to recognize that you won't be leaving the Northern Lakes Pack."

I felt for the dagger strapped to my belt—hidden under my thick sweater. "That would make things easier on us."

"Yes," Greyson agreed. "Especially because anyone who remains behind obviously has an agenda."

———

My interaction with Brock bothered me.

Not because I was scared, but because it just didn't feel right. Something about it bothered my hunter senses.

Which was why—in the dog watch hours of the night—I was still awake, sitting on my bed and paging through the hunter journals while Prince and Princess snoozed nearby.

I turned a page in the Ward journal. My eyelids were burning, but my brain just wouldn't shut off.

Does it really make sense for Brock to care that much *about the Northern Lakes Pack? It's not like he could ever do anything to the Pack even if he wanted to.*

Then again, Vant's Pack—the Low Marsh Pack—was also

pretty small, and he'd stuck his nose in Northern Lakes Pack business on more than one occasion.

I stared unseeingly at a diagram of a trap spell, when a faint howl reached my ears.

…I recognize that song.

I stood up, stuffed my feet in my slippers, and shuffled over to the window, pushing back the curtain.

Although it wasn't a full moon, it was still bright, making the white snow blue in the shade of the night and giving everything a shimmery sheen to it.

I didn't see any wolves, not even as my hunter night vision kicked in, but when I opened the window a crack I could hear.

It's Greyson.

I relaxed, resting my hands on the cold windowsill as I listened to him. His howl crested high and low in a long, soothing note that had me exhaling the building anxiety I'd been holding in my chest.

It was beautiful and ethereal—more like a song than a howl.

He paused for a moment, then started up—his howl low like the rumbles of a thunderstorm before cresting high.

My eyes drifted shut as I listened, my mind quieting.

Suddenly, sleep doesn't seem so impossible.

I sighed as Greyson sprinkled in a few bark-like yips to his howl before he started up again, inexplicably calmed by his song.

Wait…Greyson used to sing the most heartbreaking howls back when his mate bond was missing. It was the only thing that made me feel any sympathy for him at the time. But this is completely different.

I flicked my eyes open and stared outside.

He's howling…for me.

The knowledge wrapped around me like a warm blanket, and I smiled as I huddled by the window, listening.

Hopefully things with the Alphas will slow down a little. Harka is making a public statement next week about the situation. If I focus on figuring out my magic, that would probably be best. The stronger I can make the Pack, the less appealing a target we'll be.

But the idea of my magic left a salty taste in my mouth.

It wasn't that I didn't want to use it, but...what if Rio was right?

What if *I* was why my magic wasn't spreading to everyone?

I decided after Lynn left that I wasn't going to let myself get close to another wolf...but now I know why she left, and that it was all for me. But...it's not like I can just let down my walls and declare myself Pack.

The idea of being a part of the Pack was both appealing and horrifying.

The wolves kept nothing from each other—it was a miracle Greyson and I hadn't spilled our mate bond to more than Hector, Ember, Aeric, Wyatt, and Shania.

The Pack did *life* together, and they were always up in each other's business.

Can I really handle that? When I've trained to live and fight alone, without help?

I saw something stir at the very edge of the forest that surrounded the lodge and its meadow.

Greyson.

Chapter 17

Pip

I mpulsively, I shut the window, yanked off my slippers, grabbed my thick winter jacket, and ran downstairs, my cold feet slapping the wooden floors.

I grabbed my boots from the laundry room and burst out the front door as I zipped up my jacket.

I blinked as my night vision adjusted again, then thudded down the stairs.

I saw white move out of the corner of my eye and turned to see Greyson lope across the snowy meadow, his white fur sticking out against the dark backdrop of the trees.

I yanked the hood of my jacket up, then crouched down as Greyson trotted up to me.

He pushed his furry cheek against mine and released a happy whine as I sank my fingers into his thick coat.

I petted him for a minute, stroking the top of his head, then his shoulders and back.

He tilted his head, his eyes sliding shut—if he was a cat he'd be purring.

I scratched his throat for him, marveling over his white coat.

Greyson was breathtaking as a wolf. He was power and death packed into beauty. I never really let myself admire how beautiful his wolf form was. (Usually I just made jokes that his name was Greyson, but he was completely white.)

He bumped his black nose against mine, then sighed when I rubbed the spots just in front of his ears.

I laughed when he licked my face, but was surprised when he pulled away and climbed the stairs, disappearing into the lodge.

He emerged a minute later, buttoning a thin dress shirt with his sleeves rolled up to his elbows. "Who thought it was a good idea to put *button up* dress shirts in our clothes drops?" he asked.

"Hector, probably," I said.

"Probably," Greyson agreed. "Come inside. You're going to freeze out here." He held out his hand.

When I took it, sliding my cold fingers between his warm ones, he tugged me up the stairs.

"Hector would also tell you that you should be more careful about what you howl," I said when we got to the door.

"Yes, I will probably get a text for this."

Greyson opened the door for me, and I slipped inside, kicking off my boots.

"Come on." Greyson tilted his head over to the kitchen.

I followed him, curious, and let him direct me onto a stool pulled up to the giant island counter.

I pulled my arms out of my jacket sleeves, but kept the jacket pulled over my shoulders like a cape since it was chilly inside the lodge—the wolves kept it extra cold at night.

Besides one light by the entrance, the lodge was dark, but that didn't bother Greyson. He pulled milk from the fridge, sugar from the pantry, and a couple of ingredients from the spice rack.

I rotated one of the small bottles, smiling when I saw it was labeled "Dutch Cocoa."

"You're making hot chocolate?"

"I figure you need it." Greyson glanced at me, his gold eyes glowing in the darkness. "Or you wouldn't be awake."

I smiled awkwardly and rubbed my hands together. "It's been a weird year."

"You don't say?"

I laughed a little. "I just don't know how to move forward, and it's driving me crazy."

"You are a Lady Hunter of action," Greyson agreed.

I rested my elbows on the countertop and watched Greyson heat up the milk on the stovetop, endlessly stirring it.

"Does it bother you?"

"Does what bother me?"

"You keep doing so much for me, but I don't usually do anything for you. Like this. It just...reminds me how unbalanced we are."

"Pip, we aren't unbalanced." Greyson gave me a flat, unimpressed look before he checked the milk. "You are about as close to balance as I can get."

"Power balance? Yeah. But, like I said, you've been doing so much for me, and I—"

"Have been stalked more times by other Alphas than I'm willing to put up with," Greyson said. "You just said yourself—it's been a weird year. I'll do whatever I can to help ease you through this. Besides, what's fair isn't always equal. We're mates—not a business contract with a reciprocal agreement."

I silently watched him stir in the chocolate, sugar, cinnamon, nutmeg, and vanilla into the hot milk.

"However." Greyson shut the burner off, then poured the drink from the pot into two mugs. "If you would like to take some online business management courses—maybe an accounting class or four—next year, I wouldn't stop you."

I laughed and took the mug he offered me. "Think I have what it takes to build the werewolf business empire of the Northern Lakes Pack?"

Greyson smirked and beckoned for me to follow him. "You'll do."

He led me to the tiny library/den just off the great room, which had three walls of bookshelves, one TV, and a large couch that hid a bed within its cavernous depths.

He flicked on the light before dropping down on the couch, perfectly balancing his drink. I was a little more careful to settle in—concerned for my hot chocolate, which I sipped as he casually threw his arm over my shoulders and tugged me closer.

"We'll figure it out, Pip," he said.

"Yeah, but we still need better communication Mr-I-won't-tell-my-flipping-*mate*-anything!"

"I deserve that," Greyson acknowledged.

"You think?" I sipped my cocoa, and even though it had the perfect balance of sweetness and spices, the twist in my throat made it hard to swallow. "You aren't hurt or worried that I don't know what to do? About us?"

Greyson shrugged. "I told you I loved you and you didn't run off. That was the best case scenario I was hoping for."

"Wow, don't we have high expectations?" I said. "So glad I could make it over that low bar."

"You say that, but don't tell me your hunter senses didn't scream at you to run when you first found out," Greyson said.

"I've decided it's not very fun that we're mates and you already know me so well," I said. "It takes out the excitement of how I will wildly react to things."

Greyson laughed, making his chest pleasantly shake as I leaned into him.

"You do make really good hot chocolate, though," I said.

"Hector will appreciate the praise," Greyson said. "I made him grade my first few tries late last summer—one of his duties as beta."

Caught halfway between a scoff of disbelief and a laugh, I almost snorted my hot chocolate up my nose.

"I don't believe it," I said. "You're Greyson. You're perfect at everything on your first try—except for sharing important information, that is."

"Also, apparently, not hot chocolate," Greyson said. "I knew I could make a regular cup—I'd made that before. I decided it was probably in my best interest to figure out a better recipe as it seemed to be the surest route in getting your attention."

"It works. This is a lot fancier than the stuff I make back at my house," I said.

"Ahh, yes. Hector takes recipes and drinks very seriously. I made a cup using a packet. He told me he 'wouldn't feed the Low Marsh Pack such swill'."

"Woah, harsh!" I peered at my mostly drunk mug, trying to remember how I had sucked it down so fast. "But this is good. I'll need the recipe."

"Do you really think I'll share it and outsource this task?" He held up his mug, tapping the side with a finger before he offered me his almost full drink and took my mug in return and set it on the ground.

"You know...I always knew you were a good leader. But I didn't think that equated to being a good mate. I was wrong." I hesitated, the shift in conversation a lot darker. "Greyson..."

"I told you, Pip. I can wait." There was something to Greyson's voice that made me peel my head off his chest and peer up at him. The light of the room cast shadows on him that made the planes of his face stronger, and his eyes glittered in the dim light like the predator he was. He wasn't smiling—

his expression was too dangerous for that. "I'm a very patient *wolf.*"

I raised an eyebrow. "Isn't it a good thing, then, that I'm a hunter?"

Greyson's laugh was low and deadly. "Is it?"

He leaned in, and I held my breath as my hunter adrenaline—knowing something I didn't, apparently—kicked in and gave me just a small enough surge that it felt like every nerve in my body tingled.

His five o'clock shadow rubbed my jaw as he pressed his cheek against mine. His left hand slipped up, brushing my neck before he rubbed a few strands of my white hair between his fingers.

"You know." He traced my jawline with his thumb. "I have to wonder. Did your hair turn white because—as you like to complain—of genetics from your dad...or because now you match my wolf?"

Greyson caught my mug before it tumbled from my loose fingers, and pressed it back into my hands. "Sleep well, Pip," he whispered.

Before I could move, he gently bit my earlobe, his teeth scraping my delicate skin.

"You bit me!" I squawked in shock.

Greyson pulled away from me, picked up the nearly empty mug on the ground, and padded off, leaving me confused enough that I'd finally be able to sleep...if I could summon the few remaining—and lonely—brain cells I had left to wander upstairs.

"Hey—don't just walk away!" But I was too late. He was already gone. "That wolf," I said to the empty room, "is just unbelievable!"

"Don't you feel better, now?" Greyson called from the kitchen.

"You weren't supposed to hear that!"

"Then you shouldn't have said it out loud."

I stared at my hands. "It's a good thing he can make hot cocoa. I should bargain to see if he'll learn how to make popped popcorn."

"Already working on it."

"*Stop listening!*"

————

"Thank you for coming." I stood outside in the pale, anemic sunshine, sweating in my parka, balancing on the street curb just outside the welcome center. With no wind and the temperatures just at the freezing point, this was a balmy day for Wisconsin in winter.

"We ought to be thanking you," Dale said. "For our fishing vacation!"

"Yep. Yep. It was a good one," Tom said.

I shook my head. "Having you here was a…calming presence," I evasively said. It was the nicest way I could phrase that they put some of the less scrupulous Alphas in their place just by being around.

"Did ya hear that?" Tom hooted. "I should call my wife and have you tell her that!"

"It was our pleasure." Dale winked at me, then smiled warmly at Teresa, who stood next to me. "And you! Try fishing with that Jack—he knows what he's doing. And you tells your folks I says hi!" He playfully tugged her knit cap a little farther down her head and earned a giggle for his trouble.

Tom offered his hand to Dale, and the two shook hands and exchanged manly back slaps.

Tom shuffled toward his car. "Drive careful—watch for deer."

Dale guffawed as he made it to his vehicle—which was parked just in front of Tom's. "I'm not the one with the fancy jeep that's only—what—twelve years old? You've only got 150,000 miles on there. It's practically a new car!"

"We can't all have a pick-up as old as our firstborn child," Tom said.

"Yep." Dale slapped the hood of his truck—which was painted a dull red color and was probably as old as Original Jack. "She is a beaut!"

"I don't get it," Teresa whispered to me. "Are they saying older is better?"

"I think so," I said.

The Alphas opened their doors, then turned to us and waved one last time.

"Tell Greyson we expect invitations," Tom shouted, his voice echoing up the empty Main Street.

It was seven in the morning, so Timber Ridge was still fairly quiet with no cars on the street.

"An invitation to what?" I asked.

"The wedding!" Dale cackled as he climbed into his car and slammed the door shut before I could say anything else.

"Oh, I got that reference," Teresa said. "He's talking about how you and Greyson are completely twitterpated for each other."

"We are not twitterpated." I kept a smile on as I waved while Dale and Tom pulled out of their parking spots. "Greyson has a mate."

Although Hector and Ember knew about Greyson and me, they had not told their kids in the interests of keeping things…quiet.

Teresa made a noise of disbelief that was a copy-paste of her mom. "Yeah, he seems *really* interested in finding her."

Dale's truck backfired, shooting an acorn out of the tailpipe—probably the work of a rogue squirrel—and Tom beeped at him before the pair turned and disappeared down a side street.

"Okay—you ready for that hot cocoa and breakfast I promised?" I rubbed my hands together, slightly twisting my gloves. "I think we also have time for a donut or two before you head to school."

"Chocolate donuts—with cream filling?" Teresa skipped a few steps.

"We'll have to see what the café has."

"Yes!" Teresa ran up to the crosswalk, then turned around to peer back at me. "And don't think I didn't notice that you're using donuts to bribe me so I stop asking about you and Greyson. The whole Pack knows something is up between you two."

I slapped my welcome center smile on my face and laughed, but didn't comment.

Well, that's not good. We better tell them—fast. Maybe now that almost all the Alphas are gone we can call a meeting?

Dale and Tom were the last of the Alphas to leave.

Hector already said he'd been contacted by five other Alphas who would be coming out to meet me, but it seemed like we had a few days before they arrived.

Still, I wasn't moving back to my cottage anytime soon. And *no*, it wasn't because of Greyson, it was because the Bedevilments were a pain to haul around like that, and I didn't want to constantly settle and unsettle them.

"Do you think Scarlett and Radcliff are working today?" Teresa asked as she pushed the crosswalk button four times.

"Maybe?" I tried to act casual, as if I hadn't asked Teresa out for an early breakfast on this specific day because I knew the Fletchings were working. "If the café isn't too busy, maybe they'll be able to take a break and sit with us."

"That'd be fun!" Teresa hopped in place, trying to keep warm. "I like Scarlett and Radcliff."

"Yeah, they're great," I said. "Scarlett and I are going to start practicing shooting together on Saturday mornings."

"On Saturdays? I don't have school then! You guys said I could watch you. Can I come with?" Teresa asked.

It took a lot of self-control not to pump my arm.

Yeeees! She's still interested in hunters—this is going to work out great.

"Sure," I said. "If you're willing to get up early enough. We could even teach you how to shoot."

"*Really?*" Teresa beamed at me.

"Yeah. You'll have to use my fae rifle—it's a safer weapon to learn on. But first you'd need to take a hunter safety course online," I said.

"I can do that." Teresa nodded, her chin jutted in her determination.

I'd gotten permission from Teresa's parents before I even floated out this idea—I wasn't sure how they'd take to the idea of their daughter undergoing any kind of hunter training.

Happily, Ember and Hector had supported the idea— Ember used my contact with the Quillons to talk to them about finding size and age-appropriate weapons.

The light for the crosswalk switched, and I stepped off the curb into the street when I heard it—the scream of a child, coming from the direction of Pack land.

I pivoted, jumped out of the road and back onto the side-walk. "Teresa, go get Scarlett and Radcliff!"

"Okay!" Teresa zipped across the road, running for the café as I moved down the street, heading for the park that acted as the boundary between Timber Ridge and Pack territory.

I pounded across the snow-covered park, pausing when I reached the forest.

The kid screamed again, coming from within Pack land.

I ripped my gloves off as I ran—my adrenaline taking the sting out of the cold air—and felt for my thigh bandolier as I followed the sound.

The scream traveled—moving away from me—and there was something about it that was strange.

I paused long enough to suck more air into my lungs, then whistled three sharp blasts that were my metaphorical signature since I couldn't howl.

Wolves responded, their howls drifting across the still forest.

I didn't see any tracks or any sign of a child, but my hunter senses were bright with wolves. Some of them were definitely Pack, but there was a cluster I could feel out approximately where I heard the screaming kid that I didn't think belonged to the Northern Lakes Pack.

If someone took one of the Pack's kids, I'll slam them so hard into the ground we won't have to dig a grave for them.

I measured out my breathing—careful to keep it even, even with my hunter magic coursing through my veins.

The child's scream echoed in the forest, dragging me on.

I kept my eyes out for tracks, which was how I found the boot prints. There were two sets.

I can handle two wolves, but I better be careful.

I stopped to whistle again.

The Pack's howls were closing in behind me, and I heard Scarlett and Radcliff whistle back to me over my carefully timed puffs of air. Backup was on the way.

I must have run for at least two miles. I was starting to sweat, and I had the stamina to keep going, the problem was my lungs were starting to ache from the cold.

I need to at least get a visual on them!

The kid screamed again, and I frowned when I realized there was something off about the noise.

There've been several different screams, but I swear they're repeating...

I tried to mentally map out where we were, and I realized the kidnappers were arcing south, horseshoeing around

Timber Ridge and heading to the edge of Pack territory, to the boundary we shared with the Low Marsh Pack.

I heard the crunch of snow, and I paused long enough to check my footing and peer behind me.

I recognized Rio with his yellow-ish gray coat and black markings on his back and tail. Farther back was a white wolf with a brush of gray on the top of her back—Moira—and I could see flashes of Ember's tawny colored coat through the underbrush.

A howl curled around me, and Hector darted in from the side. He had similar black markings like Rio, but his fur had more of a rust undertone to it than yellow.

Seeing him and Ember, the tension in my gut loosened— we'd catch the kidnappers with them here.

River, Roanne, and Klancy—all in their wolf forms— caught up just as the wolves started to outpace me.

Even so, we were nearly on the scream—it was louder, and much closer.

I ran at the back of the group, trying to keep up as best I could, when I felt additional magic flash across my hunter senses.

The child screamed again, and I felt my insides freeze when the magic blazed in my mind.

"Wait—it's a trap!" I locked my knees and tried to scream with everything I could, but the wolves were too fast.

They skidded to a stop, sliding right over the barrier of a complex spell that glowed in the ground.

As soon as River's hind feet entered the circle, a golden barrier sprouted, encasing the wolves inside the biggest trap spell I'd ever seen.

Chapter 18

Pip

My heart leaped into my chest, and I staggered backwards, trying to take in the size.

The spell covered an area larger than the lodge, coloring everything with a golden haze.

"No, no, no, no," I whispered.

Inside the contained area, the wolves pulled together in a tight defensive formation.

Rio threw himself at the wall of the barrier, but he bounced off it, and the wall didn't even flicker.

This is bad. This is so bad.

The child screamed again—this time off to the side.

I ripped my daggers out of my bandolier and whirled around, facing two outsiders, who were casually walking toward me.

One of them held his cellphone up and tapped its surface, and the child's scream ripped through the forest.

It was a recording.

"Hunter Sabre?" the werewolf with the cellphone asked. He was taller than the other wolf and chiseled, with a cold look frozen to his face.

"Yep, it's her." His companion was Brock, the Alpha from North Dakota. We'd thought he'd left with everyone else. Apparently he hadn't.

This was a trap...for me.

I sheathed my daggers, then ran, making for the closest climbing tree.

Brock never had a prayer of knocking me out of a tree. I wasn't so sure about his companion—he freaked me out a bit because he looked so...*competent.* And if he'd gotten his paws on a spell, I didn't want to try taking him on by myself. Who knew what other fun tricks he had on him?

Climb a tree, call Greyson.

I heard one of the wolves behind me swear, and snow crunched.

I poured on the speed and threw myself at the tree, scrambling up it.

When I was about twenty-five feet up the tree, I looked down.

Brock circled the tree. "I'd climb down if I were you, Hunter."

"Yeah, like that's going to work." I clung to the tree like a koala and fumbled with my jacket as I tried to find my cellphone.

One of my wolves yipped, and I glanced at them, worried the hulking wolf was hurting them.

They were still in the barrier, crowded at the side closest to me as they howled and yipped in what I could easily recognize as a warning tone.

Are they calling for the rest of the Pack? Or—

I didn't notice the hulked-out wolf standing a short

distance from them, facing my tree, until he'd already hurled a chunk of ice at me.

I tried to dodge, but the ice was the size of my fist, and with only one hand on the tree I couldn't move fast enough.

It hit me on the back of the head—not a direct hit, more of a graze, but the wolf had thrown it with enough force that it made pain explode in my head.

"Excellent shot!" Brock said.

Against my will, my legs and hands loosened.

My phone slipped from my fingers, and my ears rang as I saw stars. I skidded down the side of the tree, ramming into branches on the way down.

I tried to grab on to something—anything—but my fingers wouldn't tighten, and my legs couldn't summon the strength to hold on as pain radiated in my skull.

I landed in a heap at the bottom of the tree, my stomach rolling from the pain. My vision was still hazy, and now I had the wind knocked out of me.

"Grab her," the competent wolf growled. "We need to move out before Greyson finds us."

"We have a unit coming—he can't beat *all* of us," Brock scoffed.

"If he activates the Northern Lakes Pack before we leave, we'll never make it off his territory. Grab her. *Now.*"

"Yeah, yeah. The money better be worth this."

The money? Isn't he grabbing me for his Pack?

I found I could breathe again when Brock walked up to me. I could hear his footsteps as he crunched across the snow.

I dragged my knees up to my chest, and waited until I could see his leather shoes in the corner of my right eye. Once he was close enough, I yanked a dagger free from my bandolier, flipped to my side, and stabbed his foot.

Brock yelped as he fell backwards into the snow, yanking my dagger out of my hand.

That's okay. I've got my second one.

The abrupt motion of my attack made me want to puke—chances were I had a concussion from that illegal snowball throw. But I made myself roll onto my knees.

Behind the barrier, Ember released several high-pitched howling yips.

Hector growled, the fur on his back bristling as he rammed the barrier.

I tried to reach for my thigh bandolier, but even with my adrenaline pumping, my entire body shook with strain.

Maybe I should try using my Wolf's Kiss magic on the Pack instead?

My thoughts were starting to come easier as the stinging pain in the back of my skull dulled.

"I told you to be careful when we cornered her." The competent wolf swept toward me—his boots, unfortunately, were the type that had steel toes and were made of leather—much harder to stab through. I saw his hand go to his ear, which was how I realized he had some kind of headset he was wearing.

Brock rolled around in the snow, holding his shoe as blood dribbled out of it. He was muttering, and I couldn't understand much between his gasps of air, though I did make out "—crazy mercenary."

That explains the wolf's competence—and why there's a unit coming to help them. But who wants a Wolf's Kiss this badly?

I briefly considered weaving a trap, but I needed concentration for that, and it wasn't going to be very strong if I was the only hunter powering it. Instead I gulped in air, and set about making my magic flow backwards.

I mentally threw my magic at the Pack, coating them in it.

Ember, Hector, and Moira started to grow larger, magic sparking in their eyes. Rio, River, Klancy, and Roanne stayed the same size, and my magic slipped off them like water.

I need to concentrate—I need to get them out of there!

The mercenary wolf was within stabbing distance.

Using my body as a shield I yanked my second dagger free, then tried to stab him in the thigh, hoping I might be able to get a major artery.

He leaped backwards with a muttered oath about hunters. My strike missed so closely it snagged on the fabric of his pants and tore it.

Before I could regroup, he kicked my dagger from my hold, which was abominably loose since my body still wasn't doing a great job of listening to me.

I tried to flop on my side so I could kick at him, but he grabbed me by the wrist and yanked me upright.

"I'm going to kill her!" Brock scrambled to his feet, snow sticking to his slicked back hair.

The mercenary wolf cocked his head as he listened to something on his headset, then shook his head. "Not yet." He tore my bandolier off my thigh.

Not yet? Wait—who would hire them to grab me and plan to kill me? Why kill a Wolf's Kiss when I could be exploited?

I glanced at the Pack, dismayed to see only Hector had retained a larger size—Ember and Moira had both returned to their usual dimensions.

But Hector threw himself at the barrier, which dented under his weight, a tiny part of it cracking like splintering ice.

I gritted my teeth as I threw more magic at them, ignoring the stinging pain as the mercenary wolf hauled me to my feet by my arm.

I heard a howl, and for a moment I dared to hope.

More howls joined the chorus, and my heart fell as I realized I didn't recognize the unique voices.

A Pack of wolves descended on us—not Northern Lakes wolves, werewolves I didn't recognize.

There had to be at least *fifty* of them. They were a cloud of colors and sizes, and based on the small clutches within the larger Pack, I suspected it wasn't one cohesive group, but several Packs combined.

Brock confirmed my guess by limping off in the direction of one of the smaller groups, who were running around the edge of the barrier.

The mercenary tugged me toward a different group that was coming around the other way.

I dug my feet in the snow and tried to resist, leaning backwards as I threw more of my magic at the trapped Northern Lakes wolves.

Even Hector was back to his usual size, and no matter how much of my backwards magic I threw at him, I couldn't make it stick.

I didn't think it was the barrier made with weird magic stopping it—I could *feel* my powers hitting the wolves.

Why isn't it working?

"Come on, Hunter." The mercenary tugged me into the center of his wolf Pack.

I felt fur brush my body, and I knew if I let them drag me away, I was done for.

Giving up on my magic, I fought the mercenary with everything in me.

I lurched forward and tried to elbow him in the throat, but he intercepted the blow and forced my elbow down. Next, I kicked him in the knee, and screamed, "*Greyson!*"

The mercenary slapped a hand over my mouth, and I bit down on his fingers as hard as I could.

He swore as he yanked his hand from my mouth, then smacked me in the back of the head, right where the ice had hit me.

Pain flooded my head with such intensity I couldn't see. I sagged in his grasp, and my legs gave out, making it easy for him to drag me along the snow-covered ground as the Northern Lakes Pack howled inside the barrier.

He hadn't dragged me far when he abruptly stopped. "He's here," he said—I think to his headset. "Watch her," he growled to the wolves who crowded around us.

Wolves started yelping and crying as the mercenary fumbled with something in his jacket.

My sight had cleared enough that I could peer between the many wolf legs surrounding me, and I saw…Greyson.

A wolf was biting his thigh, but he picked the wolf up and threw it at two who were jumping him from the front, toppling all of them.

Inside the barrier, the Northern Lakes wolves were going crazy, howling and trying to slam into the spell at the spot where Hector had managed to crack it.

"Greyson," I called, my lips numb.

Somehow, he must have heard above all the howls and cries. His eyes locked on to where I was slumped on the ground.

He took a step toward me, and I suddenly realized what the mercenary had been struggling to get out of his jacket—a gun.

He swiveled so he had it pointed at me, then nodded to his packmates, who parted so I—and the gun—was visible to everyone in the area.

"Not another step, Alpha Greyson," the mercenary said.

Greyson froze, and an unnatural quiet settled over all the wolves.

"She won't be any good to you if she's dead," Greyson said.

The mercenary glanced down at me and tilted his head from the left to the right, apparently listening to whoever was talking to him on his headset. "I assume you're referring to her powers as a Wolf's Kiss?" the mercenary asked. "That's fine. I'm not here to use her magic."

I could see the muscles in Greyson's shoulders tighten through the thin shirt he wore. "*What?*"

"It's what the client wants," the mercenary said. "Stand down, and none of your wolves will be hurt."

"Greyson..." I didn't know what to say. I didn't want him to risk his life—without him, the Northern Lakes Pack would be lost.

Greyson's gold eyes shot to me, studying my entire body.

If I'm dragged from here, it's not likely I will survive. Unless I can exert my will as a Wolf's Kiss on the mercenary, but that seems unlikely.

The reminder of my magic made me try one last frantic cast on the Pack. It settled on Hector and Ember, and the two rammed the barrier with rage-filled snarls that made the spell shake. But as soon as I switched my attention to the mercenary—and his gun—it left them.

Pain pulsed in my head, and I closed my eyes, until I heard the high-pitched chirp of a warbler songbird.

It's December, all warblers migrated...Radcliff and Scarlett!

I peeled my eyes open to see if Greyson had heard them, but he was still staring at me.

He must have seen something he didn't like. A muscle twitched in his cheek, his chest moved with his unsteady beathing, and he took a step forward.

"Don't move, Alpha, or I'll kill her on the spot," the mercenary warned. He racked the slide of his gun, loading a bullet.

Greyson took another step forward and I could feel his Alpha powers unfurl. Brock choked and fell to his knees, but while the mercenary gritted his teeth and almost kneeled, he retained just enough control to be dangerous.

The mercenary flicked the safety off his handgun and pushed it against my head. "Go ahead and throw your powers around, Alpha Greyson," he panted. "I only need to move a finger."

Fear filled my throat as the unforgiving metal of the gun muzzle scraped the skin of my right temple.

The mounting pressure of Greyson's powers eased, and he held his hands up in appeasement. "If you don't need her for her magic, why take her?" His voice was edged with a snarl—this wasn't good, the bond was pushing him hard.

"I don't care what use my client has for her, I only do what I'm paid for," the mercenary said. He glanced at the wolves backing him up. "We have to move out—he's stalling to give the rest of his Pack time to assemble and show up."

"Wait," Greyson called. "Take me instead."

Fear froze my heart. "Greyson, you idiot, no!" I hissed.

The mercenary scowled at Greyson. "*Why* would I take you instead of the hunter when it's the hunter my client wants? That is the worst stalling technique I've ever seen. Gold unit, move—" He abruptly went silent and stared at the snowy ground.

I thought I heard a crackle on his headset—whoever hired him was speaking. My throat squeezed shut as around us, wolves shifted, encircling me again.

I gulped as one of them sniffed my neck and licked its chops.

"Hold." The mercenary held his arm up. "Your offer has been accepted, Alpha Greyson."

"What? No!" I tried to sit up, but the pain in my head made the world swivel around me in a way that made my stomach flip.

"You will submit to a knockout spell," the mercenary said, ignoring my shouts. "Or the deal is off."

"Fine." Greyson set his jaw.

"Greyson, don't do this!" I begged as the wolves moved away from me. I automatically reached for my thigh bandolier, but it was gone. "Fight them!"

Greyson's eyes briefly warmed. "It's all right, Pip."

"*No, it is not!*" I growled, sounding more wolf-like than I ever had in my life.

Greyson watched the mercenary approach him. "I'm fairly certain this was all an attack against me, anyway—or they'd be more concerned about your magic."

"So?" I pushed myself onto my knees, sheer panic giving me the strength to ignore the pain that pulsed through my body. "The Pack can't—I can't—take it if…"

I couldn't even finish the sentence; it was too horrible to bear.

Greyson finally smiled—that cocky, smug grin that made my heart twist. "The Pack will survive just fine with you helping Hector now that you know your magic. And you *can* take it, Pip, if I'm gone. But I won't survive without you." His golden eyes shone with a love I didn't deserve.

This was my worst nightmare come to life.

This was exactly why I was so mad at Greyson for accepting the bond—because he was right!

Since he'd forged the bond to me, if I died he would pay a price. But I—unattached—would be unaffected by his death.

My lungs burned as panic clutched me so tightly I couldn't breathe.

It took my hunter magic kicking in again with another surge of adrenaline for me to finally take in a gasping breath. "No, no!"

The Pack went crazy inside the barrier, clawing at it as they tried to reach their Alpha.

"Take care of them, Pip," Greyson said. "And take care of yourself."

"Greyson, you can't!" I struggled to my feet, but one of the wolves who had remained near me lunged, slamming into me. I fell to the ground again. I dug my fingers into the snow and sobbed. "I love you!"

"Thank you, Lady Hunter." Greyson was still grinning

when the mercenary slapped a stun spell on him—not unlike the ones I used in my ammo—by sticking a slimy piece of paper to his neck.

Greyson sagged, and the mercenary caught him as his eyes slid shut.

"*No!*" I screamed.

Chapter 19

Pip

The mercenary tried to heft Greyson into a fireman's hold. He staggered under Greyson's weight, but fixed his stance. "We're moving out. Someone hit the hunter so she doesn't try to follow us."

"With pleasure." Brock sauntered toward me.

"Not you," the mercenary informed him. "Gold Unit—go."

The wolf who had body slammed me swung around and lunged for my throat, but I was ready. I jabbed my arm into its mouth, pushing deep so I hit its gag reflex.

The wolf reared back, its teeth slicing the skin of my hand as it pulled away, hacking.

Using the time my attack had given me, I staggered to my feet. When the wolf attacked again I kicked it in the chest, but I didn't have enough strength in me, and the wolf slammed through the attack, knocking me flat on my back.

That wouldn't have been so bad, but I cracked my head on

a frozen branch lying on the ground, which renewed the waves of pain in my head.

The wolf sniffed me, then trotted off, moving out with the rest of the invading wolves.

I moaned and curled up in the fetal position, clutching my head.

No, no, no—I can't give in. Get up! Follow them!

I managed to uncurl my body, but I couldn't do anything more than twitch my fingers as I watched the mercenary carry Greyson away, the wolves moving around him.

Briefly, I saw magic swirl around Greyson's left ankle before it was snuffed out. I didn't think it was anything the mercenary did to him—it actually felt a bit like hunter magic.

"Greyson!" I screamed as the wolves flowed around the barrier, disappearing into the woods. I got to my knees, but my legs were shaking too much—I couldn't stand. "No!"

I heard the crunch of snow, and Scarlett and Radcliff emerged from the forest, their faces white.

"I've got a fae potion—I'll give it to Pip," Radcliff said. "You see if you can break the barrier!"

"On it!" Scarlett jumped a dead bush and raced over to the spot where the barrier had been damaged.

Inside, the Northern Lakes wolves crowded around the spot, scratching and biting at it.

"Pip, here. Drink it slowly." Radcliff knelt next to me and held out a fae potion.

I took it with shaking hands and swallowed it. I was so cold and broken that I didn't even register the taste, just that I felt magic flow through my body, easing some of the pain.

Once I'd downed a third of the bottle I had to stop—I felt physically sick and almost lost what bit I had drunk.

"Take it slower," Radcliff said. "The back of your head is bleeding—you were hit pretty badly."

"They took Greyson," I said.

"I know. We'll get him back. I promise." Radcliff squeezed my shoulders, then stood up and went to help Scarlett with the barrier.

They tried stabbing and even shooting the barrier, but nothing happened.

Even with the wolves ramming it, they couldn't damage it more than they already had when they were powered up on my magic.

I sipped at my bottle, and at least fifteen minutes must have passed before I felt my hunter senses light up.

"Incoming," I dully said.

"I feel them too," Scarlett said. "Must be the Northern Lakes Pack."

"Good," Radcliff said. "We can take some of them and see if we can catch up."

We're so close to the border…what are the chances the Low Marsh Pack is helping them and they're already gone? I'd say pretty good.

Minutes later, Aeric, Wyatt, Shania, Jack, East and about a dozen other Northern Lakes wolves sprinted past. They were running so fast—with Shania, Aeric, Wyatt, East, and Jack in their human bodies and the others as wolves—they skidded out and had to turn around and come back.

"Scarlett? Radcliff? What happened?" East asked.

"Pip's bleeding—I can smell it!" Shania's voice was tight with worry.

When I opened my eyes she was by my side, the skin around her eyes tight with her concern.

"Pip?" she asked.

I fought to swallow around the ball in my throat. "They took Greyson."

"*What?*" Aeric snapped.

Scarlett explained the situation as Shania knelt next to me and peeled me off the tree so she could pull my white hair aside and peer at the back of my head.

"Then he's gone? They *took* him? Greyson?" Aeric asked.

Several of the wolves snapped and snarled—not believing it.

"He went in Pip's place," Radcliff said.

"Impossible—the Pack comes before everything," Jack said.

"Not before his mate," Scarlett said.

Everyone went still, and all eyes turned to Scarlett.

"Nah," Jack said. "That…that's impossible. Pip's a hunter."

Shania slid an arm around my shoulders so she helped support me. "Keep drinking your potion, Pip," she muttered.

East's blond hair was even more flyaway than usual as the wind stirred it up. "It's true, isn't it, Pip?"

I stared at the potion, my stomach rolling in my gut, and tried to lift it, but my body was too heavy with guilt.

"That's not a funny joke, bro," Jack said.

East slowly shook his head. "I have never seen him treat another person the way he treats Pip. He's always measured with us. But with her? He comes at her with everything he has."

Inside the barrier, several of the wolves triggered their shifts, turning from wolf into human.

One of the newly arrived wolves—I couldn't tell who it was, the pain was making it hard to track—burst toward me.

Shania let go of me and crouched defensively in front of me, but she didn't need to.

Moving as one unit, Jack and East grabbed onto the wolf and flung him tail over paws.

"Enough," Wyatt growled. "If you lay a tooth on our *Alpha's* mate, I take you down—and you won't get back up for a long time."

"You knew?" Radcliff asked.

"Greyson told us." Aeric ambled out in front of the group so he stood shoulder to shoulder with Wyatt, showing a united front. "We put it together after Aspen kidnapped her."

Rio finished his transformation and stood in his loose shorts, his shoulders heaving with anger. "How could you keep silent on this? We're *Pack*! Our Alpha sacrificed himself for *her*, and we didn't know why—we weren't prepared—" He cut himself off with a growl of anger.

"Yeah, Rio, you totally trust me," I muttered to myself. "I'm getting all the trust-y vibes off your near road-rage anger."

I'm getting salty, the potion must be starting to work.

The pain was still bad, but that might have more to do with the fact that one of the worst-case scenarios I'd pictured in being Greyson's mate had just played out before me, and I was powerless to stop it.

I shut my eyes. "We need to stop fighting and try to get Greyson back."

Rio snarled.

Wyatt held his hands up. "My dude. Chill. Hector and Ember knew too."

"What?" Rio turned around to shout at his older brother.

"And it wasn't our secret to share," Aeric added.

"We decided not to tell the Pack." My voice felt rusty, and my head was a dull ache as I made myself stand up. "Because it was dangerous when we already had all the Alphas sniffing around the territory." I paused and licked my lips as the wolves listened to me intently. "Greyson wanted to tell you all, but I was hoping to find a way to break the bond and free him." I raised a hand, then dropped it. "I screwed up. This was exactly what I wanted to avoid."

Silence fell over everyone.

They were upset—they *had* to be. I had cost them their Alpha—who was more important to them than anything.

I deserve all their anger, and more.

"We'll find him," Scarlett said. "We just need to regroup."

"How can you say that so confidently?" Jack asked, his

voice a croak that was thick with emotion. "They're off our territory by now!"

Radcliff held out a hand, which glowed. "Easy. Hunter magic."

"What?" Wyatt looked from Radcliff to Scarlett.

Scarlett planted her hands on her hips. "We cast a tracking spell on Greyson before they took him. We know exactly where he's going—south, at the moment. In a car, I think, based on how fast he's moving."

I stared at the pair, hope coursing through me. "Hunters don't have spells like that."

"It's a special family magic," Radcliff said. "We don't talk about it because what's the use of it these days?"

"I thought you said the Fletchings' family magic was related to aim?" Aeric asked.

"Ahh, yes, but like dear Pip, both of our parents are hunters." Scarlett grinned. "And while we didn't inherit our mother's perfect aim, we inherited potent strains of our dad's tracking magic!"

For the first time since Greyson had dropped unconscious, something in me loosened. "Then we can find him."

Scarlett nodded. "We can, and we will."

"But first we better break down this barrier," Radcliff said.

"And..." Aeric peered up at the sky—which was clouded over. "We better notify the Pre-Dominant as well."

———

"Yes, he was taken. The Pack followed the trail to the Low Marsh Pack lands. So far Vant is denying he had any part of the plan, but that seems unlikely. Thankfully, two hunters on hand cast a spell on Alpha Greyson, and they traced his path to the outskirts of Magiford before the spell went muted—it's suspected they put him in an anti-magic barrier which is disrupting the connection." Original Jack paced back and forth as he spoke on his cellphone. The normally cozy lighting of the lodge seemed stark, and cast a gray look on his solemn expression. He paused near me to pat my shoulder before he moved on.

"Pre-Dominant Harka has been notified. She's rallying some of her Pack, but for now she's sending scouts out to try to gather information." Sitting at the giant table near the kitchen, Olivia read off a script that had been printed off as she clutched her cellphone.

"The Northern Lakes Pack is supposed to report in to Magiford tomorrow morning, at 3 am." Tucker had his cellphone pinned between his shoulder and his head as he wrote down a few notes. He was spread out on the kitchen island. "You're on your way? Thank you."

The humans of the Pack—everyone from the rare human spouse like Original Jack to the teenage children—were on their phones, calling the fringe members of the Pack, and those who'd been sent out—like Chase—on assignments.

The rest of the Pack was doing what they needed to in preparation for the fight tomorrow.

Hopefully there'd be a fight.

Harka was madder than one of the Bedevilments when I gave them baths, but the fastest she could pinpoint the location, send in scouts for information collection, and then get ready for battle was about midnight tonight.

It's insanely fast all things considered—she can't possibly move any faster. But…I don't know if it's fast enough. It's probable they might do something to him before then.

I pressed the palms of my hands to my temples and tried to rub away the budding headache as I ignored the semi-hostile look Olivia was sending me.

"Yes," Olivia said. "He traded himself for Hunter Sabre—because they're *mates*."

Yeah, I'd had to tell the whole Pack about Greyson and me, or his actions wouldn't make any sense. The reactions so far had been…not great.

Amelia, who was sitting next to Olivia at the table, picked up the script and smacked Olivia in the face with it. "Stick to the script, or your jealousy will show," she hissed. She abruptly straightened up and returned her attention to her phone. "Hello, is this Mal? This is Amelia, I'm the daughter of Lark and Slate. The Northern Lakes Pack is in a state of emergency, and your presence is required *tonight*."

I stood up and left the kitchen, walking to the front door.

The lodge was suffocating, and I'd been banned from making any calls since whoever I spoke to wasn't going to take the news well.

I'd changed into my practice gear once I got home in preparation for the unavoidable conflict, but I layered over it my hunter jacket—which matched my practice gear and was a lot slimmer than my parka but not as warm—a black hat, and the black gloves I wore during practice matches.

I hesitated before grabbing my rifle—my thigh bandolier was already in place—then slipped outside.

Wolves were swarming the Northern Lakes territory, so it wasn't likely I was going to be attacked, but I felt a lot better with the familiar weight of my rifle in my arms.

It was early afternoon, but this late in the year the sun set by five or so, and the sky was so overcast with clouds it almost felt like twilight.

Snow was starting to fall, drifting through the air in fat flakes that quickly gathered on my shoulders and the hood of my jacket.

I walked across the meadow, my boots crunching on the newly fallen snow, and followed one of the walking trails, heading in the general direction of Aeric's house.

When I was about halfway there, I stopped.

Nothing was wrong—my hunter senses were picking up on the rapid movement of werewolves patrolling the territory, but not anything alarming.

But I just felt…torn.

I never wanted this. This was why I was so against the mate bond. But did I make it worse in my stubbornness of trying to look for a way out? Or does this just prove that I should have worked harder to break our bond?

Either way, it felt like it was my fault.

The falling snow made all the usual forest noises muted, creating a hush in the air. Normally I'd find it beautiful, but now it made the accusations in my mind deafeningly loud.

I stared up at the sky, snow falling on my lashes.

We need to get him back. But Harka can't move any faster than she already is…and without Greyson to rally behind, the Pack would struggle too much.

Fringe members had already started arriving, but the ones Original Jack and the others were calling were still an hour or half an hour out.

Could I do anything more as a Wolf's Kiss?

The thought filled my mouth with a sour sensation.

I was the cause of this, after all.

Not just because the mate bond drove Greyson to protect me above everything else, but because I'd failed the Pack. I hadn't been able to get my magic to stick to them. My failure to cover Rio was maybe understandable—I didn't think he'd ever trusted me less than this moment—but Hector and Ember?

I trusted them with my *life*.

I should have focused more on perfecting my magic—or at least taken it more seriously. If I could have correctly amplified their powers, they probably could have busted out of the barrier.

"Pip!"

I looked up, registering incoming werewolves as I saw

Aeric, Wyatt, and Shania jog down the walking trail, their hair dusted with snow.

"What are you doing out here?" Aeric slowed down to a walk, making Wyatt smack into his back.

"I was on my way to your place," I said.

"But you weren't walking." Shania skirted them both and walked directly up to me.

I adjusted my hold on my rifle. "I was thinking." I lifted my chin and straightened my shoulders—I could guilt myself later. Now I needed to be alert and helpful—if possible. "What brought you three outside? You don't look dressed for it."

Shania shook snow off her hoodie as Wyatt wiped his glasses off on his shirt—none of them were wearing jackets.

"We felt you needed us," Wyatt said.

I frowned. "What?"

"Yeah," Aeric echoed. "We just knew. Must be your Wolf's Kiss magic?"

Ahh yes, my temperamental magic at work. "Great," I said.

"It doesn't feel like Greyson's powers as an Alpha. That's a call I feel in my bones," Wyatt said. "This I feel…"

"In the heart," Shania said. "So what's wrong?"

"Nothing is wrong—the Pack needs to focus on getting Greyson back," I said.

"It doesn't feel like nothing," Wyatt said bluntly.

I tipped my head to the side, spilling snow down my jacket. "Aren't you three mad with me?"

"Why would we be mad?" Aeric asked. "It's not like you kidnapped Greyson."

"Yeah, except he was taken because he swapped places with me, and I failed to properly use my magic, so Hector and the others couldn't get out to help him."

"Pip, the Pack doesn't blame you for what happened," Wyatt said.

"They should," I said bluntly. "And some of them do."

"Look, the Pack is upset they didn't know you're Greyson's mate," Aeric said. "And they're angry and somewhat lost because our Alpha was taken away."

"It just feels like I've messed up so badly in every possible way," I said.

Wyatt settled a hand on my shoulder. "Pip, you found out you were a Wolf's Kiss just a few months ago. It's unrealistic to expect yourself to master it by now."

Shania leaned against me so our shoulders brushed. "Yeah, and you've only known about Greyson—and how to access your Wolf's Kiss magic—since Aspen kidnapped you. That was like, what, a month and a half ago? Two months maximum. An impossible mate bond and new magic is *a lot* to take in with that kind of a timeline."

The three of them leaned in, staring me down.

"You have a point," I finally said.

Wyatt nodded. "Of course we do. I'm brilliant!"

"I bet Greyson's absence is affecting your bond," Aeric said.

"That's impossible, I can't feel it," I said.

"You might not feel it, but it doesn't mean you're not connected," Shania pointed out.

"Regardless, it's frustrating for all of us," Wyatt said. "We don't know what's going on—or even *why* Greyson was taken!"

"Yeah. I'd give my best set of tires to know why they agreed to the swap if you were the original target," Aeric said.

"Well, there are a few obvious ideas," I said.

Aeric and Wyatt swiveled their attention to me. "Huh?"

"They took Greyson even though I was their original target, but the mercenary said I wasn't wanted for my magic." I rubbed my thumb on my rifle.

"Yeah, which leaves it open to an endless number of options," Wyatt said.

"Maybe, but there are two that are the most likely," I said.

"Either they wanted to cripple the Northern Lakes Pack—in which case Greyson would be the best option anyway since his tie to the Pack is stronger than mine, Wolf's Kiss or not—or they'd only grabbed me in the first place because they knew taking me would hurt Greyson, and I was the easier target."

"Could someone have put it together that you're his mate?" Shania asked.

"Possibly," Aeric said. "Or someone could have leaked it. You told Harka and Rafe, didn't you?"

"Yeah."

"Then someone from the Pre-Dominant's office might have found out," Aeric said.

"Regardless of how they put it together, I think the second option—that they were planning to take me to get to Greyson—is more likely," I said.

"Why?" Shania asked.

"Because of Aspen." Wyatt rocked back and forth, warming up to the idea as he followed my thought process. "We never found out if she was working alone or with someone else, and she very specifically wanted to take Greyson down. Since she got the wolfsbane potion, it's safe to assume she either has contacts with the black market—unlikely—or she managed to get some using Harka's clout, which could lead us back to the Pre-Dominant's office, where they know Pip and Greyson are mates."

"That's a bit more of a jump than I'd take on pure theorizing," I said. "But yeah. Because of Aspen and how little we got out of her—and the fact that someone spilled information about me to all the other Alphas—it's safe to say someone out there doesn't like Greyson."

"Or at the very least doesn't want him to become the next Pre-Dominant."

I whirled around, and was surprised to see Rio, Jack, and East meandering down the walking path.

I'd been so intent; I hadn't noticed their growing proximity.

Staring into Rio's stormy eyes, I really wished I had. He'd been the one to call out the observation as he strolled up.

He was wearing a jacket, but both Jack and East were wearing long sleeved shirts and clearly not prepared for scrambling around in the outdoors.

"Everything okay, Pip?" Jack grimaced as soon as the words were out of his mouth. "Sorry, that's a stupid thing to say when Greyson…and you're his…"

East slapped Jack on the back. "She knows what you meant."

"We were just talking about why someone would take Greyson when targeting Pip," Shania said.

"We heard," Rio said. "Did you tell this to my brother? Or Ember?"

I shook my head. "No. I've been at the lodge, and I think they went back home to check on their kids…and get ready."

"But if these bad guys are after Greyson, doesn't that mean we need to move as fast as possible?" Jack asked. "If they want to keep Greyson from becoming Pre-Dominant, they can just kill him."

"Except they chose to take him away," Wyatt said. "That's something, at least."

"Maybe, but we need to act." East grimly rubbed the back of his neck. "They make you memorize the statistics in law enforcement. Seventy-five percent of kidnapping victims are killed in the first three hours, with seventy-five percent of those remaining killed within twenty-four hours. That doesn't include human trafficking victims, but those statistics aren't encouraging either."

"At least we already know Alpha Greyson lasted more than three hours, since the drive to Magiford took longer than that," Aeric said.

"Scarlett was pretty adamant that the spell got muted

because of magic interference, not because Alpha Greyson was killed," Shania added.

"But if the person responsible does have ties to the Pre-Dominant's office, then they'll know what Harka learns," I said. "They'll know exactly what we're doing. All they have to do is complete their goal before we move tonight around midnight."

Jack groaned. "If only we had more information!"

"We could phone up Chase and ask for a ride to Magiford and do our own scouting in the meantime," Wyatt suggested.

"We're wolves, we're not trained for stealth," East said. "Pip, Scarlett, and Radcliff would be our only real options since they're better trained at hiding their presence."

"We're not sending Pip," Rio said. "Alpha Greyson traded his *life* for hers. If she wanders in and gets herself captured it'll kill him."

"I wouldn't get captured," I argued. "My hunter senses would make it impossible to sneak up on me."

"You were caught by a trap," Rio flatly said.

"Yeah, with *your* brother and sister-in-law," Aeric reminded him.

"Hector and Ember aren't Greyson's mate." Rio spat out the word like it was rancid meat. The look he gave me broke through enough of my guilt to make my hackles rise.

"Yeah, and I could tell you trusted me *so much*," I said. "That's why my magic was able to cover you—oh wait, it couldn't!"

"Your lack of trust isn't my fault!"

"I trust you," I snapped. "I trust the Pack!"

"But do you really?" Rio asked.

"If you're talking about how I couldn't get my magic on Ember and Hector later in the fight—"

"I'll write you a free pass for that one," Rio said. "You were hit on the back of the head, and you probably had a concussion. That was a high grade fae potion Radcliff had to feed you before you stopped looking like you were going to puke if you took a step. The point is you could cast your magic on those you trust. The issue is not us wolves."

"This again," I muttered. "Rio, you're not fooling anyone."

"I trust you," Rio stubbornly said. "But I can get why you wouldn't trust me after I attacked you—"

"You were dosed with wolfsbane, I know that wasn't you, and we've already said I'm not the problem!"

"Except you are! It's your magic."

"Look—I'm just bad at it. There, does that satisfy you? I'm bad at using my magic." I impatiently twitched my rifle as I glared up at him.

"A Wolf's Kiss's powers stem from their relationship with their Pack," Rio said. "If you're bad at it, it's because you don't really believe in us."

"Really? And when did you become so knowledgeable about Wolf's Kisses? Please. Illuminate me. Where did you get this information?" I asked.

Jack peered at Aeric and Wyatt. "Aren't you going to stop them?"

Aeric held his hands up. "I'm just glad he's getting some of her fiery spirit back in her."

"I'll give it a few more minutes and then do something," Wyatt said. "I'm getting wet from all this snow."

Jack turned to East. "East? Doesn't this go against some kind of city law or something?"

"They haven't gotten physical yet, so it's not a crime," East said. "But I do see your point. Pip."

"East, I swear on my rifle, if you try to tell me I don't trust the Pack, I will take you down," I said.

"I don't know anything about a Wolf's Kiss," East said carefully. "But I do know that since I became a werewolf, I've felt your presence. Remember? Jack and I told you about it."

I relaxed slightly. "Yeah, I remember."

East nodded. "You're a special presence to the Pack. You don't feel quite like an Alpha, but you're bright in our minds like Greyson is."

"Betraying you would be like betraying Greyson," Rio said. The hostility was gone from his voice, and when he stared at me he just looked...sad. "If we're part of the Pack, we can't do it."

"But why?" I asked. "I'm not a wolf." I laughed harshly. "And after today, I certainly don't deserve it. Unless, does my magic *make* you feel that?"

"Nah." Aeric shook his head. "No more than an Alpha's power makes us want to follow and be loyal to him. You might have the magic to force it, but that doesn't mean you control our emotions."

Wyatt stirred, making snow fall off his shoulders. "Pip, I think you're missing the point. This isn't about your magic— it's about our love for you. And just because you're not a wolf, doesn't mean we don't love you like one."

I stared at Wyatt for a few moments, then peered at Rio.

Rio sighed, and his broad shoulders dropped about three inches. "We forget—you are a hunter, not a wolf. You don't feel the bond that we feel with you—not through any fault of your own, it's just a difference between our races." When he peered at me, his eyes were so soft my hands tightened on my rifle from the shock of seeing Rio look, well...*nice*.

"What Rio is *trying* to say is that we can all do better," Wyatt said.

"But specifically you should trust us more," Rio piped in.

Wyatt elbowed the larger wolf. "You do realize that in acting so muleheaded you're not winning us points?"

Rio scowled at him.

"I'm just saying. When you're the only one in the Pack she

can't cast her magic on, I'm not going to be at all sympathetic," Wyatt said.

I watched, unable to pin down exactly what I was feeling.

Shania brushed my shoulder. "Pip?" she asked.

I forced a smile. "It's a lot to think about."

"It is," Wyatt agreed. "And it's not something we have to solve now. Come on. Let's get out of this weather. But—first. Pomeranian Puppy Powerup!"

Wyatt swept me up in a squeeze that was tight enough to make my back crack and warm enough to make my lips twitch.

"You're gonna have to stop doing that," Rio told him. "Now that the whole Pack knows she's Alpha Greyson's mate."

"He hasn't minded this long." Wyatt dropped me and patted the top of my hood.

"Yep, he knows he's got nothing to worry about." Aeric scooped me up and hugged me just as tightly. "If it weren't for him, our little hunter and her dog-vibe would be forever alone! Single, lonely, and miserable."

"I greatly appreciate how full and fulfilled you seem to think my life is," I muttered into his chest.

Aeric laughed as he released me.

"My turn!" Shania hugged me next. She—thankfully—didn't pick me up. That would have been a little weird since she was a touch shorter than me. But she did rock me from side to side and snuggle in like a cuddly dog. "You're like a drug."

"Thanks for the compliment?" I said.

Shania laughed, but held my hand when she let me go and tugged me along the path, heading back to the lodge.

The guys joked as we walked back, with Shania making the occasional comment. I couldn't miss the tension in their shoulders, the strain that occasionally showed on their expressions.

They're just as worried about Greyson as I am, but they're smiling for my sake.

When we reached the lodge, the snow was still lazily falling, and Wyatt's and Aeric's shirts were wet.

I watched them climb up the stairs to the porch, but there was some part of me that couldn't set foot inside just yet. Yeah, I was being a coward. I didn't want to see the humans or any packmates who were hanging out.

"I think I'm going to go talk to Hector," I said.

Wyatt paused on the stairs. "One of us should go with you."

"I have my rifle."

"You were almost kidnapped. That's not enough of a precautionary measure," East said.

"Fine. Rio, you up for a walk?"

Rio scrunched up his forehead in clear dislike.

"You can shift into your wolf form," I offered, not entirely unselfishly.

I'd chosen Rio because I didn't really want to talk, I needed to think. Rio was most likely to let me stew.

"Fine." Rio slipped inside—presumably so he could shed his shoes and clothes.

"You sure you're gonna be okay?" Jack asked.

"Yep!" I tried to smile, but I couldn't even manage my welcome center smile at the moment.

"Think about what we said," Aeric said.

"Will do!" I managed a false cheerfulness.

"Call us if you need anything," Shania said. "In fact, call us when you're finished talking to Hector, and we'll make something for dinner."

"You should tell him what we talked about—that Greyson was probably taken because someone is after him and it might be connected to Aspen," Wyatt said.

I nodded, but East—incredibly observant—cocked his head. "Or do you want one of us to call him?"

"Why don't you call ahead?" I asked. "And tell Original Jack and the others—please?"

East smiled, flashing the gap between his front teeth. "You got it!"

Wolf Rio shouldered through the door and stomped down the stairs. When he reached my side he peered up at me, then marched off toward the walking path that we could take to Hector and Ember's place.

I waved to my friends, then hurried after Rio, following him into the forest.

Chapter 20

Pip

R io was the perfect walking buddy. He walked quickly enough to keep me moving, but not so fast that I was huffing to keep up, which gave me space to think.

Am I really as special to the Pack as Wyatt and Rio said I am?

Wyatt wouldn't lie, but he would try to spare me pain—we were friends, after all. I would say I wasn't inclined to believe Rio either, except…it was *Rio*.

Rio never hesitated to bite me, or bodily slam into me, or give me a verbal shut down. He wouldn't lie—it wasn't in his nature.

Which means he's telling the truth. But is there evidence for it?

With certain packmates, absolutely.

I could see it in the way Wyatt and Aeric subjected me to Pomeranian Puppy Powerups, and Jack and East still shadowed me. It was in the way Hector and Ember always checked on me, and their warm smiles and open invitations.

But what about the rest of the Pack?

Lynn obviously loved me as Pack, even though she left. Maybe that's proof that my perspective can't be entirely trusted?

I'd taken the Pack's quiet acceptance of me as toleration. But maybe I was wrong?

Scarlett and Radcliff haven't been allowed to join in practices, even though they helped track Aspen. They're still in their apartment over the welcome center, too. They haven't been moved into actual Pack territory. But I've been here years, and they've been here for a few months. That's not really comparing apples to apples.

Rio nudged me hard, yanking me from my thoughts.

I automatically grabbed for my hunter magic, but I didn't feel anything. No werewolves were near us—besides Rio, anyway.

But I had almost walked straight into a low branch.

I stared at the branch, then at Rio's fluffy form as he prowled ahead, snow dotting his coat.

I don't know that I will ever fully grasp how the Pack feels. I don't have a wolf form, and while I can connect with them, it's all based on my magic. Maybe Rio's right, and the key is my feelings for the wolves and not the other way around.

I had purposely chosen not to trust the Pack—at least not in the deep way my magic required—because of the losses I'd experienced.

Holding back was so much easier than trying time after time, when I'd already lost my hunter parents, my wolf parents, and then Lynn and Hudson.

Or so I thought.

I'd always believed I'd turned out fine after the death of my parents, but maybe it had done a number on me. I was scared to love. How sad was that?

More than anyone in the world, the Pack—who has guarded me from crazies, sacrificed their time to protect me and train with me—deserves my love. Whether or not they trust me doesn't matter, because they as a Pack have unanimously moved to help me—even the fringe members who don't know me that well.

What they'd done for me showed where their heart was.

So where was mine?

With the Pack…and with Greyson.

I stopped walking.

Greyson changed his entire life for me—multiple times—and he hasn't blamed me. He loves me despite all of that.

Rio whined.

When I glanced at him he moved closer to me, his ears flattening as he whined again. Slowly—as if he was afraid I'd bite him—he moved in and pushed his nose into my hip, then peered up at me, watching my reaction.

I stared into his eyes, and felt my magic swirl inside of me, pacing like a caged animal.

I am a legacy, a Sabre and a Ward, a Wolf's Kiss who has been trained by hunters, and raised by wolves. I can have the courage to reach for the Pack that has supported me through all of this…even if it means I might be hurt in the future.

Inside me, my magic shifted.

All my anxiety and guilt moved. It didn't fade, but it was smashed down by my choice of love—because that was the only kind of thing that could counter my frantic thinking.

The tree branches stirred, and the wind suddenly picked up —swirling around Rio and me, tossing snow back into the sky instead of coating the ground.

The wind played with the tips of my jacket, but my white hair under my hood was undisturbed. The weight of my rifle in my hands was suddenly a lot more real, and I was conscious of its texture under the pads of my fingers.

I looked at the orange-streaked sky, and with my magic coursing through my veins, I thought I could feel it: my mate bond with Greyson.

It was hovering at the edge of my senses, reaching for me

—though even now it still couldn't get past my defensive barriers.

"We're not going to wait to go get Greyson until tonight," I said, my voice unnaturally loud from the muted quiet of the trees. "We're going now."

Rio had been wagging his tail faster and faster so his whole body moved, but at my words he planted his large paws and howled, raising his head to the sky as his wolf song soared above the trees.

Moved by the bright edge of adrenaline that swamped me, I started walking. "Come on, Rio. Let's go get Hector and Ember."

Rio cut off his howl and loped past me, his tail wagging wildly.

We reached Hector and Ember's house in about three minutes.

I lingered in the trees, staring at their brightly lit windows.

How do I go in there and tell Hector, the Pack beta, that I want us to head out now, *when it goes against all strategic plans?*

I frowned, and the front door banged open.

Ember—her tawny coat extra golden in the white of the snow—and Hector—the brush of black on his back and tail stark in all the white—bounded outside.

I blinked, shocked as they both loped up to me, their ears perked.

Hector and Rio exchanged a few playful barks and nips, and Teresa stood in the doorway.

"Go kick some butt and get our Alpha back!" she shouted.

I stood up straighter. "How did you know?"

Teresa pointed to her parents. "They went nuts and transformed about three minutes ago. Amelia and Tucker are on their way to pick me and my brother and sister up. We'll be okay."

"Okay." I started to turn back down the walking path.

"Hey, Pip?"

I turned back around, my heart breaking a little when Teresa leaned against the door, her posture wistful. "I'm glad you're Greyson's mate."

"Me too," I said, and for the first time, I meant it.

I waved, then followed Hector, Ember, and Rio back into the woods.

The trio trotted around me as I picked the paths that would take us back to the lodge.

A few minutes into our walk, two more wolves joined us. I instantly recognized the wolves' mask-like patterns—it was Klancy and Roanne.

They both greeted me with tail wags and perked ears, then fell into place with Hector, Rio, and Ember.

Ember and Roanne romped together for a few steps, then together they broke off into a howl, their duet beautiful as Ember went high and Roanne sang low.

As soon as I caught up with them they cut themselves off, all signs of good humor leaving them.

Their eyes glittered in the dim sunshine, and they stalked down the path, leaving paw prints in the snow.

River joined us a minute later, then Moira, followed by Remy and Forrest.

By the time we were almost to the lodge, I found myself at the center of a Pack of about twelve wolves. That was when I saw two snow flecked shapes waiting for us in the middle of the trail.

Radcliff and Scarlett shifted as we got closer. They were both dressed in hunter combat clothes like I was, and carrying crossbows with at least one sidearm each in thigh holsters.

"We heard the howls," Radcliff said. "All the way back in the city park off Main Street. Something felt like we had to come."

The wolves stared at the siblings, none of them moving as snow fell.

Scarlett rubbed her thumb on the side of her crossbow. "I know we're not Pack, but…"

Hector peered up at me.

Your move.

"We're going to get Greyson." I was mildly surprised when none of the wolves moved, but there was something in me—my magic, probably—that *knew* they were aware of what I was planning.

"We could tell," Radcliff said, confirming my gut feeling.

I nodded and studied the pair. They'd pulled up their hoods like I had, but I could see the painful hope in their eyes.

"Will you come with us?" I asked.

Scarlett puffed up her chest and lifted her chin while Radcliff smiled.

"We'd love to," he said.

They slipped through the wolves to stand in a position that flanked me, and we walked on.

When we reached the lodge, wolves trotted in from all directions, emerging from walking paths and forest underbrush. Snow dotted their fur, and muted light from the sky made their bright eyes and black noses stick out in the monochromatic landscape.

I could feel their certainty and their readiness to fight—it filled my soul, and I somehow knew in my heart that they were watching my every move, every twitch in my fingers and blink of my eyes.

Not to find fault, but because they were *listening*. They were following *me*.

I was about halfway across the meadow when the lodge's front door was flung open, and more wolves poured out.

Aeric and Shania were bright spots in the Pack with their red coats, while Wyatt stuck out with his dark brown—almost black—fur. East—a dusty gray color with a charcoal colored muzzle—and Jack—brown and gray—ignored the porch steps and jumped off the side, landing in the snow with quiet huffs.

I couldn't count fast enough to number the wolves, but it had to be almost all Pack staying in the territory—somewhere between fifty and sixty wolves.

I saw a few stay behind on the porch, whining with flattened ears as they took a few steps toward the stairs, then looked back at the lodge.

I waved to them. "Stay," I said. "We can't leave the territory unprotected." I paused, debating with myself for a moment. "Jack, I want you to stay with them."

Jack whined.

"I know, but the kids need to be protected," I said.

I also wasn't certain hauling a high school kid off to a fight was the responsible thing to do, even if Jack was strong.

"We also need to make sure Vant doesn't attack while we're gone," I added.

Jack brightened at that reminder, and he climbed his way back up the porch, his tail wagging.

The other wolves already standing there relaxed, their ears finally lifting off their skulls, and one of them started a howl—which set the whole Pack off.

The woods came alive with the Pack's song.

There was a sort of magic to it, one that brought all my senses into focus so I could hear the quiet tap of snow falling on my jacket and the whoosh of my own exhale. Strangely, I felt a connection to the Pack, too. I could almost feel the way their chests expanded as they sang, and the heat they gave wrapped around me as they drew closer, while the soft crunch of snow as the wolves moved was still audible to me over their song as they raised their muzzles to the sky and howled.

The Northern Lakes Pack was ready for war.

That's great—the thought came from the analytical hunter

part of me that refused to get entirely caught up in the magic of the Pack—*but how do we carry out an attack when Greyson is in Magiford, several hours away?*

Before I could do more than form the thought, an explosion of magic rocked the meadow.

A stone gateway with a twisted metal gate formed. The gate swung open, revealing blackness and haze for a split second before three creatures burst through the portal.

Silvery colored with black socks, muzzles, and horns, I recognized the unicorn-like night mares that belonged to Queen Leila.

The unicorns' black manes fluttered in the wind, and they screamed—a sound like breaking glass. Their riders clung to their backs, but I recognized them despite all the movement.

The ponytail of purple hair was practically Lord Linus's trademark, and Chrysanthe was hard to miss with her blond hair and brightly colored coat.

Chase, the final rider, flung himself off his mount's back before it stopped moving.

His yellow eyes were intense, and he was wearing his dark colored Director of Security uniform from the Night Court—which meant he was actively on duty.

And he came here? Despite working?

"Pip," Chase called.

The wolves parted for him as he jogged up to me.

"Chase, what are you *doing* here?" I asked.

"I felt it." Chase paused a few feet short of me and glanced at Scarlett and Radcliff standing behind me. "Your call."

My eyebrows traveled up my forehead, and I tried not to squeak. "From all the way in Magiford?"

Chase nodded.

I tucked my chin into my chest.

Woah, have I been selling my Wolf's Kiss powers short. My magic is way stronger than I ever gave it credit for.

"You're going after Greyson," Chase said.

"Yes."

"I'm coming with you," Chase said.

"As are we!" Lord Linus affectionately patted the neck of the night mare he was riding.

"It's our fight," I said. "I couldn't ask you to."

"You aren't asking," Chrysanthe said. "We're offering."

"Allies fight together, do they not?" Lord Linus grinned and turned his night mare in a circle.

"Thank you." My eyes flickered from Lord Linus to Chase. "For coming."

"It's our honor," Lord Linus said.

"You're Pack," Chase said simply.

"But you're with the Night Court, now," I said.

Chase tilted his head. "The Northern Lakes Pack will always be mine, even if my own family has expanded, even if I'm far away. I'll feel your call, Pip."

I threw my arms around the taciturn wolf, squeezing him in a tight hug that he returned.

Lord Linus tactfully cleared his throat as we parted. "Then…shall we be off? Where are we going?"

Chase looked at me, and I turned around. "Scarlett? Radcliff?"

The Fletching hunters' smiles were so big, and I could feel their pride the same way I could feel the certainty in the wolves around me.

"We were able to pinpoint the general area the spell disappeared in," Radcliff said.

"And we cross referenced it with street view on Google maps," Scarlett said.

"Google maps? What's that?" Chrysanthe asked.

"A human creation," Lord Linus said. "Think of it as a magic atlas that requires a phone or screened technology to activate."

I was more than a little curious how Lord Linus knew about Google maps, but Radcliff and Scarlett's genius was a far more pressing matter at the moment.

"Does that mean you'll be able to picture the area and have the night mares drop us off there?"

"Even better. We know what the entire three block area looks like," Radcliff said.

"We'll get the portals to drop us off in a safe zone, and based on what information Pre-Dominant Harka shared with us about the area…we think we know what building they've got him in," Scarlett said.

Chase nodded. "Brilliant reasoning," he said.

"No." I smiled at the pair, sharing their grin. "Brilliant hunters."

Around me the wolves raised their muzzles and howled once more as Lord Linus motioned for Radcliff and Scarlett to approach the gate.

We were going to Greyson, and we were going to free him, and smash once and for all whoever had been trying to destroy him—and his position as Alpha.

Chapter 21

Pip

"—**F**oolhardy to go in without us backing you up! Watch the building —you can make certain he's not attacked, but can't you at least wait an hour?"

"Mmhmm," I said noncommittally as I listened to Harka on my phone.

I don't know how she got my number, but after we showed up at the giant warehouse and scared the fur off the four scouts she had scouring the area, she'd immediately called me.

"*Pip. My team has confirmed there are at least a hundred different wolves who have gone in and out of that warehouse. It's not something you want to attack on a whim.*"

I stood next to a grimy brick building that looked like it could give me a disease and peered out into the street. "So I take it this has to be the work of more than one Pack?"

"*Yes. There have been wolves from the Packs belonging to Brock and the Alphas who attacked you in Timber Ridge, as well as several known mercenary squads.*"

"Fancy that," I said.

Scarlett and Radcliff had done as good as they'd promised, and taken us to the block where the tracking spell had faded.

It was pretty obvious where Greyson was being stowed. In the three city block radius that the Pack had checked—just to be certain—there was only one building that was spelled to the gills with barriers and protection spells: a giant warehouse that, surprise, surprise, was in part of Pre-Dominant Harka's territory and belonged to her Pack.

Reportedly, Harka's Pack used to use it for car, ATV, and four-wheeler storage, but this past summer the Pack had built a new garage out in the nature preserve the Pack owned/operated out of, and the warehouse had been left empty.

If Harka's right about this being the work of multiple Packs, whoever organized this has a lot of money and political connections to pull it off, and I'm starting to suspect I know who it is. Although I don't understand why he'd want Greyson dead. He didn't seem like he wanted to be Pre-Dominant.

Besides belonging to Harka's Pack, I wasn't thrilled that all the spells slapped on the warehouse were dulling my hunter senses. I could tell there were werewolves inside, but I couldn't give even a rough estimate. I just felt the bright, minty sensation of their presence, but it was as if they were just out of reach.

My phone blared in my ear, and I reluctantly returned my attention to Harka.

"And you're not listening to me at all, are you? Your tail is in a knot because this is Greyson—I swear you mates are always so hot-headed, and it only makes things worse because you get too impulsive for safety precautions, and then the worst happens."

That made me tune in as I recalled Harka's sister had a mate. I considered questioning her about it, but Chase—in his human form—Chrysanthe, Scarlett, and Radcliff were strolling up the street.

Chrysanthe was holding Chase's hand and leaning against

him, playing "love-struck girlfriend" to an interesting level of perfection as Scarlett and Radcliff loudly complained about being lost, providing cover for the quad's presence.

Since they were looping in my direction, it meant they were finished scouting.

It was time to say goodnight to the Pre-Dominant.

"At least wait until I hear back from Rafe on whether our team is ready!" Harka continued.

"I'm not really interested in waiting," I said. "Specifically because I don't think everyone in your office is trustworthy."

"…What? Why?"

"Sorry, Harka, gotta go. Toodles!"

"Hunter Sabre! Wait just a moment—"

I ended the call, silenced my phone, and put it away. I then backed deeper into the alleyway, where Lord Linus was inspecting a beautiful pair of daggers that I'd eyed with envy, and Hector was patiently waiting, his black nose quivering as he sniffed the air.

Chase, Chrysanthe, Radcliff, and Scarlett slipped in after me.

"See anything interesting?" I asked.

Chase nodded in the direction of the warehouse. "It has posted guards—werewolves, all of them."

Lord Linus delicately rubbed his thumb against the edge of one of his daggers. "That sounds promising."

"Oh, it gets better," Radcliff said.

Scarlett retrieved their crossbows from where they'd left them by Lord Linus. "We circled around the whole place— that's definitely the spot where the trail goes cold."

"Great," I said. "Are we ready to call in the rest of the Pack?"

Hector's ears perked up as he stared at me, waiting for my judgment call.

The Pack was two blocks up, hiding in a parking garage,

but I doubted the forty or fifty wolves would be able to hide there for long.

I guess it's a good thing for us the Northern Lakes Pack is the only Pack with hunters attached. The Fletchings and I would have lit up like Christmas trees with that many wolves in the area.

"You reviewed a plan of attack with them?" Chase asked.

"Not really," I said. "We can't strategize when we don't know what the inside is going to look like."

Hector sneezed, which I took to signal his agreement.

Scarlett raised her hand. "Can I make a suggestion?"

I tilted my head in surprise. "Sure. What are you thinking?"

Scarlett and Radcliff exchanged glances, before Radcliff nodded at his sister in encouragement.

Scarlett licked her lips, then met my eyes. "I think you should focus on the Pack, not fighting."

I blinked. "I don't know what you mean."

"From what we've seen, it seems like your magic gets extra flustered when you're trying to defend yourself in addition to running your magic," Radcliff said.

"We think if you just focused on the flow of your magic, you'd be able to handle it better instead of splitting your attention," Scarlett said.

"So you're saying I should…just get hit when I'm attacked?" I asked, more than a little confused.

"No, I'm saying you should let the Pack watch your back." Scarlett swallowed hard, then added, "And Radcliff and I would like to stand with you and defend you, too."

"If you allow it." Radcliff grimaced. "We can understand why having a Fletching at your back might not feel…great."

"That's not true," I said. "You two have helped the Pack—and me—more than enough times to clear the Fletching name." I paused. "But I'm not sure I can focus like that. I'm not a wizard, I'm a hunter. All my life I've been trained to counter and defend. Just focusing on my magic seems impossible."

"Their proposal makes sense." Lord Linus elegantly twirled his daggers without looking at them. "If this is a chess board, you aren't a queen piece—that would be Greyson."

"Great, so I'm the useless king?" I asked.

"Not at all." Lord Linus's purple-ish-blue eyes sparked with a dangerous amount of fae delight. "You're a hunter—you are an entirely different game from chess. You're a playmaker, not a piece to move around in battle."

I glanced at Chase, who had his arms tucked behind his back. He frowned slightly. "I haven't witnessed your magic in action, but I do imagine they are right. As a Wolf's Kiss, your role is neither wolf nor hunter."

I nervously chewed on my lip, then glanced down at Hector.

Slowly, he nodded—he also agreed with the Fletchings.

It's not that I'm against the idea…it just seems like a risky thing to experiment with in a battle to get Greyson back. But having my magic fail would be catastrophic.

I sharply exhaled and offered my rifle to Radcliff. "Great. Okay. Scarlett and Radcliff will have my back, but Hector, can you pick a wolf to hang with us?"

Hector huffed his agreement.

"Then let's call the Pack in. Either of you want to howl for them?" I glanced between Chase and Hector.

Hector stared back at me, remaining motionless.

"Wouldn't it be better for you to call them in?" Chase asked. "A verbal call would alert the mercenaries to our presence."

"Oh." I rubbed the pommel of the daggers strapped to my outer thigh—playmaker or not, I wasn't giving up my daggers. "Sure."

The problem was, I wasn't entirely sure how I had put out the call back on Pack territory.

But I guess I'm going to find out.

I'd felt my Wolf's Kiss powers kick in when I'd made the decision to come get Greyson, and that was when the wolves had started arriving.

I'd assume it's the same process: tamp up the magic, and be decisive.

I shut my eyes, blocking out the ripe smell of the alleyway and my cold surroundings, triggering my magic so it flowed in reverse.

I then took a deep breath, and thought of Greyson.

My mind taunted me with the memory of how he'd looked when he traded himself for me.

I must get him back.

Hector made a noise.

I could feel my magic brim around me, so I cautiously opened my eyes again, flexing my fingers as my Wolf's Kiss magic flowed around me stronger than it ever had before.

"Yep. Yes." Chase took a step toward me, then forced himself to back up. "That'll do it."

Hector whined a little as he also lifted a paw, his movements jerky as if he was fighting the urge to come in closer.

"Impressive," Lord Linus said.

"It's almost like an Alpha's call," Scarlett said.

"It makes sense," Lady Chrysanthe said. "Is she not uniting the Pack in his absence? I was under the impression only Alphas can do such a thing."

"Correct." Radcliff ducked his head out into the street. "And your call must have gone far enough, Pip. I can feel the Pack moving."

I could, as well. The bright spot where they'd lit up the parking garage in my senses started to move, drawing closer to us.

"Wouldn't it be best to exit the alleyway and get into position?" Lady Chrysanthe suggested.

"Yes," Chase agreed. "Pip?"

He and Hector watched me, unwilling to move until I did.

I squared my shoulders, took a breath, and checked my magic one last time before I stepped onto the street.

I crossed the road, frowning a little as I tugged on the cuffs of my hunter jacket.

The street was quiet. I couldn't even hear any sounds of traffic—the area was silent.

When I reached the sidewalk just in front of the warehouse, I heard quiet taps on pavement, and turned, my throat catching at the sight of the Northern Lakes Pack.

When Greyson called the Pack, they answered with a chorus of howls, their voices raised as they came together as one.

But for my call...the Pack was silent.

Their eyes were bright spots in the dimness as the afternoon faded into the night, and their nails clicked on the broken pavement, but they were as silent as my call had been.

The hair on the back of my neck prickled as I felt the absolute attention of every wolf. They stared at me not with judgment, or even expectation, just...waiting. For my orders.

Maybe being Greyson's mate is what's best for the Pack, too, since it ties me back to them. Because this is a crazy amount of power I have over them. I can't believe they trust me with it.

But they did.

I spotted Ember's tawny coat, Wyatt's dark brown fur, and Aeric's red highlights in the Pack, but it was actually Moira—with her white and gray coat—and Roanne and Klancy who stood at the front of the Pack.

Even that was a display of trust—my closest friends weren't leading the charge. Rather, they all believed in me enough that they had come in a mix.

As the Pack trotted closer, I felt my resolve to trust them harden, and my magic flowed over them.

The wolves grew in size—they'd always been larger than their wild counterparts, but now their backs were about as high as a grizzly bear's, though they kept their leaner build.

Previously they could comfortably press their faces into my hip. Now they could reach my shoulder.

"Well." I folded my arms across my chest as the Pack stopped a few feet short of me. "This appears terrifying."

Radcliff chuckled in a nervous, respectful sort of way.

"My Sovereign would find them dignified but adorable," Lady Chrysanthe said in a way that made me think she wouldn't necessarily agree with the label.

I leaned back on my heels. "Hector? If you'd select my guard?"

Hector silently stalked toward the Pack, his tail swaying with his movements.

I shifted so I could study the warehouse—we needed to rush in, now, before they realized we were out here. "There's a spell on the door, isn't there?"

"Fae design," Lady Chrysanthe reported. "It reinforces the doors, and makes the locks impossible to break down."

"Lady Chrysanthe and I could possibly wield enough fire power with our magic to knock them down," Lord Linus said. "But it will take a little while to build the spell."

I tilted my head as I studied the door. "That won't be necessary. Aeric? Wyatt?"

My two closest friends shouldered their way out of the Pack, trotting up so they stood on either side of me.

It felt weird—they were practically eye height for me, and I had to throw my arms high so I could rest my hands on their shoulders. "Break it down."

"I beg your pardon, *break it down*?" Lady Chrysanthe repeated.

"Your trust in your companions is...*charming*, Hunter Sabre," Lord Linus said. "But they might hurt themselves."

I glanced first at Wyatt's dark face, then Aeric's darkened mask. "Break it down," I repeated.

Moving as one, Aeric and Wyatt jumped up the stairs and slammed their bodies into the large double doors.

The doors broke off their hinges, twisting the metal door frame, and went skidding at least twenty feet into the warehouse before finally stopping.

Shouts of surprise leaked out of the now wide-open warehouse.

Scarlett fitted a bolt into her crossbow. "*Woah*," she said.

Radcliff already had his crossbow raised. "Seconded."

I glanced at the rest of the Pack. "Let's go."

As soundlessly as they'd arrived, the wolves raced past me and burst into the warehouse.

Scarlett, Radcliff, and I were a little slower to approach, lingering in the doorway so we could get our bearings.

The warehouse was filled with werewolves and had so many spells in it, it made the inside of my nose buzz when I took a breath.

About five wolves had been kneeling on the floor in a circle. The area between them was ringed with spells, but it looked like they'd been in the process of starting to break down some of the charms.

It's a good thing we came when we did—they're clearly prepping to leave.

The wolves had to be mercenaries—they looked too competent as they re-closed the fae spells they'd been moving. They immediately convened together and backed up against the far wall of the warehouse, taking up a defense position.

The other wolves that filled the ground floor of the warehouse? They weren't nearly as smart.

I spotted four different Packs—and their Alphas.

Brock was there—which was hardly a surprise. Two of the remaining three Alphas were the wolves I had half killed with my baseball bat back at my cottage when I thought they were hurting Prince, and the last one was the Alpha who had tried jumping me on Main Street—the wolf with the watermelon-crushing thighs.

Together, the four Packs outnumbered the wolves I'd brought to Magiford, but they were caught off guard—gaping in shock—and had huddled in their clearly defined groups, so as the Northern Lakes wolves raced across the cement floor of the warehouse, filling in the space between the Packs, they isolated the groups, keeping them from teaming up or working together.

Hector, Ember, Aeric, and Wyatt threw themselves at one of the Packs of roughly twelve wolves.

Only half of that specific Pack were actually shifted into their wolf forms. The others were rushing to shift—making them sitting ducks for the next thirty seconds to a minute. Hector and Ember took advantage of that time, ripping through the shifting wolves as Aeric and Wyatt—being the size of bears—physically blocked their much smaller opponents.

The rest of the Pack rushed to do the same with the other Packs.

East threw himself at one of the shell-shocked Packs, toppling two wolves with well-placed body slams.

Lord Linus ducked past them, the fae markings on the blades of his daggers glowing as he channeled magic. When he stabbed a wolf, it fell to the ground, twitching.

I guess Timber Ridge is a lot safer whenever the Night Court tour bus is in town than I realized.

Chase and Lady Chrysanthe stood back-to-back, both wielding handguns and taking down any wolves who approached the duo.

River and Moira joined East, scattering that particular

Pack and herding several of them straight to the braced Chase and Lady Chrysanthe.

Excellent. I don't think we need to worry about these Packs...but what about the mercenaries?

I scanned the rest of the warehouse, holding tight to my magic as I ignored the sounds of live bullets, wolf yelps, and angry snarls.

I grimaced when I glanced at the ceiling.

Harka's Pack apparently had so many toys they'd stored some in a shelving system installed as a kind of makeshift second floor. There was a metal scaffolding that wound snug around most of the building to allow access to the system, and there was what appeared to be a small office space with a large tinted window and a sturdy door.

About ten wolves—all in human form and toting guns and silver edged weapons—were on the scaffolding.

It wasn't the weapons that made me guess they were mercenaries, it was the calm, cool way they held themselves as they secured their spots on the rigging, loaded their guns, and started lining up their shots.

"Radcliff, do you know how to use my rifle?" I asked.

Radcliff loaded a bullet into the chamber. "I see them." He crouched down so he could better brace himself, aimed, and hit the mercenary who was farthest away, shooting him at an angle through an opening in the ceiling shelving system.

Since he was using my spelled bullets, the wolf crumpled, knocked out with a sleeping spell.

I dug out my two extra magazine cartridges from the deep pockets of my jacket and handed them off to Radcliff. "Are you *sure* you didn't inherit your mom's magic, too?"

Scarlett laughed, but she didn't respond as she aimed at one of the Pack Alphas and shot, her spelled crossbow toppling him—causing instant chaos among his Pack.

My smile slipped as I watched the mercenaries who had been handling the magic circle.

All five of them were still standing, and while they were staying on the wall, they shot at any of my wolves who got too close to the magic circle they'd been in the process of disassembling.

I rubbed my nose, trying to block out the smell of blood and the high-pitched squeals of pain before I checked on the Northern Lakes wolves, smoothing out my magic to keep it on them.

What's so special about that spot that warrants all those spells? There's nothing there. And where are the rest of the mercenaries? The ten on the scaffolding and the five on the ground can't be all of them.

The Northern Lakes wolves had worked their way through two of the Packs by this point.

Aeric and Wyatt were trying to attack the five stubborn mercenaries on the ground, but the mercenaries took turns firing their handguns, giving themselves time to reload so there weren't any holes in their defense.

East jumped one of the two remaining Alphas as he was in the process of shifting.

The Alpha screamed, and his wolves went wild—splitting up as they ran straight into my wolves, who took them down with ease.

Then, the door to the office up on the rigging opened, and mercenaries came charging out—crouching to avoid Radcliff's shots. Their boss came out with them, half hiding behind two especially large mercenaries so Radcliff couldn't get a shot at him.

"Hunter Sabre. You just couldn't wait."

"Hey, Rafe," I shouted. "Can't say I'm sorry we crashed your house-moving-party."

Rafe rested his forearms on the railing of the scaffolding and shook his head. "Would it make a difference if I told you I didn't want this?" He had to keep his voice loud to be heard over the yelps and whines of the werewolves.

"Not really," I said. "Your sister was a psycho, and I'm pretty sure she got her wolfsbane from *you*. Just a guess, but you were also the one who so kindly emailed all the Alphas in the area about me, right? You put a lot of people at risk with that move."

The two mercenaries who had been protecting Rafe moved, heading for the far stairway of the scaffolding, which would dump them out by the other mercenaries who were guarding the magic circle. More of the mercenaries followed their lead, crouching to make themselves a smaller target—though Radcliff got two of them anyway.

Yeah, there's something in that magic circle. They wouldn't be so intent on keeping it, otherwise.

"Aspen went a little too far in her zeal." Rafe ducked behind one of the shelving systems, hiding from Radcliff's aim. "But I at least tried to limit the collateral damage of my attack."

"If you're trying to make an excuse, don't bother." I glanced at the magic circle out of the corner of my eye. "You can try to sound kind and apologetic, but in the end you still kidnapped Greyson and tried to have me killed."

"I didn't have a choice," Rafe said. "My family is in danger."

"And picking on me—who has done nothing but get kidnapped by your crazy sister—will solve that. Yeah, that sounds sane." I tapped the toe of my boot on the floor, and glanced at the magic circle again.

"You personally couldn't help me in any way," Rafe said. "Not after I realized you would never leave the Northern Lakes Pack. But you did have the misfortune of being the mate of Greyson, and a much easier target than he is."

"So all of this was for Greyson?" I asked. "But *why?*"

Fated

"I said earlier, for family. Sorry, Pip. I like you—I wish you had waited for my aunt." Rafe made a raspy, barking noise, and the mercenaries jumped down the last few stairs, a group of six of them rushing in my direction.

My hunter adrenaline flooded my system, raging with the instinct to fight.

It took every ounce of restraint that I had to keep my Wolf's Kiss magic flowing properly and just *watch* as the huge mercenaries rushed in my direction, their handguns raised.

Scarlett and Radcliff stepped up on either side in perfect unison.

Scarlett shot the wolf heading the attack, while Radcliff shot the back two before his magazine ran out.

Cursing, Radcliff hurriedly replaced his magazine while Scarlett reloaded her crossbow and shot another mercenary, leaving two almost on us.

My hunter magic pulsed in me, but I stood my ground and focused on my magic.

Sweat made my jacket stick to me, and my breathing hitched—I was within the two remaining mercenaries' range.

They racked their weapons, but before they could squeeze the triggers two huge wolves stepped out of the shadows—one yellow-ish gray, and the other a distinctive red color.

Rio and Shania.

Rio snapped his jaws on one mercenary's arm—I was pretty sure he broke the bone from the way the mercenary shouted.

Shania bit into the second mercenary's shoulder and dragged him down, making him bend backwards before she threw him with a snap of her head, tossing him into another enemy wolf so they both collapsed.

Blood flecked Shania's mouth and Rio's teeth, and the duo growled as they towered over the incoming mercenaries, their message clear.

265

Did you really think we'd leave her unguarded?

The thought came to me so clearly, with tinges of both Rio's and Shania's voices in it, that it caught me off guard.

I didn't hear words through my magic. I got impressions at best.

Wolves didn't really communicate with words—more like ideas and feelings. But Shania and Rio's dedication to guarding me was so strong I could almost hear them—that was definitely a Pack thing.

Greyson has to be somewhere around here—that has to be his doing.

My eyes strayed again to the magic circle, where I could feel webs of spells, and I swear I felt something from the spot.

I set my shoulders. "Take the magic circle!"

Rafe loped down the scaffolding, rattling it. "You're disengaging from me so easily? Come on, Hunter Sab—" He abruptly ducked, barely missing the shot Radcliff had taken at him.

Next to me, Radcliff made a "*tsk*" of irritation.

"Good call, he does seem to be hiding something of interest there." Lord Linus's daggers glowed as he wiped blood off them onto the fur of a fallen wolf before he strolled in my direction.

The Northern Lakes wolves surged around me, springing toward the mercenaries.

The mercenaries rapidly fired, and two of the Northern Lakes wolves yelped, falling back.

"Moira, River!" I shouted.

I felt my magic flicker in my chest as I watched with horror as River struck the ground and skidded a few feet. Moira collapsed where she stood, her ears flattened as she whined.

"I've got the white one." Lord Linus sheathed one of his daggers and knelt at Moira's side.

"Understood," Lady Chrysanthe said. She left her spot at Chase's side and raced for River.

"Chrys!" Chase shouted, his eyebrows lowering with his concern.

"Guard them, Chase," I yelled.

Chase sprinted after her, and the rest of the Pack surged forward, pinning the mercenaries.

I ran up to the magic circle. When I got close enough I could see the area within the circle was threaded with what I suspected was an illusion spell given the way the image wavered when I was up close.

Rio sniffed the circle, growling when his nose brushed the surface and received a bolt of electricity.

"So it affects wolves...what about humans?"

I brushed the surface of the fae spell, which didn't react.

Most fae magic didn't work on wizards and all their subsets —including hunters.

But when my fingers touched the magic—which felt shimmery and insubstantial, yet as sharp as a blade—I could feel something *more* to it.

"What's wrong?" Scarlett asked, cursing under her breath when her shot fell short of Rafe—she and Radcliff were still trying to get him. "He's like a cockroach!"

"I imagine that's how he's survived all of this—unless his aunt knows," Radcliff dryly said.

"There are a bunch of fae spells woven in here, and something else," I said. "It's an old kind of magic that I've never felt before."

"Careful," Chase shouted. He reloaded his handgun and shot a mercenary, toppling him. "If you haven't felt it before, there's a chance it could be elf magic."

"*Elf* magic? But they're all dead!" Radcliff shouted.

"Yeah, and Aspen fed a bunch of wolves batches of wolfsbane—an elf potion," I said. "Either someone has uncovered elven artifacts, or their ways aren't as lost as we thought." I tapped my finger on the surface of the magic shell, causing ripples that ruined the near perfect appearance of the illusion.

For a moment, I felt something in my hunter senses. Was there a werewolf behind all the spells?

Greyson!

I tapped the shield again, but the bright spot didn't ping on my senses. "But whatever the elven part of the spell is, it's not the part that makes the barrier. I should be able to step inside."

For a moment, the only sound was the steady discharge of bullets and the snarls of wolves.

"Your call, Hunter Sabre," Radcliff said.

At my side, Rio snapped off a nod in his werewolf body.

I peered up at Rafe, who was belly down on the scaffolding, making himself the smallest target possible, his phone clutched to his ear.

Is he calling Harka?

I didn't think the Pre-Dominant was in on her nephew's scheme—she'd hand chosen Greyson to be her replacement and was bargaining hard to get him to accept it. Her actions didn't make any sense if she wanted him dead.

But who else would he be calling?

A side door burst open, and at least thirty mercenaries rushed in, squeezing the Northern Lakes Pack between the new line of battle, and the mercenaries still holding their position at the wall.

Based on the way they were sweeping, they were clearly trying to drive us away from the magic circle.

Which means it's either Greyson inside this spell, or something even more incriminating.

Given, however, that I could feel a prickle in my hunter senses, I was pretty sure it was Greyson.

Which is good enough reason to try it, even with the risks.

"I'm going in," I shouted.

"I'd advise, then, that you *hurry*." Lord Linus attempted to drag Moira backwards, but she was so massive from my magic he wasn't making much progress. "Because we're about to lose this area."

I took a deep breath, braced myself for the possibility of pain, and stepped inside.

Chapter 22

Pip

I felt the fae spells brush across my skin with no resistance and no residual effects. Whatever all the spells were, they wouldn't hurt me.

But when my left foot—the last part of my body to remain outside—cleared the circle, I felt my magic cut off.

The unknown spell...

My hunter senses collapsed, leaving me with the horrible mixture of feeling like I'd been blinded and deafened, even though I could see everything going on outside the circle and hear the howls, live rounds, and shouts.

My mental shield—which was what protected me from an Alpha's powers—shattered, falling away, and I couldn't feel the flow of my magic.

I was utterly defenseless, without the magic I'd grown up *breathing*, but I stayed stuck in the circle despite every instinct screaming at me to leave, because Greyson was there, chained to the ground.

His long, lean body was collapsed on the floor, face down,

his fingers shaking as sweat made his long-sleeved shirt stick to his back.

"Greyson!" I threw myself to his side, my knees banging on the cement ground—which was covered with glowing flourishes that I assumed were the maybe-an-elf spell.

I touched his shoulder, wincing when I felt my soul shudder as my body tried to process magic it didn't have.

How long have they kept him like this? If this is what I feel...how much worse has it been for him?

Greyson peeled a golden eye open for a heartbeat. "Pip."

Outside the circle, the mercenaries had succeeded in pushing the Pack back so our wolves barely blocked the front of the magic circle. What was worse, though, was since I was cut off from my magic, some of the wolves were losing their larger, more powerful shapes.

I've got to get Greyson out!

I inhaled, then coughed—even my breathing felt limited without magic trickling through my blood.

"Looks like you've united the Pack," Greyson said, his voice rusty. "They wouldn't have been able to follow Hector here...which means it's you. That's good." His eyes drifted shut again.

"Greyson!" I snarled. "Greyson, don't you dare die here! I'll never, ever forgive you if you die here! I'll—I'll marry a human out of spite!"

Greyson's eyes opened, and he managed a scoff. "I'm not so weak that I can be defeated by the little plans of *Rafe*," he scornfully said. "And you could never marry a human—you'd never find one who could put up with you."

"I'm glad you think so highly of your mate." I pulled on his chains—which was how I realized they were magic forged, and were one of the fae spells cast on the circle.

If it's magic, that means I can't break them without destroying the spell.

The logical thought had to fight through the panic that was threatening to overrun my system as my magic was still *gone.*

It was getting harder to concentrate, much less breathe.

"Greyson, how do we get you out of here?"

"I imagine saying please to Rafe won't do anything."

"Would you be serious?"

Greyson groaned as he rolled over onto his back. "Sorry. Being serious has been beaten out of me. All that's left is my stunning humor. And my looks—right? I can't feel much right now so I can't tell, but I don't think Rafe is *that* petty."

I growled as I glanced outside the circle.

Without their power ups, or the power of their Alpha, the Northern Lakes Pack was being pushed back so far they could barely defend the last line of the circle.

We must get out of here, now!

My heart was throbbing painfully in my chest with both worry for Greyson, and the vast *darkness* I felt press around my mind without my hunter abilities lighting up.

"Your chains are part of a spell," I said.

"Yeah."

"I can't break spells." There was a hysterical edge to my voice. "There's no hunter magic for that."

Greyson finally managed to sit up, a grimace twitching across his face for only a second before he managed to hide it —which let me know just how badly he was hurting.

Briefly, I felt a flutter of magic—not mine, hunter or otherwise. It was something entirely different—something soft and silvery like moonlight, and when it brushed against my senses it gave my mind a moment of relief, but I felt immense pain and something *else.*

"Pip," Greyson said. "Leave the circle."

"Not without you!"

"Go reunite the Pack, beat Rafe down—preferably with a

baseball bat since you are extra dangerous once equipped with one of those—and then you can crack this circle open."

It was a solid idea, but even as I felt like every nerve I had was on fire—screaming for magic—I couldn't move. "I can't leave you like this," I whispered.

Greyson smiled painfully at me. "I survived this long, I'll be fine for a few hours more."

I miserably shook my head, then gave in and leaned into him—careful not to make him take any of my weight. "But you're hurting so much…"

"…How do you know that?" Greyson asked, his voice urgent.

"I don't know!" Hot tears of frustration stung my eyes as I felt the foreign silvery magic brush against me again. It was both warm and terrifying in how I could feel that it wanted to surround me the same way my hunter magic did. "I can just tell—it's the only thing I can tell since this stupid elf spell has me cut off from my magic!"

"Wolfsbane is elven made, and it's unable to override a mate bond," Greyson said. "If it's an elf spell…maybe our bond can work despite it?"

"And? How can that help?"

Greyson yanked me against him so our heads almost knocked together.

I tried to wiggle free—concerned my weight would hurt him—but paused when I felt the rising wave of anxiety lessen.

My magic was the only thing I'd ever known that had stayed with me—constant.

As much as I was trying to hold it together, without magic flowing through my blood, without my hunter senses trickling information to my mind, it felt like my brain was slowly crumbling. The natural response to that was sheer, unadulterated panic.

But with Greyson pressed against me, he filled my senses as

he always did—to the point where I didn't feel the gaping vacuum of my magic, it was more like a small but bleeding wound.

I could think clearly.

In that moment, I knew Greyson was right.

The best plan was for me to get out of the circle, power up the Pack once again, and beat the crap out of Rafe while someone—probably Lord Linus and Lady Chrysanthe, the two *fae* who were conveniently here and very powerful—dismantled the spells.

But.

I didn't like that plan.

I didn't want to leave Greyson, even with my clear thinking restored to me.

The silvery magic brushed my mind again, and I finally recognized it. That was when I knew…there was a second way.

A way that was far more terrifying, because it meant accepting that moonlight magic, the offer of a mate bond.

In accepting the bond, it might end with me being unable to fully use all my hunter magic once this was over. Lynn's mom had said it could break a hunter's magic. That must be why it was considered so taboo: a wolf-hunter mate bond ended with either endless pain for the wolf, or broken magic for the hunter.

But hadn't I told Teresa it wasn't magic that made the hunter?

Leave the circle, get your magic. Later, consider the possibility of a mate bond. Greyson won't resent me for his pain—he's told me before he accepts it as the price. He's stronger than I am, he can survive.

The urge to let things keep going as they were was a sweet temptation.

Greyson was willing to bear the pain of our incomplete bond, I'd finally grasped exactly what my powers as a Wolf's

Kiss were, we could win this fight against Rafe with or without Greyson as long as I was able to help.

The silvery magic brushed me again, and I could feel Greyson's worry for me in my bones.

Except…can I keep going like this? In my heart?

I wanted our bond—I'd realized that when Greyson traded his life for mine. But could *I* bear the pain of knowing what Greyson was experiencing…because I wanted to keep all my magic?

Or would it slowly crush me, sapping away at my spirit? Because in the end, I needed to be able to live with myself once all was said and done.

I loved the Pack, but none of them would view me breaking my magic as a betrayal—it would simplify things, actually.

And Greyson…he'd never want broken magic for me. But this was my decision and my sacrifice to make.

I felt torn between restoring my hunter powers—which were *air* to me and the only thing I had in my life from before my parents had died—and Greyson.

Outside the circle, the battle raged.

Hector howled, rallying the Pack.

Ember and Shania jumped a pair of mercenaries as Rio fought tooth and nail to stay by the magic circle—trying his hardest to keep an exit route open for me.

Radcliff was out of bullets for my rifle and had switched to his crossbow while Scarlett swapped her crossbow for a handgun. Beyond them, Lord Linus stabbed a mercenary with his daggers while Chase and Lady Chrysanthe dragged fallen wolves away from the front line.

"Pip," Greyson said, his tone urgent.

I looked up at Greyson, peering into his golden eyes, where —with the smallest hint of our bond touching my consciousness—I could read his concern and determination to protect me from the world if it came to that.

And I made my decision.

I reached for the silvery magic, and when I could feel the faint sensation of Greyson, I accepted it, drawing it into me— because I loved my insufferable white wolf that much.

The bond magic filled my senses. I saw the moon in the dark sky with misty clouds playing at the edges while the sound of wolf howling filled my ears and the scent of pine and mossy turf tickled my nose.

And then, that beauty shattered when I felt the bond connect to me—a hot and heavy presence as it tried to make room inside my heart and head for Greyson.

Holy—this is—

I couldn't even finish the thought, it hurt too much. Hot pain carved into my chest, and I screamed as pain crested through me like waves, following the mate magic that made a torturously slow inspection of my body.

But the pain wasn't the worst part—I knew that would end soon.

No, the truly horrifying part was when I felt Greyson in my mind.

He was a strong, solid presence with his thoughts hitting me a million miles per hour in his worry.

I wasn't alone in my head. He was there, too.

"Pip," Greyson shouted. "Reject it—let it go!"

I gritted my teeth and dug my fingers into his arm, but I stubbornly held on to the magic.

I'd thought being without magic was scary—having another person *with* you like this…this was real terror.

I'd chosen to shut myself off from the Pack—I knew that now. It had taken a lot for me to reach for them. But that was minuscule compared to what I could feel of Greyson as his mind moved in tandem with mine.

Greyson could see every part about me—the good, the ugly, the petty. He could see how cowardly I'd been in my fear that he'd come to hate me, how I failed the Pack by keeping them out of my heart.

He'd be able to see how much it hurt when I wasn't allowed to run with the Pack, and how I'd been selfish enough to let him bear the burden of our relationship, and how I sometimes hated the humans of the Pack for what they'd say to me, even though I knew they were hurting worse than I was.

Now, he'd even know that I was the one who occasionally shook Rio's sodas in the lodge fridge so it sprayed everywhere whenever he opened one!

He'd see *it all*.

We might still be two bodies, but with this bond we were now one mind. *How can Greyson still love me with a bond like this?*

I screamed as the pain of going from a lone hunter to suddenly being *bound* so close to Greyson made my mind shudder in my skull.

Greyson pulled me closer so I was flattened against his chest, and tipped his forehead against mine.

"I can love you," he spoke directly into my ear, "because you're you. I didn't take the bond because I expected a perfect mate."

I pulled back just enough so I could peer into his eyes. "You promise?" I asked, my heart and tone desperate.

"Pip, I will *always* love you," he said. "That's the magic of a mate bond—it's not something shoved on us. It's something we choose, *because* we love. No matter what."

Pain still wracked my body, but dimly, as the bond settled into place, I could feel the truth in Greyson's heart.

He was being honest. He'd love me from here on out. We were bonded mates, there was *nothing* that could come between us.

I huddled my shoulders up and let go of my last fears, then mashed my lips against Greyson's.

It wasn't romantic or as glorious as our previous kisses. It was something half desperate but just as determined as I locked my lips to his and felt the last of the bond fall into place.

Greyson's lips on mine were just as reckless, marking our promise.

We were mates—there was no going back.

Greyson slipped his hand behind my neck to support my head, and I tensed up as his fingers evoked a hot, burning sensation that made me flinch—my bond mark.

I dug my fingers into his shirt as the pain from the bond made one last pass through my body before it disappeared.

For a moment, everything felt unbearably new, and then I felt Greyson chuckling deep in my heart.

Not too bad, eh, Lady Hunter? His thoughts were just as velvety and alluring in my mind as his voice was to my ears.

I can't believe that worked, I thought.

Me either. You have terrible timing.

I was just about to launch into a familiar fight with him, when I realized the pain was finally gone, and our desperate kiss had morphed into something closer to fire.

The ground beneath us cracked, and I felt the magic spells encircling us evaporate under the all-consuming onslaught of our bond, which had finally been finished.

Blown away by the sudden sensation of magic making its way beyond the broken elf spell, I opened my eyes and finally pulled back from Greyson. I laughed as my hunter magic settled back into my soul—stronger and more potent than I'd experienced before—and rubbed against the minty sensation of Greyson's own powers.

Rafe was right to fear Greyson, the future Pre-Dominant, and the Alphas of the region weren't wrong in their fear of what I, a Wolf's Kiss, could do.

But a wolf and a hunter, bonded together?

The world had better watch out.

We weren't unevenly bonded; we were perfectly matched. Woe befall anyone who thought they stood a chance against us.

Free of the elven spell that blocked our powers, I tapped my magic.

Once again the Northern Lakes wolves grew, my magic powering them up—only now, they were even stronger. Because when Greyson stood, he unrolled his Alpha powers.

Several of the mercenary wolves dropped to their knees under the pressure of his powers, but the Northern Lakes wolves raised their muzzles, howling out a song as all their voices slowly entwined into one beautiful, haunting melody.

Greyson's eyes glowed in the shadows of the warehouse. He didn't say anything, but when he shifted his gaze up to Rafe, the Pack broke apart, surging forward.

East and Wyatt pounced on the newly arrived mercenaries from behind, having snuck around behind them when the Pack was singing.

Hector and Ember lunged together at the wolves guarding the base of the scaffolding stairs, dragging them away.

Greyson pressed his forehead against mine for the briefest of moments. "I'll be right back."

"Yep," I agreed. "You've got this."

He smiled, then set his sights on the mercenary who was actively shooting at Rio.

I raised my gaze from the battle, to the far end of the warehouse, where there was a second staircase for the scaffolding.

Hah—I won't even have to turn off my Wolf's Kiss magic for this!

"Hey Scarlett, Radcliff. You feel like hunting?" I called to them.

Radcliff peered back at the staircase I was studying, then looked up at Rafe—still crouched on the part of the rig that was near us. "Ohhh, yes, Hunter Sabre. You are good."

"Never send a wolf to do a hunter's job." Scarlett racked her handgun with a satisfied grin.

"Come on." I unsheathed my daggers and made my way through the fight, leading the way to the abandoned end of the warehouse where the second stairway was.

I moved quietly as I climbed the steps and focused on making my strides even so I wouldn't rattle the walkway as Scarlett, Radcliff, and I inched along.

Rafe never looked at us, he was too busy watching his plan —whatever it had been—fall apart.

Only ten mercenaries remained when I ghosted up behind him. I placed one of my silver edged daggers at his throat and planted the other directly over his heart.

"Tell them to stand down, Rafe," I said.

Chapter 23

Pip

R afe startled, but I was surprised when he sighed deeply. "It's the end. Even if I fought you and won, Greyson would just carve me into pieces."

"The likelihood of you winning against me when I've got your heart and throat in my palms is less than miniscule, Rafe. Be smart," I warned him.

"Yeah. My men are almost down, anyway. And all of it was for nothing." His voice grew low and twisted with bitterness.

"If you go feral on me now, I won't give you the satisfaction of dying," I warned him. "My fellow hunters here have spelled ammo with your name on it."

"I'll give up." Rafe held his hands out, away from his body. His usually kind voice was jarringly jaded. "It's just...I tried. I just wanted one thing, and I couldn't even have that. Aspen was right—our family is cursed."

"Stop stalling, and call them off, Rafe."

"Men, we surrender." Rafe's voice was loud, but it was without inflection.

The mercenaries stopped and raised their hands in surrender as the Northern Lakes Pack surged around them.

Greyson eyed me up on the scaffolding, but he wisely said nothing—though I could feel both his pride that I'd bagged Rafe and his concern that *I'd* bagged Rafe eating at him through the brightness of our shiny new bond.

Radcliff and Scarlett took over for me, giving me a chance to slip out in front of Rafe and study him.

The look in his eyes bothered me. He had the same desperation Aspen had, and the light in his eyes was dimming—not to match Aspen's unhinged determination, more like he was falling to pieces because he was losing much more than a battle.

"Why, Rafe?" I asked. "You're Harka's heir. You were going to inherit a powerful Pack. Wasn't that enough? Or did you have to be the Pre-Dominant?"

Rafe laughed humorlessly. "I'm well aware I lack the strength to be the Pre-Dominant. That was Aspen's unfounded hope for me, but I never thought it'd be possible."

"Then why?"

Rafe shrugged. "I'm a wolf. I'll do anything for family." He glanced down at Greyson. "I thought maybe I could reason with him through you, but in attempting that route, it only made me realize that it didn't matter. She'd be destroyed."

"Who would be destroyed?" I asked.

Rafe twitched, then pressed his lips together, holding the answer in. "You tricky Wolf's Kiss," he said after a moment. "You almost had me with your voice and magic. No, I'll not say anything more. You may as well call my aunt and tell her all I've done."

That answered the question on whether or not Harka was involved—though I hadn't thought she was, particularly after we faced down the mercenaries and Packs.

She's too strong for this kind of show. She would have chosen more competent forces—and with higher numbers.

I heard a commotion downstairs and felt Greyson—both through our connection, and from the way his Alpha powers raged through the warehouse like an inferno.

Leaving Rafe to the Fletchings, I leaped down the stairs, landing with a roll, and popped upright in time to see new werewolves—some in human, some in werewolf form—crowding the door Aeric and Wyatt had busted open.

My eyes were hooked on the beautiful wolf who stood in the entrance, who had gorgeous white fur swirled with gray and dotted with black—particularly on the backs of her ears.

"Lynn," I breathed.

Lynn swiveled to face me and howled—a note I recognized through Greyson as a howl of finding Pack.

Next to her, in his human form, was Hudson, bearing a baseball bat. "Pip?" he shouted. "Everything okay? We felt your call halfway across the city."

I took a few jerky steps across the warehouse. "You came for *me*?"

"Of course!" Hudson tapped his bat against his leg as he eyed up the mess. "You sent out a call for Pack."

Lynn yipped and trotted across the warehouse. She jumped over a few fallen wolves, then stopped at my feet and peered up at me before pushing her face into my stomach.

I crouched so I could throw my arms around Lynn's furry shoulders. "Thank you," I whispered, unable to express how much it meant to me. "Thank you," I repeated.

She licked my ear, then pulled away and set about inspecting the fallen. I could tell by the way her nose quivered and her ears twitched that she was starting to sort out the unconscious wolves from the injured ones.

A few wolves I didn't recognize sauntered through the open door and joined her in her task, Hudson trailing behind them.

"Lynn's hubby and a few others from our Pack came, too," Hudson said. "So did Pre-Dominant Harka—though she's pretty upset."

"Harka's here?" I asked.

Greyson skulked closer so he stood directly behind me, and I could feel his caution radiating through our bond.

I twisted around slightly so I could peer up at him. "Was she...?"

"Not involved," Greyson said. "I'm pretty sure she was the reason he didn't kill me outright. He arrived only about twenty minutes before you got here—she'd been keeping him at the Cloisters with the search for me."

As Greyson spoke, a new crowd of wolves—in both human and wolf form—crowded the doorway.

"The Pre-Dominant is here," one of the wolves shouted, "and calling for the arrest of Rafe—"

Harka strode into the warehouse, breezing past him, though she slowed down to take in the carnage. She briefly shut her eyes, and when she opened them again they were steely with resolve.

"Alpha Greyson, Hunter Sabre. I'm glad to see you are both well." She tried to smile at me. "And it seems I owe you an apology, Pip. It was wise to infiltrate the warehouse when you did. It never occurred to me..." She trailed off and stared at the ground.

"We'd like to officially hand over Rafe and his men, as well as the Alphas he recruited, for a trial," Greyson said.

"Are you certain?" Harka asked. "You're well within your rights for trial by combat—particularly with Rafe."

"If he'd taken Pip I wouldn't have spared him," Greyson bluntly said. "But when I traded my life for hers he at least had the restraint to leave her alive when killing her would have been the easiest way to ruin me. That is the *only* reason he isn't already dead."

Harka grimaced. "I understand. On his behalf I thank you for this mercy—though I'm not certain he'll believe it is."

"That's my guess as well." Greyson's shoulders relaxed, and when he threaded his fingers through mine I jumped—not because of the contact, but because of the electric feeling it produced when we touched.

So the mate bond is going to take some time to get used to, good to know.

"I'll admit, that does play into my willingness to be so… benevolent." Greyson glanced down at me, and I could feel him probe the bond to make sure I was uninjured.

I ignored him as I peered out through the door onto the rapidly darkening street, feeling foreign prickles of magic. "Are there more than wolves outside? Or…?"

Greyson tensed next to me, but Harka held up her hand. "I called up a task force from the Curia Cloisters when I realized Rafe was behind this. Normally I wouldn't bring the Cloisters into wolf politics, but I want things to be done by the book and beyond reproach. Particularly since this is my second relative to fall."

Harka's expression was hard as a team of eight supernaturals wearing matching uniforms entered the building.

Interesting…but I want answers.

I pulled my focus back to Harka. "But why did Rafe do it? It didn't seem like he wanted to be the next Pre-Dominant."

Harka shook her head. "He couldn't be—he's strong, but he's not a candidate. If Greyson truly refused the position, then Maya Williams or Kim Seo-Jun from Chicago were my next choices."

Ahhh yes, they were quite strong—and smart enough to be willing to join forces between their Packs, so they wouldn't need the brute strength like Greyson has in his Alpha powers.

"Then why do this?" I tried to push the invasive warmness of the mate bond back from my tired mind as Greyson again reached out through the bond. *How on earth did he keep this hidden as long as he did when it has the power to be so reassuring it makes you brainless?*

Harka gazed past Greyson and me. "I have a hunch, but I'll have to question him to know for certain."

Greyson and I followed her as she made her way to the spot where we were holding Rafe.

He was sitting on the lowest stair with Radcliff and Scarlett standing on either side of the staircase, their weapons inches away from his temples.

East was awkwardly standing on the stairs behind him, but I could tell he was positioned so he could easily launch himself on top of Rafe if he tried to attack me, while Ember stood in front of him.

Powered up as she was, Ember towered over the sitting Rafe, and her lips were pulled back in a silent snarl that showed her teeth.

Rafe didn't seem to notice. He was staring at the ground, the fight completely out of him.

What could possibly be so important to him to make him react like this?

When we arrived at the stairs, Harka nodded to Ember.

Ember actually looked to me and Greyson before she took a few side steps. She moved so Harka could partially stand in front of her nephew, but still gave her a clear shot if he tried to escape.

Harka's hands briefly twitched into fists. "Rafe."

Rafe slowly looked up, his eyes dead and listless. "Hello, Aunt Harka."

"Why?" Harka asked. "Why did you do this?"

Rafe blinked slowly. "For family."

Harka shook her head. "She's been gone for years."

"But I had to try," Rafe said.

"No, you didn't!" Harka's voice was harsh and angry. "She

never would have wanted this—for you *or* Aspen! And you've both thrown your lives away knowing that!"

Rafe shrugged. "It doesn't matter if it's what she would have wanted or not, family is more important than that."

Harka groaned—a noise that came from deep within her soul and had the same musical quality to it as a howl. She stared up at the warehouse roof. "This is my fault that I ever allowed you and Aspen to *think* like this!"

Harka spun on her heels. "Alpha Greyson, I'm afraid I owe you a very long explanation, but I don't think this is the ideal place to give it."

Greyson nodded. "I agree. I'd like to secure the area and get Rafe's henchmen hauled into a holding cell. The Northern Lakes hunters used spelled ammo on them—it's probable they'll start waking up in half an hour or so, and I want them secured before then."

Both Scarlett and Radcliff stood taller at the reference to their positions, and I saw Scarlett fight a smile as Radcliff proudly puffed up his chest.

"Understood." Harka glanced at her wolves—who were fanning out in the warehouse in an orderly manner, making notations as the Curia Cloisters task force got to work.

I watched in fascination as the task force members started cuffing wolves. With the variety of supernaturals in the ranks, it was interesting to see how they divided and conquered.

A red-haired woman—who had to be a vampire slayer based on the way she was inspecting the wounded—spoke with a handsome vampire—who casually clocked a stirring wolf in the head, instantly knocking him out again.

"My husband—Beta Colton—will take Rafe," Harka continued. "The task force will accompany him. Would you like to send a few wolves along to ensure everything is done to your satisfaction?"

"Klancy, East." Although Greyson said their names at a

normal volume, I could feel the touch of Alpha powers put into their names—but what really made me shiver was that I *felt* him call the Pack through our bond and could feel his power, even though my magic was still shielding me from the effects.

Klancy and East trotted up to us, and Greyson motioned for them to follow as we stepped away.

As we left, Beta Colton approached Harka. I saw him briefly rest his hand on her lower back—a touch of reassurance—before he expressionlessly faced his nephew.

The red-haired slayer and the handsome vampire joined them and officially took an unprotesting Rafe into custody while Greyson spoke to Klancy and East.

"I want the two of you to go with the task force to the Cloisters to ensure Rafe is properly secured," Greyson said. "You can go in your wolf forms, but once you arrive at the Cloisters I want you to take on your human forms so you can talk."

Klancy and East surprised me by looking from Greyson, to me.

They said I felt like a different version of an Alpha…

"I'll take my magic off you," I said. "Otherwise I don't think you're going to fit in any vehicle the Cloisters send." I tugged my powers from them, and Greyson rubbed his jaw as Klancy and East returned to their regular sizes.

"I can feel it when you use your magic," Greyson said.

"Makes sense. I can feel it when you use the Pack bond," I said.

"Really?"

"Yeah. Klancy, East, we'll be going to the Cloisters as well when we finish clean up here, so wait for us to arrive. I'm hoping our fae allies will feel generous enough to take us all home once everything is finished," I said.

"I hope so as well." Greyson's voice was deceptively cheerful. "We have some unfinished business back in Timber Ridge."

"The Low Marsh Pack?" I guessed. "We already figured out the mercenaries took you out through their land."

"They didn't just use the Low Marsh territory to get out of our territory as fast as possible," Greyson said. "They had their gear stored there. Alpha Vant watched them load me."

I whistled. "Are you sure you don't want to go there now?"

"Yes." Greyson chuckled, his voice raspy. "I want you to call the wolves who stayed behind to make certain the territory is secure, but we won't be making any moves just yet. I want Rafe and his cronies fully collared before we take down Vant."

Chapter 24

Greyson

Pip yawned and tilted her head back. "Ugh. This is not ideal."

"What part of it?" I watched her as she was splayed out over a stone bench that I didn't imagine was that comfortable to cuddle with.

"Going before the *Regional Committee of Magic* at three in the morning to give our testimony about the events that happened." Pip groaned and rubbed her face.

I nodded because it seemed like she expected some kind of response from me, but truthfully I was only half paying attention to her. I was still too taken with the brightness of our bond.

It was just…*shining*.

I couldn't see it physically, but I could feel Pip at the back of my mind. It was somewhat similar to my consciousness of the Pack, but a thousand times stronger.

Her presence just hummed. Despite the nightmare of a

night we'd had, her spirits were high, her soul blinding in my mind. But she was *there*. The black hole that I'd experienced for the past few months was gone, completely extinguished by the fullness of everything that was Pip.

I think I understand why mates rarely outlive each other…it would be impossible to go back to the way it was before now that I know Pip like this.

"I get why they called the emergency meeting," Pip continued, unaware of my scrutiny. "This is the second one of Harka's relatives to target you, which is shady enough to involve the committee." She flipped onto her belly, and the ponytail her white hair was pulled back into—which was a little tangled from the night's events—flicked off her neck. The movement revealed the black paw print that was emblazoned on the back of her neck, which was probably the only thing that could have knocked me out of my reverie.

I grinned like an idiot and took a step closer so I could graze the mark with my fingers.

Pip paused for a moment at my touch before her entire body sagged—relieved by the comfort that flowed back and forth between us through the bond.

She was quiet for a moment, then her fingers twitched and she continued raving. "And yeah, Harka involved a task force from the Curia Cloisters, which does warrant committee attention even though she did it to keep everything by the books. But really, this couldn't wait until I at least got a nap—Greyson, are you even listening?"

"No," I said. "You're too distracting." I reached out through the bond and touched my consciousness to hers, grinning when I felt the flood of her emotions.

We really are bonded.

Pip groaned. "I swear you're worse than a teenage boy. Could you please *focus*?"

"Sure," I agreed. "On you?"

"Great. Wait. What? No!"

I grinned when she flipped around to scowl up at me. Her expression stayed dark for a grand total of five seconds before she held her arm up.

Able to guess what she wanted via the bond, I took her arm and pulled her into an upright position, then sat down on the bench next to her and wrapped my arms around her, scooping her against my chest.

"You can't ever do that again," she muttered into my shoulder.

"What? Pull you up?"

"No. Trade your life for mine like that."

"Ah."

"Will you promise?"

"Not a chance."

"*Greyson.*"

I slid my left hand up her spine and rested it on her shoulders so I could rub the back of her neck with my thumb. "Pip, our hearts are linked. I will always do what's best for you, even if that means endangering myself when you don't want me to."

"Maybe what's best for me is having you survive," Pip mutinously grumbled.

"That's what you think," I said. "But I do have a higher chance of surviving—and with your hunter training you stand a greater chance of being able to save me."

Our bond bubbled between us with Pip's unrest.

I flicked the tail of her ponytail, then kissed her forehead. "But that's probably going to be a fight we're going to have all our lives."

"You can bet on that."

"But we made it."

"We did." Pip pried herself off my chest so she could grin up at me. "And we're mates. Even though everyone said it was impossible."

I studied her for a moment, and a part of me dreaded the question I was about to ask. "You didn't feel forced?"

"To accept the bond? Nah." Pip started to yawn, then held a fist over her mouth to muffle it. "I told you from the start, I was angry about our bond because I didn't want us to have an unequal relationship. That's no longer an issue. It's just a little...different. Though it is going to take some time to get used to you just...*being* there." Pip squirmed a little, and I could feel it through the bond when she mentally spooked at the tightness of our bond. "But you were never the problem. Just like you decided not to reject the bond because it was me, I was so upset *because* it was you. Because I cared for you—and yes, eventually fell in love with you—and I didn't want to put you through that kind of pain."

I nodded slowly as I stared at Pip's lips, barely registering that I heard movement inside the council room.

Pip must have felt it through our bond, though, because she peered at the door. "They're almost ready for us, aren't they?"

"Yes," I confirmed. "But we still have time to cut and run."

"Why would we do that?"

"So we could go make out?"

"I'm spattered with blood and dried sweat, and I have the worst breath right now," Pip said.

"I wouldn't mind."

"*We're not making out.* At least not right now."

"How about when the meeting is over?"

"*Greyson,*" Pip said, sounding just as growly as a wolf.

I laughed, especially when I could feel Pip's shy delight poke through our bond.

How could I ever have even thought *about denying the bond?*

Regardless, it didn't matter. I had Pip, and our bond. She was safe, and the Pack was stronger than ever.

The region might be aware that Pip was a Wolf's Kiss, but it didn't matter. With my Alpha Powers, her Wolf's Kiss magic, and our bond, our Pack was going to become *impossible* to beat.

Chapter 25

Pip

T he night stretched on from the Regional Committee of Magic meeting to being involuntarily cross examined by a bunch of nosey Alphas who had shown up because 1. They wanted to know what had happened, and 2. They wanted to ask me (since Greyson was busy) questions about my supposedly impossible bond.

It took *hours*, but in the end Lynn was able to shoo them away, earning me about five minutes of rest, because sometime after six in the morning I got a message from Young Jack.

> *Vant's ranting in downtown Timber R.*
> *Can I bite him?*

For a second, I froze and almost dropped the styrofoam cup of coffee I had reluctantly made myself since the waiting room I was sitting in lacked both hot cocoa and mimosas.

I opened my mouth to shout for Greyson, but he flung Harka's office door open. "What's wrong?"

I blinked, and I'll blame the going 24 hours without sleep that it took me so long to realize he could feel my alarm through the bond. "Trouble back in Timber Ridge."

I held up my cellphone, but it buzzed again. This time with a message from Original Jack.

Pip—there's a bit of trouble on Main Street T.R.
Vant is here with five of his wolves—he's not doing anything, just shouting.
We have twenty-five wolves here since fringe members kept arriving all night, and Police Chief Henry has deployed all of T. R.'s police officers.
We don't expect much trouble, but thought you'd want to know.

"Sounds like it's time to head back," I said.

"I'll have Hector stay behind—could you ask Scarlett to stay, too?" Greyson asked. "We'll take everyone else back with us, but I'd like them to stay until Harka finishes with her statement."

"Got it. I'll text Lord Linus and ask him to meet us outside for transportation in…five minutes?"

Greyson nodded and disappeared back into Harka's office while I opened up my group text with the Fletching siblings.

Never a dull moment…but if Vant tries to launch an attack which keeps me up for another twenty-four hours with making statements and processing paperwork, I'm going to turn violent.

———

The sun was barely peeking up over the horizon, casting the brick buildings of downtown and their snow-covered roofs in a beautiful golden glow when we arrived in Timber Ridge.

I staggered through the gate, and it took my hunter senses a moment to settle from the confusing spin of magical teleportation before I could confirm Chase, Lady Chrysanthe, and Lord Linus had dumped us in the park just off Main Street.

Greyson exhaled sharply and slumped against me—he still didn't do great from the massive shift to his sensitive werewolf senses that came with moving through three locations in less than two minutes.

I wrapped an arm around his waist and tilted him against me—to steady him more than anything since he didn't put much of his weight on me—then peered back at the night mares and their riders.

"Thank you for the drop off, and for the help today. Er, I mean last night. Your help in both the fight, and in transporting us was, well, we wouldn't have made it in time," I said.

Chase nodded seriously. "Of course. I will always answer when the Pack calls."

"He means that," Lord Linus added. "He actually bolted in the middle of his shift—after notifying Queen Leila and King Rigel there was an emergency. I've never seen anything like it happen before."

"I am honored to be included as a friend of the Northern Lakes Pack and to be allowed to fight alongside you," Lady Chrysanthe said.

"Yes, you are," Lord Linus agreed. "Because you hope to marry into the Pack."

The fae lord laughed when Lady Chrysanthe turned bright pink.

Chase nudged his night mare so it once again faced the stone lined portal. "She does not hope, she intends."

Lord Linus stopped laughing. "Wait—intends?"

Chase rode through the gate.

"That wolf! Chrys, did you actually *confess* to him? Are you two a—to borrow the human colloquialism—a *thing* now?"

Lady Chrysanthe's pink blush threatened to turn red as she hurriedly urged her mount through the portal as well.

"Lady Chrysanthe!" Lord Linus paused long enough to mock salute Greyson and me before he and his night mare loped through the portal, which disappeared with all three members of the Night Court.

"I knew it wouldn't take much," I said, smug with satisfaction.

"Original Jack's text message said Vant is on Main Street?" Greyson kept his arm slung over my shoulders, but he did straighten up.

"Yep."

"Ember, I want your team with us," Greyson said. "Klancy, take your team back to the lodge and check the building. Then get Moira and River settled at their places and do a sweep of our territory. I want to make sure Vant hasn't already started anything while we take him down."

Klancy stalked off, the majority of the wolves following him. They went slow for Moira's and River's sakes—while they'd been dosed with fae potions, they were still recovering from getting shot.

Only Ember, Rio, Aeric, Wyatt, East, and Shania stayed with us. A smaller group, but probably the strongest fighters in the Pack.

"Does Vant even have enough wolves to start anything?" I asked. "The Low Marsh Pack is small. He's probably mistakenly banking on the idea that you'd be out of the picture shortly, and the Pack would go crazy."

"I'm hoping you're right." Greyson tugged on my shoulders, pointing us toward the parking lot and—beyond it—Main Street. "But after the past few weeks…we're not taking any chances."

The snow crunched under my boots, and I double checked my daggers as we stepped off the snow-covered park lawn and into the parking lot, which was gritty with sand and half-melted salt.

"Do you want your rifle, Hunter Sabre?" Radcliff asked.

"Nah—I still don't have replacement ammo," I said. "Plus, if a fight goes down, I'd be a bigger help if I used my Wolf's Kiss magic." I frowned at that reminder.

"Not too stoked you don't get to revel in blood and carnage?" asked Greyson.

I narrowed my eyes at him as we joined the sidewalk. "My preferred method was always my spelled ammo—not blood. But, yeah, just focusing on my magic during a fight goes against every other hunter sense I have."

"Instinct," Greyson said knowingly. "It can be a painful thing."

Ember made a half wheezing/half yipping noise that even I could interpret as laughter.

"She's making fun of you for when you were trying to hide the mate bond, isn't she?" I asked.

"Yep."

"Good. You deserve it. Here we go!"

We followed the curve of Main Street, slowing down when we saw Vant and his five wolves.

"—with Greyson gone, and Hector is only a beta, the Northern Lakes territory will be annexed by surrounding Packs, but it is obvious due to the close proximity of the Low Marsh territory with Timber Ridge, that the Low Marsh Pack will engulf Timber Ridge into our territory," Vant declared.

He was standing in the middle of the street, like an idiot, while his wolves were crowded on the sidewalk in their human forms, fidgeting in obvious anxiety as they peered from the ten or so Northern Lakes wolves, to the police officers leaning against their cars, to their ranting leader.

Vant slipped his hands into the pockets of his trousers, slightly messing with the fall of his suit coat—which fit him well enough to underline the breadth of his shoulders and give him an extra jolt of intimidation that I'm sure he used to advantage on his Pack based on the way they were pressing themselves against a brick storefront.

"When Timber Ridge is given over to the Low Marsh Pack, there will be changes," he said. "The welcome center will be replaced, and the wolf children will no longer attend school with *humans*," Vant said with revulsion.

Original Jack stood with his arms folded across his chest, talking to Police Chief Henry—whose moth-like eyebrows were wiggling up and down double the speed they normally did.

The Northern Lakes wolves had taken on their human forms, and a bunch of them turned in our direction before we reached them—either sensing Greyson's presence or hearing our footsteps.

Vant remained oblivious as Young Jack trotted up to us, a big grin splitting his face.

"Pip—and Alpha Greyson! Welcome home."

Young Jack tipped his head to Greyson—even though Greyson had his Alpha powers locked up so tightly I couldn't feel them at all. He then bounded up to me with the glee of a puppy, so I gave him a side hug, figuring it was better than a full on, impromptu Pomeranian Puppy Powerup.

Judging by his happy sigh, I must have still given him a pretty potent dose of my puppy pheromones—or maybe he was just looking forward to seeing Greyson mop the streets with Vant.

"Thanks, Jack. Any problems—besides Vant?" Greyson asked.

"Nope." Jack popped the p of the word and grinned. "I don't think Vant can even be considered a 'problem'. We just didn't move because Pip texted us to wait, and Chief Henry hasn't shot him because Mayor Pearl told him to stand his ground about five minutes ago and waddled off to City Hall. Not sure what she's up to."

We'd reached the police line-up by that point.

It was kind of cool to see, actually. The Northern Lakes werewolves—even the fringe members who didn't live in Timber Ridge—were standing with the police, leaning against the cars or talking to the humans in lowered tones.

They did stop whatever they were doing to bow their heads to Greyson—even the police officers, except Chief Henry, jolted a little into motion.

"Pip, Alpha Greyson!" Original Jack beamed. "I am glad to see you looking so well. Congratulations on the bond."

"Thank you—and thanks for holding the place together while we were gone." Greyson finally stepped away from me so he could deliver a slap to Original Jack's shoulders.

"Of course," Original Jack said. "Though, I hope you don't mind me asking, but could you take care of this quickly? The kids start walking to school by seven, and I don't want to give Vant any chances to hurt them."

Greyson patted his pants for his nonexistent phone. "Sure —this should only take a minute or two."

Vant didn't notice any of this—a testament of just how unchecked from reality he was, though we were downwind from him, so he was just deaf and blind, apparently.

"The Low Marsh Pack will, of course, accept any Northern Lakes packmates who wish to join. Though you will find our Pack is not so weak willed as the leadership that Alpha Greyson had—there will be no kindness, and humans are *not* our equals, nor will they be treated as such."

"Wow. I knew he was a creep, but I didn't know he was this bad," I said.

A younger police officer I recognized but didn't know personally crouched down to scratch East's ears. "Pretty sure he's been hiding this long as Alpha Greyson was around, and now that he thinks Alpha Greyson is dead, he's talking as big as he believes he's been all along," she said.

I tilted my head. "You know about Vant?"

"Sure," the police officer confirmed. "Since East got changed, Chief Henry has had us memorize information on all the Packs that directly surround the Northern Lakes territory—so we can spot them if they try to impede on Timber Ridge."

When I glanced up at Greyson he raised his eyebrows, and I felt a hint of surprise through our bond.

He didn't know about this either. Hmm…

I grinned a little, relaxing more and more by the moment as I watched our intermingling people. "Regardless, based on how the Low Marsh wolves look, something tells me this is going to be *very* rewarding."

The Low Marsh wolves were staring at Greyson—and me—with wide eyes and rapidly paling faces.

They would have backed away if they could have, but they'd already pressed themselves against the freezing bricks of a store.

"Supporters of Greyson's—like Beta Hector and Ember—will be exiled out of the Midwest to find a Pack in a different region," Vant continued. "Though Hunter Sabre will remain in Timber Ridge."

A Northern Lakes wolf—unable to keep it in any longer—laughed, then tried to cover it up with a cough.

Vant—who'd been scowling at the welcome center—spun around with a snarl, but froze when he saw Greyson and me standing with our packmates and the police.

"What?" Greyson said when Vant turned a sick hue of green. "Aren't you going to continue? You have so many great plans for Timber Ridge." Finally, Greyson let his Alpha powers uncurl.

"Impossible. They had you—I saw it with my own eyes—" Vant shut his mouth with a click so loud even I could hear it once Greyson's powers slammed into him.

His eyes widened, but Greyson's magic was so potent, it was holding Vant in place so he couldn't collapse to his knees like his mind was screaming at him to do to acknowledge the stronger Alpha.

Greyson's powers started to press in on the Northern Lakes wolves—I could feel the spirit of the Pack stiffen through our bond—so I tapped my Wolf's Kiss magic, giving them their own power boost that let them at least stand normally as Greyson's powers flared around us.

Young Jack fidgeted next to me, blinking in surprise, and Ember sat like a dog panting with smugness.

Greyson cracked a smile at me that was so slight it was more a hint of a curve than anything else, then turned his golden gaze—which was warm in color but harder than granite—back to Vant.

"Vant, you threatened my mate, my Pack, and our town." Greyson's voice was quiet, but unyielding—like a lake frozen by subzero temperatures. "You're going to pay retribution for this."

Before Greyson could continue, I heard the roar of a car engine.

A small, boxlike car that was a maroon color that hadn't been popular in cars for at least thirty years—pulled onto Main Street about two blocks up. The tires squealed as the back fish-tailed a little on some ice.

Since it wasn't seven o'clock yet, all the lights on Main Street were yellow. The car *gunned* it, driving down the center of the road and hurtling toward Vant.

I think I recognize that car, my mind bleated at me.

The car smashed into Vant, proving it had to be even older than my original estimation—and possibly with a bumper made of steel or something—because besides a slight dent, the car was fine and rolled up and over Vant. Though based on the way it bounced as it rolled over him, the suspension was probably going to be off.

The car screeched to a stop, and Vant—flat on the ground —groaned as he was face down into the pavement. He slowly sat up, coughing and moaning.

Wolves are tough, so while Vant was probably struggling to breathe and probably had a broken bone or two, there was no way he was suffering from internal bleeding or anything life threatening.

At least, he wasn't until the car started backing up and rolled over him again.

This time, Vant didn't try to get up, he just moaned into the dirty street.

The car's parking lights came on, and the front door creaked open as Mayor Pearl—recognizable with her bowl-cut curls and ever-present scowl—got out of the car.

Because of the cold weather she was wearing a long wool trench coat that fell to the calves of her slacks, but she still carried her umbrella as she marched up to Vant.

"You—you no good degenerate," she declared. "Will stay. Away. From. Our. Town's. Wolves!" She punctuated every emphasized word with a smack of her umbrella on Vant's head.

Vant whined and tried to roll away from her, but she determinedly followed him, still smacking him with her umbrella.

Chapter 26

Pip

Jaws dropped around me, but I broke into a loud whoop and clapped. "Go Mayor Pearl!" I shouted before breaking into a hunter whistle for celebration.

Mayor Pearl straightened up at the noise, adjusted her hold on her black umbrella, then marched in our direction.

Greyson glanced at a few of our packmates, and four Northern Lakes wolves trotted down the street—very wisely sticking to the sidewalk instead of risking jay walking in front of Mayor Pearl—then scraped Vant off the road, taking him into Northern Lakes custody.

Ember, Rio, and two human-shaped wolves headed for the Low Marsh wolves, who showed an interesting mixture of distress and relief as they watched their Alpha get dragged down the sidewalk, the toes of his dress shoes scraping the ground.

"Henry." Mayor Pearl wiped an imaginary fuzzy from her coat when she finally reached the line-up. "I dented the car running over some trash."

"That's fine, dear," Henry said. "I'll just pull it around and take it to the auto shop over my lunch break."

"Thank you."

"Have a good day at work." Henry—much taller than his petite wife—stooped over to kiss her wrinkled cheek. "Alpha Greyson, Hunter Sabre. Welcome back home." He winked at me, then slowly made his way to the still running car. When he got in and slammed the car door, Vant squealed.

Mayor Pearl rested the tip of her umbrella on the ground, and slightly leaned on it as she peered up at Greyson and me.

"Mayor Pearl," I said since neither of the city leaders seemed inclined to be the first one to speak. "I didn't know you had it in you! Way to go!"

Mayor Pearl sniffed. "He was threatening Timber Ridge —*and* its wolves. As deluded as he was, I didn't think a fine was going to make him rethink his life's choices. I opted to knock some sense into his silly skull." She narrowed her eyes as she peered up at Greyson. "Should I expect trouble from that loud, overly opinionated wolf woman for this?"

"You are referring to Pre-Dominant Harka?" Greyson asked. "No. It won't be an issue. Vant was clearly threatening humans. You're allowed to retaliate. It was our failing as wolves that we didn't act before you felt your actions were necessary."

Mayor Pearl nodded stiffly and seemed prepared to march onward, ignoring the chaos she'd caused in her wake.

I mashed my lips together as I looked from Greyson to Mayor Pearl.

No, I'm not going to let it end here. This was a big deal—Mayor Pearl stepped in for us.

The more I thought about it, this was the third time she'd helped us.

She'd sent officers when the Fletchings attacked the Pack, she'd blocked Harka from entering Pack territory with her sheer tenacity, and now she'd run over an *Alpha* for us.

Considering we acted more like we were locked in an uneasy truce when it came to the city, that was *a lot* to do on our behalf without bringing it up.

"Mayor Pearl." I took a couple of steps after her, but paused when she turned around. "You called the Northern Lakes Pack...Timber-Ridge's wolves?"

"Yes."

"Why?"

Mayor Pearl rested the tip of her umbrella on the ground again. "Because they are, aren't they? The Northern Lakes wolves are *our* wolves."

"Even if you fine us?" Greyson asked.

Mayor Pearl scowled. "Alpha Greyson. I would have thought you'd know me well enough by now: I'd fine my own children if they broke the law. No matter how much you care about a person, laws must be abided by or chaos will reign, and that won't do a lick of good for anybody!"

Amused, I glanced up at Greyson.

"The Northern Lakes wolves belong to Timber Ridge—the whole city knows it," Mayor Pearl continued. "And as long as I breathe, *nobody* is going to hurt them, or this city! I've seen to that since Alpha Hudson was a young man, and I'll still be seeing to it by the time the two of you spawn some children of your own!"

Now it was my turn to be shocked while Greyson smirked and leaned against me so our shoulders brushed.

"I understand, Mayor Pearl," Greyson said. "We wolves are lucky to have you."

"You are," Mayor Pearl said.

"Have a great day, Mayor Pearl," I called.

"I shall!" Then, with her umbrella resting on her shoulder, Mayor Pearl sallied off.

"If humans could be Alphas, she'd be the Pre-Dominant," I mused.

"Who are you kidding? She'd be the Dominant." Greyson curled an arm around my shoulders and drew me closer to his side.

I didn't protest because he radiated heat I could feel through my hunter jacket, and it was a pretty cold morning.

"Come on," Greyson said. "Let's head back to the lodge."

"What about Vant?"

"Chief Henry is going to hold him in one of the temporary jail cells with Northern Lakes wolves on a rotational guard basis."

"Great. Then let's go home. I want food. And maybe some popcorn."

"Whatever you want, mate."

———

Scarlett and Radcliff met us back at the lodge with an update on all the proceedings, but Harka didn't arrive in our territory —with Hector, and the remaining wolves in tow—until around three in the afternoon, with a little help from a Night Court night mare.

After sleeping for most of the morning, I'd woken up with the *need* to be back in my cottage, so Greyson, Radcliff, Scarlett, and Teresa had helped me pack up the cats and head back to my cottage where we'd done a bit of cleaning.

(Or rather where Radcliff, Scarlett, Teresa, and I did some cleaning. Greyson shoveled my front porch, but then he broke a cellphone when Hector called him and he'd forgotten to turn his ringtone onto vibrate, then spent quite a bit of time on Radcliff's borrowed phone, because I certainly wasn't lending mine to him since Lynn had texted me several of Phil's baby photos.)

"Are you sure I should start my hunter training with

daggers?" Teresa asked. She was seated at my small kitchen table, carefully paging through the Ward family journal.

"Yes," Radcliff said. "Daggers are a great basis for any number of weapons you can choose to specialize in. They also have a number of uses, and they are beginner friendly…relatively speaking."

Teresa turned a page in the journal. "Except Pip's taken multiple wolves down with a baseball bat, and that seems like it'd be easier to start with."

Scarlett finished washing the Bedevilments' food bowls and set them aside to dry. "You know, she has a point."

I scooted past her, sweeping up a few cat-hair-dust-bunnies that I'd missed earlier when I vacuumed. "Start with the daggers," I advised. "They'll teach you about balance, and give you the leverage you need against an enemy since you're smaller and not fully grown. Once you're more muscled and have more strength to your swing you can use baseball bats, and then from your dagger training you'll know where to aim to cause knockout hits."

"Yes, you need a proper foundation." Radcliff shut the door on my washing machine—where he'd just finished throwing in a load of towels—then turned to Teresa. "And in the meantime we can get you signed up for an online hunter safety course, and then we can practice target shooting, which is where the *real* fun happens!"

"See, your mother's Fletching blood runs deep in you," I joked. I closed the door to my bedroom—where Greyson was still on the phone—so our talking didn't disturb him. "Though, I'll admit, I prefer my rifle, too."

Radcliff cleared his throat and glanced back at Scarlett.

"We wanted to ask you about that," Scarlett said. "We enjoy our lives here in Timber Ridge."

"Okay." I nodded as I looked back and forth between the siblings.

"And since it seems that there will be a fourth hunter in the city," Scarlett grinned at Teresa, who giggled, "we were thinking perhaps this would be a good time to restructure."

I watched Radcliff casually pet Prince—who was frozen in shock that someone was daring to pet him—without seeming to notice he was doing it.

They're nervous. What is this about?

"What do you mean by restructure?" I put my broom away, a little spooked by their manner.

"Well." Scarlett folded her hands in front of her. "You're a legacy—the last of the Sabres and the Wards."

"Yes," I said.

"But the Fletchings have our little brother—who actually inherited the Fletchings' main magic—and the whole family," Scarlett said. "So…we were wondering…" She trailed off and slightly twisted her hands.

"Aw for crying out loud—you're taking too long," Radcliff said. "Pip, I want to be a Sabre, and Scarlett wants to be a Ward."

I blinked hard. "What?"

"You can legally adopt us into your family line—it happens all the time in hunter families, like our dad becoming a Fletch-ing," Radcliff said. "Since you'll be busy doing stuff as a Wolf's Kiss, Scarlett and I were thinking we could keep your families going."

I stared at them, trying to take in the sheer immensity of what they were asking for.

"We won't have your magic, but we could at least keep the names and traditions alive," Scarlett said. "And of course, any kids you have with Greyson who are born hunters could join either family and take over. We'd just be regular family members."

"I'm…honored you'd want to join my family—either fami-ly," I said, meaning it.

When I'd first been orphaned, there wasn't a single hunter family besides the Quillons who had offered to take me in. Because I was a legacy I couldn't be adopted into a family—like Scarlett and Radcliff were requesting—because I needed to keep my family names going.

But they're offering to join my family...so I won't be a lone hunter anymore.

I swallowed around the knot in my throat. "You'd really want to be a Sabre—and a Ward?"

"Yes," the siblings said together.

"We've been thinking about it for a while." Radcliff gave Prince one last pat—the cat immediately set about licking that spot clean when he finished. "We love it here, and we love working together as hunters with wolves."

"But we're selfish enough that we don't want to go find our own Packs," Scarlett said. "We love the Northern Lakes Pack."

"Of course," Teresa piped in. "That's because they're the best!"

Scarlett grinned at Teresa, but Radcliff kept his eyes on me.

"What do you think, Pip?" he asked.

I had to mash my lips together to keep from laughing in joy.

For so long I'd felt stretched between two worlds, with no one walking with me.

Now I had it all—a mate, a Pack, and a hunter family.

"Yes," I said. "I'd *love* for you both to join my family."

Scarlett and Radcliff pulled me into a three-person hug.

"I'm so excited!" Scarlett said. "We already talked to our mom about it and learned how to do it."

"There's a lot of paperwork," Radcliff sourly said as he stepped out of the hug.

"Does this mean *I* could be a Sabre or a Ward?" Teresa asked.

I laughed. "In a couple years, once you've gotten your hunter certification, yes. Of course you can."

There was a knock on my front door—the prickle of my hunter senses said outside were several werewolves, who must have come under Greyson's direction because he popped my bedroom door open and was making tracks for the front door.

The door opened, letting a blast of cold air in, and Aeric, Wyatt, and Shania slipped inside.

"Woah, that's cold." Shania rubbed her arms and shivered. "I am actually feeling these temperatures!"

"It's not that bad," Aeric said.

"Pipe down, Canada," Wyatt said.

"Alpha, we're here to tell you Pre-Dominant Harka is almost here," Shania said.

I paused, limply holding my broom. "Harka? Here?"

"She wanted to talk," Greyson said. "I thought this was a suitable place."

"Oh, sure. Invite the most important werewolf in the Midwest over to my dusty cottage that I haven't lived in for weeks," I said. "That sounds great."

"You know, I'm really glad even though you two are mates and you get mushy sometimes, you still act the same," Aeric said.

"That's because—if you're paying careful attention—their fighting is flirting," Wyatt said.

"If you're going to stand around and make jokes, can you at least sweep or something?" I asked.

"Sorry, we can't. We're here to deliver the news and then get out," Shania said. "Though Ember asked us to bring Teresa to the lodge."

"Okay." Teresa carefully closed the Ward family journal and put it on a spot where one of the Bedevilments wouldn't knock it off the table, claw it, or damage it in one creative way or another.

"We'll come with." Scarlett retrieved her coat, hat, and gloves. "It wouldn't do for hunters to stand in on regional were-wolf business."

"Pip is going to," Aeric said.

Radcliff put his hat on, then handed Teresa hers before he took his cellphone back from Greyson. "Because she's the Alpha's mate and a Wolf's Kiss."

"Hmm," Aeric said. "Does that mean she gets to come with us on Pack runs, now? And what about Pomeranian Puppy Powerups? I still want to get those."

"Aeric," Wyatt said. "Stop bothering Mom and Dad, or you're going to get us grounded. Come on!"

Wyatt yanked his friend back outside by the collar of his shirt, and the wolves and bundled up hunters made their way outside.

The door was closed for a grand total of five seconds before it opened again, this time admitting Pre-Dominant Harka into my cottage.

"Hello, Harka." I hastily washed my hands as the Pre-Dominant shed her boots and brushed snow from her dark hair.

"Good afternoon, Alpha Greyson, Hunter Sabre." Although Harka smiled, there was a tiredness to her eyes, and her smile was wan at best.

"Can I get you something? Hot cocoa or...hot cocoa?" I glanced back at my cupboards and winced. "Sorry—I'm not much of a tea or coffee person."

"That's very kind of you, but no," Harka said. "I'm here to give you something I owe you: an explanation."

Greyson led Harka over to my kitchen table—which had three chairs and just enough room for all of us to sit at.

Harka planted her elbows on the table and threaded her fingers together, then briefly pushed them against her chin.

"I'm sure it didn't escape your notice that both Aspen and Rafe cited family as the reason for their actions."

"Yes," Greyson said.

"I imagine you think it has something to do with loyalty to me?" Harka prompted.

Greyson stared at Harka, and I shrugged.

Harka rubbed her eyes. "While my niece and nephew love me, it's their parents they love more than anything else—their mother specifically—and to a detrimental degree when they perceive others as a threat to her."

"I thought their parents died," I said. "Weren't they mates?"

"Gen—my brother-in-law—died when Aspen and Rafe were teenagers," Harka confirmed. "My sister, Cedar, didn't die…she went feral."

I shut my eyes, momentarily feeling compassion for Aspen and Rafe.

No matter how screwed up they were, no one should have to watch their parent lose their mind, humanity, and their very selves until only a mindless beast remained.

That would be enough to traumatize anyone.

I jumped when Greyson set his hand on my thigh. It took a moment before I felt his grim determination through our bond.

No, neither of us will die until we're old and ready to go. Greyson's a wolf, and I'm a hunter. There's not a Pack in the world that can take us on.

Slowly, I slipped my hand under the table and set it on Greyson's, feeling weirdly shy—which was only compounded when I felt Greyson smugly purr through our bond, though he quickly sobered up when he returned his attention to Harka.

"I'm sorry for your loss," Greyson said. "Though I had heard as much prior to coming to the Midwest. You had her mercifully killed?"

Chapter 27

Pip

Harka took a deep breath. "And now we expose my own shortcomings, and perhaps the reason *why* Aspen and Rafe felt it was fine to sacrifice so much for family. No, I did not. Since I was the Pre-Dominant, I used my power and influence to have Cedar hidden. She's still alive—and still feral—in a secure facility owned by my Pack."

"*What?*" Greyson said.

"But that means...she's been alive and feral for *years?*" I asked.

Going feral from your mate dying wasn't a temporary fit like a dose of wolfsbane. It was permanent. If Cedar was going to be one of the rare mates who survived her husband's death, she would have pulled through within *days*.

But it's been years...

"Why would you do that to her?" I asked.

Harka massaged her forehead. "Because I was too cowardly to let her go. Colton—my husband, though he was only my beta at the time—warned me not to do it. But Cedar and I had been through so much together. I just couldn't make the order. Rafe and Aspen knew, of course. They'd grown up in our Pack, so I didn't hide anything from them."

Harka paused. "They understood how final it was and knew she wasn't coming back...but while I've felt guilt for Cedar, they've been determined to keep her alive no matter the cost." She glanced at Greyson. "I hadn't understood just how deep that desperation went, until Rafe made his move."

"But I still don't understand why that would make them target Greyson," I said. "He has nothing to do with this."

"Except when he takes over as Pre-Dominant, I'd have to tell him about Cedar," Harka said. "As the Pre-Dominant I can keep Cedar alive, but since she's feral I'd *have* to inform Greyson once I leave my position, as the Pre-Dominant is kept abreast of all ferals in the region. And I've known since I first met Greyson that he would undoubtedly order me to have Cedar killed."

Greyson said nothing and unflinchingly met Harka's gaze.

"I don't know for certain, but I *think* Aspen was hoping that if she could discredit you, maybe I would be inclined to choose Rafe as my replacement," Harka said. "At the very least she wanted me to push out my plans to leave my position."

"Cedar is why you want to retire even though you're so young," I said.

Regional Committee member was typically pretty close to a life-long position. At the very least the member always served until they were of advanced age, but Harka looked like she was maybe in her mid to late forties.

"Yes," Harka slowly said. "I've always known that keeping her alive is a sign that I'm not the right wolf for this position. About the time I was considering who to choose as my replacement, you were brought in—Greyson—because of Pip. You were the strongest in the Midwest—you had to be for the Pack's sake—and I couldn't find a fault with you, so I resigned myself to Cedar's fate. Aspen and Rafe apparently did not."

"But Rafe knew you wouldn't make him the Pre-Dominant," I said. "He mentioned it himself."

"Yes," Harka agreed. "But as he's my heir, he was privy to my second choices after Greyson: Kim Seo-Jun or Maya Williams."

"Having met both of them, neither strike me as being willing to let ferals live," Greyson said.

"No, but they aren't as strong as you, and they're aware of it, so they'd have to politically bend and make sure they had allies backing them up. That's where Rafe planned to bargain with them," Harka said. "My Pack is still one of the strongest in the Midwest. If he offered to politically back the new Pre-Dominant in exchange for his mother's life, it'd be an excellent bargain."

I narrowed my eyes as I recalled one of the meetings with Harka. "Rafe did try feeling you out, Greyson, when the Alphas started showing up. He mentioned ferals, and you gave him a hard no. That was when Alphas started attacking me."

"That was also when Rafe and I found out you two were mates. According to his private phone, text, and his secret email that my people found, after that meeting Rafe contacted the other Alphas, seeking to capture Pip. I imagine he thought she'd be the easier target," Harka said.

"Did he send out the email—the one about me being a Wolf's Kiss?" I asked.

"No—and yet yes, in a way," Harka said. "We found emails from the address used to email the Alphas in a separate, private email account of his. They appear to be from Aspen. Best we can tell from the emails is that Aspen temporarily stole the flash drive after the Fletching fight, copied the files from the drive, then put it back. She set up the email about you to send at a later date as a last-chance effort in case she failed to ruin

Greyson's reputation. An email to Rafe's secret account makes it obvious he knew the pre-scheduled email existed, and he gave Aspen the email addresses. He is somewhat guilty, but it still was not entirely his idea."

Those siblings…how could they spend so much time with Harka and come out so horrible?

But in a way, I could see why they thought and operated the way they did.

Wolves were generally some of the most straightforward of supernaturals—it was their nature. But in watching Harka bend the rules for the sake of her sister—their mother—it probably taught them a lot of lessons Harka wouldn't have wanted them to interpret that way—like the dogmatic way they both insisted family came before everything.

No wonder Harka was so upset with Rafe at the warehouse. When she told him "she wouldn't have wanted this" she was talking about Cedar.

"I think he was still hoping he could sway you to Magiford, Pip, until he learned you and Greyson were mates," Harka added.

Greyson leaned over slightly to pet the top of Princess's head. She was sitting next to the table, looking cross—probably because none of us had any cups for her to knock off the table. She was so shocked by the sign of affection that she sucked her head into her shoulders and just froze while Greyson unthinkingly scratched the top of her head.

"I can understand the heartbreak," Greyson said. "But I'm disappointed in you, Harka, that you didn't realize Rafe was capable of this, given you must have realized why Aspen did what she did."

Greyson settled his golden gaze on Harka, who stared down at her hands.

"Pip could have gotten hurt," Greyson said. "And if she had been, I would have started a war. All because Rafe talked the Alphas up to it because he didn't dare ask me to my face, or —the far more obvious path to success—suck up to Pip and get *her* to ask me to spare Cedar."

I briefly reflected on that idea and realized it was a much better plan than anything Rafe or Aspen had enacted.

I am way more of a bleeding heart than Greyson. If Rafe had told me about his mom—especially given she's feral because her mate died—I would have endlessly petitioned Greyson to let her live until he eventually gave in. Without any bloodshed, or one-man revenge teams. Just pure annoyance.

Hmm. This was probably an example of why Greyson was as powerful as he was.

I'd better stay on my toes. There is no way I'm going to let him win all the mental warfare games in the future. Maybe I should take up sudoku puzzles or something to keep my brain fit.

I shook the errant thought out. "It's also disturbing that both Rafe's and Aspen's gut-reaction, plans of attack always involved violence. Exactly *what* did you do to ensure Cedar's safety, Harka?"

"Nothing that involved bloodshed—except my own Pack's," Harka said. "Cedar has attacked a few of our members—particularly before I found the safest method to house her. But I will admit I have been brutal in my set downs of anyone seeking to become the Pre-Dominant—before Greyson came to the Midwest—because I knew I couldn't afford to lose. Even so, I will admit this is my fault—and my responsibility."

Harka leaned back in her chair and finally met Greyson's eyes. "Obviously I'm not fit to lead the Midwest wolves, given my history of making exceptions for family. This is your last chance to decide, Greyson: do you want to be Pre-Dominant?"

Greyson looked at me.

"What?" I asked.

"We're mates," Greyson said. "That means this is also your

choice. Particularly because more responsibilities would fall on you and Hector whenever my presence would be required in Magiford."

Woah, that's a good point. Do I want to take on more responsibilities for the Pack?

I thought of Shania and the other newly-turned wolves, and Teresa and her aspiration to become a hunter, and even the way Mayor Pearl checked in on me more than I wanted at the welcome center.

Even if Greyson turned down the position, I think I'm going to be more involved in Pack operations as a result of everything. And I know, now, that I can rally the Pack similarly to the way an Alpha can. So... would it be so bad?

I shifted uncomfortably in my chair. "I think Hector and I can handle it. The biggest issue would be that we'd need to make some kind of agreement with the Night Queen so you can come and go as needed through portals—because having a second residence in Magiford is not an option. I am not dealing with a bunch of disappointed wolves when they want to go for a run and you're staying in Magiford for a week."

Maybe I can get everyone to make the welcome center be the new main location for Pack issues when Greyson is out of the area.

As a plus, if we were ever attacked, Mayor Pearl and her car were only a few blocks away.

"An understandable concern," Greyson said. "I'm sure we can work something out with the Night Queen—she still openly states her Court's need for funding."

I felt him mentally lean into our bond—probably trying to make sure I wasn't lying to him.

The feeling of just having him...*there* was still so new and foreign to the absolute control my hunter senses put over everything. I physically jumped, surprising Princess so she hissed and ran off, her paws tapping against the wooden floors.

Greyson flinched in return, and though his expression didn't change, I caught a slight clenching of his jaw.

I tried to reach for him through the bond, and when we brushed I attempted to push my acceptance—and even a little bit of glee at the thought of making all the werewolves trek to the welcome center whenever they needed something.

Greyson grinned—I think more because I had mentally reached for him than that he was particularly worried that I'd hate the idea of being left in charge.

Harka patiently sat in her chair, letting us wordlessly exchange…whatever you wanted to call all of this.

"There will be more logistics to work out—and we'll need to tell the Pack—before I am confident in accepting the role," Greyson said. "*However*, I want to make it clear that I'm not coming on as a replacement, but a protégé for at least six months and up to a year, possibly even two."

Harka blinked. "Really? I would have thought you'd want to replace me as soon as possible."

"Besides the failure of your niece and nephew and your weakness for family," Greyson acidly said, "you have proven to be a good leader for the wolves. As long as I—or others—are in a position to make sure that weakness doesn't affect your actions, I am satisfied. Besides, more than anything, we need time."

"Why?" Harka asked. "Nothing will change—you'll still be the Pre-Dominant."

"Ahh, except, the region just found out I'm a Wolf's Kiss in November." I raised a finger and slightly wagged it. "This week they're going to find out Greyson and I are mates—we had to report as much to the Regional Committee of Magic, and they publish their meeting minutes for the community. That's two power boosts to the Northern Lakes Pack in the span of two months, when the Pack was already well known for its change survival rate and size," I said. "If Greyson becomes Pre-Dominant now, that's way too much of a power climb in just a few months. It'll make some wolves panic, while others will believe something sketchy has happened, maybe that Greyson tried to force you out."

Harka whistled. "I did not think of that possibility, but it is true. If I left and Greyson became Pre-Dominant—no matter the reason—more than a few Packs would rebel." She glanced at Greyson. "I'm impressed you two were able to realize that in such a short span."

Greyson shrugged. "Actually, I hadn't been thinking of that at all—though Pip is correct. I was referring to the fact that I know almost no shifters excluding werewolves, and if I am to represent them on the Regional Committee of Magic, I'll need time to meet them and better understand what I'm dealing with, as well as your wisdom in how to deal with them."

"Ahh, yeah that's a point I hadn't thought of," I said. "Nice thinking."

Greyson's expression relaxed into a slight curve of his lips that had the faintest hint of his cocky grin. "I'm the wolf, and you're the hunter. Between the two of us we'll have all fronts covered."

Oh, yikes. That smile is going to kill me one day—look away! Look away before I agree to do something stupid!

I cleared my throat and pointedly looked at Harka with a smile.

"I can do that," Harka said. "If it would make you feel better, I can hire on one of your wolves as a sort of auditor to ensure my actions are above the books. But…" She hesitated.

"You're still concerned about Cedar," I guessed.

Harka briefly shut her eyes.

I saw Greyson's slip of a smile snuff out, and as he rolled back his shoulders, I knew what he was going to say.

It's so sad…but Cedar won't come back—her mate died. And no one can reach a feral wolf besides their mate…except…

"Leave her for a few months," I impulsively said.

Greyson frowned at me, and Harka furrowed her eyebrows in surprise.

"I'm sorry, what?" Harka asked.

I glanced between the two Alphas. "Leave Cedar for now. Rafe is going to be imprisoned, there are a lot of adjustments in the future, and this has been an emotionally rough time for everyone here. We can push it off a few months, and deal with it in the future."

"I appreciate the sentiment, but this was my mistake," Harka said. "If I deserve to even be an Alpha anymore, I need to—"

"Four months," I said. "Maybe six. Come summer, we can talk about it again."

Greyson stared at me, and I swear between our bond and his eyes it felt like he was reading my heart.

Maybe he was, because he shrugged. "Six months," he said. "Then we'll talk about it again."

Through our bond, I felt his absolute confidence in me pulse, and it warmed my entire body.

I fretted about the bond for absolutely no reason.

Yes, Greyson still had places I couldn't follow him—like his position as Pre-Dominant, and Pack runs—but this was enough.

We'll see about that.

It wasn't Greyson's voice in my head, more like the idea of his thoughts.

I twitched in surprise, and Greyson's cocky smile was back in full force, which let me *know* it was his doing.

I rolled my eyes at his good humor, then turned my attention back to Harka. "Keeping all of this in mind, I'm sure there will be lots of logistics?"

"Yes," Harka said. "I'll start by having you attend my monthly meeting with the shifter leaders, Greyson…"

I stood up and walked to the kitchen, intending to make some hot cocoa, if not some popcorn—after that kind of conversation, I needed it.

I stopped on the way to crouch down and pet Prince, who was squishing one of his catnip mice.

This has been an ugly story with so much beauty in it for Greyson and me, I thought as I tickled under Prince's chin. *Please, please let me make it beautiful for someone else, too.*

Chapter 28

Pip

I pulled my knit hat farther down my head, then twitched the braid I'd tucked my white hair back into as I tried to distract myself.

Running gloves, check. Winter-worthy hiking boots, check.

I adjusted the zipper of my hunter jacket and made sure my gloves were tucked into my sleeves.

Prince and Princess sat on the couch, watching me with their usual judge-y expressions.

"I'm overthinking this, aren't I?" I asked them.

Neither responded.

I shifted my weight from one foot to the other as my hunter senses intensified, creating such a bright and minty sensation in my mind that I could practically taste it. As such, I wasn't too surprised when something scratched at my front door.

I took a shaky breath, then winked at the Bedevilments. "Don't wait up for me."

I opened the door and stepped outside into the cool night

air, my breath turning into silvery puffs that looked like miniature clouds in the soft glow of the full moon.

Greyson leaned into my hip, radiating warmth through
both his body and our bond.

I brushed the top of his head, then had to hold in a gulp as
I stepped off my front porch with him, joining the Pack on my
lawn.

There were at least seventy wolves present—the most I'd
ever seen on a Pack run.

But when Greyson made the call that I'd be joining the
Pack on my first run ever the week of Christmas, fringe
members from all over the territory came in addition to the
core Pack.

Aeric, Wyatt, Shania, Hector, Ember, East, Jack, Moira,
River, Rio—even Chase—were present.

The wolves silently watched me—motionless except for the
way light reflected off their eyes, creating an odd glow.

Greyson glanced up at me again as he stalked along by my
side. I left my hand on his shoulders when we stopped and
stood before the Pack.

The hair on the back of my neck prickled as my hunter
magic—unused to being the center of so much werewolf attention—spiked.

*Maybe this was a mistake. Maybe I was just being an idiot for feeling
like I didn't belong to the Pack because I'd never been on a run. This whole
thing is stupid. It's a bad idea. I—*

In perfect synchronization, Aeric and Wyatt tipped their
heads back and howled, their voices arcing high in a friendly
call.

Chase added his low howl in, and East, Jack, and Shania
were a breath behind—finding a natural harmony.

The whole Pack joined in, all of them raising their noses to
the sky and closing their eyes as they howled for me—not the
call of the hunt that had chased after me in our practices, and

not the happy yips of those excited by the prospect of a Pomeranian Puppy Powerup.

This was the song of greeting—of welcoming a packmate home.

I exhaled in relief, my breath a little shaky as my eyes felt hot and itchy with emotion.

Greyson gently leaned into me, poking his black nose into my belly, before he too raised his muzzle and added his voice to the choir.

Greyson's howl didn't join the others. It matched the song, but it stuck out, going high and low in a call I felt through our mate bond.

He's calling to me.

I hesitated, filled with the need to add my voice to the mix, but for all my joy at being included, I wasn't a wolf. I didn't want to howl. Instead, I followed my gut and yanked off one of my gloves so I could fit my fingers to my mouth and performed a hunter whistle—one that was long and high-pitched that was typically used to call out an ally.

The wolves molded their song around my whistles, and it was shocking to hear just how well it all meshed—as if the beautiful but eerie wolf howls needed the piercing hunter whistle to ground them and bring the song back.

When I felt the song winding down I stopped my whistle and replaced my glove. Greyson cut off his own note, then he nudged me and started trotting down my short driveway.

I followed him, and when we got to the spot where my driveway joined the gravel path that turned into a road, the rest of the Pack finished howling and joined us.

We started at a jog, the Pack finding their spots around us.

Aeric and Wyatt loped next to me while Shania and Ember stayed behind Greyson and me.

Young Jack shot out to the front, where he was shortly

joined by East—who body slammed him when Jack didn't notice Moira and almost ran into her.

Hector roamed—I think he was filling in for Greyson as he'd sometimes be out in front, and other times slow down and drift to the back to check on any stragglers.

River released a happy yip that a few other packmates mirrored. She stopped briefly to sniff a patch of snow, then ran to catch up, almost ramming into Rio when she raced past him.

Besides the occasional yip and barks of the Pack, the only noise was the tap of my hiking boots and their paws on the frozen ground.

I found my rhythm, my breath evening out as my hunter stamina kicked in. At this pace I could keep up with the wolves for an hour easy, but I knew they sprinted at times, so I wasn't positive how long I was truly going to last.

I felt Greyson mentally lean into our bond, feeling me out.

When Hector surged past us on one of his checks, Greyson huffed at him.

Hector gave a short little howl before he burst past East and Jack—taking the lead. He split off from the road, leading us into the underbrush.

While I had good night vision, I faltered for a moment or two as I followed the wolves into the forest—passing through the crosshatch shadows of bare trees, and slipping under the branches of tall pines, firs, and spruce trees.

I could see the branches and roots in the ground, and physically everything was fine, but it wasn't as easy of a run, and the wolves were starting to speed up.

It knocked my cadence off for a moment, until I felt my hunter magic make an abrupt reverse, and my Wolf's Kiss powers started flowing, and it had a strange, werewolf inflection to it.

I couldn't say exactly what it did, except just like the way it made the wolves *more*—larger, stronger, etc—I also felt…more.

Sounds were louder, the icy air almost had a sweet taste to it I hadn't noticed before—though that might have been the mental high I was riding.

When I saw the large shape of a fallen tree trunk, I was able to easily boost myself over it. It wasn't with the ease that Greyson and the others leaped over it, but I managed it more easily than I would have by myself.

I laughed as I kept up with the wolves.

We'd had a melt two days before, so the ground had only a dusting of snow, and the trees hadn't yet gathered much frost on their branches in the cold, clear night. There weren't many stars in the sky—the moon shone too brightly for that—but the night was inexpressibly beautiful, with no wind and the air soft and muted and the feeling of the Pack surrounding me.

That's what's different—the Pack!

Usually, my Wolf's Kiss magic drew from within me and spread to them. But now, I could feel it drawing upon the Pack and applying to *me*.

It's taking their strength and leveraging it for me—that's why I can keep up more easily!

Aeric playfully rammed his side into my hip.

Greyson snarled at him a little, but I grinned, tapped Greyson on the shoulder, then ran faster.

Aeric's yip turned high like laughter, and Greyson huffed as he raced after me, kicking snow into the air.

But if I can draw on their abilities for myself…can I do it for others, too?

I locked my legs for a moment, the thought blooming in my mind.

Rio gave me an annoyed *"Aroo"* when he almost rammed me from behind, while Shania circled around me, wagging her tail.

The Pack whirled around me like a canine hurricane, and I slowly turned in the direction of the lodge. "Sorry, I want to try something. Come on!"

———

We arrived at the lodge—a few of the wolves singing every so often, marking our progress through the forest.

When we popped into the meadow I could feel the confusion—Greyson's through the bond, and even a bit of the Pack's puzzlement through his own reaction.

I was practically chortling as I raced up to the lodge.

Most of the Pack stayed behind, except Shania.

I think—somehow—she knew what I was doing, because she yipped and howled in excitement, getting the rest of the Pack riled up.

The door creaked on its hinges when it opened. "Pip?" Original Jack stood in the doorway, his face cast in shadow by the warm light of the entryway behind him. "What are you doing here?"

"Get everyone inside to put on their warm clothes and boots, and come out here," I said.

"Are you sure about this? There could be a lot of hurt feelings." Original Jack paused and slightly tilted his head. "Although…you've got that look in your eye—the one that says you're a hunter."

"Because I am," I said. "Please, Jack?"

"Okay. We'll be out shortly." Original Jack pulled the door shut and disappeared inside.

I clapped my hands and hopped a few steps in my glee. Shania waited with me—her tail wagging wildly.

I scratched her back for her, then dug my cellphone out of my pocket and made a call to the Fletchings.

By the time Original Jack had gotten everyone—from the

Fated

kids like Teresa to the adults like Noah and Original Jack himself—in their winter things, Scarlett and Radcliff jogged out of the woods, dressed in their hunter gear.

"We left our car parked on the road in," Radcliff said. "What's up?"

"Is something wrong? I thought tonight was the big night you were supposed to join the Pack on a Pack run?" Scarlett peered at the swarm of wolves, who were standing silently in the moonlight.

"Everything's great," I said. "Maybe even wonderful. Now...line up!"

"Line up? Why?" Tucker asked—though he and Amelia moved to stand next to Radcliff and Scarlett.

"Isn't it enough to be the most special-est girl in the Pack, or do you need us all to witness how *amazing* you are?" Olivia scoffed. She was wearing a headband that was definitely going to leave her cold since it didn't cover the top of the head, but hey—it was her choice to freeze.

Greyson growled and flashed his teeth, which made Olivia immediately shut up.

I absently patted Greyson's back as I ignored the catty teenager and watched the last of the humans—including Noah, Original Jack carrying Rory, and finally, Teresa—leave the house.

Teresa shut the door, but she came down the stairs at a turtle speed, her misery obvious in the way she dragged her booted feet and hung her head.

My heart twisted in my chest.

But it's going to work. I'll make it work!

Teresa glanced back at the lodge as everyone else lined up, her shoulders stiff.

"Line up," I repeated as I approached Teresa. "Hey." I rested both of my hands on her shoulders—I could barely feel

331

her through the thick cushion of her winter jacket. "Do you trust me?"

Teresa blinked. "Of course."

"And you know I love you, right?"

"Yeah."

"Then trust me—as a fellow hunter. I wouldn't drag you out here for nothing. Okay?"

Teresa paused a second then nodded, her dark eyes solemn in the moonlight.

After what happened to her, it's amazing she can trust anyone outside her family.

I impulsively hugged her and clenched my teeth so hard I could feel it in my jaw.

This is going to work. Not because it's going to make any difference for me, but because it will change so much for the better in the Pack. It's not about me, it's about the Pack.

"Pip?" Teresa said into my hunter jacket.

I squeezed her again—maybe there was something to these powerup hugs after all—then stepped back. "You're Pack," I said.

I walked down the line of humans, coming next to Rory and Original Jack. "You're Pack—both of you." Next was Olivia. "You're Pack."

I continued on, telling each human that they were Pack. It wasn't so much for their sake as for the sake of my magic. I was trying to nudge my magic into remembering that just because they were human, didn't mean they weren't Pack.

My palms grew clammy inside my hunter gloves, and I lowered the zipper of my jacket as my rapidly spiking worry that this may not work made me sweat.

I stood stone still, paralyzed with the fear that it wouldn't work, when Greyson sat down next to me and pressed his nose into my hip.

I dropped my hand over his shoulder, and I could feel his reassurance through our bond.

He didn't fully know what I was planning, but he had a hunch. And even as I looked into his white, canine face, I could feel his unshakable faith in me.

You can do anything—you're my *mate.*

I nodded at him, inhaled, then reached for my Wolf's Kiss magic. But instead of unspooling it from myself and throwing it to the wolves, I threaded my magic through the wolves and pulled it back to me, then turned to the humans.

Please work. Please work. Please work.

I stretched my fingers wide as I mentally draped the magic over the humans.

It has to work. It has to work. It has to work.

I held my breath, smiling slightly when I felt the magic stick to them—now I could only pray that it would take.

"Pip?" Original Jack asked. "What are you—wow." He paused and tilted his head back, rapidly blinking as he looked around the meadow.

Amelia spun in a circle. "I can *see.* It's dark, but I can see!"

Just a little more…

I poured more of my magic on the humans. "Hey Teresa," I called. "Want to go for a run?"

Teresa took a shaky step, then another.

My throat squeezed as I waited—*hoping.*

Teresa took off, running faster than any human normally would, her steps sure as she raced around Rio, who howled in joy for her.

I turned to watch her, barely noticing when Greyson slipped away.

Amelia, then Tucker, and—shockingly—Olivia were just moments behind her.

Amelia's parents bounded up to her, and she kept pace

with them, my Wolf's Kiss powers flowing through her to give her enhanced speed and night vision.

"Pip…"

I turned around and saw tears in Original Jack's eyes.

He'd set Rory down—who was playing with his parents in their wolf form. Since he was young he wasn't as fast as everyone else, but both he and his parents were delighted—he giggled like crazy as he ran between them, swaying wildly back and forth in the snow suit he was wrapped up in.

I slowly approached Original Jack with a little grin. "Do you like it?"

"It's your magic?" he asked.

"Yep," I said. "It doesn't have a ton of use—as far as I can tell, it just affects night vision—possibly daytime vision—speed, stamina, and maybe a touch of reflexes. It doesn't give you werewolf strength, and we'll have to be careful because it absolutely does *not* give you the werewolf healing speed," I said.

"But we can run with the Pack," Original Jack said. "Teresa will be able to run with her parents, and I…"

I smiled up at the man who'd done so much for the Pack—including me. "Yep. You'll be able to run with your wife," I finished for him.

Original Jack opened his mouth, but the few tears that dripped from his eyes were too much. His shoulders shook, and he took in a ragged breath.

I wrapped my arms around the older man. "Thank you—for everything."

Original Jack patted my back, but before he could say anything in return, a gray and white swirled wolf rammed his side: his wife.

I laughed as the two sprinted off together.

"Us, too?" Although Scarlett phrased it as a question, based on the way Radcliff was jumping up and down behind her, they could feel the misty touch of my magic.

"Of course," I said. "You're Pack—and family."

Radcliff pumped his hand in the air and hollered. Scarlett's smile was smaller, but no less happy.

"Thank you," she said.

"Come on, let's try this out!" Radcliff elbowed her before he took off running. Scarlett was a second behind him, but she caught up fast and yanked him by the collar of his hunter jacket—momentarily choking him—so she could take the lead.

East and Young Jack loped up to them, playfully circling around them.

They ran past more of the Pack, which was when I caught sight of Ember and Hector playing with their three kids. Teresa was laughing, her face lit up with joy as she ran, able to catch up to Ember as her mother tried to dart to the side.

"Are you ready?"

I turned around in time to see Greyson trotting down the stairs, shrugging on a light jacket. He must have retrieved the jacket—and the black boots he was wearing—from the lodge.

"For what?" I asked.

Greyson's laughter came out with a puff of mist. "To run!"

Shania immediately howled, lifting her nose to the sky. Wyatt, Aeric, and East copied her, starting up the wolf song once again.

I chewed on my lip as I eyed Rory and the younger kids. "We can't bring the children—I'm at my limit with everyone standing around like this, and it's going to be harder to keep everything up when we start running."

"I'll stay behind to watch them," Original Jack started to offer.

"No."

"Nah."

I swiveled, peering from Olivia and Tucker to Moira—who was standing on the porch of the lodge wearing the bag-like, shapeless dress spun for her by her fae bracelet.

"The three of us will handle it," Moira announced, nodding to Tucker and Olivia.

"Are you certain?" Original Jack asked.

Olivia gave a teenager shrug that was full of attitude, but there was no mistaking the love in her voice. "There will be more runs in the future," she said. "And you've held *all* of us when we had to stay behind while our parents ran. We can wait."

Original Jack swept both Tucker and Olivia up in a hug.

Around us, the wolves howled, and I could feel my magic kick it up a notch.

The younger kids dutifully ran back to the lodge, Rory leading the charge. The teenagers and adult humans stayed with the Pack.

I shouldn't have a problem covering this many people...

There were some tight shortcomings to this magic—I could tell I couldn't cover nearly as many humans as I could wolves. I'd been at my absolute limit with the kids added into the mix, but I was guessing it was going to be harder to keep the magic flowing right if we were all running.

I saw a familiar shape trudge back toward the lodge.

One extra isn't going to put me over the edge, and given her circumstances, the whole Pack will watch out for her.

"Teresa," I called. "Come with us."

She glanced back at Moira, who made a shooing motion, then bounded back out to the Pack, laughing as Rio romped along next to her.

The Pack started howling again—this song was as bright and big as the moon in the night sky.

Greyson threaded his hand through mine, then tugged. The two of us started the run, leaving the meadow before the wolves flowed around us.

My magic pumped through my veins, making the run easier.

We ran through the shadows of trees with the moon shining bright overhead.

My heart throbbed in my chest in rhythm with the movement of the Pack, and my breathing matched Greyson's—our hands still linked.

I don't know how long we ran—it felt like forever in a moment, and with my magic fueling me my muscles burned, but they didn't give out or quiver from the tireless drive of the wolves.

We slowed down when we reached a half-frozen river that ran between two steep embankments. Greyson turned, leading us upstream.

Scarlett and Radcliff fearlessly jumped back and forth across the river with Young Jack and Wyatt—while East snarled at the four of them, no doubt informing them river-jumping was illegal.

The humans, thankfully, did not copy the daring siblings. They ran with the wolves they loved—Teresa swaddled between her parents, Original Jack loping alongside his wife as if his aches and pains no longer existed.

When I could tell my magic was starting to unravel a bit—I was getting tired—I squeezed Greyson's hand.

He tapped the top of my hand and pulled me a few steps farther so we made it around a bend, revealing a partially frozen waterfall.

It was small—the shelf the water dropped down to fall into the next level of the river was just a little taller than me—but frosty white and beautiful.

There were frozen ice shelves along the side of the river, and some stalactites of ice that were stuck to the shelf.

The Pack slowed to a walk, but Greyson pulled me along up the gentle slope, stopping when we reached the level of the waterfall.

He led me out to the ledge, sticking to a dry spot that put

us right next to the waterfall but—most importantly—gave us the perfect view of the playing Pack.

Greyson wrapped his arms around my shoulders and pulled me in, tucking me against his chest. Together, we watched the wolves and humans run together and heard the crunch of snow under their feet, the playful "*Aroos*" of the wolves, and the humans laughing.

"You gave them this gift," Greyson said. "Even though some of them have been snot nosed punks to you for years?"

"Yeah." I rested my head against his shoulder and let Greyson hold more of my weight. "Because the Pack loved me, even when I kept them shut out. I can do the same for the humans—who love them so much."

"It seems like there was more to being a Wolf's Kiss than even us wolves knew," Greyson said. "I'd have never thought it meant you could unite the whole Pack—wolf, hunter, and human."

"Me either." I yawned. "There are some limitations. It's harder to hold on to."

Somewhere in the group I heard a human yelp—Noah, I think—and the thump of him faceplanting when the magic accidentally slipped off him and he lost his night vision.

"Sorry," I called. I attempted to push more magic to him, but I fumbled the movement.

Greyson rubbed the back of my neck, tracing over my paw print mate mark. "Take a moment to recover. They'll be fine sitting here for a few minutes."

"Okay." I let my magic go at once, and was relieved when the laughing continued.

It's almost like the punchline of a joke...I was so stubborn to be alone, when my strongest magic can bind people together.

But now, I wouldn't have it any other way.

I impulsively slid my arms around Greyson's waist. "Thanks, Greyson—for including me in the Pack run."

"Of course, mate." Greyson tilted my chin up so I looked at him.

I could only stare into his eyes as he tipped his head lower, his lips brushing mine.

My eyes fluttered shut, and I slid my hands up his chest to grab on to his jacket for balance as I felt his lips twitch into a smile against mine.

"Ew," Wyatt announced—apparently having decided that the middle of the forest was a great time to shift into a human. "Young Jack, avert your eyes. Mom and Dad are flirting again."

"Should we sing them a love ballad or something to set the mood?" Aeric asked, because he and Wyatt seemingly shared one brain between them. "Also, I don't like the grittiness of this snow. I wish I had shoes."

"It never ceases to amaze me that they both survived long enough to make it to adulthood," Greyson breathed against my neck.

"Someone distract East so he's not tempted to fine our Alpha and Wolf's Kiss for public displays of affection," Aeric said.

"Is that a thing?" Wyatt asked.

"If it's not, I bet it'll be soon since Greyson can't keep his paws off Pip and she works downtown," Aeric said. "The library needs new carpeting."

"You two are wearing kilts in snow and freezing weather. Shouldn't you shift back?" Scarlett stood on the bank of the river—she glanced at Shania, likely hoping for support, but Shania was getting a belly rub from Teresa and didn't seem to care.

"This is a *skort*, I'll have you know!" Aeric yanked up the hem of his skort to show off his bulky shorts underneath. "And it cost me a fortune!"

"I did *not* need to see that," Amelia said.

I rolled my eyes and was about to add my own two cents, but Greyson gently tilted my chin again and kissed me long and hard, and any thoughts of retaliation died in my brain.

We kissed until the Pack started howling around us, and I couldn't stop laughing.

This is how it's supposed to be.

I kept on laughing as I hung on to Greyson—who was giving the loudest howler, Rio, a look.

Wolf, hunter, and human. Together.

Epilogue- Greyson

Greyson

"We're going to be *late!*" Pip leaped over the side of the lodge porch, landing in a secure crouch as her dress flared around her.

So that's why she insisted she wanted to wear sandals and not heels like Roanne was pushing for.

"It's not like they can start without us," I pointed out. I opted to go down the stairs, because I didn't care what time we arrived.

"I can't decide if you're excessively chill, or just arrogant." Pip checked the skirts of her dress. I didn't know anything about women's fashion, but Roanne had informed me Pip's gown accentuated her athletic form with its scoop neckline, high-low white chiffon skirt, and delicate golden lace overlay that wrapped around the waist and sleeves.

I just knew she looked incredible.

Maybe it's about time the Pack invest in a black-tie restaurant for Timber Ridge.

Of course, we could always just use our transportation to

visit something in Magiford, but our method of travel had a bedtime it very stubbornly stuck to, except in cases of emergency.

"I'm whichever one you find more attractive."

Pip rolled her eyes, but switched her attention to the shawl she was bringing for the heavily air conditioned Curia Cloisters since it'd gotten snagged on her opal ring.

Our ride arrived then, slowly picking her way around the lavish barn we'd built for her.

As part of me becoming Harka's official protégé, I'd made a contract with Queen Leila.

She lent us one of her night mares—a particularly big boned mare named Solar who made for a pretty unconvincing unicorn even though she had the silvery coat and black horn of her brethren because she always had an annoyed look on her long face, and her ears were constantly pinned—and we paid the Night Court a monthly rental fee and built a brand-new barn for the mare in addition to feeding and caring for her.

While Solar refused to let anyone ride her, which was hardly surprising since she belonged to the wild herd of night mares but had answered the call when Queen Leila had asked her animals for a volunteer, she did allow some of the Pack, particularly the kids, to brush her.

Teresa must have brushed her that morning. Solar's thick black mane was braided and tied off with gold ribbon that matched Pip's dress, which Ember had helped her choose weeks ago.

"Solar!" Pip waved to the mare. "We're heading for the Curia Cloisters."

The mare stopped about ten feet short of us and gave us the stink eye.

Pip pulled an apple out of one of her two secret pockets—

the other most likely held a dagger or firearm. "I have our payment." She approached Solar and held out the apple.

Solar stared at it for a few moments, then delicately took it from Pip's palm. As she eyed us a little more, the stone gateway assembled behind her, proving the mare's immense abilities, even if she did look like a draft horse that had been squashed down to almost pony size.

"Okay." Pip swung around and smoothed her skirt as she studied me with a critical eye. "Hector is staying behind to keep the place secure. East, Aeric, Wyatt, Rio, Shania, Ember, River, Remy, Forrest, Radcliff, Scarlett and Young Jack went down last night to scout the area since everyone is still aggressively paranoid about us getting attacked. The rest of the Pack is staying behind."

She stepped closer to adjust my golden tie.

I'd reluctantly let her force me into dark gray slacks and suit vest over a dress shirt for the occasion, even though I was quite possibly going to die in the summer heat if we stood outside for more than five minutes.

But, given the way her eyes traveled up and down my body —and the familiar glow of approval I could feel through our bond—I was inclined to think I could stand a little thing like heat if the stupid outfit made her this happy.

"Then let's head out," I said.

I would have offered her my arm if I was civilized, but I'm just a wolf, so I spun her around and draped my arm over her shoulders and did my best to wipe as much of my scent onto her as possible.

We'd only had one or two minor incidents with Alphas eyeing up Pip since Rafe's attack, but given what we were about to walk into, I would have rented out a billboard reminding Magiford of our bond if billboards had a better return-on-investment.

"To the Curia Cloisters!" Pip called as the mare entered

the portal ahead of us. She subtly slung her arm around my waist, providing the extra touch that helped ground me as we stepped through the portal.

The emptiness of the portal was bad enough, but going from the forest to the Night Court—which, at least, was experiencing daytime at the moment, but the place smelled like a florist had gone wild—to the Curia Cloisters that brimmed with the scents of supernaturals was still enough to make my senses swirl.

Experience was slowly helping, but touching Pip had proven to be the best prevention and cure for any sickness portal traveling might stick me with.

"Thanks, Solar," Pip called as the world still swirled around me.

I blinked a few times and stabilized enough to realize Solar had dropped us just outside the main entrance, right by the doors.

Many would say she'd done it for our convenience, but I was pretty sure it was because she liked to stand in the middle of the main parking lot and glare at all the cars that came through until she got bored and left.

"In we go—wow that feels nice." Pip checked me through the bond, making her presence stronger in my heart, as she pulled open the door and we stepped into the bliss of air conditioning.

I adjusted my arm on her shoulders. "Are you sure you're ready for our plans after all of this?"

We passed a few fae, and a gaggle of wizards, but besides the staff, I mostly smelled wolves and shifters in the building.

"Yep," Pip said. "I don't think I can prepare any more than I already have."

"We could wait," I said. "My power level might need to be higher for it to really work."

"You've proven that you're more dominant than Harka," Pip said.

"Being more dominant isn't going to change anything about the situation," I said.

"The ceremony will." Pip stubbornly mashed her lips together, then peered up at me. "Don't worry about it, Greyson. I'm a Wolf's Kiss, and your mate. I'm all about doing impossible things."

"It's kind of unfair when you think about how overpowered you are." I teasingly squeezed her shoulder.

"I don't want to hear that from you—the most ridiculously powerful Alpha to ever breathe, with the confidence to match."

"And I'm all yours. Lucky you!" I winked as we pushed open the door to the assembly hall.

The assembly hall was one of the largest rooms in the Curia Cloisters and boasted three floors—the main chamber we were walking into, and two balconies for additional seating.

The main floor of the hall was filled with wolves from all over the Midwest, though I saw a trio of vampires that I was pretty sure came from the infamous Drake vampire family— they were the only vampires strong enough to be out in the daylight like this, and as their leader, Killian Drake, was the Vampire Eminence of the Midwest, he was somewhat famous for poking his nose into all things supernatural related.

Shifters had taken over the two balconies—I recognized a few panther shifter prides, some bears, and a fox or two, but for the most part I just sensed—and smelled—how different they were from wolves but could pick up the faint animal musk all of us shape shifters had.

Lord Linus was seated on the main floor of the chamber in the front row of chairs. He was inescapable with his black-purple ponytail and his star spattered fae tunic. Chase and Lady Chrysanthe were sitting with him—probably to represent the Night Court as our ally.

Harka stood on the small platform at the head of the room, her hands folded behind her. Her husband, Beta Colton, stood behind her, along with a few other wolves from her Pack, while East, Aeric, Wyatt, Shania, Scarlett, and Rio all stood in front of the platform.

I couldn't help the smirk that spread across my lips as we walked down the aisle, heading for the platform.

Pip's steps were sure, and she casually brushed back a lock of her white hair that had come undone from the elaborate braid Roanne had done for her. She was confident—even though we were surrounded—and unbothered by all the wolves.

I couldn't smell any sweat or changes in her body from anxiety, and her presence in the bond was steady.

Maybe I need to think about importing more hunters into the Pack as possible romantic partners.

I glanced at Scarlett and Wyatt who were standing shoulder to shoulder, and a part of me wondered.

We reached the line of Northern Lakes wolves. Aeric and Wyatt gave Pip thumbs up, while the rest of them subtly bowed their heads to me.

Harka beckoned for us to join her on the platform, and I kept my arm over Pip's shoulders as we climbed the stairs together.

"Are both of you ready?" Harka asked.

"This isn't about me," Pip said.

"No, but you'll get dragged into the spotlight with me whether you want to or not," I said. "Given what we are and what's about to happen."

"We're ready," Pip assured Harka.

Harka nodded, and I could read a faint sense of relief off her that it was finally happening.

She's been looking forward to this day more than anyone else.

"Werewolves and shifters." Harka's voice was loud and

powerful, and it immediately silenced the hushed conversations the wolves and shifters had been holding among themselves. "Thank you for attending today's meeting. I'd like to officially introduce my protégé: Alpha Greyson of the Northern Lakes Pack, and his fiancé—and bonded mate—Hunter Phillipa Sabre."

Epilogue- Pip

Pip

"This isn't a good idea," Harka said.

I ignored her as I settled my skirt and stood, waiting in a small, gym-like room.

"You said I could ask for anything by agreeing to go public as your protégé this early in the process," Greyson drawled. "This is my price."

He was standing some feet behind me, his hands tucked into the pockets of his slacks, no doubt looking unbearably handsome with Radcliff and Scarlett standing at the wall behind him.

We'd come straight here from the ceremony in which Harka had officially recognized Greyson as her protégé.

What the wolves and shifters didn't know was that Greyson had already taken on about a third of her workload.

If all went as planned, he'd stay as her protégé for a year— possibly two—but take over the majority of her work by the end of the year.

Between our wedding in early autumn and trying to deal

Fated

with the influx of humans interested in trying to become wolves—not to mention all the werewolves petitioning to join the Pack—announcing Greyson as the full Pre-Dominant would attract too much attention when we couldn't really deal with any more than we already had.

The title of protégé was little more than a screen to make the power shift easier on the Pack.

I rubbed my thumb over the opal stone of my engagement ring as I waited. It was *freezing* in the room for the comfort of the wolves, so I adjusted my white shawl around my shoulders as my heart beat frantically in my chest.

I should have brought a spare set of clothes to change into for this.

Aeric and Wyatt—both in their wolf forms—flanked me, ready to act if I failed and my life was in danger. (Though with Greyson in the room, I doubted that would be necessary.)

"Hunter Sabre, I'm honored you want to help Cedar," Harka said. "But she's gone. Her heart was irreplaceably broken with the death of her mate. I can't reach her—and I'm her sister and the Alpha of her Pack. Neither Aspen nor Rafe was able to reach her, and they're her *children*."

"I know," I said. "But I have to try." I turned to face Harka and motioned between Greyson and myself. "Because I'm not willing to let that kind of tragic story keep playing out for mates. Werewolves have lost too much as magic has died out, but everything I've experienced—with Radcliff, Scarlett, the Pack, and my own magic tells me it's because we supernaturals don't help one another enough. So I have to try."

Harka studied me for a moment, then nodded.

I returned my gaze to the door, another reason for wanting to help Cedar lurking in my heart.

I need to try, because I refuse to let Rafe—or psychopaths like Aspen—use family like a weapon and a shield to hide behind horrific behavior, when the truth is we're stronger together.

349

My heartbeat steadied, and I felt my hunter adrenaline kick in, making my thoughts clearer.

The door on the far side of the room creaked open, and Beta Colton and another wolf from Harka's Pack walked in, dragging a cream colored wolf who had what would have been beautiful dark and light brown markings on her ears and back if her hair wasn't matted and greasy.

She snapped her yellowed teeth at Colton and the other wolf, who dragged her in with leashes. Her eyes were empty of the light that made it easy to tell a werewolf from a regular wolf—she was entirely animal instinct as she growled, the clumpy fur on her back bristling.

They'd put a wire muzzle over her mouth so you could see her bare her teeth, but she couldn't bite, and something about that broke my heart.

Poor Harka. She loves her sister so much—it must hurt beyond every-thing to see her like this.

I risked glancing at the Pre-Dominant, and some of my less-than-sympathetic thoughts about her niece and nephew withered when I could see the raw grief in her eyes.

Cedar writhed, trying to get free from the leashes, but Beta Colton and his packmate held fast. She snarled at them before she caught sight of me, then her growl took on a frantic, manic quality to it.

"We can't risk letting her go." Beta Colton grimaced a little, the muscles in his arms bulging as he forcibly held Cedar back. "Will this work?"

"Yes. Thanks." I slowly sidled closer. "Hopefully it won't take long for me to figure out if I can do anything or not."

My hunter senses were screaming at me that she was a danger, and I was painfully aware that—since I'd be chan-neling my Wolf's Kiss magic—I was going to be a sitting duck if she got away from the others.

Aeric and Wyatt pushed in behind me, their soft fur brushing my legs.

But that's what it means to be a Wolf's Kiss, and to be Pack—to trust others to protect me when I can't.

I swallowed hard as I knelt down, studying Cedar.

She twisted and snapped, spattering the floor with strands of drool. Her nails were overgrown, and based on the crusted pattern on her legs she'd been chewing on her own limbs.

She hopped in place, frantically trying to wrench away from Beta Colton's hold before straining at the end of the leash to snarl at me.

"Greyson?" I asked.

Technically, an Alpha couldn't force a feral to do anything —as Harka had mentioned. But Greyson had raw strength. He might not be able to make her behave, but he could freeze her where she stood.

Greyson strolled up behind me, unrolling his Alpha powers.

I felt them—strong and overwhelming—as they brushed against my hunter senses and easily flicked off.

His powers were so potent it made Wyatt, Aeric, and Colton shake a little as they fought the urge to bow their heads to him—or possibly kneel.

Cedar thrashed a few steps, then stilled when Greyson's powers latched on to her. She growled—her fur still bristled, and she was still drooling rivers, but at least she was motionless.

I chewed on my lip for a moment to make certain she wasn't going to suddenly break free of Greyson's grasp, then I tapped my magic, feeling it make the slow reversal so it switched from the sharp sense of my regular hunter magic to the stronger Wolf's Kiss magic.

With my Wolf's Kiss powers whirling around me, I could more strongly feel Aeric's and Wyatt's connection to Greyson—and, more interestingly, the Fletchings' faint attachment to him as well.

What was perhaps even more shocking, was that I could feel the ties of Harka's Pack, and distinctly Harka's ties to Greyson…and it wasn't one of overseeing.

That's subservience. I stared at Harka as I tried to make out the feeling. *Even if she hasn't passed the title over to Greyson, in her heart, she's done.*

That moment, more than any other interaction I'd had with Harka, told me what a great leader she really was.

It took a strong person to recognize their own faults, but it took a true leader to know when to pass power on to another because of those faults.

But does that mean when Greyson really does become the Pre-Dominant, I could possibly affect more wolves than our Pack? If they put themselves in a subservient position to him…

That would be a puzzle to bring up on a different day— one when I wasn't facing down a feral wolf.

I tentatively reached out and brushed my Wolf's Kiss magic against Cedar.

She peeled her lips up so high I could see her pink gums, and it distorted the shape of her nose.

She stank horribly—both her fur and her breath—and for a second my hunter instincts nearly got the best of me and cut off my Wolf's Kiss magic.

Stop it! I told myself. *I'm a hunter, a Wolf's Kiss, and a mate—I can empathize, unite, and match her strength. I can reach her, and I'm not so weak that I'm going to back away from this with my tail between my legs!*

I took a deep breath, exhaled, then looked into her eyes. "Cedar."

Nothing in her changed.

"Cedar," I repeated, this time using a little more of my magic.

Don't enhance her, for the love of all the popcorn in the world DO

NOT enhance her abilities! I mentally shouted at my magic as I directed a little more to her.

Now that I could feel Harka's attachment to Greyson, I was hoping I could feel Cedar the same way I could feel Aeric, Wyatt, and the rest of the Pack through Greyson.

Wouldn't it be possible to use mathematical properties and say if she's below Harka and Harka is below Greyson, then I should be able to reach her through Greyson?

It was a shaky concept at best, but it wasn't like I had much else I could go on.

I sent a pulse of my magic through Greyson—which then passed through Harka.

Based on the strangled noise Harka made and the sound of Greyson shifting behind me, they must have both felt it.

It reached Cedar, and I had to clutch my gut to keep from retching at the horrible sensation it ignited when my magic brushed her consciousness.

Everything was twisted and upside down, or maybe it was closer to being trapped underwater with my lungs burning for air but no ability to tell up from down.

"Cedar," I said again. "I'm here to help."

Cedar's frame shook as she tried to break out of Greyson's mental hold on her—I had to do this fast, or she'd injure herself like this.

"I know you lost your mate, and that you must feel immense pain because he's gone...but there is so much more to live for." My voice broke a little, and I felt a ball of emotion at the back of my throat as I faced her down.

As I peered into her wild eyes, I couldn't help but feel like this was a chance to tell her—what I'd want Greyson to know if I died first. Because I'd already lost so many loved ones, I knew.

"You lost a part of yourself." I pushed against her a little harder with my magic, enduring the lungs-burning-underwater feeling. "That's never going to go away. But the pain will get a tiny bit better. Not every day, but maybe every year, then every month. There will be times when it will come back with a vengeance and you'll feel like you couldn't possibly go on, because the pain is too much. But there are so many more people who love you—so many other people who *need* you."

Cedar's lips slowly lowered so her teeth no longer showed.

She stared at me, but I still couldn't feel any humanity in her—just the chaotic, lost, upside down feeling that made my stomach swirl.

"You've got to come back," I said. "It's painful and awful, but you're strong of heart. And I know—because I know Harka—that you must love just as fiercely as she does."

And then…I felt something.

It was distant, like the pinprick of a star in the night sky.

Desperately, I tried to throw more of my magic to her, making another pulse of it shoot through Greyson and Harka.

But it couldn't reach her.

There's still—maybe—a part of her left, but there's no way I can reach her. Harka's right about that. However…

"I need you to reach for me—for this way out," I said. "No one else can make this choice for you, and my magic can't get deep enough to you. You have to get to me, and then I can help pull you out."

Cedar stared at me as I held my breath. She wasn't panting as much, and she'd stopped drooling uncontrollably.

That's a good sign.

I gnawed on my lip for at least a minute while she stood in absolute silence before I reached out with shaking hands and stroked the top of her head.

Cedar's ears flicked, but otherwise she didn't react.

Slowly, carefully, I started to unbuckle the wire muzzle.

Next to me, Aeric growled in displeasure.

"I know it's risky," I said. "But I just have the feeling it needs to be done. Besides, if she reacts badly, I trust you both to cover for me."

Aeric huffed and licked his chops, but he and Wyatt crept closer, their shoulders pressing into mine as they moved so they were closer to her and ready to strike.

I pulled the final strap through the last buckle and removed the muzzle, setting it on the ground.

Cedar stared at me—her eyes still glassy—for several long seconds, then she lunged, her lips bared in a snarl.

My heart exploded in my chest.

But before Wyatt and Aeric could grab her, Cedar scrambled backwards, crying as if she was in immense pain.

She whined pitifully as she lay on the ground, her breathing pained.

"Cedar," I said. "*Please*. Please choose life."

I extended my magic again, straining as I tried to reach that faint glimmer.

Cedar slowly stood. Her entire body shook, even though Greyson had rolled back his powers before I'd taken the muzzle off her.

Cautiously, like a wild wolf, Cedar stepped closer to me, stopping at the end of her leashes.

I heard Harka take a breath filled with the painful gasp of hope, but I kept my focus—and my magic—on Cedar.

I stared into her eyes, heartsick.

Please work. Please. Please let me break this horrible cycle.

"Come home," I said. "Your Pack misses you."

Cautiously, I held out my hand.

Cedar stared back at me.

I held my hand out for so long my arm started to burn, and the minutes felt like hours.

Just when I was about to drop my hand, Cedar stretched as far as she could so her muzzle brushed my fingers, and I felt it: the tentative, faint touch of Pack brushing my magic.

Mentally, I grabbed on to the feeling and yanked hard, pulling all the way through Harka, Greyson, straight back to me where I flooded her with my magic.

I scrunched my eyes shut and poured my magic into Cedar, blocking out the shouts of surprise and the strange sensation of fur turning into skin as I kept my arm thrust out in front of me.

When the faint touch became something more permanent and heavy in my mind, I cautiously peeled an eye open.

A horribly emaciated woman was crouched on the ground in front of me. Her hair—black like Harka's—was snarled and wild, and the bones of her body stuck out too prominently, but I could still see the same fierce, protective love in her eyes that I'd seen in Harka's.

I smiled, my eyes filling with tears. "Hello, Cedar."

Harka yelped and scrambled to us. She was on her knees and embracing her sister before I got my shawl untied.

"Cedar, Cedar." Harka clutched her sister and rocked back and forth as Cedar collapsed into her arms, crying as well.

"H-Harka," Cedar said, the name coming out slightly slurred as her voice was almost beyond understanding from years of disuse.

I offered my shawl, which Beta Colton took from me as he crouched at Cedar's other side and tucked the shawl around her.

"Welcome home, Cedar," he said, his voice tight with emotion. "We've missed you so much."

I exhaled and inched backwards before I stood up.

I took a few steps, then reached for Greyson—knowing where he was even though I didn't see him.

Greyson moved in, propping me against his side for stability as I tried to put myself back together after using so much Wolf's Kiss magic in one go.

"You're not going to join the celebration?" Greyson asked.

"Not yet." I peered back at the reunion, and was happy to

see that Harka was now smiling and laughing through all of her tears as she rested her forehead against her sister's.

"I may have been the one to call Cedar back," I said, "but I wasn't the reason why she chose to come back. I just made it possible."

Greyson wrapped his arms around my waist and tugged me closer. "So what next?"

"We go home," I said. "And I add to the Sabre and Ward family journals everything I've learned. You become the next Pre-Dominant, I'll teach everything I can to Scarlett, Radcliff, and Teresa…and maybe we see if we can convince any other hunters to join other werewolf Packs."

Greyson tilted his head and smirked in a way that used to kick up my self-defense instincts.

"What?" I asked.

"Nothing," he said with too much innocence. "I was just congratulating myself."

"For what?"

"For the brilliant decision to accept my mate bond with you, Lady Hunter."

"It turned out better than I ever hoped for," I admitted.

"It did, didn't it?" He leaned closer, and even after more than six months of being bonded, it still made my spine prickle with over-awareness. "You're a lot of trouble, but you're worth it."

"*I'm* trouble? *You're* the one who recklessly bargains with his life, accepts potentially hazardous mate bonds, and tears head first into danger!"

"More decisions I'm proud of," Greyson said.

I gaped at him in disbelief, and he chuckled lowly, then took advantage of the moment to kiss me senseless.

"*Aroo!*" I'd never heard a howl tinged with disgust, but when I laughed and stepped away from Greyson, Aeric had his head down and his paws covering his eyes.

Wyatt wagged his tail at us and crooned what I suspect was supposed to be some kind of romantic love song, because Aeric made a dry-heaving-hacking noise.

I rolled my eyes. "Scarlett, Radcliff, we're heading out," I said.

"Where to?" Radcliff pushed off the wall and stretched while his sister crouched down to scratch Wyatt in front of his ears.

"Home," I said. "Back to the Pack."

THE END

For free short stories and more information about the Pack of Dawn and Destiny Series, visit kmshea.com/freebies

If you enjoyed Pack of Dawn and Destiny, please check out Leila's story in the Court of Midnight and Deception series.

Other Series by K. M. Shea

ADDITIONAL NOVELS

Life Reader

Princess Ahira

A Goose Girl

About the Author

K. M. Shea is a fantasy-romance author who never quite grew out of adventure books or fairy tales, and still searches closets in hopes of stumbling into Narnia. She is addicted to sweet romances, witty characters, and happy endings. She also writes LitRPG and GameLit under the pen name, A. M. Sohma.

Printed in Great Britain
by Amazon